THE LOST
Quest for the Lost Keys

Printed in the United States of America
First Edition
June 2018
ISBN 978-0-9962753-2-3
ISBN (eBook) 978-0-9962753-3-0

Cover Design and Interior Format
© KILLION
THE
GROUP INC.

THE LOST

ELWOOD JOHNSON

The Vigenere Cipher

```
B C D E F G H I J K L M N O P Q R S T U V W X Y Z
B C D E F G H I J K L M N O P Q R S T U V W X Y Z
C D E F G H I J K L M N O P Q R S T U V W X Y Z A B
D E F G H I J K L M N O P Q R S T U V W X Y Z A B
E F G H I J K L M N O P Q R S T U V W X Y Z A B C
F G H I J K L M N O P Q R S T U V W X Y Z A B C D
G H I J K L M N O P Q R S T U V W X Y Z A B C D
H I J K L M N O P Q R S T U V W X Y Z A B C D E F
I J K L M N O P Q R S T U V W X Y Z A B C D E F G
J K L M N O P Q R S T U V W X Y Z A B C D E F G H
K L M N O P Q R S T U V W X Y Z A B C D E F G H I
L M N O P Q R S T U V W X Y Z A B C D E F G H I J
M N O P Q R S T U V W X Y Z A B C D E F G H I J K
N O P Q R S T U V W X Y Z A B C D E F G H I J K L
O P Q R S T U V W X Y Z A B C D E F G H I J K L M
P Q R S T U V W X Y Z A B C D E F G H I J K L M N
Q R S T U V W X Y Z A B C D E F G H I J K L M N O
R S T U V W X Y Z A B C D E F G H I J K L M N O P
S T U V W X Y Z A B C D E F G H I J K L M N O P Q
T U V W X Y Z A B C D E F G H I J K L M N O P Q R
U V W X Y Z A B C D E F G H I J K L M N O P Q R S
V W X Y Z A B C D E F G H I J K L M N O P Q R S T
W X Y Z A B C D E F G H I J K L M N O P Q R S T U
X Y Z A B C D E F G H I J K L M N O P Q R S T U V W
Y Z A B C D E F G H I J K L M N O P Q R S T U V W
Z A B C D E F G H I J K L M N O P Q R S T U V W X
A B C D E F G H I J K L M N O P Q R S T U V W X Y
```

CHAPTER 1

DREAM

THE ROOM IS THICK WITH the stench of sweat and fear. Mostly fear.

I look down at the bomb with tears stinging my eyes. My mind is blank. I know nothing of bombs—how to make them or how to diffuse them. I follow the wires running here and there, a spiderweb of confusion. Is there an on/off switch?

I know everyone in the room is depending on me, hoping and maybe praying that I'll know what to do. To know how to save our lives.

I take a deep cleansing breath, hoping and praying that this will help me calm down and focus on the problem at hand. It doesn't. My breath comes out raggedly. I see my hands shaking, then realize it's not just my hands. My whole body is vibrating with the certain knowledge that death is imminent.

Argh! I let out some primeval roar as I fight to gain some sense of control.

Think!

I retreat into my mind, the walls of this subterranean prison receding, replaced by synapses and grey matter. I recreate the bomb and its wiring in my mind. I try not to focus on the timer counting down at the front of the device.

It's a crude box containing explosives of indeterminate origin. On the face of the box, a timer. Running from the box are several wires. Stop. Several is vague. Get specific. Eight wires. Four leaving the explosive device and running away to my left. Four more identical to the others running away to my right. Why two sets? Why four per set?

In each group of four, two wires are red and two are black. No multi-colored wires like in the movies. No cute rhymes to go from violet to red to blue to green. I'm no movie star, I don't have a pair of wire cutters handy, and I'm not moving them from one wire to the next while the tension builds and scary music plays. The only thing I hear is my heart pounding its base notes deafeningly in my ears.

Two black wires, two red wires. I reach to grab the set that runs off to my right. I attempt to separate the wires so that I can see where each one of them runs. I fumble with shaking fingers, clumsy like a newborn reaching for a nursery toy. I command my left hand to join my right, thinking maybe two spasmodic hands are better than one.

I somehow manage to get ahold of a red wire. I feed the wire between my hands, bringing my eyes close to the trail of red. I see this wire enter the device and disappear into the explosives. I reverse course on this wire and see that it runs around the main box, down to the floor and into another box I hadn't notice before. It looks like a car battery, maybe slightly larger.

I notice that all four wires disappear into this same box. I drop to my knees rather clumsily, groping at the box, worrying that my spasms will detonate the bomb.

I open the box, lifting a lid that is haphazardly placed on top. The wires are connected to this box, blinking lights and bare circuitry revealing them to me. I quickly take in this new element, and despair spreads through my body like a warm drug newly injected into my bloodstream. I have zero ideas about defeating this bomb.

I sit back on my haunches, squatting in front of the box. My breath comes in ever more sporadic gulps. I shake my head and clench my teeth so hard I think my jaw might break.

No! I shout, but not aloud, strictly inside my head.

I think of the timer and guess I have less than a minute now. I glance at the faces in the room, silently communicating my apology. They stare back mutely, tears freely flowing.

Seeing them brings renewed determination. I must at least try. At the very least. Make an attempt.

I roll forward from my squat to my knees, leaning forward and looking into the box. Four wires. Four red blinking lights. Two red wires. Two black wires.

Here goes nothing, I think, and reach forward to the nearest red wire. The wires are all secured to metal prongs in a fashion that reminds me of the twist ties that you use to secure a loaf of bread. My fingers touch the bare copper wiring that is wrapped around the metal prong. It sends a shock through my body. My hand recoils and my heart stops.

Geez. Static electricity. Not funny. That could've set off the bomb. But it didn't. Does that mean this particular wire isn't live? It is not the one carrying the deadly charge? I don't know. I mean, I. Don't. Know. After taking a second to restart my heart, I reach again and begin untwisting the wire. It comes free in my hand.

Nothing happens for just a second. And then everything happens at once.

The red flashing lights begin blinking quicker in a clockwise fashion around the wire and light that I have just removed from the prong. The lights gain speed in their circular pattern. And then they go out. No more blinking or flashing. No more light.

My eyes are wide, my breathing fast. I don't know what this means.

Another second passes. A low hum builds.

No!

A flash of light, a deafening sound, slightly delayed, and then nothingness.

Nothing.

Emptiness.

Darkness.

CHAPTER 2

HOME

I WAKE UP DRENCHED IN SWEAT, feeling like I have just stepped out of the swimming pool. I'm not dead. The explosion never came. It never comes. But the dream hasn't stopped coming. Every night for the past week. I know what this means, this time around.

The Quest is coming.

The past year has been a strange one. At times, days and weeks have seemed like a lifetime. By the same token, time has passed so quickly that it seems like yesterday that I sat and read Mom's letter and placed the Key around my neck.

At this thought, I unconsciously reach my hand up to the Key that hangs from my neck. I finger it as if to gain some assurance from its weight. I dip my head and read the symbols of the key. The circle, the crossed arrows, and the triangle. A space and then the eye symbol. Turning the key over, I see the word *Faithfulness* inscribed in flowing script.

Another Quest and another Key await.

I feel better prepared this year. I spent this past summer and school year doing what I can to improve my skills and ability. I have worked at public speaking. I have been training in self-defense and martial arts with a special trainer, Master Shi.

Master Shi revealed himself to me just after my return from ancient China. He showed me the birthmark of the eye—the symbol that he is my Guardian during the Quest years. A Guardian during the time that I am not on Quests. A Guardian here at home.

Master Shi comes from China, from an order of monastic men

who are trained and skilled in a special martial art. He left the monastery to gain an education that along with his marital arts ability, would serve to educate me in my ability to recover the keys of the Quest.

We have trained in meditation, martial arts, public speaking, and in general I have become a more well-rounded individual. He has put me through exercises that have been painful at times and also embarrassing at times, but the end results are hard to argue. I feel if not ready, much better prepared to face the challenges that lie ahead.

I shower, brush my teeth, floss and gargle, then dress. I return to sit on the edge of my bed. And wait.

TODAY IS MY BIRTHDAY. I'M fourteen.

I don't know when the Key around my neck will take me to the Training Center. I know it will be today; I just don't know when. Yet another question that I never had an opportunity to ask last time.

After a minute of just staring out my window, waiting for my feet to fall out from under me, I stand and move to the full-length mirror. I look hard at my reflection, wanting to see a drastic change in my appearance due to my advancing years. I don't see it. I look pretty much the same. Black hair trimmed short, more from a lack of interest in styling the hair than from any sense of style. The glasses are still perched on my sharp nose, blue eyes staring back at me. I lean closer, trying to see a trace of whisker on my cheek and chin. Nothing yet. My voice is deeper and my Adam's apple more prominent. Other than that, not much has changed.

My gaze moves to my body. I'm still whip thin, although to my eyes my musculature has improved ever so slightly. I have grown a fraction, I know this because new clothing and shoes were needed throughout the year. But I wouldn't call it a spurt. I've added just over an inch in height and ten pounds in weight. I'm certain all ten pounds are pure muscle.

I raise my right arm up and curl it into the traditional flexing pose. My bicep looks like it houses a medium egg underneath the skin. I'm not going to be featured in any muscle magazine, but I'm proud of my egg.

I've been doing a lot of biking this past year, back and forth to school and Master Shi's house. I've also taken to Sunday bike rides with Dad. All of this adds up to some small definition of leg muscle. I don't have huge calf or thigh muscles, but again, to my eye at least, some definition has taken place.

I move away from the mirror and without thinking move to Mom's room. It's empty like always.

Dad is gone on a business trip. He was really beat up about being gone for my birthday, but I told him not to worry. I assured him that my birthday would be just what I wanted it to be.

I couldn't tell him that I was excited to see Gene and Li, of course, but I let him know that things wouldn't be too dull without him.

The biggest coup came when I convinced him that I didn't need my aunt to stay with me. Master Shi came by and between us we convinced Dad that I would be fine. Master Shi would come by each day, or I would go to his place. He would ensure that I had enough to eat and that I was in all ways taken care of.

Freedom from my aunt was the perfect birthday gift.

Knowing I wouldn't be disturbed, I sat on Mom's side of the bed.

"Here we go again, Mom," I say aloud.

Mom was a Buddy of the Quest, but had died on my twelfth birthday, before she could tell me of my destiny. I was left to read it in letter form last year today.

I can practically feel Mom's arms around me today. My birthday. The day she died. I bask in her embrace, imagined and wraithlike though it is, until I begin to feel she is moving away again.

I stand and make my way down the stairs, always thinking of the inscription on the topmost stair. Great-grandpa Jakob had been a Brawn of the Quest, leaving a message for his family on the underside of that stair.

Moving into the hallway leading to the kitchen, I look at the newly hung family picture of Dad and me. We both had great conversations over the summer together. We spent time fishing and riding bikes; we even went camping once in the mountains. We talked more than we ever had. I discovered Dad wanted to talk, he wanted to be for me what I had lost in Mom. It was a pleasant discovery, one that made a huge difference this year. Dad and I have found a new groove. We spend a lot of time together, and we're okay talking about Mom. We both miss her and that will never go away. But we found that through each other we can find joy in the shared memory of her.

For these reasons, we decided to take a picture of the two of us and add it to the hallway of family pictures. I think Mom would be happy. The picture is the two of us at our campsite in the mountains near our home. We both look like fish out of water, and we were definitely out of our element. But I told Dad that I felt so close to him and Mom during the trip that our awkwardness was worth it. He agreed. We took the picture, and both of us think that if you look really hard, you can see Mom with us there in the mountains.

I smile and tentatively touch the picture, as I have taken to doing. Our new family picture is complete in my eyes.

I decide on a hearty breakfast, remembering the cold caves of the Training Center. I even have some bacon, the kind that is already cooked and you just have to warm up. That is Dad's and my idea of cooking bacon. Gene probably wouldn't approve, but I take what I can get and it works for me.

Still nothing from the Key.

So I return to my bedroom, irrationally thinking that I need to be sitting on the edge of my bed like last time in order for the Key to activate.

I wonder if Gene and Li are already there. Have they met our Guide? Are they waiting at the huge stone table for me? Or are they sitting on their beds waiting just like me?

A knock at the front door interrupts my thoughts.

CHAPTER 3

MASTER SHI

MASTER SHI IS WAITING ON the front porch when I open the door. He smiles wide and holds a gift.

"C'mon in, Master," I say, sweeping my hand in a gesture of invitation.

"Good morning, Jake. Happy Birthday!" he says, holding out the gift in both hands.

"Thank you!" I say appreciatively, receiving the gift in both of mine.

We walk back through the house and out onto the back patio. We sit in two chairs facing the backyard, enjoying the warm summer sun as it climbs into position. This is our familiar ritual on the days he has come to visit when my dad is gone.

"Master ..."

"Today ..."

We both begin to speak at the same moment. We share a laugh and then I motion for him to go ahead.

"Today is the big day, Jake. I feel like we have accomplished much over the course of the year. You added confidence and power in measurable amounts. You are ready for your next adventure," he says.

I sense he is not done, so I simply nod and smile.

"I should like to remind you of the Five Points that Liu Ji shared with you one year ago today," he says, sitting forward and turning to face me.

"Point One: keep a record," he says this like a question, testing me.

"I have kept a record this past year," I say economically.

The Master nods.

"Point Two: unearth hidden talents."

We both share a smile.

"As you know, I have worked at unearthing talents, which has brought much pain and embarrassment. In spite of this, I think we have been successful," I say.

"Agreed," he says with mirth.

"Point Three: stay close to family and friends."

"Dad and I have forged a new relationship. We are so much more open with one another. We spend tons of time together—well, at least more than before. I think this works for Point Three," I conclude, my eyes shining with emotion.

"Yes." He says it all with this one word. "Point Four: do for others what has been done for you," he continues.

I shrug. I don't know about this one.

"May I share a story with you?" Master asks. I nod. "Do you remember Amber from the ice cream shop? I tasked you with finding out about her pets and the toothpaste she uses? Do you remember this exercise? The exercises designed to help you unearth your hidden talents?"

"I remember," I say. Amber was a shy girl—probably about sixteen—who served me ice cream. Master Shi asked me to find out if she had a pet and what toothpaste she used, attempting to help me get over my shyness and embarrassment in front of strangers. She has a dog named Pandora and uses Crest toothpaste."

"Do you remember the boys that were huddled in the corner staring at you while you spoke with Amber?" he asks.

I nod again. "One boy in particular was staring daggers at me while I engaged Amber in conversation. At the time, I couldn't understand why he was upset. I mean, I was a thirteen-year-old kid talking to a much older girl. His jealousy was irrational."

"Well, I have taken an interest in Amber since that day. I suspected that you had sparked something within her with your kind inquiries. She has since dumped that jerk boyfriend you saw that day, traded in her glasses for contacts, and is confident in her smile and in herself. You did that for her with just a few questions and a genuine interest in her," he comments with eyebrows raised.

"Come on, Master Shi. I'm sure there is more to it than my

asking a few questions that day. I mean, I was so nervous I think my voice even cracked," I say, deflecting his praise. It sounds out-landish to me.

Master Shi is shaking his head. "No, I had a chance to speak with Amber recently. She told me that her newfound confidence is due to a chance encounter at work that helped her see herself in a new light. That encounter was with you. She remembers you, although not your name. You made a difference. Point Four is coming to be," he says.

I'm shocked enough that I can't find words.

"Point Five: enjoy the journey," he continues with his list.

I smile. "I think I'm getting better with that, too," I say.

"Agreed," he says. "You are progressing nicely."

I shake my head a little in frustration. "Yeah, but I still get ner-vous, bile is still dangerously close to spewing out, and hives are just a nerve-wracking breath away."

"Jake, you cannot expect to erase all of your challenges at once. We have made good progress, and I suspect that this progress will serve you well today," he says, clearly referring to the impending Quest.

I think of my dream. I almost say something to the Master about it, but decide I'm too embarrassed to mention it.

He looks at me for a long moment. He knows when I am about to say something. He waits for it, but it doesn't come. He looks a little disappointed, but quickly erases the emotion from his fea-tures. He points to the gift I'm holding in my hands.

"Go ahead and open it," he says, excited once again.

I'd almost forgotten about the gift. I tear open the packaging, a cardboard box is revealed, like a box Amazon.com would use to ship an order. Removing the tape from the box, I peer inside to get a first look. My brows come together. It's another, smaller box.

"I thought I'd have a little fun with you," Master Shi says with a chuckle.

I drop the bigger box, coming away with the smaller box. I remove the tape from this one and peer inside. I look at Master Shi with a smirk. Funny. The smaller box holds an even smaller box. This box looks like a jewelry box—you know, with a velvet exterior and a clamshell opening. I hinge open the lid. After seeing what is inside, I look a question at Master Shi with a cock of my head.

He leans forward and points to the object inside.

"I thought long and hard about something that might aid you on your Quest today. While I don't know where and when you are headed, I tried to come up with something universally applicable," he shrugs. "This is what I selected."

Inside the jewelry box sits a ring. I pluck the ring from its cushion and turn it over in my hand.

"There is nothing remarkable about the ring itself," Master says. "It's what is held within the ring that is important."

I reach to the ring, wanting to discover what lies within. It is large enough to contain something within it. It looks sort of like a class ring. Big and bulky, with a wide blue stone set in the top. I slip it onto my right ring finger; it's a perfect fit. I twist it, looking for the button or whatever that opens the ring.

Master Shi reaches a hand out.

"You must not open it now. Wait until a moment of need presents itself, then the ring will open and reveal its contents," he says cryptically.

"Um, well, how will I know when I need it, if I don't know what is inside?" I ask a perfectly logical question.

"The ring will know," he says, like this is completely reasonable and will make sense to me.

I just stare at him, waiting for the punch line or further explanation. Nothing comes. He leans back as if the matter is closed now and gazes off into the trees. I shrug and drop it; obviously nothing more is coming from Master Shi. I recognize his posture from the last year together. He's done speaking.

We sit on the back porch for several more minutes. He neither speaks nor looks in my direction. Then, suddenly as if some unseen force has poked him, he gets to his feet.

"I must be going, Jake. I'll come by this evening with a birthday celebration dinner. Until then … good luck," he says, then moves through the door without so much as a handshake.

CHAPTER 4

THE BEGINNING

I WATCH MASTER SHI'S RECEDING FORM move through the hallway leading to the front door. I look down at the ring and twist it around a few times with my thumb. I don't normally wear any jewelry, not even a watch, and the ring feels foreign. I get up and move through the house to the front door. I peek out the side window and see Master Shi pedaling his bike down the driveway and then turning left on the sidewalk, heading for home.

Not knowing what to do, I find myself heading for the familiar territory of my bedroom. I pull out my cell phone and notice a message from Dad. He's wishing me a happy birthday and tells me to have a great day. I check the time stamp and see he sent it early this morning. I must've been in the shower when the text came through. I type a quick reply and tuck the phone back into the front pocket of my jeans.

I reach to the nightstand next to my bed, stretching for the Sudoku book that I leave there with a pencil.

I never make it to the book or the nightstand, because I'm falling. Falling to the floor. And then through the floor.

Even though I know what's happening, I can't help but reach out to try and brace my fall, hands flailing about helplessly.

I'm falling through the tunnel at impossible speed.

My Quest—and the Key—are active once again.

MY FEET FIND SOLID GROUND again, and I look around at the familiar scene. It's been a year, but now that I'm here it feels like yesterday. I see the familiar light coming from the end of short hallway.

Sensations return like long forgotten dreams. Nausea. Vertigo. Confusion.

I walk toward the light, half expecting Gene to appear and grab me up in a big bear hug. I guess I should add the sense of déjà vu to the others I'm feeling.

As I reach the light, I hesitate at the corner. I'm not sure about the hesitation, it just feels like the thing to do. I peer around the corner, searching for familiar shapes, familiar bodies.

The long, open hallway of the Training Center looks just like it did a year ago. Three hundred yards separate me from the far wall. The lighting, the walls, the stone table and chairs—all exactly the way we left them.

I am the first to arrive today, which disappoints me. I'd feel more comfortable if Gene or Li were here. All of my insecurities come rushing back, and it's like the past year never happened. Gone are my instruction period with Master Shi and my time with Dad. For the briefest of moments, I wonder if I've dreamed it all up. Maybe I never left this place. Maybe I dreamt the whole past year.

I shake my head. I don't have room for nonsense. Focus on the situation and think logically, I tell myself, still shaking my head. Do I stay here and wait for the others or do I head forward and take a seat?

I decide the confident, rational thing to do is go take a seat. Two hundred eighty yards to cover, since this time I haven't covered any ground past the entrance yet. I focus on my math, knowing this will help me tamp down my anxiety. I wonder if my stride has increased its length since last year and decide counting my steps will tell the tale. If my stride has stayed the same, 11.2 inches, then I will require exactly 900 strides to reach the table. If my stride has become longer due to growth, it will require less.

I reach the table in 869 strides. I quickly do the math in my head, calculating that my stride has increased fractionally to 11.6 inches. Not much difference. I shrug. Oh well, it kept me busy on the walk over.

I think about sitting down, but decide I'd rather stand. So, I kind of lean against the table with my back.

My mind wanders to the imminent reunion. Will Gene look the same? I wonder what a year has done to him. Is he taller, slimmer, and calmer? Yes, maybe and no are my automatic answers to my own questions. Thinking these thoughts makes me chuckle aloud.

I think of Li. I wonder for the thousandth time what she is doing right now. Has she changed? What has she been up to? Has she thought of me a thousand times? Or a hundred times? Or maybe just ten times? I think I'll take ten times and be happy.

I blow out an audible breath of air and shake my head. What's wrong with me?

"I am surely missing something, standing here watching your mind churn through so many emotions. Care to fill me in?" a voice sounds behind me, causing me to jump. It's usually Li who sneaks up on me, but this voice is different.

I whip around to face the voice.

The voice belongs to a bemused looking woman. She is moving toward the table from the rear of the room, opposite from where I entered, with an unspeakable grace. Her movement is so fluid, she appears to be gliding. The fact that her long robes flow to the floor, covering her feet, add to the sensation. The woman is tall and athletic looking, with long white hair. I try for a moment to imagine the color of her hair in younger days. I decide on red, but don't know why. Her eyes are a clear and piercing green. She looks like an angel.

I realize that I have not answered her question or responded in any way other than with my stare. My mouth drops open, but words don't come out.

"I've scared you and for that I am sorry. I can't help myself sometimes. Old habits die hard," she says with that same bemused look. "It is a pleasure to make your acquaintance, Jakob Kimball."

She has reached me now. She is offering an outstretched hand, although it is not in a position that suggests a firm handshake. Rather, it hangs as if I am to take it and bring it to my lips in some strange medieval way, like a lowly subject kissing the hand of the queen.

Unbidden, my hand reaches to hers and clasps it in a cupping manner, wrapping around her fingers only. I can't bring myself to move her hand to my lips, so I give it an awkward squeeze/shake and release it. My hand falls lamely to my side.

This brings a bona fide laugh from within her. "Forgive me, Jakob; I am not accustomed to your ways. I suppose we should shake hands in a gruff, firm manner. Is that correct? Never mind, it is of no consequence." She waves at the air. "As you can plainly see, you are the first to arrive. The others will arrive shortly. We have no time to lose, there is much to discuss."

With this statement, she seats herself on the opposite side of the table from me. I continue to stare at her like some kind of idiot. She jumps up.

"Oh my! Forgive me, I am so preoccupied with this Quest that I have forgotten to introduce myself as your Guide." She offers a courtesy with these words.

Realization dawns on my face. The Guide. Of course, I think to myself. I guess it makes sense that we have different Guides for different Keys and Quests. Why hadn't I considered her a Guide? It was logical to make that assumption, but I hadn't. I thought that our Guide would be the same as last time. I should've known, though, when she appeared. I mean, I hadn't ever seen anyone else in this room who wasn't a Guide.

I'm rambling. And worse yet, I'm rambling to myself.

"Um, I'm going to go wait at the entrance for the others," I stammer.

She waves a hand pleasantly as if to say it's a wonderful idea.

Wow, I have not started this Quest well.

TWO THIRDS OF THE WAY to the back entrance, I hear the familiar whooshing sound that accompanies an arrival. I quicken my pace, excitement building within, but I'm also dismayed to feel nervous and a bit scared. I stop short when I see who comes around the corner.

Li. And Gene.

They must've arrived at almost the same time. They see me as they come into the full light of the cave.

"Hey-oh! Jakers beat us to the cave!" Gene says. "Hey, little buddy, it's great to see ya!"

Gene has his arm around Li in a companionable way. Li is studiously avoiding my gaze. That's different, I think.

"I ran into Li, literally, when I dropped into the cave. It looks like this place needs some air traffic control, ya know what I mean? We can't have the Chosen droppin' on top o' one another before the

Quest even starts. I coulda smashed Li into pieces," he runs on, all the while crushing Li in a one-armed squeeze.

Li wriggles out from under Gene's hug. "Gene, you're doing a pretty good job of smashing me to pieces right now," she mumbles in an annoyed tone.

"Whoops! My bad. I'm just so dern excited to be back with you two. I can hardly contain it, I'm so wound up," he says, the apology lost in his fervor.

A year has passed, yet Gene looks pretty much the same as he did the last time I saw him. He is fractionally taller, but not noticeably so. His bright red hair is the same. He has probably lost a few pounds, but still carries more than he should, I guess. His gregarious personality certainly hasn't changed at all.

All of this sameness has a calming effect upon me. He's the Gene I know and love. The Buddy that I have come to rely upon in so many ways. I smile.

"It's good to see you again, Gene." I greet him, stepping forward into his space. I know he'll sweep me up in a hug when I do so. He doesn't disappoint. Bone-crushing hugs follow—another welcome, familiar feeling.

"So, Jake, did ya hear us a comin'? I couldn't help but notice that you were already on the way over to the entrance," he says, hooking his thumb over his shoulder in the direction of the rear entrance. "I know you couldn't have covered all those strides in such a short amount of time, so you musta had some warning, right?"

I just stare.

"How many steps did it take you this year to cover the distance tween here and the table? Have you grown a bit? It looks like maybe a little." He squints his eyes at me, as if this will help him discern minute changes. "Yeah, it looks like you're a bit sturdier in the bone and maybe a little taller. Attaboy, Jake!"

One year away and I had forgotten the torrents of language that pour from Gene with such ease. I feel like I am being swept under by a tidal wave of words. He's asked at least three questions and hasn't waited for an answer even once. I think about answering, but realize he isn't finished.

"Wow! I have so much to tell the two of ya! Y'all are not gonna believe what happened to me this past year. Holy moly, I can't wait for the Sharing Room either; I gotta tell you 'bout Chloe and ... and well, everything!" he gushes.

Gene takes a breath and in doing so, looks up to see the Guide waiting patiently near the stone table.

"Jakers, why dinnit ya tell us the new Guide was waitin' for us?" he says.

I give him a look to let him know that he's been talking the entire time. He chuckles and slaps me on the back.

"Oy! Hello, Madame Guide. We'll be with ya right quick," he calls as a greeting. Li is shaking her head at Gene. I just smile.

Gene waves us forward and begins taking his long strides toward the Guide. I hang back an extra second and fall into place next to Li.

"Hi, Li," I say, hating that my voice wavers. I'm at a loss as to what to say next, so I latch onto something I used in my summer work with Master Shi. "Um, your hair looks so shiny, what shampoo do you use?" I instantly regret the words. So stupid.

Li snaps her head over to look at me, shock in her eyes. Her right hand automatically reaches up to the long braid hanging over her shoulder. She laughs, and it seems to break her out of whatever haze she was in upon arriving.

"Hi, Jake," she says with the laugh still in her voice. "I am very particular about my shampoo, if you must know. I found a brand I like when I lived in America, and now I order it from the internet. The brand is Kérastase." She is smiling at my ridiculous question. "What brand do you use, Jake?" she asks, the humor still there.

"Umm ... I don't ... I think it's Suave or something. Dad just buys it, I guess," I stumble, not ready for the return question. Nobody ever asked me that before.

"Suave, huh?" Gene pipes up and joins in. "How very suave of you to ask Li about her hair. Is that the burning question you've had for the past year, Jake? I wonder what Li uses to wash her shimmery hair? Have you been practicing that question all year? It sounded a bit rehearsed, buddy," Gene teases with a smile, moving back ahead of Li's and my pace.

I just shake my head, my embarrassment clearly showing in my face. A whole year's worth of training down the drain. I feel like crawling into a hole. I've made a mess of the whole deal. My eyes find the floor and I keep them locked there.

I feel a hand on my arm. "Thank you, Jake," Li says with warmth in her voice. "I needed that. I was feeling a bit odd upon arriving here again, and you helped pull me out of it with your question. I guess it all feels a bit strange to both of us."

I glance at her and smile a small thank you. She leaves her hand on my arm for an extra second and then lets it drop.

"Ya know, Jake, I think you're onto somethin' with that hair schtick. I think I'll remember that for next time I see Chloe," he says, then rehearses the words aloud. "Hey, Chloe, your hair is positively radiant today. What kind of shampoo do you use?"

And to think I had been looking forward to this day.

CHAPTER 5

REVELATION

GENE FALLS BACK INTO LINE with Li and me. He shoe-horns his way in between us and swings an arm around each of us.

"Okay, so I can't even wait another second, you guys are not gonna believe how last year went!" Gene says, excitement getting the better of him. "Chloe and I are gonna get married. I mean, not right away, we're fourteen for Pete's sake and we live in Texas, not Arkansas!" He laughs at his own joke; it must be a southern thing. Li and I don't get it. He moves on like we do. "I'm only kiddin'. I'm just so happy."

"Wait, is Chloe the girl you talked about with the red hair and freckles like yours?" Li asks, alert. I, too, remember a few passing references when we were in China together. We both look at him now, having been sucked into the powerful Gene gravitational pull.

I surprise myself when I hear words pouring out of my mouth. "Yeah, Gene, you'll want to be careful if you two have kids, they might spontaneously combust."

Both Gene and Li stop and stare at me, Li leans around Gene to get a good look at me. They're both looking at me like I have two heads.

"What?" I demand.

"Wait, was that a joke, Jakers? Did you just make a funny? Wow, I mean it was a little nerdy with the whole spontaneous com-bustin' bit, but overall, I'm impressed. You musta had quite a year too if you're crackin' wise now," he grins. "First you're talking all smooth-like to Li about her hair and now you're throwin' jokes out?"

Li is smiling at me, but she lets Gene do the talking. My lips curl up a little, but I don't say anything.

"It's like I don't even know you. What have you done with Jake?" Gene jokes as he playfully shakes my shoulders in mock anger. I shrug his hands away and turn forward, beginning our walk again.

"Anyway, as I was sayin' before you both so rudely interrupted, you are not gonna believe who I met during the summer—"

"Your Guardian," Li says matter-of-factly, stealing Gene's momentum.

"Wha—oh, I see. I get it. Mr. and Mrs. Smarty Pants also got a visit too, huh? Well, way to steal my thunder, you two. Way to go. I hope you're proud of yourselves," he says glancing between the two of us. I let him know from my expression that I've had a visit also. I flash a look at Li, congratulating her on deflating Gene so easily. It almost seems like we're teaming up on the poor guy.

"Ya know, I *am* the Buddy here. And the way you two are lookin' at each other, I gotta take exception. You two gangin' up on me like this—" Gene stops, and his eyes go wide. "Oooooh, no way!"

Gene continues to move his eyes between Li and me, and then back. Over and over again.

"You two!" he says, pointing an accusatory finger at us. "You two!" he repeats as if stuck on these words, not knowing how to move past them. It doesn't take long for Gene to find the words.

"You two are in love! Perfect. Great." Gene starts pacing circles around Li and me. Shock registers on my face. Li looks the same. We race one another to go completely red in the face. "Now we're not the Chosen trio, we're the Chosen duo and their third wheel." He raises his arms up and throws them down to slap his sides, looking very much like a child throwing a tantrum. I would laugh if I weren't so afraid that Gene might pop me, or maybe I'm worried because he might be right.

"Uh, Miss Guide, ma'am," he says, turning toward the stone table and the woman standing beside it. He starts moving in her direction, double-timing his steps. "I'd like to propose a change in the guidelines. Can I bring my girlfriend along to even up the situation here? I'm serious. We used to call the Sharing Room the Awkward Room, but now any room these two are in with me as a third wheel now becomes an awkward room. Dernit all!"

I haven't moved; I'm in shock. Li gives me a slug in the arm. I turn to see her smiling at me. She moves her head toward the front, signaling me to get a move on. Li seems unaffected by Gene's outburst. I'm definitely affected.

As we reach the table, Li gives Gene the same slug in the arm she gave me. "Gene, will you take it down several notches? Jake and I are not in love. We're fourteen years old," she says evenly. "We don't even know what love is, but what we do know is that we are friends. We share some things that nobody else shares. You know, our mothers died. Only the two of us get that, okay?"

Gene looks dubious. My turn.

"Gene, Li is right. We're fourteen years old. We've found a friendship that is important to the two of us." I hesitate and then move on. "Just like the friendship I have with you. It's important to me too. Trust me, you are just as big a deal to me."

Gene smiles a bit, slowly coming around. I decide try to joke with him again.

"I mean, don't get me wrong, Li is beautiful, and you're are a big oaf, so it's different, you know?" I say with a smile.

"Big oaf, huh?" he says slowly, thinking.

"Our big oaf, though," Li adds quickly, emphasizing the first word.

"I get it, guys, and if your friendship is close and different from mine, I guess that's okay with me," Gene says, then turns to the Guide.

"Well, Guide, o wise one, let's get this party started, shall we? The Chosen three are here and ready to roll."

The Guide has been silently watching this whole drama play out with amusement on her face. "Ah, the energies and insecurities of youth. It's a pity that I've grown old, Gene," she says with a wink.

For the first time that I can remember, Gene is completely flabbergasted by the Guide's wink. His jaw drops, and his cheeks match his hair for color. The Guide starts laughing; Li and I join in quickly.

I think I'm going to like this Guide.

Gene turns to me, "Yeah, well, I think I liked the old stuffy Guide better." Everything seems back to normal now, with Gene reading my thoughts again.

"Just giving you a dose of your own medicine, as they say,

Eugene," the Guide smiles with mirth. "Now let's get down to the business at hand," she adds, settling into her seat.

I IMMEDIATELY NOTICE OUR GUIDE DOESN'T rise to speak as the first did. She seems content to sit with us and discuss the new Quest in a more familiar, intimate way. It's not a presentation or speech, rather it's a discussion and planning meeting.

Old habit kicks in and Gene sits in the far seat, with me in the middle and Li to my right. Gene and Li seem to have taken in stride the fact that we have a new Guide with us for this Quest. The atmosphere around the table shifts from joviality to tense seriousness, as each one of us shifts our mindset.

The Guide begins without preamble. "The Quest that you embark upon today is unique. Unique because the Key you seek was lost." She allows this to hang in the air. One of the two lost keys. "And this Key was recovered by your parents," she adds.

If the air was tense before, now the tension feels almost suffocating. Li sucks in a breath. Gene makes a sound that I can't interpret, his face is easy to interpret through: shock.

A smile from the Guide, a kind smile.

"I'm sure that several questions are begging for preeminence in your minds right about now. Please allow me to attempt to answer each of them in turn." She leans forward as if to grab our attention more completely. I don't think that's possible. She has all of us.

"First, it would be well to remember that we are not retrieving the Eight Keys in order according to your way of keeping time. Time is a humankind invention and is not relevant to our retrieval order. The Keys are ordered according to virtue—the characteristic that accompanies each Key. Each virtue builds upon the previous one. To bring them all into harmony as we near the end of this world, that is our mission. This will allow peace to reign finally and forever."

She pauses to allow us to digest this information.

"Your previous Guide felt it important to let you discover the virtue that the first Key held. Faithfulness. Today, I will tell you that the second Key is the Key of Integrity. We will speak more of this later. But for now, you need to know that you will be striving to add integrity to faithfulness."

I stole another glance at Gene and Li. They looked enraptured, completely given over to the Guide.

"Second, because this Key was originally lost and subsequently found by others— in this case, your parents—you are free to retrieve the Key, even though two of your parents are still alive. The original protectors of the Key are dead." I find myself trying hard to keep up with this Guide. The amount of stunning information is dizzying.

"Although your parents are alive, they cannot have shared any information with you regarding the location of the Key. If they had, this Key would not be able to be retrieved. Your parents have known since they successfully completed their Quest that you might seek their Key while they were still living."

A deep sadness creeps into my heart, knowing that I would not have this shared experience with my mother. There would be no silently exchanged acknowledgements between her and I, like I supposed there would be at the end of the Quest with my companions. No knowing hugs and shared emotions—nothing like the bond that should be there.

I snap back to the present upon hearing the Guide's voice start again. She is looking deeply into my eyes. "Each one of you has received something from your parent, however, to aid you in this Quest. It may be a tangible object or an intangible teaching or lesson. You will have to discover on your own exactly what has been given to you."

Again, I look to either side of me to take in Li's and Gene's expressions. Li is stoic, as usual. Gene's eyes are wide, and he has a hand shoved into a pocket. Apparently, Gene knows what he has been given; surprisingly he does not give voice to his shock, which shocks me.

"As with your previous Guide, I was also a Chosen." She reveals her Key to us. "I was not successful in protecting my Key."

Gene is practically apoplectic upon hearing this latest bombshell. I try to imagine the war going on inside Gene's mind. I know he desperately wants to speak but is wrestling with himself to stay silent. It's like watching a toddler try to keep from grabbing the candy that has been placed before him with instructions not to touch it. A virtually impossible task—both Gene's and the toddler's.

Li sits with her trademark calm exterior, but her eyes give her away. She is shocked, intrigued and appalled, all at the same time.

As for me, I'm having trouble processing the whole thing, I admit. Confusion is the main feeling here.

"Your parents retrieved the Key that I lost. I was part of a Chosen trio that turned to treachery. I am the only one of the three not to relinquish this," she says, her knuckles white as she holds onto her key. She is reliving some unseen nightmare as she speaks to us.

"Although I wouldn't give up my Key, I was also unable to protect it from the other two. I was deceived by them and left behind …" the Guide trails off, now clearly completely consumed by her memories. A single tear streaks it way down her cheek.

The room is silent. Nobody moves. Nobody breathes.

The Guide regains herself then and draws a shuddering breath. "This is a dangerous Quest. The Key you seek has been wielded by Evil for decades. Those who have controlled it did not give it up easily to your parents. It required everything of them— every ounce of skill and intellect they possessed. They are true heroes. *My* heroes. They saved me from my shame and guilt. They redeemed me. You do not know your parents as I do. It is my hope that during the Quest you will find pieces of them along the way. Pieces that you do not see now, cannot see now." She finishes her sentence, eyes boring into mine.

I offer a slight nod. She returns it. Something passes between us and somehow I know that I will see my mother in a new light by the end of this Quest. Perhaps a light I have been hoping for, to illuminate so much that I don't know about mom, about Sarah.

The Guide straightens.

"Now, you will be traveling to postwar Berlin, Germany. You will arrive days after your parents left. They retrieved the Key and secured it, knowing that a new generation would be back to collect it shortly. Their Quest was painful and difficult. I have no doubt that yours will be likewise. "Evil reigned for decades after I—after the Key was lost. Over one hundred million people lost their lives in the time between losing the Key and its recovery. Countless others suffered difficulties, emotional and physical, that may be considered worse than death. "The importance of this Key cannot be overstated. It must be recovered and returned here." The Guide's eyes shone with a fierceness and passion that did more to drive the point home than her words.

"The weapons you will face are more deadly and sophisticated than your previous Quest. The Evil forces are desperate to regain control of the Key, and their numbers are legion. These are hard men who won't be 'buddied' easily. And, finally, the codes, ciphers and tricks are more complex than you have seen." She offers this as she moves her gaze from Li to Gene to me.

I tried to think of what I knew of World War II era technologies and ciphers. I had heard of the famed Enigma machines, which were used to create and send coded messages and the Native American coders of the United States. But I lack specificity about the subtleties of the systems. Time to study, I think.

"Like before, you have three days here at the Training Center to prepare yourselves for this daunting task. Your training will be fierce—harsh maybe to your thinking. We must not fail. We cannot lose this Key again." The Guide seems worn out and leans back into her chair.

"Each of you will be treated equally in all three disciplines. This means that all three of your will practice Brawn, Brain, and Buddy skills. You will need all of your considerable abilities to succeed." She falls silent and retreats into her mind. She appears tortured by her past. It's obvious that guilt racks her mind and body.

"Madame Guide?" Gene says quietly, unable to contain himself, but at least using some restraint.

The Guide opens her eyes and looks at us like she is surprised to see us. She has been jolted out of her memory, momentarily confused.

"Please, you may call me Elizabeth," she says, her voice small.

"Miss Elizabeth, may I ask what happened?" Gene asks.

The Guide shakes her head. "I cannot tell you, because my failed Quest is your current Quest, though I am sure you will discover details as you pursue the Key."

Gene nods, conceding this point.

"Miss Elizabeth, you are not to blame. You kept your key. It is the others who shoulder this blame. Don't beat yourself up about this, our parents succeeded, and we will succeed too," Gene assures her, trying to cheer the woman up.

She smiles a sad smile. "You three are still so young, I worry about you. I know you have good intentions—so did I and my companions." She leans forward, the ferocity returning. "Gene, you still misunderstand faithfulness if you seek to remove blame from me and lay it on my companions. We were three but were to be one. We sat in the Sharing Room, just as you have done. We believed in ourselves, just as you do. I failed them just as much as they failed me. If one of us fails, we all fail. Just because I did not remove my Key from my neck, does not excuse my failures to my companions. And to humankind. To the innumerable souls who lost their lives, to those who lived in misery and subjugation, to those who counted on me. Think of those you know and love back home," she pauses. "What will they do if they cannot pursue virtue and character, how will their lives turn if humankind turns away from the eight Keys. They turn to vapid, empty pursuits of selfish desire …"

The room feels like it is closing in on us, depressing and sad.

"But, as you have rightly said, Gene, your parents have indeed succeeded!" she says, working to infuse joy and positivity into the room once again. "And you will, too. I will work to prepare you, doing everything in my power to see that you are ready."

She smiles and we all take our cue from her.

Gene sees his opening and leans forward slapping the table loudly. "Excellent! I assume that we'll have the same situation as far as the language goes? Everything'll be translated for us. And hey, German language with an alphabet like ours, so no confusing symbols and such, right? So that's something!" he looks around for support.

"That's right, Gene. You will hear the language as your own and vice versa."

"Plus, we can wear regular clothes on this gig, right? No more slippers and robes. Jeans and a T-shirt sounds just about right to me, huh?" he says, turning to me for confirmation. I look down at my own jeans and T-shirt. I nod.

"Okay, then, let's talk about the next three days," Gene continues, prompting Elizabeth.

She nods and begins laying out the plan.

"Mornings will be Brawn sessions, to get our blood pumping early. Afternoons will be Buddy sessions, and evenings are reserved for Brain. Only on the final day will you work on your individual areas.

"Like last time, I have assistants who have volunteered to work with you in sharpening your skills. I am the Master Buddy of this Quest. The Master Brawn and Brain will be revealed later.

"One final word to you all. A couple of you were carrying electronic devices such as cell phones when you were carried to the Training Center. Please know that these devices are not allowed during your Quest. Therefore, they have been left behind, don't worry, they have not been damaged in any way. You will find them close to the spot where you were taken," she explains.

Gene pats his pants pocket with a dismayed look. "Man, I was hoping to exchange contact information with the two of you. We didn't get a chance at the end of the last Quest and I was wantin' to talk to the both of you during the past year. Oh well, I s'pose we can do it the old-fashioned way, ya know, write it down on a piece of paper. Or we can just tell Jakers, here, and he'll lock them away in his sturdy melon." He says this last part while slinging an arm around my neck.

CHAPTER 6

TRAINING

W E MOVED DIRECTLY FROM THE stone table into the Brawn Room, where the three of us huddled together, discussing the change that had taken place in the room since our last visit.

The room's dimensions were the same, of course, but were laid out differently. There was what looked like a firing range toward to the back of the room, with targets hanging yards away. Shelves that must be gun racks lined the wall closest to the range. Pistols, rifles and automatic machine guns lined the shelves. To the right of the range and rack were the more familiar mats for grappling and wrestling. Gone were the staffs and weaponry of early fifteenth century China.

"Yeah, so this is different. The stakes have definitely gone up." Gene speaks aloud what we are all thinking.

The Guide enters the room at that moment, along with several assistants and what I assume to be the Master Brawn of this quest. He looks like steroids might have been in his past, his very recent past. He is tall and muscular, with no neck showing. His shoulders just grow into his head. He and the assistants are all dressed in what I assume to be vintage World War II military gear.

"This is Hans, and he will be your instructor for the Brawn portions of your stay here. Please pay careful attention to his directions," Elizabeth says, then turns and leaves us.

"Of course his name is Hans. Have you ever met a guy that looked like that named Gary or Stevie? He could be my long lost brother," Gene mumbles under his breath.

I think he couldn't be Gene's brother; he has blond hair and blue eyes. Gene sees my look.

"Okay, maybe a distant cousin," he acquiesces.

Hans stands rigidly before us with his feet spread wide and his hands clasped behind his back.

"I am Hans. And these are my assistants," he says, only moving his eyes to indicate his assistants. "We must quickly prepare you in the use and care of the common weapons of the period. Have any of you had any practical experience with firearms?"

As he speaks, I imagine that he is speaking with a movie-like German accent. He may be speaking German for all I know, but it translates perfectly to my ears. I wish I could hear the accent, so I fill it in myself. This causes me to miss his question. He is staring hard at me.

"What?" I blurt out, suddenly afraid.

"Have you ever handled a firearm?" he repeats. I seriously can't get the accent out of my head. I'm adding it every time he speaks. I shake my head to purge the accent.

He takes my shake as an answer, which in this case is perfect because it is also accurate. I haven't so much as held a gun before and always had a goal to never do so. Another resolution down the drain.

"Are you hearing anything I am saying?" Hans barks at me. I haven't heard anything. Had he said more after asking me the direct question? I'm not sure.

"I'm not sure this is the best time to zone out, Jakers," Gene whispers.

Li steps forward. "Sir, I am fundamentally opposed to guns, I prefer to use my body—" she begins.

Quick as lightning, Hans draws the pistol he has holstered at his waist, points it at Li's chest and pulls the trigger.

Boom! The firearm discharges with an explosive sound that reverberates through the room. My ears are ringing. I'm pretty sure I shouted or more probably screamed, and I rush to Li's side. She goes down from the shot, blown back and down by the round. Gene also falls to her side, yelling at Hans at the same time.

Bright red liquid covers Li's chest.

I gasp and fight the initial gorge that rises. Then I realize it's not blood. It … it looks like paint.

Gene and I both turn to Hans in confusion. Li groans and rubs her chest, her hand coming away painted red. She struggles into a seated position.

"Seriously?" Gene's shout filters into my ears now, but still faintly.

"You are lucky it is just paint. The enemy you will encounter is not 'fundamentally opposed to guns' and will not hesitate to pull the trigger," Hans says without a trace of emotion.

"Oh, it's on now, you big freakin' German," Gene says as he stands up and moves quickly toward the gun rack.

Hans's weapon explodes again, deafening me a second time, and Gene spins around like a top. Red paint covers his shoulder. Gene's face is a mask of anger now, red and contorted in fury. He takes another step toward the guns. I quickly glance to Hans, who is raising his pistol to finish Gene off.

But he never gets the chance.

I just now notice that Li has moved from her seated position. She must have moved like a ghost, because neither Hans nor I noticed her approach. I see the blur that is Li colliding with Hans, her foot meeting his wrist. The gun clatters to the floor.

I smile.

Li doesn't waste time on a smile. She is already moving into her next kick, then a fist strike to Han's neck and he sinks to his knees.

"On the ground, Li!" Gene shouts triumphantly.

I turn to see him wielding a large shotgun. He pulls the trigger just as Li disappears behind the huge form of Hans.

Boom! A rack of the slide. Boom! A rack of the slide. Boom!

Small paint balls bloom on Hans's chest and arms. I notice paint blooms on the assistants' chests and arms as well.

"Stop!" Hans's voice bellows above the din.

Remarkably, Gene obeys the command. His chest is heaving, the anger is still written on his face.

"I am NOT fundamentally opposed to guns," Gene grinds out, each word punctuated with a clipped pause. "I know how to use them, and will not stand by and see you fire a weapon at an unarmed girl to prove a point. *Sir.*" Gene drops the weapon to the ground. He stalks over to where Li is still prone on the ground, brusquely passing Hans, moving him aside. Li accepts Gene's hand and they both move back to my side.

Hans is examining the paint on his own body.

"Well done, Eugene," he says, satisfied with Gene's aim.

"Save it, Hans. I don't want your praise for firing a weapon at other people in anger," Gene says, the adrenaline and anger draining away.

Hans just nods his head. He shoos the assistants away and out of the room with a wave of his hand. I assume they are going to get changed. He turns his full attention to the three of us.

"Ms. Li. Please accept my apologies. Often I act in a brash manner, projecting my own beliefs and personality onto others. Forgive me," Hans concedes, sufficiently humble.

"Apology accepted," Li acknowledges with a nod of her head. "Perhaps you can show me how to use these weapons so that I might use them as distractions. They seem to be perfectly capable noisemakers," she offers this olive branch to Hans. He accepts it with a large smile.

"I think I understand your meaning. You would like to learn to use them so well that you will know just how to miss your target, yet still come close enough to stop them from shooting you, yes?" Hans asks, his smile spreading.

"Yes. Well placed shots don't necessarily mean hitting your opponent, and there are other options that I would like to practice with you," she adds, casting a glance at Gene and me. "Alone," she adds mysteriously.

"Fine. We will find time for your mysterious 'other options' later," Hans answers, then turns to face Gene. "Eugene, you handled the shotgun with comfortable ease. May I assume that you chose this weapon from the rack in a period of intense focus, that this is your weapon of choice?"

"That assumption is half right, I guess," Gene remarks. "I chose this particular weapon because I could see that it was loaded with paintballs, therefore it would be relatively safe to discharge, and might be effective," he offers a smile. "But, yes, I like a good shotgun. I knew I could stop this nonsense fastest with the pump action."

"There is one thing I would like to know. I shot you in the shoulder. While only paint, there is a punch to our rounds, how did you manage to still use the shotgun?" Hans asked, his voice clinical now.

"You shot me in the left shoulder and yes, it packed a wallop, but adrenaline and anger do wonders for a guy. Now, if it had been in the right shoulder, I may not have had as good an aim or enough strength for three shots," Gene trails off while shrugging his shoulders, suggesting the discussion was not important.

"You are very strong, Eugene," Hans finishes, turning his attention to me.

I was hoping we could delay this part a bit longer.

"And what of you, Jakob?" he asks.

I just shake my head. He gets the message.

"Well, we'll just train you on a pistol and see how we progress from there." Hans pauses and offers more. "I understand that this is difficult for you, as young as you are, but you must protect yourselves while on your Quest. You are going into a very dangerous situation; it will be chaotic beyond imagination. Four countries control Berlin at this time, although the term 'control' should be used loosely. All four want what the Key can give them—power. They don't understand what it represents, but they want to control it, possess it, and prevent the others from obtaining it."

Hans runs out of steam, worry showing through his rough exterior. His emotions are laid bare now, I can see that he is committed to helping us in whatever way he can. Gene and Li recognize this also, I see it as I look at their faces. They both nod. Gene steps forward.

"Hans, we appreciate your help very much. Let's get started."

AFTER A COUPLE HOURS IN firearms training, the three of us sit in the cafeteria eating a slow lunch. Each of us is buried deep in our own thoughts. I suspect we are all overwhelmed with the new destination, and the new weapons associated with it.

I look at the pistol sitting next to my tray. I am carry it with me always through the next days of training. It is loaded with paint shot, but still, the sight of it seemed so incongruous. I'm not a guy who would normally carry around a gun. Not to mention that I'm fourteen years old! Is it even legal to carry a firearm at my age? I don't know, and then I suppose it doesn't matter. We are headed to a different era, a different time with different rules. A place, from Hans's accounts, where there are no rules.

Li catches me staring at the gun and misreads the situation.

"Do you have to keep it on the table? I mean, you're staring at it like it's some kind of prize. It's a terrible weapon," Li objects, disgust plain in her voice.

I look at her, surprised at her vehemence. I shake my head.

"No, I'm not staring at it out of rapture. I'm staring at in in awe, I can't believe the situation. Plus, I don't like the way it jabs into me when I sit down," I say, rubbing the holster on my waist. "I can put it away if you'd like."

She just shakes her head, I think my explanation helps her see it in a new light.

"No, you can leave it. I get it now."

"You're not half bad with that piece, Jake," Gene says between mouthfuls of food. "Your marksmanship improved pretty dern quick."

I shrug. "It's all math and physics again. I can do the calculations quickly in my head and make the necessary adjustments to hit the target. But that is in a controlled environment—no fear, no adrenaline, no nerves. Introduce those elements and I don't think I could hit the broad side of a barn," I add, borrowing the phrase Gene had used earlier in the day. I don't know exactly what it meant, but I know Gene knows.

"I'm counting on not hitting anything," Li comments.

Li had been exceptional in our training. She is the best shot of the three of us. Her accuracy even shocked Hans. Only I understood why she was so intent on becoming a crack shot. She wanted to ensure she didn't hit anybody mortally. I remember something she told me during our first Quest: *"We want to put our opponent out of the fight, not out of life."*

Even Gene was hesitant about using too much force.

"I ain't got no interest in shootin' anybody. Back home, we hunt for food. When we fire our weapons, we do so because we are shootin' at food. You may not agree with it, but for us it puts food on a table with seven hungry boys," he had told us earlier today.

As we finished up our meal, we gathered the weapons we're now required to carry and headed for the Buddy room and our next block of training. The Buddy room is straight down a long corridor from the cafeteria. As we leave the "chow hall," as Gene calls it, we pass by the junction where we had fought assistants last year. They had come at us from three directions, cutting us off. As I look down the hallway that I had fought in, the hairs stand up on my arms and neck. A tingle zips through my body. My hand automatically drops to the holstered pistol.

"Something's not right," Li says quickly.

"I feel it, too," I agree.

Gene brings his shotgun up and pumps the action.

Suddenly, Li pushes Gene into the wall, just as a projectile passes by his ear. Li bends at the waist, limbo-like. She does this while pushing me into the corridor that I was just staring down. Another paint ball passes just over Li, only because she is doing the limbo. Paint splatters on the corner at my head height, unable to reach me because I was shoved around the corner.

Li is back upright with her pistol in her right hand, firing away down the corridor. She begins running toward the unseen assistants, zigging her way toward them, all the while firing her paint.

I blink my eyes, as I see her run up the wall for three steps, defying gravity for the briefest of moments. Paintballs zing by where she was just running. She regains the ground and tumbles into a roll. Light blazes into existence, as Li must've have lit a flare. The assistants are crouched in a defensive phalanx near the Buddy room entrance.

Li is on them now, legs kicking and palms striking in a blur. In another instant, the assistants are down and Li is applying plasti-cuffs all around. I finally come to my senses. I round the corridor and run toward Li, my pistol raised and ready to fire. I know that there is nobody else to concern myself with, but I can't help it. Gene matches my pace and we sprint to Li.

"Uh, Li, what exactly is it that you've been doin' this past year again?" Gene says with a trademark grin. "'Cause what you just done looked like somethin' out of a movie."

"Collect their guns, Gene," Li says, ignoring the question while she finishes up binding the attackers.

Gene and I jump into action.

"Not you, Jake. Let Gene do it," she says. "I need you over here."

I stop and reverse direction, making my way over to her, stepping over prone figures.

When Li turns to me, my eyes go wide. She's been hit.

"You've been hit, Li!" I almost shout, dropping to my knees next to her. Red paint blooms on her left calf.

Li waves her hand dismissively. "A ricochet. It's nothing. I need you to see this." She redirects my attention to a downed attacker. He is unconscious, eyes closed. Blue paint has colored the back of his head. Blue paint from Li's weapon.

Li looks at me with a mix of anger and fear. Tears are in her eyes.

"This is why I hate these things." She's clearly referencing her gun. "I was firing at them, not coming close to them, just to keep them down and hiding, so that I could get close enough to disarm them," she shakes her head, trying to rid herself of the image of this attacker. "But this guy stumbled and fell into the path of my paint. There was nothing I could do."

As she is speaking, the attacker begins to stir and his eyes flutter open.

"He's fine, Li," I say, looking to reassure her.

She gives another violent shake of her head.

"I know he's okay. It's just paint right now. But soon it won't be paint," she turns to me, her eyes wild. "I can't do this Jake. I can't do it!" She throws her arms around me, her body shaking against mine. I tentatively reach around and comfort her.

"Li, we'll figure this out, okay? Maybe we can use rubber bullets or non-lethal darts or ..." I run out of words.

Just as quickly as she folded into me, she pulls away. I have no idea how to act in this situation. I turn to find Gene looking at us. In the back of my mind, I register shock that Gene hasn't taken this opportunity to give us grief. Maybe this past year was good for him, too, I think.

Li notices Gene as well. She offers a weak smile. "What? No pithy comment? No teasing remark about Jake and me hugging?" Li says, injecting some small amount of humor into her voice. "Uh, Gene, what exactly is it that you've been doin' the past year again?" Li says, her voice matching how Gene sounded earlier.

Gene laughs. I follow with my own laugh. Finally, Li laughs out loud. The adrenaline and tension sluice away.

"Well now, about fifty-two jokes and smart remarks came to mind while I watched the two of you fall into each other's arms, but I stopped myself from sayin' 'em," Gene says. "But now that you've given me permission—"

Li cuts him off. "Good job, Gene. Way to show that newfound maturity. Let's head into the Buddy Room and see what's next," she says, quickly stopping him from revving up all the way.

Gene heaves a sigh. "I'm not sure I like my 'newfound maturity,'" he speculates, but just follows Li into the room.

CHAPTER 7

SECRETS

OUR GUIDE LEADS BUDDY TRAINING.

"Gene and I will work together today, and Li and Jakob will pair up," she assigns briskly. Before she can continue, Gene takes up the challenge.

"Uh, Madame Guide, Elizabeth, I kinda think it's best if we steer clear of the words 'pair up' when referring to Jake and Li," he's warming to his role. "They might get the wrong idea," he continues with a wink toward us.

"And the real Gene is back," Li intones with a roll of her eyes.

I muster up all of the courage I have and reach over to grab Li's hand in mine. I do this while staring straight at Gene with a serious look. I almost pull it off, but the corners of my mouth begin to turn up.

Li squeezes my hand and flashes Gene a big smile. My smile blooms now too.

"Jake? What in tarnation is going on with you?" Gene asks with an eye roll of his own. "Another joke from you? I can't handle you anymore."

Then the Guide shocks us all. She intertwines her hand with Gene's and uses her silkiest voice.

"Who said anything about Jake and Li, Eugene?" she purrs with a sultry wink at Gene.

His eyes flare wide and then he pulls his hand away from the Guide like she's on fire. "Oh, I get it. Let's all gang up on Gene. Is this how it's gonna be?" he grumbles, acting pouty. "Elizabeth, please control yourself, I am practically spoken for."

We all have a good laugh, relaxing into our roles here in the

Buddy Room.

I am well aware that I haven't let go of Li's hand and that she hasn't let go of mine either. It feels comfortable, like we fit.

"Uh, guys, you can let go of each other's hands now." Gene notices that we haven't let go either.

Li offers a smile to Gene but says nothing. And she doesn't release my hand.

Gene tips his head back and up to the ceiling and lets out an exaggerated sigh. "Seriously. This is going to be a long Quest."

I realize the Guide is staring at me, and I feel the familiar flush of red rush into my face and neck. She offers a smile and small nod. I can't read it. Why the smile and nod? Li gently removes her hand from mine (reluctantly, it seems to me), but maybe that's just my imagination.

"What would you like us to do?" Li prompts the Guide.

Elizabeth turns to Gene, directing her words to him. "Gene, I have a secret that I am not sure that I can trust you with. I need you to convince me that I can share it with you. Once you have the secret, the exercise is over."

She turns to Li. "Li, you are the secret keeper; Jakob, you are the secret finder. Okay? Begin."

I watch for a moment as Gene jumps right into the exercise, questioning the Guide, getting to know her. I watch Gene because I have no idea what to say to Li. I don't know how to begin.

Reluctantly, I turn to her. She chuckles at my expression.

"You look like you'd rather face the attackers again with your pistol than have to face me, Jake," she says, bemused. She is clearly not going to help me out any.

I shrug her off, hoping to buy a little time. Her little joke about the attackers gives me an idea.

"So, about the attackers, I saw you like run up the wall and back down to avoid some paintballs. Did you learn to do that this summer?" Now it's my turn to wait her out.

"I guess so. I worked heavily on my Brawn abilities, including some new understandings and techniques," she answers vaguely.

Whether she knows it or not, she's given me an opening. "Some new understandings and techniques? Tell me more about that. Did you gain a new teacher or teachers this past year?" I prompt, silently thanking Master Shi and his training over the year. He introduced me to debate and listening to people, then taught me to use their words to direct further questioning, drawing out the information required.

Li leans back in her seat, retreating into memory.

"Yes, some new teachers were arranged, and they taught me some fairly advanced martial techniques."

"How did they go about teaching you these techniques?"

Minutes pass. Questions are asked and answered. Li responds to my questions, but I can tell that she is too relaxed. I am not getting closer to what I need to know. She is secure in her secret. I need to change course, but don't know what new course to pursue. I fall silent.

Li continues to smile at me, confident her secret is safe. I think of her hand in mine. It feels good. It fits. There is something hidden behind that fit.

I decide on a gamble.

"Did you think of Gene and me over the past year?" I ask, my turn to smile.

She looks taken aback by this new line of questioning. She recovers quickly. "Of course I did," she says coolly. Too coolly, in my opinion.

"What specifically did you think about?"

"I don't know, just wondered what you were up to and stuff like that."

"Oh? Let's talk about Gene. Did you do anything specifically to remind yourself of Gene? Do you have a memory that makes you think of Gene?"

She becomes comfortable again. I've left the correct path. She opens her mouth to speak, but I cut her off.

"You know what? Let's save that question for a minute? I have a different one." Alarm registers for the briefest of moments. Yes!

"What did you do specifically that reminded you of me?" I ask. I know I have her.

She fiddles with her hands, studiously avoiding my gaze. I wait. Success is near.

"Well, there is something that I did that reminded me of you. Something you showed me while we were in China ..."

I'm close. I do what I do best: I stay silent, waiting. I tell myself that I'm interested in knowing solely how to reveal her secret and move on with training. That's a bold-faced lie though. I want to know.

"On some clear nights, I would lie down in the grass and 'climb the sky,'" Li says, hands becoming still while she flicks her eyes up for a glance at mine.

Our eyes meet and something passes between us. I don't really understand it, but I know it's something. A slow smile spreads across my face.

"You did? You remembered?" I say, hating the way I sound.

Li nods.

We stare at one another for a minute—or longer—searching for the meaning in this revelation.

Gene breaks the spell. He snaps his fingers centimeters from my eyes.

"Earth to Jake. Whoa buddy, what happened to you? Did Li's secret send you into a coma? Was it that she can kill you with just her pinky finger? Or did she learn to hypnotize people?" Gene runs on and on. I glance up at him, letting him know that I'm back.

Gene moves on. "Li, whatever you just did to Jake, let's not have it happen again, ya hear? We need his mind clear and sharp. No more hypnosis, got it?"

Li gives Gene a serious nod. Gene leaves it, confident he's got it sorted.

I PAIRED UP WITH THE GUIDE after Li and then Gene followed. Buddying was draining, I thought to myself over dinner. I'm ready for bed and we still have a Brain session remaining today. My specialty, and I'm already spent. That can't be good, but I finish up my meal and head toward the Brain room with Li and Gene in tow.

Once again, the Guide is there to meet us. She introduces a man as the Master Brain for this quest and leaves us alone with him. This room is familiar ground to me and I automatically move to a seat along the back wall. My friends join me, sitting to my right and left.

"I am the Master Brain for this Quest. My name is Reginald, and I prefer that you call me be my given name, rather than Master."

He makes eye contact with each one of us, his way of ensuring we understand his request. He is tall and thin, with the distinct look of a British blue blood—sharp nose, erect posture, thin hair combed over and failing to cover his bald spot.

"You got it, Reginald," Gene says, our spokesperson as always. "Let's have it regarding this Quest. I mean, last Quest, Jake had this part covered, so I guess Li and I are wonderin' why we are needed here."

The Master looks happy with Gene. "An excellent query, young man! I will explain all." He looks like he is settling in for a long discourse. "This Quest is unique, as you've been told. And as far as the Brain angle, it is tricky because there may be multiple layers of encryption, so to speak, due to the Key being lost and then found."

He must register that we don't follow, because he quickly continues.

"You see, the Key was originally held by late nineteenth century Chosen. However, they gave up the Key. The Key then passed from hand to hand for the next fifty or so years. Finally, your parents acquired the Key and protected it. Therefore, elements of different eras are most likely in play here.

"Codes and ciphers are from the late 1800s, mixed with early and mid-twentieth century technology—which advanced quite rapidly, by the way. Imagine layers of a cake," he says warming to the task and looking quite pleased with his chosen analogy, making me think he has a thing for cake. "In order to get to the very bottom of the cake, one must eat all of the layers, one by one. So too with what you will probably find with this Key—layer built upon layer. It is quite a challenging problem!" he finishes, looking ready for dessert.

"Okay, that all makes a certain sense to me," Gene says. "Especially the parts about cake, but again, I don't see how that involves Li and me."

Reginald scurries closer to our table, placing his hands on it and leaning toward us. "Did your father give you a gift during your twelfth year? And did he tell you to keep it with you on each of your subsequent birthdays?" he asks, knowing the answer full well.

Gene pats his pants pocket absently, checking it contents to be sure. "Yep."

"And what about you, young lady?" he swivels toward Li.

Li gives a nod, hands in her lap, giving away no sign of where she keeps her "gift."

Reginald turns to me, his brows knit closely together. "I suspect your gift was given in a different way; maybe something passed on verbally," he suggests.

I shrug. I don't know what to say. I mean, Mom said a ton to me, and she said nothing to me with a preface of, "You need to remember this for later, Jake."

"Well, we'll come back to young Jake later, I suppose," Reginald remarks, sliding down into a chair opposite us.

"Gene, will you show us your item?"

Gene reaches deep into his pocket. A memory of him reaching into openings along the Great Wall of China comes unbidden into my mind. I smile. His hand is closed in a fist as he moves it over the table. With a dramatic flair, he opens his hand and lets a coin drop onto the table. We all crowd in, looking at the coin. It's an old penny.

"Oops! Wrong pocket," Gene chuckles. "I'm just pulling yer leg with that there penny."

Li looks like she wishes she had a knife. Again, memories. This time they're of Li threatening to permanently cut Gene's smirk into his face.

"Honestly, Gene, when are you going to grow up?" She sounds impatient.

Gene just flashes her a smile and his trademark wink.

"Here it is, in my other pocket," he says, reaching into his other pocket.

He places what looks like another coin onto the table. We are not as anxious this time to crowd forward, expecting to see a quarter, a or nickel, or whatever. But this isn't a coin I am familiar with. In fact, I don't think it's a coin at all. All heads turn to Gene expectantly.

He holds up his hand in a curious, empty gesture. "Hey, I don't know what it is. Pa didn't explain anything about it other than I should keep it on me. He reminded me every birthday morning."

I lean in for a closer look. It looks like a mix between a button and a coin. The surface that shows has a Union Jack on it. The Union Jack is on the flag of Great Britain. I reach out to flip it over, looking at Gene for permission. He nods. I pick it up to turn it over and am struck by its weight. It is solidly heavy, not like a button. I use my thumb to turn it over.

A six-pointed star is carved into the metal coin, with a circle within the star. There is lettering in the circle, but it's faded and unreadable. At the top of the circle is a royal crown. Three large letters that look like they could be initials occupy the middle of the circle. I bring the disk closer and make out Roman numerals under the initials. The Roman numerals are VI.

"It looks like a token of some kind, obviously British in origin. I'll have to study it further to get a better understanding," I say, distracted by the token.

I look over to the desk on the opposite side of the room. That is where I do my studying for each Quest. Books line the walls near the desk. The answer must be there, somewhere.

"Miss Zhang, do you have something from your father?" The Master's voice pulls me back.

Li removes a postcard, worn and creased. She presses it flat on the table in front of her, and we lean in to get a look. The image is faint; the colors have faded over time, but the message is clear. Along the top of the card are the words: Wake Up, America! Below these words is a picture of a woman asleep in a chair, who must represent America. And finally, the words, "Civilization Calls Every Man Woman and Child." We look at Li, who shrugs non-committally.

"If you're looking to me for some piece of knowledge, you've come to the wrong girl. I don't have any idea. My father gave it to me much in the same way Gene has described. I am supposed to carry this with me ..." her voice trails off as she searches her memory for more. She shrugs again; there is nothing more.

I slowly reach toward the card, signaling to Li that I am going to pick it up. I want to make sure that she is okay with this, and she gives a little nod. I turn the card over. There is handwriting in a flowing script that is unintelligible. The ink has faded too much to be read. I bring it close to my eyes, squinting in an effort to bring the ink to the surface, clear and sharp. I shake my head.

"It's not legible. I don't know what it says, and who knows if that is even important to us," I tell my comrades.

"Well then, we have a coin or token and a postcard of unknown origin, and we have no idea what these mean, or what we are to do with them," Gene says cheerfully. "It sounds just like a Quest! Ya know what I mean? We have ourselves a genuine mystery."

It wouldn't be a Quest with Gene if he didn't use *gen-you-whine* at least once. I can't help but smile and notice that Li's lips curl up slightly as well. Gene slaps both of us on the back.

"That's the spirit! This is gonna be fun, just like old times. Mysterious items left for us to puzzle over, a foreign place in history to explore, and absolutely no idea what we're doin'. It's perfect!" Gene finishes by standing and stretching. "Is anybody ready for a midnight snack? 'Cause I'm ready. The best part about this ol' training center is that ya never know what time it is, so I can call it midnight and hit the kitchen for a snack." He looks to Li and me for support in his quest for a midnight snack. Li isn't interested and Gene can tell. I'm lost in thought and miss Gene's look.

WHAT DID MOM LEAVE ME? I reach into the memory files, searching for something related to our Quest. The funny thing is I have catalogued each and every memory of Mom. They're all organized in my hippocampus, which is the part of the brain that stores long-term memory. I've spent what probably amounts to days or weeks searching my brain for every little memory of my mom. That happens when your mom dies so early—you want to remember everything about her, everything she said, everything she did, because these memories have to last a lifetime. And forgetting seems like letting her die all over again. I can't let that happen.

As I retreat into myself and search my memories, I cannot come up with anything even remotely related to postwar Berlin or even anything related to war at all. She never spoke of anything like what I need. Frustration wells up inside of me, threatening to burst up and out of me, geyser-like. I take a deep breath, pushing back the frustration and even tears.

I feel a hand on my forearm. It rests there for a moment and then slides down to my hand. The hand squeezes mine reassuringly and then is gone. I know it's Li. She must know what I'm doing, and where I am currently in my memories. She understands and lets me know, without words.

I open my eyes to find all three watching me, all with concern showing on their faces. The question goes unspoken, but I answer it anyway.

"I don't know what Mom left for me," I murmur with a sharp shake of the head. "I can't think of anything she said or did that relates to our Quest." And then I add something as if to reassure them, but I know it's more for me than them. "I remember everything she said and did, trust me."

Reginald smiles warmly. "We do trust you, Jake. I suppose that this particular memory is there, but without proper context it seems benign. May I suggest that you will recall the memory at the exact time you need it, and not a moment before."

I nod, unconvinced. I'm certain that Gene and Li also see that I remain unconvinced, but they let it go.

"Well, Reginald, is there anything else for us tonight?" Gene says with a congenial slap of the table. "If not, I'll be headed over to the chow hall in search of that midnight munch."

Gene stands and when he sees Reginald's nod, he heads for the door.

"Jake, I'll see ya back in the room," Gene calls over his shoulder with a wave of his hand and then disappears.

"Well, I think I'll go find Hans and put in some work on my so-called 'secret option.'" Li says, standing and moving toward the door.

"Li," I call, stopping her before she leaves the room. "Thank you." I know that she'll understand what I mean. I still feel her warmth on my arm. She smiles and heads out of the room.

It's hard being fourteen, I think to myself. I've never been more confused about my emotions, especially toward Li. I stare after her for several moments, silently wondering how to catalogue how I feel. Can this be quantified by a mathematical equation? I'm out of my depth with girls and feelings I decide, and push the impenetrable mystery that is the female away.

"May I stay for a while and read up on our destination?" I ask, turning to Reginald.

"Of course. I have put together a primer for you, over on the desk. I would start with those documents," he says while rising. He runs his long fingers over his clothing, absently attempting to smooth the wrinkles. "Well, I'll leave you to your studies then."

I stay at the table for a moment, working to push away the ghost-like tendrils of memory. Of my mom. Of Li's touch. Of my growing unease with this Quest. Despite my attempts, I think again of Mom. I fear that without a token from her, I will fail at this task. The voice of the Guide, Elizabeth, comes loudly into my mind, her passion filling every corner: *"We must not fail—this key cannot be lost again."*

I cannot fail, and though I don't have a token or memory that I can cling to, I do have the books sitting over on the study desk. I have my mind. I can add all of the information on that desk into my memory and hope that this will work for now.

I move to the desk and open the file folder that rests on top of the stack. I easily fall into a comfortable rhythm, inhaling facts and images like I imagine Gene is doing right now with his midnight snack. The image makes me smile. We are the same, he with his food and I with my facts and figures. We both have insatiable appetites.

With this thought, the walls of the room fade away and I delve into the Berlin that existed in 1945, a Berlin in chaos and ruin, governed by four countries; the city itself separated into four little fiefdoms. I commit a map of 1945 Berlin to memory and turn the page to gobble up more information.

CHAPTER 8

TOUGH

I'M AWOKEN THE NEXT MORNING with a shock. Li rushes into our room, fully clothed and brandishing weapons. I work to shake the sleep away as words rush at Gene and me.

"Get up! Combat training starts now! Throw something on and grab your weapons. I managed to grab them while training early this morning with Hans." Li's staccato words sound like a weapon themselves, rapid-fire. She turns back to the doorway or opening, since there are no doors in the Training Center, and peers out into the hallway. She's keeping watch and allowing us some privacy, all at the same time.

Gene rolls out of his bed in his boxers only. He sees me throw my blanket back, fully clothed, and stops short.

"Jake, did you sleep in your clothes?" he stares at me in confusion.

I don't waste words, just nod. Last night I had time to think about our previous Training Center experience. I remembered that on Day Two we had early morning combat practice, so I guessed that today was the same. When I got back to the room last night, Gene was already into full snore mode. I changed my underclothing and dressed completely before laying down to sleep.

Sometimes deductive reasoning pays off. This morning is one of those times. I pick up the pistol I used yesterday, checking the magazine for the telltale blue paintballs. The magazine is full. I push the clip back into the gun and rack the slide. For a second, I wonder what my dad would think if he knew that I was now familiar with a pistol I could strip, clean, and reassemble. I won't set any records, but I am serviceable.

I turn to see Gene hopping on one leg trying to get his pants on. He sees me smiling at him.

"Hey, maybe a heads-up next time, huh buddy? Ya know, a little shake of the shoulder before you crawl into bed," he grumbles, finally managing his pants. He changes his voice to what he must think sounds like mine as he reaches for a T-shirt. "Gene, you're a good buddy of mine, so I wanted to give you a shout about my latest genius theory. Wear your clothes to bed tonight, okay?" he intones in his Jake voice. He has his T-shirt on now and moves to his socks and shoes.

"More dressing and less talking, big guy," Li says sharply, her eyes never leaving the hallway.

"Well, you could've figured it out for yourself. Li did," I say with amusement. I know Li was dressed and prepared, using the same deduction I had.

"That's why I have you! So I don't have to figure it out!" Gene sputters in exasperation, his "figure" turning to figger.

He's dressed now and bends down to pick up his shotgun. He opens the breach and checks the load. I catch a glimpse of blue. He closes the breach with authority and turns to Li. "Let's rock 'n' roll," he says, moving toward the doorway.

"Jake, stay behind us and cover our backsides," Li commands, comfortable in her role. I notice that she has a pistol in each hand, and an ammo vest takes up most of her upper body. We all wear goggles, a nod to safety. She removes something from the vest and tosses it into the hallway.

The hallway lights up brightly. A flare of some kind.

"Let's move."

I feel ridiculous with my gun pointed at our rear, doing a sort of sideways shuffle in an attempt to follow Li and Gene while watching behind me. We reach a corner. Gene rotates to the rear and I move to the middle, just behind Li.

To our left is a dead end, to our right is the main corridor that leads to the Brawn Room and then further down to the open entrance hall with the stone table.

Li throws another flare, which blooms bright revealing attackers tucked into cross hallways that open onto the main corridors. Too late, they duck their heads back around corners.

"Jake, give me cover fire. Do not hit me. Shoot high up on the walls on the right side. I'll be moving down the left side. Empty your full clip and then stop firing," Li orders succinctly. "Gene, if I were them I would have a force coming at us from the rear as soon as they hear gunfire. Take them out."

Li pulls something from her vest and hands it to Gene. They share a meaningful look that I can't interpret.

"Now, Jake!" Li says and turns the corner, bringing both her guns up high, firing rapidly as she runs.

I pivot around the corner, raise my gun and carefully pick out the space on the right and pull the trigger. The sound is deafening.

Li covers the distance between her and the first attackers like a champion sprinter. I see her out of the corner of my eye. She holsters both of her weapons—they must be empty—and sprints up the wall. How does she do that? I turn fully to watch her now. She is climbing the wall at the corner where attackers hide just behind. Unbelievable, I think. She drops down on top of the attackers, and I know she's got them.

It doesn't take long for me to empty my clip. I pull back around the corner, just in time to see attackers round the corner down near our room. I count six of them. Gene's shotgun sends them scattering. Boom! Pump action. Boom!

I realize I have a weapon too, so I eject the clip and reach to my pocket for a replacement. My only extra. Li thinks of everything. I slam the new clip into the pistol, rack the slide and raise the gun. My timing works, because Gene is out of shells. While he reaches for more shells, I pull the trigger in rapid succession, crouching down slightly behind Gene.

I count four attackers still running toward our position. My paint flies wild but manages to cover Gene. The four duck into a room about halfway to us. I guess they are reloading as well.

"Jake, on the count of three, I am going to throw this," Gene says, showing me something that looks like a grenade. It's a paint grenade, I guess. "We are going to rush their position in the confusion. Disarm them and slap the cuffs on them, okay?"

I nod, holstering my empty weapon.

Gene's count reaches three and he tosses the grenade underhand. It lands and rolls right to the opening of the door. What a throw, I think. Gene mumbles something about horseshoes.

Blue paint explodes in a loud concussion, and Gene and I are up and running toward the opening. Gene gets there ahead of me and swings his shotgun like a baseball bat at an arm still holding a gun.

Time slows.

I see Gene step into the man cradling his arm, snapping his hand into the attacker's face. He goes down in a heap. I see two attackers down, covered in blue paint. The final attacker stands at the back of the room, arms raised, ready for a fight. He's lost his weapon, I see it in the corner of the room.

Gene approaches the attacker carefully. They circle one another warily, sizing each other up.

I move through the room, ensuring the others are out of the fight. I slide cuffs onto wrists, binding them together.

I sense movement and look up to see Gene sliding inside a wild punch, spinning the guy and choking him into unconsciousness. I watch, not thinking to breathe, until the guy slides heavily down to the floor.

I sit back, breaths now coming shallow and fast. I stare at the paint covered attackers all around me, numb to the whole thing. I shake my head. I can't do this; I can't do the real thing, I think. It won't be paint later. And that is something I can't be a part of, I won't. I feel vomit rise quickly and I just catch it in time, forcing it down. Barely.

Gene looks and me and recognizes my plight. He comes over and pulls me up. "We need to go see about Li, okay?" His voice steadies me, his eyes boring into mine.

I nod.

Gene moves to the room's opening and checks the corridor. He waves me forward and we jog down the hall, back the way we came. Gene checks around the corner again, holding me back protectively. His body relaxes visibly. He steps out into the open hallway.

"Hi Li! Nice to see you are paint-free," he says, trying to inject joviality into his voice.

Li doesn't speak; she just looks at Gene and then sees me coming around the corner. She doesn't look good. I assume that neither do Gene and I.

"Let's get to the Brawn room," she says curtly and turns down the corridor.

W E STAGGER INTO THE BRAWN room, where Hans waits in a chair. He looks the three of us over for a moment, then stands.

"Where are the attackers?" he asks.

Li jerks her thumb over her shoulder. None of us speak. We collapse into chairs lining one wall.

Hans hasn't moved, he continues to appraise us.

"Hans, this isn't going to work. The paintball games are one thing, but the real thing is something else," Gene says hesitantly, trying to find the words. "Jake almost threw up because he was imagining the real thing. He won't be able to pull a real trigger with real bullets that bring real blood. And neither will Li, we already know that. To be honest, I've kind of shut off the thought that it'll be real out there. I can't do it either. I won't."

Hans looks from Gene to Li, and then from Li to me. Something changes in his face that I can't understand. He moves slowly toward us, grabbing a chair and pulling it over to sit in front of the three of us.

"I hoped that you would feel this way; Elizabeth did too," he reports, his voice tinged with relief. "You are the Chosen. You are builders, protectors, guardians of humanity and all that is good in the world. To take life and wield weapons of destruction so cavalierly seems contradictory."

He pauses to let this sink in. Hans doesn't seem so big and callous all of a sudden.

"However, those who oppose you feel no such hesitancy. There may come a time where Good must end the life of Evil, but not now. You are fourteen. You are innocents." He stands and moves toward the weapons rack.

"I believe I have a solution. It may not fool Evil and its minions for long, but I hope it will provide you enough time to subdue the opposing forces." He lifts a particular weapon. "Several weapons have been retrofitted to carry wax bullets."

"What about rubber bullets?" Gene asks. "I've heard about rubber bullets and other non-lethal kinds like them."

"Rubber bullets will not be invented until 1970, unfortunately. Long after the time you are traveling to. However, wax bullets were a kind of predecessor to the rubber bullet. They will stun a person, bruise them, and maybe even knock them down. You must use this time of confusion to subdue them."

"How will we obtain such weapons?" Li asks. "I assume we will not be able to take these weapons with us."

I think back to our last Quest. Li had left early to procure weapons and supplies needed. Would she do so again this time?"

"You are correct. You will need to acquire these weapons after you arrive on site. A cache of these weapons has been left for you, in a particular place. A place unknown to me or anyone here."

Confusion registers on all three of our faces.

"They were cached by your parents," Hans says simply.

"Wait, what?" Gene objects. "Are you telling us that you allowed us to think we were going to use real bullets this whole time, all the while knowing you had an alternative?" He works to control his temper.

"Why not just say on our first meeting, 'Hey team, your parents used wax bullets and left some weapons behind for you guys, so don't stress out about using live ammunition and turning into cold-blooded murderers. Instead, you got us all worked up about 'secret options' and Jake's over there trying not to puke ...'" Gene's bluster runs out of steam.

"You should know by now, Gene, that we cannot make your decisions for you. You must be allowed to work through your Quest using your own moral compass," Hans explains slowly.

"You shot Li!" Gene's voice is loud and strained.

Li puts a steadying hand on his arm. "We have made our choice, Master. I believe I see the wisdom in your actions. Without your ... antics," Li struggles for a better word but can't find one. "Without your antics, I would not have worked so hard on my 'other options,' and we would not have learned about our moral compass. Fine. Let's move on." She stands, pulling Gene and me up with her.

"We don't have more time to lose. Show us how to use these wax bullets, and whatever else you have for us."

Hans nods, coming to his feet. "First, I will show you how to operate and troubleshoot the wax weapons. We will practice firing them—they present unique challenges that you need to be familiar with. Second, we will train on the Close Quarter Combat tactics of the era. Subduing the enemy is now our primary focus."

HANS SPENT THE MORNING WORKING with the weapons that fire wax bullets. We even donned some padded protection and shot one another in various places to understand the impact. We found out the wax bullets will still do some damage, albeit non-lethal damage. Just what we need and want.

Following our wax training, we separated into two groups and learned the CQC tactics of the World War II era. It was called Defendu, and we read from a book titled "Get Tough" that was used to teach such tactics during the war.

Li and I were paired together initially because of our similar height and build. Gene and Hans were paired for similar reasons. Knowing height and build were the end of Li's and my similarities, I approached this next phase of training with not a little fear.

Eventually, Li and I fell into a familiar pattern of marital arts training. Li is obviously a master of the arts and had clearly added to her repertoire over the past year. She appears impressed with my training.

"Did you take some classes over the past year, Jake?" she asks while watching me warm up. I am moving through my forms.

I just smile at her. She cocks her head, curious. "This ought to be fun then," she says, warming to the task of finding out just what I have learned.

The room tunnels down to just the small space that Li and I occupy, my vision focused only on the challenge.

She comes up me in a traditional opening strike. I move my left foot back, pivoting on my right while my arms come up to block and parry away her rigid palms. She spins quickly into a kick aimed at my ribs. I step forward, closing the gap between us, moving behind her swinging leg. My rigid palm catches her leg, and I use my momentum to carry me downward. My other hand flashes out in a strike toward her planted knee. She manages to deflect my strike at the last moment. I use our momentum to roll onto my shoulder, intending to take out her still planted leg and bring her down to the mat.

Li has other ideas, though. She defies gravity again, leaping lightly into the air. I pass under her, helpless now to avoid her descending blows. I am beaten. She stops the blows short with a smile.

"Wow, Jake, you have learned a lot. Who is your master?" Li asks, reaching a hand out to me, pulling me to my feet.

I just smile at her again, resuming my stance, ready for another chance.

"Don't make me hurt you Jake, I'm asking nicely for now," Li says with a laugh.

I drop my stance, as if I'm going to tell her my story. I see her relax her posture and I leap into action, choosing an attack I just learned for Master Shi. Li leaps up to meet me in mid-air and we collide in a flurry of strikes and kicks. I get the better of it and land with my hand stiff against her neck.

Li can't believe what just happened. I can't either.

Neither can Gene.

"Whoa! I feel like I just snuck up on Romeo and Juliet's dyin' scene. Jake, did you just beat Li at her own game?" Gene says. "Seriously, what just happened?"

Li shoves my hand away and scrambles into a sitting position. She looks halfway furious and halfway impressed.

I stand with a smile and head to grab some water.

"Uh, Jake … it is you, right? What have you done with the old Jake?" Gene questions me. With my back turned, he turns his attention to Li. "Li, did you let him do that to you?"

"No," she answers shortly.

"Excellent work this morning; it is now time for lunch. After lunch, please meet me at the Buddy Room," the Guide's voice reaches through the room. She must have entered when I went for water.

"C'MON OL' BUDDY, TELL US what you been up to this past year. Li and I are dying to know," Gene begs me at lunch, sending food particles everywhere. "Seriously, Li almost died at your hand this morning. And she woulda died not knowing who taught ya."

"I would not have died," Li says tersely, stewing over her lunch.

I put my fork down and take a quick look around the cafeteria. Hans and Reginald sit about twenty yards away against the far wall.

"My Guardian taught me," I answer.

"I knew it." Gene says. "When do we go to the Awkward Room? 'Cause I need to hear y'all's stories and you'll want to hear mine, too."

"I don't know if we'll have time this trip for the Sharing Room," I counter.

"Well, I'm gonna ask Elizabeth about that after lunch," Gene replies. "We need some time to share, don't ya think?"

Li and I both just shrug and focus on our lunch.

"Seriously, you don't think we need to share? 'Cause we do," Gene asserts, then lets it go so he can dive into his lunch again.

AS WE ENTER THE BUDDY Room, I notice three grizzled old men scattered around the room, each with an empty chair opposite him. Elizabeth is standing off to the side.

"Good afternoon," she says in greeting. "Today I would like you to befriend these three gentlemen. Please choose a chair and begin when ready."

The three of us look at each other and then move off randomly toward the men. I am the last to find a seat.

The man in front of me looks ancient and is dressed in military uniform. I know from my studies that he is wearing the uniform of a World War II infantryman. The bars on his uniform tell me he's a captain. An officer. His cap sits in his lap, hands wringing it nervously.

"It is a privilege to meet you, Captain," I say, noticing the surprise that registers in his eyes. "My name is Jakob. Jakob Kimball."

Other than the brief surprise that flared in his eyes when I called him Captain, he makes no indication that he has heard me.

"I am grateful for your service to our country, for securing our freedoms at such a cost," I say, hoping to register something with him. Still no acknowledgement.

"My great-grandfather served as well. Jakob Sigurdsson," I offer, running out of ideas.

"What theater did he serve in?" The soldier says.

"Mediterranean theater, Italy," I answer.

The soldier nods and stretches out his hand.

"Ray Hudson," he says as he shakes my hand.

"I can't believe that you're the only one of the three of us to get a soldier to talk," Gene marvels, shaking his head. "First, you beat Li this morning at her own game, and next you beat me at mine.

We might as well go on home now, Li. Jake's got this."

"Well done, Jake," Li says. "You've really grown during the past year. Your Guardian must be quite effective."

I look at her, a little hurt that she ascribes my success to the Guardian. She sees the look.

"No, Jake, I don't mean that you didn't have anything to do with it. Obviously you had to be willing and put in the time," Li rushes, trying to cover her gaffe.

I wave her off.

"I understand what you mean and you're right. My Guardian is amazing. He really helped me out this year." I smile and add, "Look at it this way, I've only wanted to throw up once and I haven't tried to quit yet … so a definite improvement, right?"

Gene and Li laugh. I join them.

"Man, Jakers, I can't get used to you crackin' jokes to us. It's like Li startin' to count her steps and measuring every room automatically," Gene says.

"Who says I don't do those things?" Li shoots back.

"Oh, geez, somebody please save me," Gene beseeches, raising his hands to the sky.

CHAPTER 9

SHARING

A S WE FINISH UP OUR dinner, we receive a surprise. Reginald, the Master Brain enters the cafeteria and approaches our table.

"Good evening; there has been a slight change of plans. Rather than joining me in the Brain Room, please meet the Guide in the Sharing Room," he says to us, then turns to me. "Jakob, if you could meet me in the Brain Room afterward, that would be most appreciated."

I nod. Reginald retreats and leaves us to finish up.

"Finally, a stop at the Sharing Room. I reckon Elizabeth saw the need for us to get together after all," Gene says.

The Sharing Room has shrunk since the last time we met. Or we have grown. I perform the quick calculations in my head, knowing it isn't the room that has changed. Li, Gene, and I sit knee to knee in the small space, the Guide stands with us, just outside the room.

"It's been hard not to notice that much has transpired over the past year of your lives, and I thought it best that you get this out of your system, so to speak. It won't do to have you surprising one another during your Quest with unknown or unshared experience. I will leave you to one another," Elizabeth says and then slips away.

"Ladies first," Gene offers.

"No, I think I'd like to hear from you first, Gene. You have been pretty anxious over the past couple days to get some things off your chest," Li says with a smile.

"Well, if you insist," Gene returns the smile.

"I do," Li replies.

"Okay, I guess I should start with this," Gene begins, holding out his right hand. A ring occupies his middle finger. The ring is not familiar to my eyes. Or to Li's, apparently.

"Are you showing us your promise ring, Gene?" Li teases. She earns one of Gene's trademark too-loud laughs.

"Ya know, in a manner of speaking, I guess ya could say this is a promise ring. As in, I promise you're gonna hit the hay," he says. I don't know what he means. I shake my head to let him know.

"In English, please," Li prompts.

"What? You guys've never heard of 'hit the hay'? It means to go to sleep."

Li and I shake our heads simultaneously.

"Well, you remember the ring that Mr. Wang gave me that I used on his lying brother? Course, it turned out both Wangs were lying. Anyway, I had that ring on when we were brought back to the Guide's office after we grabbed the key. And well, I still had it on when we were sucked out of the office and back home."

Realization dawns in my mind. Gene took what he called the knockout juice back to our time with him. I find myself leaning forward in the cramped space, anxious to hear more.

"Now I see I got your attention. That's right, I brought some of the knockout juice back to Texas with me," he says with a smile. "I call it 'bacon fat' now. Ya know, 'cause it renders people unconscious."

We laugh at the memories of our first stay in the Training Center. Gene was obsessed with having bacon that trip.

"So, it causes victims to hit the hay," Li says, incorporating Gene's lingo and telling him she's listening.

"Exactamundo," Gene says, satisfied. "So, I get to thinkin', maybe I can find a way to duplicate the bacon fat, ya know, make more of the stuff, 'cause I figure it'll come in handy in the future. Why not incorporate what's worked before into our current circumstance." Gene sits back, looking a little uncomfortable. "I decided to test it in our current world." He is definitely less enthusiastic now.

"Gene, which one of your poor brothers did you test it on?" Li gulps.

Gene squirms more. "Rexie," he says in an almost inaudible whisper.

"Is he okay?" Li asks, alarmed.

"What? Oh yeah, he's fine. The bacon fat worked like a charm and good ol' Rexie was good as new a couple hours later," Gene shrugs. "But I just kinda feel bad, because I couldn't tell him what really happened. He suspects something, but doesn't know what exactly. And I think Magnus and Axel suspect something too—they were there when I did it to poor Rexie. I mean he had it comin', he took a swing at me and I figured it was the perfect time to see about the bacon fat," Gene says these words in a rush, still looking to find some peace about the deal.

"Rex isn't the only person I used it on," he adds quickly, almost like he's trying to sneak this little bit of information by us.

I start. *What?*

"What?" Li asks, sitting up straight. "Gene, please tell me you didn't use your bacon fat on Chloe."

"Huh? Why would I do that? Oh, no, no, no," he says, putting his hands up in a defensive gesture. "I would never use it on Chloe. I … um … well … I may have used it on her boyfriend—her boy-friend at the time."

Li leans forward, eyes closed, and brings her hands up to rub her face like she just heard some terrible news.

I'm just dumbfounded, staring wide-eyed at Gene.

"I know, I know. I don't know what I was thinking," Gene says, shaking his head. "But let me go back a little. So, after I had done my little experiment on Rex, I decided to see if I could find someone who could help me determine the formula of the bacon fat. I knew it had to be an organic compound, 'cause a when I got the stuff." Gene is now warming to the task of sharing his story.

"I know this guy that runs a small pharmacy; not one of those highfalutin Walgreens-type places—just a small-town kind of establishment. Pa won't let us frequent the 'abomination of a mon-strosity'. We give our business to local folks. And anyway, I like old Charlie, the owner. We've struck up a bit of a friendship over the last year or two.

"Well, old Charlie is a chemist and a pharmacist, and I reckon he can help with the bacon fat, plus I think I can trust him. Anyhoo, long story short, turns out old Char-lie is a Guardian—my Guardian. I s'pose that's why he'd gone out of his way to become friends with me in the first place." Gene arches his back in a stretch, looking for some relief in the cramped quarters.

"Charlie takes me into the back of his old shop and lo and behold, it looks like a high-tech laboratory back there. His hobby, he tells me. I tell him about the bacon fat, he tells me he's my Guardian, and we become buddies.

"He tests the bacon fat, discovers its origins, determines that we can get more of the stuff and last, but not least, he designs this new ring and delivery system." Gene finishes, coming full circle back to the ring. The ring is much smaller than Mr. Wang's ring, more unobtrusive and streamlined.

"Old Charlie told me that the needle on the old ring was old technology and thick, that's why people felt it so much, apparently. This new ring uses a much smaller needle to deliver the bacon fat, you hardly even feel it now. I know firsthand—Charlie used it on me, so I'd know how it felt to be rendered."

Gene pauses as we all take in the ring and its implications.

"Anyway, old Charlie is also a tough old guy," he continues, retracting his hand, effectively putting the ring away and moving on. "He's been working with me on CQC techniques. In fact, some of the techniques I was shown here, he has already worked with, so I guess I have a leg up there. He's helpin' me become more well-rounded, I've learned tons about chemistry and science and things like that, so that's also cool." Gene sits back. "I guess that's about it."

"No, it is not, Gene. You haven't told us about the other person you rendered, and why?" Li reminds him pointedly.

Gene was clearly trying to avoid this topic. He's clearly uncomfortable.

"I'm walking back home from old Charlie's pharmacy one day during the summer, when who do I run into? Chloe, that's who, only she's with this Neanderthal of a boyfriend by the name of Johnny. He's a football player an' I know he's messin' around with steroids, or HGH, or whatever, ya know—bad chemicals idiots put in their bodies.

"So, Chloe and I start to talkin' and I think things are going real good. Chloe is startin to see what a great guy I am and how much we have in common and why she'd be better off with a guy like me."

I wonder if Chloe is really thinking these things, or whether

Gene is projecting them from his mind onto hers, but I let him continue his story. I'm completely wrapped up in the drama.

"Somewhere along the way, Chloe's hand ends up in mine for a piece and Johnny decides he's had enough of my showing him up with his girl. There is a bit of a confrontation, I convince him the 'performance enhancing' chemicals he's putting in his body have messed with his system. Ya know, the power of suggestion is mighty strong with the weak-minded."

"I convince him and Chloe that he's feeling a bit woozy, I lean in to steady him, and bam, I inject him with the bacon fat. He goes down in a heap. I haul him up and over my shoulder, and become Chloe's hero," Gene finishes, and his voice is tinged with regret. "Look, I know I shouldn't a done it. I got caught up in the moment. I feel terrible and I know I gotta come clean with Chloe, but I just haven't found the right moment," he adds quickly, but sounds unsure about what he truly wants to do.

"So, you brought back an unknown compound from ancient China, felt like it was a good idea to use on your brother without knowing how it might affect somebody in our time, then before you know if it's totally safe, you use it again to trick a girl into dropping her boyfriend and liking you. Is that the gist of it?" Li demands, not happy at all.

"Well, when you put it like that ..." Gene mumbles pathetically.

"Listen, Gene, Chloe sounds like a real nice girl, but you need to tell her the truth. And you can't go around using this bacon fat to render whomever you see," Li chides.

"I know, and I'm gonna tell her just as soon as we get back. It may wreck our friendship, but heck, I'll bounce back, I mean we're only fourteen, right?" he says, but his words lack conviction to my ears.

"What about your dad, Gene?" I ask, wanting to steer the conversation away from the bacon fat, and also curious to know what his dad thought of Gene's successful return from the first Quest.

Gene brightens. "Oh, Pa and I are really making good progress. During the summer, I tried to spend whole days with him, just him and me. I think we're getting better at this father and son thing. He's startin' to see me in a whole new light and I see him differently too, I guess."

"Great, Gene! I'm happy to hear that," I say, genuinely thrilled for him. My thoughts turn to my dad and our relationship, but I push them away, saving them for later. Right now, I want to focus on Gene.

"Did you receive advice in China?" Li asks hesitantly. I guess she thinks maybe Gene didn't have a conversation like she did with General Xu.

"Yep. I forgot to mention that, but I'm guessing we all did. I'm keeping a journal now, which was one of the five points of counsel that Pang gave me. The other four are: be open minded, be well-rounded, spend time wisely, and have fun," Gene reports, his normal glee returning.

"One last thing, I have rings for the two of you also, ya know, just in case you get in a tight jam." He reaches into his pocket and removes two small packages.

He unfolds some protective fabric and holds out his hand to us. In his palm are two rings: one obviously made for Li and the other must be mine. Li's is beautifully crafted in silver with a center stone that looks like jade. The one I suppose is mine looks like a normal band of platinum, the top forming the shape of a shield.

"I hope you like them. Remember, the rings only hold one dose of the bacon fat. To inject the fat, spin the ring around so that the stone or shield is under your finger so it faces the palm, then give a quick, sharp squeeze. Turning the ring under the finger causes the needle to extend, the sharp squeeze injects the fat."

Li and I take our rings and slide them onto our fingers. Mine only fits on the middle finger. I see that Li's fits nicely onto her ring finger.

"Looks like they fit, I had to guess on sizes, hoping they would fit at least one finger, and hey, I got something right," Gene says happily. "Who's next?" he finishes, sitting back.

Li and I share a look.

"I'll go." I say.

"I SPOKE WITH GENERAL LIU FOLLOWING our gigantic Go game. He counseled me on five points as well," I say jumping right into what I think of as my past year recap. "The Five Points sounds similar in many ways to Gene's. They are: keep a record, unearth hidden talents, stay close to family and friends, do for others what has been done for me, and enjoy life.

"One of my favorite things that has happened because of the counsel from General Liu is that my dad and I are figuring out how to be happy together without mom. We ride bikes together, spend more time talking, and even went on a camping trip. We've found sort of a good spot without mom."

I take a breath to steady myself. It feels good to share with these two. I didn't realize how much I needed this until Gene started. I realize that these few hours are critical to our success as a Chosen trio.

"Dad and I even had our picture taken by a friend—have you noticed that everyone knows somebody who is a professional photographer these days? Anyway, we framed our little family photo and hung it in the hallway next to all of the others with mom. This was a big step for us.

"We know it's okay to continue creating memories with one another, even though we both miss Mom like crazy. It's okay to show each other our sadness, our emptiness. I guess we found out that we fill up the other's heart, replacing sadness when one of us is low. It works for us."

I finish with a shrug, not sure that I am communicating my feelings well. Gene's eyes are shining when I sneak a peek at him to judge his understanding. I guess that means I'm doing fine. I don't dare look at Li.

"So, Dad and I talk about Mom openly now. We relive our memories, sharing our perspectives, and this will help us to not forget. Dad's perspective is so different from mine, obviously, and I see Mom with new eyes. I think that's cool. And I can tell Dad likes to see his wife from a son's point of view."

I show a small smile to both Gene and Li. Li is hugging herself tightly, eyes brimming with wetness. I want to reach out to her, but don't have the courage.

"The counsel to stay close to family and friends has worked out well. I … um … well, I consider the two of you my closest friends." I laugh a little to cover my embarrassment, and then my words come out in a rush before I can stop them. "Maybe that sounds weird, I don't know you that well, but I don't have any lifelong friends. I want to share everything with the two of you because I want to be close to you both." I trail off and find a spot on the floor to inspect. I feel Gene's big arm pull me close.

"Jakers, if I'd a known you were gonna tug on the ol' heart strings like this, I woulda brought a box full of hankies," he assures me, doing what he does best, making us all comfortable with his odd sense of humor.

Li laughs a small laugh that sounds almost like a hiccup. "I'd like to meet your father, Jake," she says.

Our eyes meet, and a knowing look passes between us. Gene for once pretends not to notice.

"Yeah, me too. We need to get together outside of this cave and outside of history," Gene says. "But 'scuse the interruption Jake, carry on."

"Shortly after returning, I met a man named Mr. Shi.

"Turns out, Master Shi—as I call him—has been preparing his whole life to be my Guardian. He originally lived somewhere in China. He's kind of vague about the exact location, I get the sense it's some sort of secret. A hidden order or something. He became a master of a specialized kind of martial art—" I stop short as Li sucks in air and her eyes flare wide.

"I knew it! Oh my goodness!" she says, then her, staring at me like I have two heads. She doesn't say more, so I decide to continue.

"He has been training me in his specific branch. It's pretty cool, I have to admit, but I have a lot of work to do." I stop and smile at the memories with Master Shi.

"He also helped me with Point Two of my counsel, to help me unearth hidden talents. He claims that I have it within me to be a powerful public speaker. Or at least learn how to strike up conversations with people."

I smile shyly at Li. "That's why I blurted out that stuff about your hair and shampoo, I've been doing these exercises with him where I go into a place like a restaurant or ice cream shop and he gives me tasks to complete. For instance, he tells me I need to find out if the server has any pets or what toothpaste or shampoo they use, stuff like that. It's pretty ridiculous, but it has helped me become more comfortable with people. I'm not at Gene's level yet, but I'm working on it. Um … I think that's about all. At least those are the things that relate to the Five Points."

"Any special friends back home?" Gene leers while doing some weird eyebrow wiggle.

I anger myself when my eyes involuntarily flash to Li. Li stares back at me with intense eyes, waiting for an answer. Gene catches the glance to Li. He starts laughing.

"Well … the thing is … um … when I'm with Master Shi, I feel I work hard at the things he assigns me, but when I'm at home or school, I usually just fall back into my comfort zone. You know, I'm quiet and thoughtful." I quickly add, "And I like it that way most of the time."

I break eye contact with Li, finally able to break free from her tractor beam-like stare.

"So, to answer your question, no I don't have special friends back home," I finish. At least I hope I'm finished.

Li appears satisfied. Gene just continues to look between Li and me, but he lets it go.

"Li, I think we're ready for the grand finale," Gene prompts.

"AS YOU TWO KNOW, I spent some time with General Xu Da and I received counsel just like you," Li begins. "And like you, I was given Five Points of focus. The first of which was identical to both of yours: keep a record. Second, I am to develop my latent talents. Third, I am to educate my mind. Fourth is to see the best in others. And finally, I am to enjoy the journey. My list is much like both of yours; we must have many similar qualities and opportunities," she says with a smile.

"Also, like both of you, the theme about our fathers continues. My father and I have also been working hard to have more of a relationship. I have always felt small under father's gaze, but this summer I realized that he felt something similar under mine. I had been so consumed with how I was feeling that I hadn't noticed nor cared about his feelings.

"Something opened up in my heart and mind; I saw my father's grief for mother, I saw his pain at not knowing how to be both a father and mother to me, I saw how much he needed me to fill some of his emptiness," Li brushes a tear from her eye with a slender finger. "When I stopped thinking about our relationship selfishly, things began to open up. Father travels a great deal, but when he is home, we spent many days together in our gardens or in his study just talking and sharing. Already, I can't wait to get back from this Quest and talk to him as much as we can about our shared experience in Berlin."

Li stops and I can see her mentally shifting gears.

"During the summers, Father and I live at our place in Hong Kong. Just after my birthday, he had to leave for three weeks on business. This isn't uncommon, so I settled into the house and started to consider how best to go about fulfilling my commitments to General Xu. As I'm thinking about this, a bunch of monks in orange robes file into my yard.

"Turns out, the leader of this group, a Master Zhao, is my Guardian. Not only that, he has a scroll with General Xu's seal on it. He hands this to me and tells me that his order of monks have been keeping this scroll for hundreds of years, preparing for that particular day."

Li sees the shock that registers on our faces.

"I know, I was taken aback as well. The monks moved into the quarters on our property and began their tutoring. I was introduced to what General Xu called educating the mind. The monks have a philosophy that melds mind and heart, a way to free the body from the normal bonds of this earth."

Li turns to me now. "I think that Master Shi must be from this same order of monks. He must have lived there in his youth before he struck out to pursue his destiny in preparing to be your Guardian. I think this because the moves you used on me this morning were the exact same that I have been taught this past year. I didn't think for a second that you would be capable of executing such moves. You caught me by surprise and beat me."

She says this coloring in the cheeks, still unhappy about being beaten, especially by me. I wonder about her theory, it makes sense to me. I make a note to ask Master Shi about it upon my return.

"Anyway, a great deal of our time was spent in meditation, as I educated my mind, subduing the impulses that I am prone to: anger, rash behavior, uncontrolled thoughts and fears. I know you both have expressed curiosity about my ability to run along walls and defy gravity in some cases. It's not that simple, and very difficult to explain, but through the meditations of the mind and melding them with the martial training I have received, I can do things that before seemed impossible.

"I know what you've seen in the movies and on the internet about Shaolin monks and whatever, but that is mostly embellished and exaggerated. The true art is found with these monks. Their monastery is deep in the western mountains of China, near Tibet. I don't know how much contact, if any really, these monks have had with the outside world. They were full of wonder when we traveled into the city of Hong Kong proper.

"I guess that leads me to the last thing I would like to share. I have found a friendship with a cousin, Faith, who also lives in Hong Kong. I have felt like I need to have more friends who are girls. It's just my father and me at home. I need female friends, especially some that are my age. As I've said before, I don't have a lot of friends back in China due to jealousies and other issues. Of course, maybe I could try a little harder, too.

"Anyway, I spent time with my cousin over the summer while I was in Hong Kong and really found a different side of me coming out and I think it's important. She is such a girl, and I need that. I need to know what that feels like for me. No offense guys, but even your friendship can't fill that need."

We all laugh.

"So, it has been a good year. Hopefully, I have mellowed some and am finding peace and harmony within my mind and heart. My father and I are great, better than ever, and I have a cousin who teaches me what it feels like to be a fourteen-year-old girl."

Li finishes with a confident smile, comfortable with Gene and me. I recall our first encounters together and am amazed at how far we have come together.

"Well would ya look at the three of us, working hard to fulfill the measure of our destiny? One more day and then we are thrown into fire, so let's go see about what else we need to do to prepare, right?" Gene says, capping off our sharing session on a high note.

Remembering last year, I reach my hand into our little circle and let it hang there.

"I am with you through whatever may come!" I say.

Li and Gene smile, happy that I remembered our ritual, and reach their hands into the circle in turn.

CHAPTER 10

HINT

I FIND MY WAY TO THE Brain Room, remembering Reginald's request from dinner. I still feel the warm glow of friendship and camaraderie from our Sharing Room experience. I enter the room and find Reginald hunched over some documents, lost in study. I approach silently, not wanting to disturb his mental process, being especially sensitive to the process myself. I wait for several minutes.

Reginald stands and stretches his back. I take this moment to give a little cough. He turns around, startled a bit.

"Oh, Jakob, I didn't hear you approach," he says ruefully. I smile, showing him I know the feeling.

"Why don't you fetch a chair and sit next to me here."

I do as he asks, dragging a chair over from my usual desk, joining him at the table.

"Brilliant," he says as I join him. "Now, please tell me what you have studied to this point." He motions to the stack of documents and book in front of him. He has brought the stack from the desk over to the table.

"I believe I have completed my reading of the first stack of information," I report.

His eyes reveal shock. "Goodness me! You've already gone through the entire stack? Well then, it seems I have underestimated you. But, this is good. I have been thinking about your Quest. While you are travelling to postwar Berlin, I believe you should also cover a period of much earlier history.

"Think of it as a supplement to your knowledge. I hope it is relevant and proves useful to you. You see, the Key itself was originally lost near the end of the nineteenth century—the Key originally intended to be safeguarded by the Chosen during the British Empire. If possible, I would add this reading to your list."

He waves a hand to a stack of books and documents ten inches high.

"I'll get right on it," I say, thinking about skimming off more sleep time.

"There is one other thing, Jakob," he says.

I sense a hesitancy in his voice. I nod, giving him permission to go ahead. He stands abruptly, wringing his hands while he begins to pace. He doesn't say anything for a long minute. I begin to wonder if he is going to say anything at all.

He stops suddenly and wheels on me.

"I knew your mother," he blurts. "That is to say I trained her here at the training center."

I don't know what to say, or if he is waiting for me to speak. I remain silent.

"She was a student of French. She used to say that she loved the language," he says with a faraway look.

I remember very little of her love of French. On occasion she would mention her trip to France with Dad before I was born. She also would use little sayings in French, but I didn't understand them. I don't speak French. She would translate them for me sometimes. I think hard, trying to recall anything important. Nothing.

"Well, while she was here," he waves an arm to indicate the Training Center, "she would always share these sayings with us and her fellow Chosen. Her favorite, as I recall, was this: 'Make friends with those who would be quick to criticize.'"

That doesn't ring a bell in my mind.

Reginald shrugs. "I don't know if that helps at all, but I thought I should tell you."

He waits. I give him a shrug.

"I'll have to think on it, Master, I'm sure it will come to me when I need it," I say, wanting to encourage him.

"Well, I'll leave you to your studies," he says, attempting to hide his disappointment.

THE FOLLOWING DAY, GENE, LI, and I see each other for the first time all day at dinner. Our third day in the Training Center has been all individual training. It's good to see the others and share our meal together.

"Whew! I'm as tired as a one-legged man in a butt-kickin' contest," Gene offers up his wisdom between bites. "I think I'd rather spend the entire day workin' with Hans in the Brawn Room than working to get those crusty ol' guys to say a word."

Gene is referring to his work of Buddying the soldier volunteers in the Buddy Room.

"I gotta tell ya 'bout this one fella. He was a tough nut to crack, but once he did, he wouldn't stop yammerin' on about this and that." Gene has shifted into full southern drawl mode, with the added bonus of speaking with his mouth full. Thus, Li and I are treated to a shower of food bits and indecipherable words.

"These old guys are the strong silent types, but it got me to wonderin' about what they were like when they were younger. I couldn't imagine they were just as mute in the glory of their youth, which was when they were in the war, right? So, I brought this up to Elizabeth—"

"I'm sorry, Gene, but don't you think you should show the Guide some respect?" Li says, not happy with his use of her given name.

"Li, please, I'm as respectful as they come," Gene protests, earning him a shake of Li's head and a roll of the eyes. "Elizabeth insisted that I call her by her first name. She's great, so easy to talk to and all ..." Gene gets a faraway look for a second that has me nervous for the Guide.

"But, back to our regularly scheduled program. I asked Elizabeth about the assistants. Why are they all old dudes? I mean, shouldn't I be working with guys in their prime? I don't reckon I'll be meeting up with any soldiers in their old age." Gene stops and puts down his fork, leaning in toward Li and me. "And ya know what she said? She said, 'You're right, Gene.' And with a wave of her hand all of the old geezers got up and marched right outta the room!" He finishes with a wave of his hand, looking like a magician with a wand.

Li and I don't say anything in response. Gene waves his hand in a flourish again, thinking maybe we missed it the first time and giving us another chance to respond. He's not happy.

"Do I have to spell it out for ya? I passed the test!" Gene exclaims. "Eliz—or the Guide was testing me with the old guys, and I was supposed to figgur out that this was all wrong. Ta-da!" he brags, acting like he hears a crowd cheering somewhere in front of him.

"Gene, have you ever wondered why both of our Guides have been a Buddy?" Li asks dryly.

"What?" Gene is startled to be pulled back from his imaginary accolades.

"Have you wondered why both Guides have been a buddy?" Li repeats.

"No, not really, but I guess it's probably 'cause a Buddy makes the best Guide," Gene answers, rushing to present his case. "Think about it, having a Brain lead a Quest doesn't make sense, 'cause they'll probably be too caught up in formulas and theories and whatever. Brains are too scatterbrained—no offense, Jake," Gene theorizes. "And Brawns, well, let's face it—somebody'd probably just get themselves killed with all the anger and testosterone flyin' around," he stops short when he sees our faces.

"Er … it's just a theory though, I'm probably way off …" he mutters, suddenly looking around the cafeteria for a hole to crawl into.

"Gene, do you feel a lot of testosterone coming off of me?" Li asks with mock sweetness. "I'm a Brawn, after all."

"Uh …" Gene stammers, looking to me for help. I let him know that he's on his own with this one. "Is that what I said? I can't remember the specifics. Like I said, it's just a theory and definitely wrong …"

Li sits unmoving, allowing the silence to eat away at Gene. He looks like he's melting into nothing with each passing second. Finally, Li speaks up.

"Would you like to hear my theory, Eugene?" she says in the same sugary voice.

Oh! This is going to be good, I think, and look for a place to shield myself from the upcoming blast.

"I think that we have Buddy Guides for one simple reason—our Buddy needs tons of help, Eugene. Tons upon tons."

Gene's head starts moving like one of those bobble-head dolls.

"Yep! You got it, I mean, you nailed it, Li. I need tons of help. In fact, I wonder where Eliz—the Guide is right now. I could probably use some extra time with her. I need extra help, so maybe I'll just go on ahead—" Gene begins to stand and collect his tray, but Li's hand comes down on it, stopping his progress. He sits down quickly.

"But, you haven't finished telling us about your day … *Buddy*," Li says, using Buddy like it's a foul word.

Gene stares at us, moving his bugged-out eyes back and forth in a fast twitch. He licks his lips. "Well, I don't know what else to say. It was just routine stuff that I failed at, and …" he is cut off by Li's laughter.

"I'm just messing with you, Gene. You opened yourself up to it and I took the opportunity to give you grief. Relax." She's still laughing, and then quickly sobers up. "But I wouldn't repeat your theory again. Ever."

Gene laughs and leans back. "You had me there, Li. I can't believe it, but you had me. I guess I got myself into trouble with that nonsense about Brawns and Brains. Geez, Li, I thought just maybe you were gonna come across the table and pummel me into oblivion." He turns to me now. "What do you think, Jake? Did ya think Li was going to destroy me?"

I blink my eyes a couple of times, acting like I hadn't heard any of the conversation. "What did you say, Gene? I guess my brain was just a little scattered," I deadpan. Li bursts into a new fit of laughter. She leans into me like she needs me to hold her up as her body shakes from the giggles.

"Oh, very funny, Jake. I get it—Jake and his newfound sense of humor, huh? 'Cause I said you were scatterbrained." Color is flooding his neck and cheeks. "You two are a real comedy act."

L I STRAIGHTENS UP AS THOUGH her laughing fit is subsiding and grabs my shirtsleeve. She pulls it up to her eyes, wiping the tears of laughter away.

"Oh cute, Li, very dramatic," Gene says drily, beginning to stand again. "I'll just go find a different table."

Li puts a hand out to stop Gene, this time gently. "Come on, Gene. Admit it, you were having fun with us here. This'll probably be the last time we have to relax and have a laugh for a while. Let's enjoy it. Just because this time it's at your expense instead of ours doesn't mean you can't laugh with us," she looks at him with a smile.

"Alright, alright, ya twisted my arm and I'll stay with you," Gene relents, back to his normal self. He settles in and I recognize the look; another long monologue is coming.

"So, before you guys decided to play your little improvement game, I was just gettin' started about my grueling day." He warms to the task quickly. "After the old guys all file out, the Guide tells me that I have done well to recognize the issue."

Li and I share a smile as we notice that Gene has referred to the Guide by her title.

"The Guide then goes on to explain that I will need to recognize small inconsistencies with our situations going forward. She tells me that this is the next level of Buddying, to notice that people don't match their surroundings. To see who doesn't belong, and to make smart decisions based upon this knowledge." I'm always amazed to see Gene switch in and out of his good ol' boy routine. One minute he's laying it on thick, the next he's talking as if he's a college professor. He's a chameleon in this way, I think to myself. It's probably a good Buddy skill to have in one's arsenal.

"So then a bunch of young soldiers file into the room. They find their places and the Guide asks me to determine who doesn't belong. I am to mingle with them and study them to determine who the mole might be. As I get started, the Guide throws one more curveball at me—maybe all of them belong, she says. Maybe there is no mole." Gene shows his consternation with this new wrinkle.

"I feel a little like Jakers now, scrutinizin' their uniforms and their hair and everything." He smiles at me. "It's kinda fun playing Buddy detective, so I move among the guys, laughing and carryin' on, when I notice two things. First, one of the guys' uniforms isn't quite right. I don't know exactly what's wrong, but I know it isn't right. Second, when I speak to him, I detect the slightest of accents." Gene leans in toward us, the climax of the story approaching.

"I know if I can hear his accent that he is speaking to me in English, but that it's not his first language. The magic translator isn't functioning between us, because it's not necessary with

English—even accented English." Gene is now even closer to us, fully leaning across the table. "Then I know that this guy is an impostor. His uniform is off somehow, and his accent is American, like the others." Gene, never one to shy away from the dramatic, pushes back and jumps to his feet, pantomiming grabbing the impostor by the collar and hauling him up. "I grab the guy, yank him up out of his chair and haul him before the Guide. 'Here is your impostor, Elizabeth,' I say triumphantly."

Gene sits back down, pleased with his performance. "It turns out that I'm right, but the Guide doesn't just let it go. She asks me how I knew and I tell her. She then asks me what was wrong with the uniform. I tell her that I don't know."

"'What if he's just an immigrant and his accent is normal for the period of World War II?' she asks me. I don't have an answer for her. So she continues to tell me that if I don't know what's wrong with the uniform, I might have made a mistake with the accent. She's pushing me, ya know, to be sure. She asks me what kind of accent the guy had. I think about it and tell her that I think it's Russian or somethin' close like that, and she nods."

Gene is in full storytelling mode now.

"'Gene, you must be sure before you act, you cannot afford to make mistakes. In this case, you were correct in singling out the mole, but you can't tell me why he's the mole exactly. I need you to think hard and tell me why, right now,' she tells me, a little scolding in her voice. So, I visualize the uniform in my mind, and I see it!" Gene exults with a slap on the table. "His rank insignias don't match! He's wearing enlisted patches and officer pins." He shows us his wide, toothy smile. "He was a Sergeant-Captain! Okay, I didn't know the ranks—the Guide had to tell me—but I knew that it was messed up."

Gene is slowing down now, and I find myself a little disappointed that his monologue is coming to an end.

"You two're letting your chow get cold, so I'll finish up my captivatin' story so you can finish," he notes, a finger directed to our trays. "After this exercise, we spent the rest of the day deciding who didn't fit and buddyin' up to those who did. Sometimes all of them fit. Sometimes I found the mole. All in all, it was a successful day," he finishes proudly, then stands up. "I'm going to go get seconds on some of this chow and then when I get back, I want to

hear all about what you guys were up to today," he calls over his
should as he moves off to the buffet.

CHAPTER 11

BULLETS

I TURN TO LI AFTER WATCHING Gene descend on the buffet like a lion on a downed gazelle. "Why don't you go ahead and tell us about your Brawn training next. My day was full of boring studying and the like," I tell her.

"I doubt it was as boring as you say, but I'll go next. That way I can really settle in and concentrate on your scatterbrained attempts to tell us how your day went," Li teases with a smile in her eyes.

I smile back and give a little roll of the eyes. "What did you just say?"

"Exactly," she says, still smiling. I find myself staring at that smile. It seems to have its own gravitational pull. *Yeah, Jake, bring out the nerd,* I think with a small shake of my head. Seriously, gravitational pull?

Li misinterprets my staring and headshake. "What? Do I have something in my teeth?" she says, automatically doing what all of us do when we suspect an offensive food particle is hanging out in our teeth. After clamping her mouth shut, she runs her tongue around all of her teeth, in search and destroy mode.

"No, Li, you misunderstood," I laugh, and then hesitate to explain. "Um … I was just looking at your smile. I … well, I like your smile."

A tray slapping the table interrupts us, and I never find out what Li is going to say in reply. Couldn't Gene have waited another minute? I would have liked to know what Li was going to say.

"Geez, you two; I can't leave you alone for a minute without one or the other of ya expressing your undying devotion," Gene fakes exasperation, taking back the upper hand in the joke department. "So, who's up?"

"I had a ton of fun today with Hans and his band of tough guys." Li says tough guys ironically, a clear indication that she handled all of them. "We started off this morning getting comfortable with the wax-bullet weaponry. The shotgun is fun, but too scattered for my tastes; I like the precision of placing a shot exactly where I need it.

"We experimented with placement of the wax bullets. Throat shots seem to be a good opportunity—enough damage to scare the attacker, but no threat of accidental mortality. But throats are small and a hard target to hit consistently, so we also found knees will buckle … and other soft parts of the anatomy are susceptible to a wax bullet." Gene and I both wince involuntarily.

"Otherwise the bullets feel more like a heavy punch to your body. The key, of course, is to momentarily distract them with what they'll assume to be live rounds. A few seconds is all I need to get close and use my natural martial arts skills to neutralize the targets.

"So, are you hoping to carry two pistols?" Gene asks, and I think he wants to keep a hold on the shotgun.

"Yes, I like the weighted balance of a weapon in each hand. Plus, it gives me more shots to use without the need to reload."

Li shifts in her seat before she continues; almost as if she is subconsciously reassuring herself that her twin pistols are still strapped on. With this thought, my eyes automatically go to her waist. The pistols are there.

"The biggest trick with the wax bullets is making them work with automatic weapons. Nobody wants to go into a gun battle with revolvers, so Hans and his team have been working to ensure that I understand the mechanics of the guns, so if there is a jam, I will be able to fix it."

Out of curiosity, I had done some research on the origin of the wax bullet. It has been in use since around 1805, mostly used by magicians to fool people with tricks such as the bullet catch. Today, wax bullets are readily available and fly at speeds higher than paintballs. I wasn't able to find much information regarding wax bullets in the 1940s.

Li's voice called me back to the cafeteria.

"After finding my comfort level with the bullets and guns, I asked Hans to put me into as much protective gear as possible," she pauses for a breath. "I needed him and his assistants to shoot live rounds at me."

Gene and I both sit up and begin to speak. She talks over us both, no small feat.

"Hold on guys! Let me finish. I'm here safe and sound, aren't I?" We both are unhappy about this news but have to admit she does look fine. "I can't practice eluding the bullets, using the skills the monks taught me, against fake bullets. It's not the same, they don't travel as fast through the air. It would be a fatal mistake not to practice against the real thing.

"So, I bundled up and we played some games involving firing live rounds at me while I attempted to avoid them and get close enough to disarm the attackers." She winces at her memories. "I was hit quite often early on and even with the armor, those bullets hurt me badly."

Gene is captivated with the whole story. "The armor probably slowed you down though, right? So, how accurate a judgment can you make when the armor weighs you down?" he asks.

"You're right, Gene, but my thought process was if I can do it with the heavy armor, then it will be that much easier without it in live situations. Over the course of a few hours, I was able to dodge all but the closest bullets. The most dangerous parts of this are right before I get close enough to disarm them. I don't have time to dodge the bullet, so we worked even harder on my final leaps and attacks.

"And if they have machine guns or other rapid-fire weapons, well then, none of my training matters. So, let's hope for pistols."

I look at her and a few sarcastic remarks run through my head about hoping for guns to be pointed at us, but I let them all go unsaid. I am beginning to long for fourteenth century China.

A smile creeps onto Li's face, again reliving the day. "After I was given a chance to rest and ice some of the bigger bruises, we moved into close quarters combat. Now that was fun. You guys probably remember being instructed in Defendu, the common CQC techniques of the day. They were all created by a British man who took from many disciplines to create his own highly effective system of defense and attack.

"Well, all of these guys, including Hans, are specialists in this method and they were determined to train me in it as well, rather than rely on my own training. So I told them to bring it on. If they beat me, well then, I would learn their methods. But if I beat them, we would do it my way.

"I had them all down quicker than they could say, 'Go.' They felt cheated, so we did it again with the same result. Although this time, Hans gave me quite a battle. He is so strong, and much quicker than you would think."

Is that jealousy I am feeling, I wonder? I shove it away as quickly as it came.

"The rest of the day was spent in a variety of situations: one against five, then eight, then a dozen. On some exercises, I would start pinned down by a guy, or up against a wall, and so on. I won most of the time and feel good about the challenges of Brawn in the upcoming Quest."

"Li, would you tell us if you didn't feel confident about your chances?" Gene says with a wink.

"Of course not," Li answers.

"That's what I thought. Well I for one sure am glad to have you on our team. Nobody kicks keister like Li kicks keister," Gene crows. He stands up and says to me over his shoulder, "Hold that thought, Jakers. I need to make one more run to the buffet for some dessert."

I stare straight ahead, thinking about Gene teasing Li and the last time he left and came back. I don't want that again, so I reach into my memory and start to order the events of the day.

Li snuggling up next to me while she snakes an arm through mine and holds it tight pulls me out of my thoughts. "Let's really give Gene something to talk about this time," she says, mischief in her voice and all over her face.

I freeze. I don't know what to say or do. My mind implodes, sweat breaks out on every surface of my body, and my jaw drops agape.

She starts laughing, and I can't tell if she is laughing at me or playacting for a returning Gene. For his part, Gene is standing a few feet from the table, shaking his head. I do notice that for all the disgust he is showing, he is careful with the mound of cake balancing precariously on his plate.

L I'S LAUGH IS INFECTIOUS, AND I find myself laughing too. I sound like a hyena; my laugh mixes with my nerves to come out sounding painful. This makes Li laugh harder as she leans into me further. And then just as quickly, she gently extricates herself from my arm and sits up straight. "Oh, Jake," she breathes, allowing the words to linger like some grand secret has passed between us.

"What?" Gene demands as he sits back down with his cake. "Oh, dern, I forgot a blasted fork, I'll be right back." He looks like he doesn't want to leave for fear of what Li and I might do.

This makes me laugh again, my normal laugh this time. I turn to Li to tell her about Gene's awesome look. She appears shy and nervous. What?

She turns quickly to me. "I'm sorry, did I push it too far? Did I make you uncomfortable? I'm sorry," she repeats herself as she finishes in a rush.

I'm shocked. Li seemed so confident and poised a second ago. Now she looks like she's going to crawl into a tight ball.

"No. No, it was great. I'm the one who should be sorry. I froze. I ... I wasn't ready for ... well, for the whole thing. I'm sorry," I stammer lamely.

She still looks hurt. I take a quick glance at Gene, Hans has tied him up at the buffet. They look deep in conversation. Good.

"Li ... um ... I'm not great with these kinds of things. You know, like flirting and stuff. Plus, I don't know how to improvise very well. But it was fun. I'm glad you did it." I shake my head, what a doofus. "What I mean to say is it was nice, Li. I liked it. It was fun ... and funny ... and stuff." Not going to win any awards for that little speech, Jake, I think to myself.

Or maybe I will win something, I rethink things as Li's hand finds mine.

"Thanks, Jake. It was fun, wasn't it? I like giving it to Gene; usually he is the one having all the fun," she says, withdrawing her hand.

I stare straight ahead, lost in thought. I have no idea what just happened, nor do I know how to interpret the whole deal. I have a lot to learn, I think, and choose the path of least resistance in my mind. I go back to things I know, like reviewing what happened today.

Gene returns and it's time to tell my side.

"You guys know that what you do is interesting and what I do is mostly tedious and boring, right? Well, Li's stuff *is* fascinating, and Gene at least makes his sound fascinating," I start.

"Is that more humor, Jake?" Gene says drily.

Li giggles and leans into me again. I guess we're back to driving Gene crazy with our antics. I don't understand it, but hey, I'm game. I lean back into Li with a smile. Gene looks nauseous.

I've completely lost my train of thought. The seconds tick by as I try to remember what I was saying.

"And ... ?" Gene prompts.

"I started with all of the documents relating to Berlin from mid-1945 back to the turn of the century. Remember, the Key was originally lost in the late 1800s, so I wanted to cover as much ground as possible.

"I read about the British Empire, the conflicts and problems stretching across the globe and brought it up through the first world war and then on into the second."

Gene's head falls back, and he begins snoring loudly.

"Nice," Li comments.

Gene brings his head back to normal. "Hey, if you two are going to try to get under my skin with your giggling and snuggling, then I'm going to pretend to snore through Jake's boring recap." He smirks at both of us.

Li and I share a look of disappointment.

"Hey, I wasn't born yesterday, and you can't trick a trickster," Gene reminds us with a wide smile and his thick drawl. "You gotta get up purty early in the morning to fool me."

Li stares at him defiantly for a second and then slips her arms in between mine and snuggles in close.

"Keep going, Jake, don't mind him." She practically coos this, her eyes never leaving Gene's.

Somehow, I'm now caught in the middle of their little contest of wills. Who's going to blink first, I guess. Well, I don't mind if it means more contact with Li. *Let the games begin!* I think, and settle into Li.

Gene looks like he's trying to hold in his anger, his flared nostrils giving him away.

"As I was saying, I went through as much history as I possibly could in the allotted time. After studying, Reginald and I worked through the common codes and ciphers employed during both wars and in the late 1800s.

"Again, we have a ton of ground to cover, so it made for an intense day. I worked with the famous Enigma machine," I say, but from the blank looks on Li's and Gene's faces, it wasn't as famous as I thought. "I also learned about how the codes and ciphers were passed and recorded on all sides of the wars."

Gene and Li were continuing their staring contest. I decided to put them to the test.

"Anyway, after this, Reginald and I got a little bored and decided to head up top in search of this little Mexican place Reginald swears is within walking distance from the caves. I told him I didn't think it was a good idea, but the thought of great Mexican food won out and we headed out."

Nothing registers on either face.

"Once we left the cave system, I find out we have been transported to the deserts of Arizona, right next to where they built the first atomic bomb," I explain, drawing from some of what I had read today. "Turns out the restaurant is further away than Reginald remembers, and we almost pass out on our way there because of the heat. Just when we think we can't go any further, a truck driver picks us up on the side of the road.

"Anyway, long story short, the place is called 'Atomic Tacos' and I have the best burrito I've ever tasted." I stop.

Gene's head snaps over to me, and I swear I hear a sucking sound as his eyes peel away from Li's.

"Did you say burrito? Where?" he turns and cranes his head in the direction of the buffet. When he doesn't see anything, he turns back around.

"The End," I announce, acting like I'm wrapping up my day.

"Cool, Jake, I'm sure that will pay off when we get to our destination," Gene sounds vaguely sarcastic.

"Yeah, Jake, you are incredible with that memory of yours." Li says, distracted by her war of wills with Gene.

I just shake my head and laugh at their ridiculous game, but if the game involves Li snuggling into me, I'm, well, game.

"Chosen, will you please gather your things and join me in my office?" The Guide says, having appeared out of nowhere. Her words are more of a command than a request.

CHAPTER 12

GLOBE

FIFTEEN MINUTES LATER, WE ENTER the Guide's office. I look around, eyebrows coming together in confusion. The office is completely different from last year. Our Guide then had kept a very Spartan office, almost bare.

The desk and chairs are the same—they haven't changed, but the walls are covered in paintings—old paintings, but not too old. I judge them to be from sometime in the nineteenth century, which is consistent with what I know of our Guide. Freshly cut flowers adorn the room along with live decorative plants. The office smells fresh and floral, whereas before it only smelled musty and old.

The fifteen foot square room also houses a palpable tension. The Guide waits for us, and she makes no effort to hide her concern. Worry lines cover her face, originating from her eyes and eyebrows and spreading from there to the rest of her face, all culminating at pursed lips.

Elizabeth, the Guide, must at one time have been an incredible beauty. For the first time in three days, I really study the woman who had helped us through the training process of this Quest. So much sadness permeates her eyes and her being that it is easy to overlook the strength and beauty that define this woman. I try to imagine what she has seen and suffered; I try to see the heartache she feels. I want to somehow soak it up and draw it away from her. I know sorrow. I know heartache. This binds us together.

I glance at Li and guess from her posture and eyes that she is feeling the same things that I am. She knows, too.

For his part, Gene is smiling some secret smile at the Guide. I look again at the Guide and see that her eyes dance a little from

Gene's smile. She relaxes some due to Gene's smile and unspoken communication. At that moment, I understand the true power of Gene's abilities. With all of his posturing and good ol' boy antics, he really does find the center of a person. He knows what brings them happiness and makes sure that what the person feels from him is the important feeling of love and acceptance. He brings to the surface all the good that lies within, no matter how buried or how scarred.

Gene catches me looking between him and the Guide. He looks into my eyes and nods his head slightly, as if to acknowledge that he knows what I see and it's fine with him that I see and learn. He is comfortable and confident. Not perfect, nope, but definitely someone I need, whom we all need.

"Lady and gentlemen," the Guide begins, "our time together is coming to a close tonight. After consulting with Reginald and Hans, I have decided to send you into the globe this evening rather than waiting for morning. The cover of darkness may help you arrive and settle safely—at least more safely than in the light of day."

The churning in my stomach begins to stir and burble imme- diately. I feel like I do when Master Shi is sending me in to get information through a conversation with some unsuspecting soul, only intensified a hundred times.

"As soon as you arrive, you are to locate your contact, who will hopefully provide you with information directing you to the sup- plies and information you need to begin your Quest."

The Guide is working to keep her composure, as evidenced by wringing her hands so hard I think she might break a bone or two.

"The forces of Evil will oppose you from all quarters. There are many who will seek the Key. Beware of who you trust and who you share your Quest with, for deceit and treachery follow the Key."

The Guide glances at the three-foot tall globe that stands between us.

"Please bring your keys out from under your clothing and gather at the globe," she instructs us, rising out of her seat and moving toward the globe.

The three of us rise simultaneously, automatically going through the motions required of us. Keys appear in our hands, mine trembling visibly, and we form a tight circle around the globe.

"Gene, place your arm around Li, and Li do likewise with Jake."
The Guide's voice is all business now.

"Remember to place your keys on the X I have marked at the
same time." She pauses, draws in a deep, shaking breath. "May you
be blessed in your Quest."

We nod at the Guide; I feel Li's arm coming around me, squeezing me tight in a protective gesture. We lean forward in concert,
like synchronized performers, each touching our key to the map,
bracing for what we know is coming.

The first time I fell through this map and traveled through space
and time, I didn't know what to expect and so didn't feel any
nerves about this portion of the Quest. Tonight I'm scared about
the falling and the feelings of heat and helplessness. There is something about doing this a second time that brings a more solid
apprehension, as if the knowing is worse than not knowing.

These thoughts pass quickly as I am forced to concentrate on
the falling, the spinning, the heat, and the speed. As soon as I begin
to sense these things, they stop. We are unceremoniously dumped
in a heap onto a floor that feels similar to the cave flooring we
have left behind.

"THAT'LL NEVER GET OLD, WILL it?" Gene mumbles as
he extricates himself from limbs that aren't his and pushes
to his feet. Li and I do the same.

What comes next is the unavoidable staring around, trying to
get some bearings in our new situation. It's like we have passed
out and awoken in a never before seen room, we all spin in slow
circles, craning our necks in every direction.

We are in a broken building. By broken, I mean bombed out, a
mostly destroyed burned-out shell of a structure. Rubble is everywhere, small bits and large chunks littering the floors and streets
outside. The building was four stories when whole, and we are
on the first floor, in what must've been someone's office. An old,
rubble covered desk sits near the glassless window. Two of its legs
are missing, so it is cantilevered awkwardly.

I stare upward and have an unobstructed view of the sky with
its moon and stars winking as if oblivious to the devastation below.

The roof is missing completely from what I can see, with parts of concrete floors also missing. The building looks like four walls were built, but the floor and roof were forgotten. Black soot clings to everything, some places darker than others.

The darkness presses in on the room, building and street ominously, giving a sense of dread and fear. I try to imagine what it must've been like when people inhabited the places, listening to the air raid sirens, wondering if that day was the day their building would be hit. My body responds to my thoughts with a cold shiver.

My reverie is interrupted by what sounds like small explosions, quickly followed by someone tackling me forcefully to the ground. It's not until I'm on the ground that I register that the explosive sounds are bullets blasting into the walls around us.

Li tackled me. I turn my head to see Gene crouching next to the window, shielded by the walls.

"Stay down, Jake," Li says, serious and focused now. She scuttles over to Gene's position.

"Do you see anything?" she asks.

"Not really, the muzzle flashes are coming from the building across the street, I think from the alley," Gene responds. "But I don't see any actual people, it's too dark."

More shots shatter the silence and blast into our room, none doing any real damage.

"Who are they? How did they know we would be here? Are they after us or what?" Gene asks in rapid-fire fashion.

"There are two core possibilities. First, the guys out there knew we were coming and have staked out our location, waiting for us. Second, it's just random soldiers thinking we are somehow the enemy," Li reasons.

As I listen to the two of them, I shake my head. I assumed from what we were told at the Training Center, that we were coming after the fighting had ended. So that rules out Li's second theory. But, how would anyone know that we were coming? That just seemed impossible, so Li's first theory didn't work either.

"Either way, it doesn't matter right now. What matters is that we get out of here and find our supplies as soon as possible," Li whispers. I know when she refers to supplies, what she means is weapons.

"What, you're not going to slink around and take out whoever is out there shooting at us?" Gene says softly, with a hint of laughter.

"Funny, Gene. I don't know the lay of the land. We just got here, plus it would be nice to have those wax bullets to use as a distraction," Li answers. "I think we concentrate on getting out of the line of fire and regroup to come up with a better plan."

She scuttles out of the room, disappearing into the gloom. Gene and I follow her out with our eyes, knowing she is scouting out our retreat. It's too dark to see his facial expression, but I imagine he has a smile on his face. That's just Gene. I'm just happy I haven't thrown up or broken out in hives. Maybe I'm getting used to danger, I think. What a crazy notion.

"Crawl back to my position, I have a way out," Li whispers.

Gene and I do just that, and quickly.

"I didn't see any movement from the alley," Gene reports. I guess I'm a little slow about gun battle tactics, because it takes this statement to realize Gene was watching to make sure the shooters didn't cross the street and close in on us. Or worse, cut off our escape.

"Thanks, Gene. That doesn't mean they don't have more units in different locations, so keep your heads down and stay right behind me."

I stick to Gene and Li, following their quiet movements out the back of the building and into an alley. We pick our way in and around rubble and trash, moving away from the shooters. I don't know if I'm projecting my own anxiety or what, but I sense a deep despair and gloom hovering over the city. This part of the city feels abandoned, like some strange post-apocalyptic movie. It's eerie. Of course, it is the dead of night, so that must have something to do with it, I think, trying to reassure myself.

After zigzagging for a couple of blocks we come to a wider street. I can tell Li is weighing the risks of rushing into the open space.

I see something across the street and tug on Li's sleeve, leaning in close to whisper.

"Can you see the sign that has been hammered crudely into the post across the street?" I ask, pointing in the direction of the sign.

It reads, "You are leaving the French sector." The sign also carries an image of the French flag—blue, white and red vertical stripes.

And a sign directly below the French sector sign reads, "You are entering the Soviet sector," along with a red flag with a hammer and sickle in the top left corner.

Li looks around, head swiveling in all directions. She is looking for something, making a decision of some kind. Finally, I see she has made it. She brings Gene and me in close.

"Jake, get a good look at this street, those signs, and our surroundings. We're going to find a little hidey-hole and talk this out for a few minutes. I think we've put enough distance between us and those guys taking potshots at us."

I gaze around the street, locking everything into memory. As an afterthought, I look directly up to the sky and take a mental picture of the stars and moon.

L I LEADS US INTO A building, backtracking a half block into the buildings we have recently put behind us. We huddle in the corner of a room that looks like all the rest we have passed, rubble and dust everywhere.

Li shoots me a look to indicate I should begin. I know what she means.

"Okay, at the end of World War II—well, at least at the end of the war in Europe, Berlin was taken by Allied forces and divided into four sectors. So essentially, the city is divided four ways. We are in the French sector, near the border of the Soviet sector.

The Soviets are from what we now call Russia; back then it was referred to as the Soviet Union and was a communist country, or more accurately, countries," I say, emphasizing the last s in countries. I check for comprehension. I get nods in return.

"So, West Berlin is occupied by the western Allies—France, Great Britain, and the United States. Again, divided into three chunks. The whole of East Berlin is occupied by the Soviet Union.

"The Soviet Union allied itself with the others during the war against Nazi Germany; however, very soon they will be on very different sides of a new conflict—what history now calls the Cold War. In 1961, a wall will be built to keep East Berliners from escaping into West Berlin. It will be called the Berlin Wall and will become infamous. A symbol of the war between democracy and communism; between the United States and the Soviet Union.

"In 1987, United States President Ronald Reagan famously gave a speech in Berlin where he said, 'Mr. Gorbachev, tear down this wall!' and two years later it did come down," I report, stopping because I realize I am getting caught up in the history, which won't necessarily help our current predicament.

For their part, Gene and Li look mesmerized.

"We are at the very beginning of events that will shape world history for the next 40 years or so. I don't think we want to cross that street and enter the Soviet sector," I say, drawing things back to the present. I laugh as I realize the irony in my thoughts about the present. We stand in the past and yet it is our present until we find and secure the Key.

"From my studies, I know that the French sector is the northernmost portion of West Berlin. If we move south, we will run into the British sector and then further south the U.S. sector.

"Knowing that crossing that street back there sends us east, I believe we should make our way southwest and see if we can locate our contact," I finish and lean back a little to give them space to consider what I have said.

"Li, how did you find our contact last time? You went ahead of us and found Mr. Wang's home," Gene remembers. I can hear the smirk in his voice. "Of course, Mr. Wang turned out to be a real jerk. But we still needed him, I guess."

"Honestly, I just wandered the city, scrutinizing every home and building until I saw the Key motif in his mansion," Li says with a shrug.

"Well, I guess we wander then," Gene says, standing fully upright.

Li and I join him, and Li takes the lead, heading back out into the streets and alleyways.

CHAPTER 13

THE CHURCH

W E WIND OUR WAY THROUGH streets, following no clear pattern as Li acts as though we are being followed. We double back, zigzag, stop, watch, listen, then continue. It makes sense to do this, but I feel myself becoming exhausted with all the adrenaline spikes and anxiety.

We pass through what must've been a park or open space of some kind. I see a sign that has fallen to the ground. "Starrplatz" is translated just as it reads, meaning it is a proper name. The name of the park, I guess. The trees are all gone. I suppose they have been cut down to be used for firewood. This whole city is surreal with its dark, deserted feel. Another shiver runs through me.

We turn out of the park and begin walking down a long street with fully and partially destroyed buildings on either side. It's amazing how quickly one adapts to surroundings. We skip through the shadows, hiding in burned-out hallways, resting and watching behind piles of rubble.

A light glows further down the street, maybe two blocks further on. Man-made light burns brightly in the darkness of the surrounding city. Li seems to consider this new element, deciding at last that this represents a threat to our safety and turns right down a street, then left into an alley. It is quieter here, the light diffused.

But like moths we are drawn to the light. We carefully approach the corner that will reveal the lights off to our left. We sidle around the corner and the source of the bright light reveals itself.

A church. A large church that has suffered some damage from the air raids, but remains largely intact. Lights burn outside the structure as well as inside. A large French flag flies on the church.

Li backtracks around the corner, out of the line of sight of the church. She turns to face Gene and me.

"What do you think?" she asks.

"I saw soldiers entering and leaving the church," Gene says.

"So did I," Li returns. "It must be used as some kind of headquarters or station for the French soldiers."

That made sense, the church would be a landmark that can be easily found, citizens will associate it with a place of refuge and safety. The French are probably using it and others like it to bring structure and governance back to this part of the city.

I nod my agreement to the other two.

The others begin weighing the pros and cons of making contact with the French forces, but I recognize the familiar tickling in the back of my mind. Something important is trying to work its way to the front of my thoughts. I close my eyes and relax, letting my brain do its work.

The church sparked something in my memory. I open my eyes and take a few steps to bring the church into view again, hoping this will aid in my memory recovery. What is it about this church? Have I seen it before? I shake my head, I haven't.

The church is huge, with a rectangular tower slashing into the sky, its roof missing. Light burns from windows and in the courtyard.

"Oh!" I think I say aloud; Gene and Li turn to me. Li quickly yanks me back around the corner.

"Easy there, Li. I think our Brain just found something in his giant memory that is gonna help us," Gene says, sliding his arm around me in his characteristic way.

Li darts an apologetic glance my way, and then replaces that look with one of expectancy.

"The church, we need to go there," I say, rushing on. "My mom—I know what she left me as my token, or clue, or whatever. She used to tell me how much she loved Europe. She and Dad had traveled there often before I came along. She used to tell me that Paris was her favorite city, but nothing beat the churches of Berlin.

"I used to think it odd that she would always add this to any talk of their European travels. Paris is beautiful, but no match for the churches of Berlin. Or the beaches of southern France are gorgeous, but not even close to the churches of Berlin.

"Dad would always shake his head, and once he even said something like 'But, we've never been to Berlin.' Mom then said something like she had gone to Berlin before she met Dad.

"I don't know, it was weird, but I never paid much attention. It didn't mean anything to me then, but now I think she was passing her token along verbally." I run out of things to say, so I clamp my jaw shut and look from Li to Gene.

"That's good 'nuff for me, pardner," Gene announces with a slap to my back.

Li looks a little more hesitant but agrees in the end.

"Okay, let's go see what happens," she agrees, clearly uncomfortable and wary.

She notices that I look pained at her reluctance.

"Jake, my worry has nothing to do with your memory of your mom's token. It's just that I'm worried about whoever was shooting at us. They may still be out there," she says with a hand on my arm.

I just shrug.

As we approach the church, a soldier steps out of the shadows and stops us. I didn't see him and from Li's reaction, neither did she. She's angry.

G ENE IS SMILING.
     "Howdy there, sir!" he says, southern twang in full effect. "It's might fine of ya to greet us. Boy, are we glad to see you. We've been wandering these streets for a while and even had someone shootin' at us. Us! We aren't even armed."

The soldier looks like he can't be too many years older than us, a boy himself, really. His words come out in English, not through our translator, but through his own mouth. The English is heavily accented.

"You are American," he states, saying American like A-mare-ee-can. He scrutinizes Li the longest. I can't decide if it's because of her beauty or because she is Chinese.

We nod, although I'm confused because Gene's little speech should be translated to him as if we're speaking French. So, how does he know we're American?

"You are lost?" he continues in accented English.

"Ya could say that, but really, we are lookin' for somethin' and we think it might be in this church. Do you reckon we can go in and have a look?" Gene continues. I'm still wondering about the translation.

The guard seems not to hear Gene.

"Where did you learn to speak French?" This he says in French; there is no accent in the translation. He seems suspicious of us.

Gene opens his arms in a wide gesture, hoping to reassure this soldier that we mean no harm. "That, my friend, is a long story," he says. "Let's just say that we picked it up at a Training Center."

The soldier turns his head back to the church like he's checking to be sure that no one else has seen us. He ushers us further into the shadows, and again checks around him to ensure we are alone.

"I have met another trio of Americans that were similar to the three of you." He says this while looking pointedly at Li.

Gene's face crumples in confusion.

I think I know what the soldier means.

"You met a group of three Americans, one of whom was also of Chinese descent. Is that what you mean?" I ask.

"Yes," his eyes grow wide as he recognizes my comprehension.

"These other three, they were two boys, one of whom was Chinese, and a girl who looks sort of like me, yes?" I press further.

The soldier's eyes practically bug out of his head now. "Yes. Yes! The girl was very pretty, but yes you have the same look—same hair and eyes," he whispers.

I turn to Gene and Li to explain my theory but I don't need to. Gene looks like he is trying to outdo the soldier's bug eyes and Li's eyes are shining.

"You ... know ... these other three?" the soldier asks, trying to find the words. His brain is probably trying to reconcile what he is seeing.

This soldier knows our parents. He must be our contact.

The soldier regains some of his composure. "I thought the others must be joking with me when they said others would come. I can't believe it ..." he retreats into his thoughts for a moment. "Are you spies?"

Gene's back to himself also.

"No, sir," he says with a laugh. "But we do need to find what the other three left us. Can you help?"

"I must ask for the key phrase that the pretty girl said that you would know," he says, waiting expectantly.

I panic. What key phrase? I feel Li and Gene turn to me just as expectantly as the soldier. I can't think of any key phrase. Oh! Wait ...

"Um ... 'Make friends with those who would be quick to criticize you,'" I say, hoping the one French quote Mom had taught me was the key phrase. It had to be. Why else would she be so insistent about teaching me this particular phrase? It wasn't even very important or famous.

The soldier smiles and nods.

"I am Corporal Ray LeGendre. It is a pleasure to make your acquaintance," he says, reaching to take Li's hand in his own and bringing it to his lips. How very French, I think. And then I imagine this young Frenchman doing the same thing to my mother. I sort of scowl at him, in some weird way thinking I'm defending my dad's honor.

Li misreads my scowl.

"Jake, he is just being polite," she whispers to me, thinking I'm upset with his kissing Li's hand. Come to think of it, I guess I am. Not wanting to make a big deal of all of this, I just smile at her.

"I will escort you to the items that the others have left in my care," Corporal LeGendre says and smartly turns for the door of the church.

As we enter the church, he asks us to wait behind for a moment. He moves over to a soldier sitting at a desk and speaks to the man for a moment. They smile and talk a bit, with the seated soldier taking a glance around Corporal LeGendre to peek at Li. He is smiling, or leering. I frown.

Corporal LeGendre returns and directs us into the building proper.

"I told the Captain that you wanted to see the night sky from the tower," he tells us. "I also had to tell him that I was obliging because of you," he is looking at Li.

She nods as if this is all perfectly natural. Gene and I share a look like two protective brothers agreeing to guard a little sister. Like Li needs our help.

We enter the bell tower of the church. I look up and stare straight into the sky. The roof and some of the upper wall has been damaged, but it is mostly intact. Somehow, this doesn't give me a ton of confidence as we begin the climb up rickety wooden stairs. The stairs wind upward along the rectangular walls, back and forth, upward into the night sky.

As we reach the floor that must house the bells, Corporal LeGendre opens a hatch that allows us up to climb up and through the floor and into the bell tower proper. As we stand up on the concrete floor, I notice that only about a third of the floor has been torn away along with the wall on that side. The roof is completely gone.

The room itself is a tight fight. Three large bells hang from steel girders bolted into the brick walls. Steel beams run from the concrete floor to the steel girders, further reinforcing the bell structure. It looks like a spider web of steel crisscrossing the space to ensure these bells do not fall down the tower.

The tower and bells are fortunate that the bomb that took the roof, part of the wall, and part of the floor did not take the parts that were bearing the load of the bells. Pure luck had kept these bells in the tower.

"I have been instructed to leave you alone in the bell tower," Corpoal LeGendre says, then disappears down the stairway.

LI AND GENE BOTH TURN to me.
"Well, at least this space is small compared to what we're used to, right?" Gene says, referring to the part of the Great Wall of China that we had to search last year.

"Yeah, but I think we're only looking for our supplies here, not the key," Li responds.

"There aren't a lot of hiding places in here, guys, so let's check inside the bells and get what we came for," I say, getting down to business.

Three bells means one for each of us. I step over, between, and under the girders, making my way to the bell furthest away. I look back and see Gene coming next, followed by Li. Li has already checked the nearest bell and is shaking her head.

"I got nothing," Gene reports.

It must be in my bell then, I think. I look up into the bell and see a large bundle suspended from the bell's clapper.

"It's here," I call out while reaching up to untie the bundle, which comes away easily and I lower it to the floor. Gene moves over to open it.

"That bundle is light; it must contain clothing and other such supplies," I say, looking back up into the bell. Sure enough, there is a second bundle suspended higher up. I duck my head back down.

"Gene, you might want to come get this one, it's a bit higher up," I tell him, not adding that I'm betting it's also full of heavy weapons and supplies. I'm not ready to admit that I fear dropping the thing.

Gene and I do a little shuffle, scooting around each other and the beams. While he reaches up into the bell, I kneel down to finish going through the first bundle. There are rucksacks, several uniforms that look like they're from different countries, and mess kits. It looked like standard stuff for the soldier of the period.

"Bingo!" Gene's voice echoes from inside the bell.

I turn to see him struggling with an awkward load. He manages to get it to the floor and I join him to see the contents of this second bundle. Li joins us also.

Gene unties the twine and spreads the canvas open. Pistols, rifles, a shotgun, ammo and grenades are revealed. A smaller package is sealed within the large canvas. Li picks it up.

"Ammo," she says by way of explanation. She busies herself with loading the weapons and moving the extra ammo to our individual packs. One glance showed the wax bullets were different from live ammunition.

As Li finishes with the weapons, she begins putting on the uniform of an American soldier. She put it on right over her clothing; it was bulky and big, but not overly so. Next, her hair was whipped around and disappeared under a hat.

"Huh. Jakers, our Li just became Lee," Gene says with a smile. With her hair tucked away she looked more the part than ever, but her striking beauty was difficult to hide, at least to my eyes.

Gene and I begin to pull on our uniforms when we hear a small laugh coming from Li.

"I think we need to rethink these uniforms guys," she says. "I mean, let's face it, Gene may be able to pull off being a soldier, but there is no way that Jake and I are believable. I'm a smallish girl and … well, Jake is a smallish boy. Gene can pass for seventeen or eighteen, but we can't. No way."

I look down at my uniform. I look ridiculous, like a boy dressed in his dad's uniform. Li is right, this isn't going to work.

"Here's what I think we can pull off," Li says, emphasizing *can*. "Gene wears the uniform and escorts the two of us around the city. It's not perfect, but it's the best shot we have."

Gene and I are both nodding. Gene continues settling into his uniform, while I begin to shed mine like a snake sheds its old baggy skin. Li does the same.

"Let's keep the uniforms, just in case, if our parents left them for us, there had to be a reason. I'll get everything divided into three packs." Li says while tossing Gene a shotgun. "I think this is your baby."

Gene catches the gun in his right hand. He inspects the gun, breaches the chamber and squints an eye to look inside. Li has already loaded the weapon.

"Six wax rounds are chambered and ready to go," Li reports and then tosses a separate pouch. "Those are your extra shells. I think that pouch cinches around your waist and hangs off the hip."

Gene leans the shotgun against the brick wall and adds the pouch to his uniform. Li stands and weaves through the steel beams toward Gene. She places an item into each hand.

"These are grenades, but don't worry, they aren't the real deal. They are more like a loud firecracker, I'm guessing. Sort of like the predecessor to flashbang grenades—they make a lot of noise and light, but don't have any explosives. Non-lethal ordnance," Li informs us, sounding like a weapons expert drilling her team. "Here is the pouch that they are kept in. Gene takes the pouch and slings it across his shoulder so the pouch hangs opposite the wax shotgun shell pouch.

Li returns to the weapons canvas and kneels down.

"Jake, do mind coming over to me? It might be easier," she requests with her back turned to me. I make my way over to her. She is kneeling below the middle bell. I kneel beside her.

"Hey, just a random thought. When do these bells ring? 'Cause I reckon we don't wanna be up here when they do," Gene warns us.

"The bells aren't functional right now. Ray told me on the way up after I asked that very question," Li says, busy with her weapons.

"Ray told you? Since when did you get cozy with Corporal

LeGendre?" Gene teases.

Li doesn't respond. She just shakes her head, and hands me a pistol.

"You and I need to be a little more discreet about carrying our weapons. We won't be dressed as soldiers, so we can't just strap them on like cowboys," she explains. "Also, it would probably look pretty strange for a couple of kids to be armed to the teeth like vigilantes."

She turns to me and reaches over and pulls up my shirt, shaking it out like Mom used to with bed sheets. I recoil at her touch, wondering what is going on. Li doesn't seem to notice.

"Uh, Li, do I need to leave you two alone?" Gene says. "It looks like you're getting mighty cozy with the little guy."

"Will you two show just an ounce of maturity? I'm just trying to see how to conceal Jake's pistol. Honestly!" Li shakes her head.

I'm just staring at Li, nervous at her touch, but not wanting it to stop. She spins me around awkwardly. Now her back is to Gene. She smiles at me, her eyes warm with a hint of mischief.

"I don't think we can hide the pistol below your T-shirt, the bulk will show," she says and grabs my pack, removing the soldier shirt and holding it up. "This will do. It's baggy enough to hide what we need, and it makes sense that a teenager might have grabbed an old soldier's shirt to keep clothed in difficult times." She throws the shirt over my shoulders and buttons it for me. When she has it just right, she lifts it and the T-shirt.

"Why didn't you help me get dressed, Li?" Gene asks playfully.

Again, Li ignores him. She hands me the pistol in a leather holster. "I've loaded this for you, Eight wax bullets, point and shoot, okay? Put it in a pocket, or slide it into the small of your back at your waist, whatever is comfortable.

"These two items are smoke grenades. We may need these to cover an escape or something, so I'll have you carry them. Just fill your pockets with as much extra ammo as you can, but not to the point where it's too noticeable," she says, fussing over me like a mother dressing her son for the prom. I shove the gun into the small of my back, sling the grenade pouch over my shoulder and push the ammo into pockets.

Li has her hands on my baggy lapels. She twists her head around to Gene. He is busy with his gear, getting it all situated properly.

She quickly leans forward and pecks me on the cheek, coming away smiling a goofy smile I've never seen before.

"You look ready," she says, trying to put gruffness into her voice.

"What just happened? What'd I miss? I was looking down, getting all this gear to sit right and next thing I know, I look up an see Jake blushing so red he's ready to burst into flames," Gene says, eyes squinting suspiciously.

I can't make eye contact with him.

"Gene, what are you talking about? It's dark up here, how do you know Jake is blushing?" Li says without emotion, she's back to impersonating a weapons master.

"A guy like me can tell, and it's not that dark up here; dawn must not be too far away," Gene says. "But stop avoidin' my question, Jake. What happened?"

I just shake my head, unable to trust my voice right now. Li is busy arming herself, copying my look by putting a soldier's shirt loosely over her clothes, and stashing all sorts of gear underneath.

She cocks her head to the side suddenly, listening to something I hadn't heard. She holds up her hand. The second time around I hear it. Someone is coming up the wooden stairs to the bell tower.

CHAPTER 14

VISITOR

"IT'S MORE THAN ONE SET of footsteps," Li whispers. "Jake, get back behind Gene at the far wall. Put the bells between you and the hatch. They'll have to show themselves as they come up through the opening."

Li makes her way over to the far side of the cramped space. The hatch opens near the wall farthest from us. Three huge bells are between the hatch and us. Li sets up on the wall, behind the hatch opening. Whomever is coming up will have to turn their heads fully around to see her.

"It's probably just ol' Ray comin' ta check on us," Gene whispers.

"Shh. It's more than just one," Li declares, ending the debate.

Time slows down and I feel the familiar signs of impending action. Adrenaline dumps into my bloodstream, bile rises into my throat, and anxiety prickles and crackles across my skin like a tiny electrical storm.

The hatch opens, and a soldier's head pops up through the hatch, pulling himself up and through the opening.

"Excuse the interruption. I am Captain Bernard and I have someone with me who knows of you and needs urgently to speak with you." The soldier's voice is even, no malice and no hesitation. As he straightens, I will myself not to look at Li, who is crouched behind him. He offers Gene and me a smile and then turns to the other soldier coming up.

I don't know what to make of this situation. Who in the world needs to speak to us, who even knows we are here? It doesn't feel right to me, and from Gene's shuffling, I know he feels the same.

The second soldier straightens to his full height and turns his head toward Gene and me, breaking into a huge sneer. My breath catches. What?

My brain scrambles to make sense of what my eyes are seeing, I blink a few times to clear the image. I'm seeing a ghost—an apparition. I must be imagining things now. Maybe I banged my head on one of the bells and I'm woozy.

The ghost laughs, making a cackling sound that I thought I would never hear again. It's impossible.

"Is it too early to say good morning?" he says through the sneer.

I finally find my voice, although it doesn't sound like mine as the words come out. "Rat Face?" I'm still unable to believe my eyes.

"In the flesh!" he says, bowing deeply with arms spread wide. "How nice to see you again, Jake." He takes a step forward.

"What, no pithy comment, Gene? No greeting like, 'Howdy pardner!' from you?" Rat Face chides, clucking his tongue in disappointment. "Too bad. Well, I don't have time for chitchat, so I'll get right to it." He reaches a hand inside his coat, but never makes it.

Li descends on the two trespassers in a blur. Captain Bernard goes down from a blow to the side of the neck, then Rat Face is brought to his knees, his arms twisted behind his back.

"Ah, Miss Zhang, so nice to make your acquaintance again," he says as if we are all sitting down to tea. "I am unarmed. I simply have a message for you, unless, of course, you'd like to turn over your keys right now. No? Well then, your move, Miss Zhang."

Rat Face is a street thug, an inconsequential bit player in our previous Quest. The Wang brothers tried to soften us up, to scare us. They used him and now here he is again, this time speaking in a cultured tone, four hundred thirty years later. It doesn't make sense. My mind races through the possibilities, none of which seem possible.

"Jake, I can read you like an open book, just like your pal Gene, and I can tell you are confused trying to make sense of all of this. Here we are in a church's bell tower in Berlin, halfway around the globe from the last time we met, but how is that possible?" Rat Face speaks as if he is a professor lecturing students.

"Do you think you are all so special? Do you think you are the only ones who can skip back and forth through time? It is just like your side to keep these truths from you. I am chosen, just like the three of you—" Rat Face's voice is cut off by something Li does, causing him pain. He is breathing heavily now, and a spark of pain registers on his face for a brief moment.

"Miss Zhang, please, search me thoroughly. I am not armed. I am not a threat to you here. Now I'd be lying if I said that I will not be a threat to you in the future, but for now, I just want to pass a message along and be on my way."

Li pushes him roughly onto his face. She pins a knee in his back and gives him a quick frisking. She rolls him over and just as quickly searches over him. The only thing she comes away with is an envelope.

"Stay on your knees, you can talk just as easily from there," she barks and flicks the envelope at him.

Rat Face rolls onto his knees, pushing himself up and grabbing the letter.

"Before I read the message to you, I should tell you that I have contacts spread throughout the city. I knew the minute you arrived and was informed as soon as you arrived here at the church. I will know where you are at all times. You cannot escape me," he remarks casually. "I made the mistake of leaving you to the Wang brothers last year. I thought I would take a smaller role and allow the Wangs to exact their revenge against General Xu. I'll not make the same mistake again." Rat Face begins opening the envelope. He does so slowly and carefully like he's unwrapping an ancient scroll.

I TAKE THE TIME TO SCRUTINIZE him. I realize that he has generic features that most likely allow him to pass among many cultures and peoples easily. With a few modifications to eye and hair color, he can pass for any number of people. He is a true chameleon, which must be a useful tool in his trade of deception and dishonor. I struggle to come to terms with the fact that he was the mastermind behind our troubles in the last Quest—the puppeteer pulling the Wang brothers' strings. I make a mental note not to underestimate him again.

Rat Face has grown taller since I last saw him, and while he can't be much older than us, he seems five or six years older. His dark hair is done in the style of our current era and he even has the beginnings of a beard pushing through his skin in patches.

He clears his throat. "I address this letter to the Chosen Trio, those who mistakenly believe they can change the world. Look around you, look closely at the devastation and destruction and you will see that humans have been and will continue to mistreat one another unless someone with true power can subdue them under his rule.

"I am he who can bring about such a change. Peace and prosperity are just out of reach for the world, but I can make it happen. And you can help. Your place beside me is reserved. Join me and together we can rule in peace.

"Hundreds of millions of lives have been lost over the first 50 years of this century. Do not allow even one more unnecessary death. You have the power to change history, to bring lasting peace under our rule. Do the right thing.

"I have sent my trusted friend, Steven, to bring you into our circle.

"Do not disappoint me. I do not want to be your enemy; however, I will pursue your destruction if you defy me. Yours faithfully, The Master." Rat Face finishes and tucks the letter back into his jacket pocket. He looks expectantly to us.

Silence hangs thick in the air.

"So … your name is Steve?" Gene asks, breaking the spell of silence.

Rat Face nods. "Steven Clark, at your service."

"Your name is Steven Clark, no last name?" Gene says again.

"Clark is my last name."

"Is that a lie too, 'cause I just can't imagine you as a Steve. And with two first names and zero last names, it sounds wonky," Gene notes.

"Well that is my real name. I guess not everyone can have a name as solid as Eugene," Rat Face sneers mockingly.

"You know that we call you Rat Face, right? That seems to fit better in my mind, so I'll just continue on with that if it's okay with you," Gene counters, his voice hardening with malice.

Rat Face heaves a theatrical sigh. "Gentlemen and Lady, you have a real opportunity to avoid disappointment, pain, and most probably an ignominious death," he says. "Join with the Master; his offer is generous. Take it. Please."

"I don't know what ignomimoose means, but I do know that I want to whoop your greasy little keister, so I suggest you take this message back to your master: We are the Chosen of the Quest and we will not give in to evil. We will not be weak and give in to a lesser life. Not for us and not for humanity," Gene says in a clipped tone while walking toward Rat Face.

He ends up right in front of him. He reaches down and lifts Rat Face roughly to his feet. Gene speaks to Li without taking his eyes from Rat Face. "Li, put this poor misguided soul to sleep; he looks tired."

Li's hands move quickly, striking Rat Face sharply in the side of the neck. Gene catches his slumping form and lowers him to the floor, more roughly than he probably could have.

"What do we do with him?" Gene wonders.

"We're the good guys, remember? Let's just leave him here and go find Ray. I have a feeling he needs our help right now," Li answers.

She lifts the hatch and motions us down. We wind down the stairs quickly, reaching the bottom in minutes. We move through the church and out into the courtyard.

We find Corporal LeGendre face down in the shadows of the walls of the huge church. Li rushes to his side, dropping to her knees to inspect him.

"He's alive, unconscious though, with a bloody nose. It looks like he took a rifle butt to the face." She removes a canteen from her waist and hands it to Gene. "Go fill this up with water, I'm sure the church has some somewhere."

Gene returns a minute later with a canteen sloshing water. Li takes it and splashes some onto the corporal's face. He comes to and heaves great breaths. Li holds him steady.

"You're okay, now, Ray. What happened?"

He takes a minute to gather himself, blinking his eyes and struggling to focus.

"I was stationed here as always, watching for intruders, when the captain called my name. I turned to him and that's the last thing I remember," he says haltingly through the fog of pain.

"He must have hit you with the butt of a rifle. I'm sorry, Ray, that you are involved in all of this," Li says sincerely.

The corporal waves a dismissive hand, thinking better of the gesture halfway through. He struggles to maintain focus again.

"I know what I am doing, and what side I fight for," Ray says knowingly. "I have something to give you. It's in my right jacket pocket, can you get it for me?"

Li reaches to his coat pocket and retrieves a letter. She shows it to the corporal. He nods.

"Yes, that is for the three of you. Good luck with whatever it is you seek," he says between careful breaths. "And be careful."

Gene and I help Li carry Corporal LeGendre into the church and pass him off to some medics. They assure us he'll be well taken care of.

CHAPTER 15

LETTER I

"WHAT NOW?" GENE ASKS. "MAN, what I wouldn't give for a Mr. Chow's Noodle House right now."

"There are rations in your rucksacks," Li says. "Let's find a place to sit, eat something, and read this letter."

We end up back near the former park that we passed last night. Dawn is now fully upon us and the warmth of the coming day feels nice on my skin. We lean against a tree stump while we eat our food.

"This food is terrible," Gene complains while making sure he licks up every last crumb. "This Quest is gonna be harder than I thought."

Li and I both turn to Gene and we all laugh. Gene always thinks with his stomach.

Li pulls out the letter and offers it to me. I take it. The envelope isn't sealed shut, so I lift the flap and remove three sheets of paper that have been folded in half.

"I'm getting' that déjà vu feelin' here now," Gene intones, his voice hesitant.

The first paper is a handwritten note.

"My mom wrote this note," I say, barely managing the words.

I stare at the paper, the words floating in and out of my vision as tears threaten to escape my eyes.

> *Chosen,*
> *This letter is unique, I think. We who write it and you who read it will surely know one another. The three of us, in our time, say to the three of you, we miss you!*

Now, the Quest to gather the Key is upon you. We have recovered the lost Key and placed in a protected place until you can retrieve it for the final time.

The Key was difficult to get back from those evil ones who held it for so long.

You will require four tokens to unlock the mystery of this Key. These tokens are spread throughout the city, one in each sector. You must not leave a sector of the city until that sector's token has been retrieved; you may not be allowed back.

To safeguard the Key, we have followed the usual protocols. Brain, Brawn, and Buddying will all be required for each token.

We have left communications behind with individuals you can trust in each sector who may assist you in your Quest; use them wisely. Employ honor and honesty to find what you seek.

The first token is located in the French sector. We trust that you have found the supplies that we have left behind for you.

Now, crack the code of the French token. It is not just boilerplate material, but is complex and unique to your task.

PGBPVKCSVPP

DWNPEIH

May you be blessed in your Quest.
Sarah Sigurdsson
Buddy of the Quest

Man's greatest weakness is his love of life.

A FTER I FINISH THE LETTER, I look up at my fellow Chosen to find them both standing very close, staring at me.

I move the letter to the back of the three pages to inspect the next. It is a cipher, in some ways similar to our first code in China, but with important differences. The third page is blank.

"Wow! How cool is it to be reading a letter that your mom wrote when she was a teenager? My mind is blown right now!" Gene marvels, breaking the silence as usual. "Now, that looks like one of those thingys you solved back in China. Is it the same deal?

Do we need to find one of those boards and stuff?"

I shake my head, looking over the cipher. "No, I wish it were a Grille Cipher. This is a Vigenère cipher, and it's much more complex. This was named after a Frenchman named who perfected it."

"A visionary cipher?" Gene says, misunderstanding the French pronunciation.

"Yes," I say, letting it go. It isn't worth the trouble, I think.

"So, this visionary guy put together a cipher that's harder than the Grille version?" Gene says.

"It's different," I say. "We need a keyword or keywords to decipher the scrambled text on the second paper. But mom didn't leave any of the words."

I check the third paper again, holding it up to the light, hoping something will appear. Nothing does.

"Well, she probably gave you the keys, you just didn't know it at the time, right?" Li says, hoping to prompt my memory.

"Yeah, I guess, but the keywords are usually just random, simple words. It would be hard for mom to pass them on to me that way. I mean, she died when I turned twelve, but she said millions of words to me during our lifetimes together," I point out, frustrated by the lack of clues.

"WELL, OL' BUDDY, SOUNDS LIKE we've been in this position before, right? So, we just need to talk it out. Let's go over what we know, and not talk about what we don't know." Gene says with a wink, repeating the words I said to him last year.

"Good plan," I say.

"Do you think we should get somewhere safer, like maybe put some distance between Rat Face and us?" Gene suggests before we launch into the puzzle.

Li shakes her head. "I've been thinking about that ever since we left that bell tower. It seemed strange to me that he would approach us like that—let us know that he is here and has forces ready to stop us. Tactically, it's a terrible idea to let the enemy know that you're here. So why do it?"

Gene and I both shrug.

"I think Rat Face did it because he can't find the Key. He needs us to find it for him, or at least find the tokens that unlock whatever is keeping the Key safe. So he'll keep an eye on us, maybe scare us into working faster, or harder, or whatever and wait for his chance to swoop in and take what we find."

"I don't follow. Couldn't he have done all of that even better without showing himself to us?" Gene asks.

"Yes, but what he loses in surprise, he gains in intimidation and shock. Look at how Jake reacted to seeing the ghost of Rat Face; Jake is still off his game because of it," Li explains.

Am I off my game? I wonder. Maybe a little.

"When you are always looking over your shoulder waiting for disaster to strike in the form of Rat Face, you get worn down. Fatigue sets in and you miss things. Maybe we trust the wrong person or make the wrong move. He waits for our guard to drop, because we can't possibly be vigilant every second of every day, and he wins." Li stops to think it through. "Yeah, I think that's his plan in a nutshell."

"So how do we beat him?" Gene asks.

"Easy. Relax when we can. Don't stress out worrying about when he is going to pop up," Li says, working out the strategy as she talks. "Sarah said there are four tokens to retrieve before the Key can be unlocked from its hiding place. Worst-case scenario, Rat Face and his evil minions have stumbled onto one of them. That means we should start being vigilant after we have two keys in our possession."

"You think they already have one of the tokens?" I ask.

"Probably not, but I'm just saying that if they do somehow have one, we should be vigilant sooner rather than later," she emphasizes.

"That makes sense to me," Gene muses. "What you're saying right now is not to worry too much about Rat Face, 'cause he'll come after us later."

Li shrugs, still showing worry. "I guess that's what I'm saying, but I don't think he'll just let us totally alone, either. So, find periods to relax so we can be ready at other times."

"How about we just take this relax-then-be-vigilant thing a little bit at a time?" I suggest. "Like right now, we feel reasonably confident that we can relax because Rat Face is asleep in the tower. So, let's relax and get to work on finding our first token."

"Agreed," Li concurs.

Gene nods his agreement and brings us together in a mash-up hug.

"I'm so happy to be back together with the two of you. I know it's crazy dangerous being here at this time doing what we're doing, but still, I'm happy I'm here!"

Gene voices what we all are thinking as well, I think. We share a smile together and turn our attention back to the cipher.

"Okay, we know that we need to find keywords somewhere from my mom that will allow us to crack this Vegenère cipher. Let me see if I can explain how this works to both of you," I say, laying out the paper with the mass of individual letters.

"Let's say you want to encrypt GeneConklin. The first thing you need is a keyword of the same length. It doesn't need to be a word of exactly the same length—you just repeat the letter of the keyword until it fits. Let's use the word *noodle*. GeneConklin is eleven letters, so we make our keyword fit by doing this: *Noodlenoodl*. Are you with me so far?"

Two heads nod at me.

"Now a Vigenère cipher is basically a Caesar cipher repeated with different keywords used for each code," I start again.

"Wait, stop," Li interrupts. "What is a Caesar cipher?"

"Oh, a Caesar cipher is basically a substitution code, like if you want to encode the letter A, you might use a number 3 substitution and the letter A moves three places along the alphabet and becomes D. The person deciphering the code would just need the number 3 to know how to decipher.

"The Vigenère cipher takes a Caesar cipher and makes it much more complex by using a table of several alphabets and multiple keys. These ciphers were indecipherable for the better part of three hundred years." I look up and see confusion written all over my friends' faces. Time for a new approach.

"It will be easier to show you what I mean," I decide and remove a pencil from my pocket. I had left the training center prepared this time, with my very own pencil tucked away in my pants pocket. It made the trip with no harm done either to my pencil or my thigh.

"This is what a Vigenère square looks like. The 26-letter alphabet is written into a grid 26 times, shifting the order of the alphabet by one letter each time," I explain, pointing to the second piece of paper included in the envelope. "Notice also that to the left runs a vertical column of the alphabet and running along the top is a row of the alphabet."

GENE AND LI BOTH CROWD in on either side of me. I feel a little like a teacher sharing a moment with his students. I admit that I like the feeling of sharing knowledge.

"If wanted to encrypt the word GeneConklin using the keyword 'noodle' we would do so like this: take the first letter G from the plaintext word we are encrypting and run down the column to that letter." I run my pencil down the left-hand column and stop at the G. "The word you are encrypting always uses the left-hand column. Now, we take the N from our keyword and use the row along the top of the square." I run my pencil across the top row and stop at the N.

"The final step is to run across from the G to meet up with the N row. Running over from G and down from N leads us to the letter T. Take the next two letters, E from the text we are encoding and O from the keyword and that gives us an S." Li and Gene follow along easily now. "And continue this way through the entire word that we want to encrypt." I sit back to check on understanding at this point.

"So, this thing looks pretty simple to use, but without the keyword it is impossible to decipher, right?" Gene asks.

"Exactly."

"You have shown us how to use the square to encrypt words, but we need to decrypt words, not encrypt them," Li points out.

I smile. "I know, I thought I would show you how this is used, because once you have an understanding of the encryption process, decrypting things makes more sense."

They both nod, a signal to move forward.

"Okay, to decrypt, we sort of do the opposite of what we have just done. When you don't know the plaintext in our example GeneConklin, we only have the letter jumble and hopefully a keyword. We have the first two letters of the letter jumble as TS and the first two letters of our keyword NO." I show them the work we have already done on the first two letters of our sample encryption.

"We take our keyword letter N and run down the column until we come to N," I illustrate, again using the pencil to trace down the square. "Then at N we go across the square to find the letter jumble T." I run from the N across the square until I come to the letter T and leave my pencil resting there.

"Then we just move the pencil up the square to the letter at the very top. As you can see, the letter is a G, just as it should be, since we know our encrypted word is GeneConklin. If we move to the second group of letters, we go down the column to the O and over to the S. When we move up to the very top, we find that E is our decrypted letter. GeneConklin is starting to take shape."

"THIS IS SO COOL. THIS Visionary guy was a bad dude," Gene gets a faraway look on his face. Uh-oh, here comes a monologue. "I'm thinking of the possibilities back home. Chloe and I could pass each other these Visionary codes without anybody being the wiser—"

"Let's stay on topic, Gene. I'm sure you'll have time to daydream later," Li interjects, cutting Gene off and bringing us back to the here and now.

"Sir, yessir!" Gene answers and snaps off a smart salute.

"Um, so anyway, we know how the cipher works," I say, jumping in quickly, hoping to avoid another rant by Gene and the inevitable bristling by Li. "What we don't have yet is the keyword. And without the keyword, we are at a dead-end."

With these words, I accomplish what I intended. Both Gene and Li stop gearing up for another exchange of words and turn their focus back to our problem.

My mind begins to turn through the possibilities again. It's overwhelming to think that Mom would have given me a keyword to remember among all of the millions of words that she said to me over the years. I shake my head; it's not reasonable to think that this is how she would pass on the keyword.

"I think I'm going about this in the wrong way," I mumble aloud. Although it's mostly just for me, Gene picks up on it.

"Listen, pardner," he starts up with a slap on my back. "We know the drill at this point, don't we? Let's talk it through together. Stand up. Pace around. Spout out all that is running through that genius noggin' of yours." He pulls me to my feet.

"I mean, this is what we do, isn't it?" Gene encourages, warming up now. "We are the Chosen and we will conquer!" He raises his arms to the sky, head back in a posture of victory. He returns to a normal stance and his arm goes back around my shoulders. "Let's start at the beginning."

I smile and move the letter from Mom back to the front of the three-paper stack.

"Our parents left us this letter after hiding the tokens in the four sectors of Berlin. We need to find these tokens, moving in order from our current sector, France, to Britain, the U.S., and finally Soviet Russia.

"Mom's legacy was verbal, not something tangible like the two of you got. Why? She died before she could give me a token, but she couldn't have known that when she was a teenager. So, it was planned this way. Maybe she knew that she wasn't a keeper of memorabilia. She was a free spirit who liked to move around, traveling the country. It could be that she didn't trust herself to keep hold of a keepsake," I find myself running on, not sure that this is even relevant.

Gene steps in to help. "Keep on truckin' Jakers, keep workin' the process," he says, reinforcing me.

"So, she knew she wouldn't hold onto a keepsake, so she decides on a famous quote that she knows that she can remember to pass onto me. This results in our finding an ally, the supplies, and the letter."

I stop. I think I'm onto something. I run through it quickly, checking for holes in the theory, or to see if I'm missing an important piece of information.

"The keyword wouldn't be something that Mom passed on verbally though, unlike a famous French quote. She couldn't be sure that a single word would be something that I would remember at this specific time.

"The keyword has to be in the letter," I say, bringing the letter up for further inspection. The other two gather around tightly to read with me.

"The letter is unique!" Gene shouts. "Maybe the special word is unique, I mean, it's kind of a strange way to open a letter, right?"

"You're unique, Gene," Li remarks, the sarcasm easy to hear in her voice.

"Well, I don't see you throwing out any bright ideas! It could be unique, ya know," Gene's voice sounds pouty.

"It could be any one of these words, Gene. Let's allow Jake to keep going through his process," Li returns, more kindly this time.

"Quick, Jake, how many words are in the letter?" Gene says, rapid-fire.

"Two hundred fifty-two," I say just as quickly.

"Man, I knew ya'd already counted the words, probably without even thinkin' 'bout it. You're such a genius. Wow," Gene marvels, using his natural buddying skills to pump me up. He always knows what to say—well, almost always.

"Look at this part of the letter. The letter up to this point is more a recap and informative, then it turns to the cipher and our Quest," I reason, pointing to a line in the letter.

Now, crack the code of the French token. It is not just boilerplate material, but is complex and unique to your task.

"IT SEEMS LIKE SHE IS pointing to this portion of the letter when she writes now, like she's saying, 'Now focus on this part to crack the code,'" I note.

"Hey, look! The word unique is used again. Maybe it's like last time with the repeating words," Gene says.

I think he really hopes unique is the keyword so he can lord it over Li for the rest of time.

"Jake's mom had no idea about General Xu and our last Quest, buddy," Li points out, emphasizing the word buddy to remind Gene who the Brain was in the group. I think he catches on.

"I'm just sayin'…" he offers.

"This sentence here just sounds awkward, doesn't it?" I say to nobody in particular. "'It is not just boilerplate material but is complex and unique to your task.' It sounds forced."

Mom never spoke like that, and I don't think she ever wrote in that manner either. It doesn't flow with the rest of the letter either. It stands out. That's it!

"This sentence stands out!" I say aloud, voicing my thoughts. "Mom wrote it so it would stand out. This sentence will lead us to the keyword."

I see Gene counting to himself, using his finger to trace the words in the sentence.

"Fourteen. Fourteen words in the sentence" Gene muses, proud of himself. "Down from two-hundred-fifty somethin'. That's good. Maybe we should take them one at a time and put 'em through the square doohickey."

"Doohickey?" Li repeats, suppressing a smile.

Gene bristles. "Yeah, a doohickey. You know like a thingamabob or a whatchamacallit. Or doodad," he says, running through all of his words that mean he has no idea what the actual name is.

I'm smiling, but trying to wipe it away, because this is serious business. I fail. In fact, I break out into a chuckle. I say chuckle because men don't giggle, right? I chuckled.

Li giggles. "Honestly, Gene, you are a piece of work," she tells him. "What would we do without you?"

Li quickly goes up onto her tiptoes and gives Gene a quick peck on the cheek.

Wait. What? I thought that was our thing—something she just did with me.

Gene colors bright red. I think I do too, but for a different reason. My hand goes up to my cheek, as if I'll feel her kiss print on my skin.

Li moves around and slips an arm through each of our arms. I wonder if we are going to fall into some impromptu skipping routine.

"My boys," Li says possessively.

I'm confused.

"Well, now, young lady, don't be gettin' any fancy ideas. I'm spoken fer," Gene informs her with a huge grin. "Plus, I think Jakers here thought the peck you gave him up in the tower was an exclusive thing."

My eyes flare wide and I quickly turn to stare at the ground. Too late.

"Yep, just as I thought," Gene continues, having seen my reaction. "You thought that I didn't see that quick little action, Li. You are lightning fast, but I don't miss a thing."

"I'm impressed, Eugenie," she says, using the nickname his brothers use. She does this to tease him, her voice light and full of humor. "I thought I pulled that off without you noticing."

Gene huffs like such a thing is impossible.

"LET'S SIT DOWN AND GET comfortable. Jake needs to focus, and we aren't helping," Li says, leading us by the arms back to our spot. "Where were we? Oh yes, Gene was wondering if we should just plug all fourteen words into the doohickey."

Another round of laughter threatens, but I clear my throat, hoping to cut off the laughter before it starts. I'm still a bit torqued.

"I don't think any of these fourteen words are the keyword," I say flatly.

"Huh? I thought you just said it was in that sentence," Gene says. Li nods her agreement.

"I said the sentence will lead us to the keyword," I remind them precisely. I smile at the thought of Mom teasing me about my use of *precisely*.

Gene says something that sounds like *wull,* but I take to mean *well* and then he drifts off, adding nothing to this single word.

"'It is not just boilerplate material, but is complex and unique to your task,'" I mutter again. Something sparks in the back of my mind, but I can't exactly pin it down. I read the sentence over and over again, losing myself in the letter.

"What exactly does 'boilerplate material' mean anyway?" Gene asks.

"It means plain or ordinary, something that is just standard," I explain.

I think of the way Gene pronounces boilerplate. Boiler sounds more like bowler when he says it. His pronunciation always has sort of grated at my ears—

"That's it!" I yelp. I turn to Gene and on impulse I lean into him and peck him on the cheek, knowing that'll get a laugh. Welcome to my newfound confidence and sense of humor. Gene recoils backward, which sends Li into another fit of laughter.

"Well, I'll be a blue-nosed gopher!" Gene exclaims. "Jake's comedy just keeps on a comin'."

They laugh for a minute while I gather my thoughts.

"Blue-nosed gopher?" Li asks Gene.

"I don't know, I just heard my Granddaddy use the term all the time when I was little," Gene says, coloring.

Back to business, I think to myself.

"So, the way Gene pronounces boiler like its bowler reminded me of something my mom and dad would say," I say by way of explanation. "Mom was always using famous French quotations around the house, and now I know why. She would say them in French and then English. She would always tell us the name of the person who said the famous words.

"Well, Mom would always sort of joke about a friend of hers who would always butcher the French pronunciation on purpose, you know, his way of joking with Mom. I remember that the man who said the quote I used earlier with the corporal was named Boileau. In French it sort of sounds like 'bweh-loo', but Mom's friend would always just say Boiler."

Gene and Li are desperate to follow my ramblings.

"So, you're saying that the keyword is boiler or boilerplate?" Gene ventures, not sure of himself.

"Congratulations Gene, you followed my scatterbrained ramblings," I say with a smile.

"You're never gonna let that go, are you?" Gene says with a shake of his head.

"Probably not. But anyway, I believe the keyword is actually Boileau, the name of the guy. It's not specifically mentioned in the letter, which I think is important, because anybody could get ahold of this letter and the Vigenère square and put all of the words through the square until they find one that makes sense. This way, Mom protected the keyword from all others except us."

I let that sink in for a minute. Then I drop the other bombshell.

"I think my mom was referring to your dad, Gene, when she talked about her friend who mispronounced all the French names," I say with a smile.

"Hey, yeah, you're probably right! How cool is it that our parents did the same thing we're doing now," Gene gushes.

Li and I find ourselves nodding, caught up in a moment of nostalgia for our parents.

"Anyway, let's use the square to see if my deduction is correct." I say, slipping into business mode.

I pull the square out from behind the letter and hand the empty sheet of paper to Li. I write the keyword out on the empty sheet: BOILEAUBOIL making sure to repeat the letters until they match the length of the letter jumble. Then, below the keyword, I write the letter jumble from the letter: PGBPVKCSVPP

The paper now looks like this:

B O I L E A U B O I L
P G B P V K C SV P P

"Do you mind recording the letters as we decrypt them?" I ask her.

She just smiles and takes the paper and pencil from me.

"Okay … first letter of the keyword is B," I say, working aloud as I run my finger down the left-hand column to B. "The first letter of the code is P." I move my finger along the B line until I come to P, then move up to the column to the topmost letter. "The first decrypted letter is O.

Li writes O below the other two words.

B O I L E A U B O I L
P G B P V K C SV P P
O

"Next, we find O in the left-hand column and move over on that line to G," I say, moving up to the topmost letter. "Second letter is S."

Li puts an S next to the O.

We follow this pattern through the full eleven letter code. Li ends up handing the sheet back to me, now looking like this.

B O I L E A U B O I L
P G B P V K C SV P P
O S T E R K I R C H E

"Uh … Jake …" Gene says, voicing what we are all thinking.

"I know, it's not an English word," I say. "But it's not translating into English, which means it's a proper noun. A place name, I'm betting." I continue to stare at the word, willing it to translate.

"Is it French?" Gene asks, hope shining in his eyes. He knows we can find Ray to translate it for us.

I shake my head. "It doesn't look like French to me," I answer.

"In fact, I think it looks German."

"German?" Gene echoes.

I pick up steam now.

"Acutally, German makes sense, of course. We are in Germany, the place names here won't be in French or English or Russian just because they now occupy the country. This word is a German proper noun—a place name I bet," I reason.

"So we need to find someone who speaks German," Li states.

"Maybe …" I say, distracted by a new thought. "I pored over tons of documents while in the training center, many of which were in German. When words wouldn't translate, I knew they were proper nouns, so I began to get a feel for some simple words in German."

I turn to the other two in turn, a smile growing on my face. "This word is actually two words. And I recognize the back half of this word," I mutter, really concentrating now. "Let me try something …"

I take the pencil and write the word Osterkirche in two separate words: Oster and Kirche.

The paper now looks like this:

B O I L E A U B O I L
P G B P V K C S V P P
O S T E R K I R C H E

OSTER   KIRCHE

CHAPTER 16

EASTER CHURCH

A S WE LOOK AT THE paper, the two words translate before our eyes. Easter Church.

"Easter Church? So, it's another church we need to find," Gene says.

"We need a map," Li adds.

"Wait," I say, deep in thought. "We're not done. There are two codes or letter jumbles in this letter."

I hold the letter up and point to the second of the two letter jumbles: DWNPEIH.

"Oh, right. Do we use the same keyword?" Li wonders.

"No, I already did a quick look and it doesn't work with Boileau," I answer, hoping I'm hiding my frustration at beginning anew. "The Vigenere box can be used multiple times; a new keyword reveals a new solution. So, in a way this cipher can hold several clues."

"Well, maybe we should go find this Easter Church and see if something jumps out at us as a keyword for the second code?" Gene says.

"I think the keyword for the second code must be in the letter also," I say. "I think we need to find something that relates to the first clue."

I stand and stretch, pacing in small circles. "The first keyword is a Frenchman's name. One who my mom quoted often, something only we would know."

"Well, what about this last line then?" Li offers. "Do you recognize this line as a quote, or is it just something our parents added?"

I sit back down in between Gene and Li. I stare at the line that is slightly darker than the rest, at the bottom after the signature.

I let out a kind of yelp, then lean into Li and give her a quick peck on the cheek.

"You did it, Li!" I exult. "I think I know what the second keyword is!"

Gene interrupts me. "Okay, I see what you did there, Jakers," he starts with a knowing smile. "You think that you can hide these things from me, but remember I can read your thoughts, little fella."

I turn to him with a confused look. Or at least I hope it's a confused look, because I'm afraid he is seeing right through me. I know he can't really read my thoughts, but what he can do is pretty much the same thing. My expressions are a window to my mind, apparently.

"See, you can't pull one over me. It's all so clear to me now. You only gave me that peck on the cheek earlier just so you could find the right time to do the same thing to Li without me thinking it's weird. Well, sorry, Jake, I see right through your little plan," Gene finishes.

He's right. *Precisely*. He just detailed my plan in front of me—and Li. I gave Gene his little peck just so I could do the same to Li at some future time. *Geez, Gene!* I yell at him, silently in my mind.

"Don't be ridiculous, Gene. Jake is just excited, and I did point him to the next keyword," Li interjects, brushing aside Gene's accusation.

Gene's eyes squint, and I know he's trying to decide if Li is seriously clueless to my little game or if she is just covering for me. I know this because I turn to Li, trying to determine the exact same thing.

Li gives nothing away from her stony-faced expression. Finally, she raises her eyebrows as if to ask when I'm going to get back to solving the second code word.

Staring at Li gives me a chance to relive the quick peck. Truth be told, I'm not even sure I touched Gene when I performed my sham of a peck. But with Li, I held my puckered lips to her cheek solidly, feeling the warmth. I wonder what she thought of it.

I'm fourteen. I don't know the mind of Li. I don't think I'll ever know. I shake my head to clear this thought from my brain.

"Right, so I think I know the second keyword," I announce, pointing to the final line of the letter. "Li was right when she asked if this was also a quote—it is. Another Frenchman said it. This time the man's name is Molière."

I WRITE THE SECOND GROUPING OUT on the table while talking.

"This is actually my mom's favorite quote. She would say it all the time to me, when I was acting particularly shy or anxious. "Take risks, enjoy the moment,' she would tell me. 'Go out and experience the world, have fun!' and then she would always end with Molière's words, sort of in a teasing way. She knew I wasn't afraid to die, she just thought I was afraid to really live." I stop and hold the paper out to them.

M O L I E R E

D W N P E I H

We go through the same process as last time. Down to the M in the left-hand column, then over to the D and finally up to the top for the decoded letter, in this case an R. When we finish, the paper looks like this:

M O L I E R E

D W N P E I H

R I C H A R D

"Richard? As in the name Richard?" Gene says, staring at the name.

"Richard was a very popular name in the 1940s and 50s, I think," Li says.

I barely hear them. I'm confused too, but not for the same reasons that the others are. Richard is an English first name, but also a French surname. But I don't think it is a German name, at least not that I can think of. So where does that leave us, I wonder?

I'm pulled out of my thoughts with bump on the arm from Gene.

"You in there, Jake?" he nudges.

I haven't heard their discussion.

"Sorry, what?" I say.

"We're wonderin' what you think of this new word ... er, name?" Gene asks. "Obviously you're thinkin' somethin', 'cause you weren't listenin' to us."

I give an embarrassed smile. "Yeah, well, I'm sorry I didn't hear what you were saying," I apologize. "I was thinking about how odd it is that the name is Richard. Richard can be an English first name or a French last name, but I don't know about any German connection. I guess I thought that since we are in Germany and the church we are pointed to is in Germany ..."

"Hey, we'll figure it out," Gene says, again with the figgur pronunciation. I need to let it go.

"It could be that we will find a French soldier by the name of Richard who will help us with finding the token at the Easter Church," Li hypothesizes, trying to tie it all together.

I shrug. "Well, I guess now is the time to find the Easter Church and hope that someone there presents themselves, right?" I try to inject cheer into my voice. "The simplest thing to do is to return to the church we just came from and see if Ray can help us with a map or directions to the Easter Church."

We gather our belongings together and leave the Starrplatz, heading back toward the church the French were using as a military station.

The sun was reaching into the sky by now, fully midmorning moving toward noon.

On our walk back, I see people for the first time since we arrived—citizens of the city. I mean, not foreign soldiers. Women worked in clumps shoveling the rubble into piles, while others worked to clear it away. Children also materialized, running and playing among the ruins of this once beautiful city.

What I saw in the eyes of those we passed surprised me. I guess it shouldn't have, but it did. What I saw was hope. Hope in a better future. Though bodies were gaunt and cheeks hollow from too little food, a brightness burned in their eyes. Of course, there was much of sorrow and sadness in the faces, and maybe even a little defeat in the slope of the shoulders. The overriding feeling I sensed was one of hope for a better future and willingness to work toward that goal.

Gene had found some chocolate in his rations and had been saving it for a treat later. But now I watch as he approaches two children who can't be more than eight years old. He kneels in front of them while bringing something out from his pocket.

I see that the women have stopped their work and are also staring at the red-haired giant. It seems they don't know how to react. Should they grab the children and run? One woman takes a firm step in Gene's direction, but the other woman stops her with a touch on the arm.

Gene unwraps the chocolate and holds it out to the children. They look toward the women, who must be their mothers. The mother with a hand on her companion gives a nod.

The boys snatch the candy and it disappears into their mouths quickly. They smile chocolatey grins at Gene. He leaves the rest of the sweets in their hands, stands and ruffles their heads with his large hand.

He turns and moves toward the women. When he reaches them, he hands his entire pack of food rations over to them. They shake their heads and raise their arms in protest. I can't hear what they are saying, but I can imagine. Gene simply places the pack full of rations on the ground at their feet.

Then he does something so characteristically Gene, and yet it still takes my breath away. He hugs both these women in a huge enveloping grasp. The women look terrified at first and then seem to melt into his arms, grateful for the warmth and kindness.

Li and I have stopped moving. We just watch Gene speak kindly to these two women for a few more moments. I feel like we are intruding on something sacred, but I can't look away.

Gene slowly returns to Li and me without a word.

We begin walking in silence toward our destination again. After a moment, Li puts and hand on Gene's arm.

"Your mother and father would be proud of you, Gene," she says, her voice a bit shaky. "I'm proud of you too, Gene."

Gene just smiles and continues walking, head held high.

We come across more women sweeping and shoveling, with children always nearby. Unbidden, first Li and then I walk slowly over to these groups and leave behind our food and sweets.

As we near the church, it's Gene who breaks the silence.

"We've done good today. Done real good," he says. "If we all could remember to treat others with kindness and respect, war would just be a distant memory."

"That's why we're here, Gene. They are why we came," Li says, waving a hand in the direction of the women and children we passed.

AS WE NEAR THE CHURCH, Corporal LeGendre steps from his usual station and waves a hand in greeting. As soon as he does this, he casts around looking for threats or his Captain, or Rat Face. Apparently, no threats are visible and the corporal begins a casual saunter over to us. He meets us at the street's edge.

"Hello, I did not expect to see you return." Ray thinks something must be wrong.

"Neither did we, Ray, but here we are again," Li agrees, looking past Ray with searching eyes. "Any sign of our unwelcome guest from last night ... or this morning?"

Talking about time that is usually spent in sleep is always awkward. Do you call it night because its mostly dark and people are asleep, or do you stay technical and call it early morning? Li isn't sure and neither am I.

"The ... friend of the Captain's ... has not returned. He disappeared into the morning light just as quickly as he appeared. He must be a vampire," the Corporal says this with a smile, which turns into a cringe when the pain registers.

"Believe me when I say that the Captain's friend is way worse than a vampire," Li chimes in.

"What can I do to help you?" the Corporal asks. "Do you need more food?"

He says this while looking down the street. He makes it clear that he's seen what we did for the women and children on our walk down the street. I turn and cast a glance up the street and see that Corporal LeGendre's view of our actions would have been quite clear.

"If you have some rations to spare that would be nice, but if supply is tight then by all means keep them. We'll find other means, Corporal," Li answers.

"Please call me Ray. All of you please," he says, making sure to include Gene and I in his invitation.

"Well then, Ray it is! That's might decent of ya, Ray," Gene smiles while putting his arm around the guy in a welcoming gesture. "The little man here, Jake, has read the letter you gave to us. It's pointed us in a certain direction, but we need a map or some directions. Do you think you might be able to help?"

"Certainly," Ray says with confidence.

Gene turns to me, inviting me to get on with it.

"Have you heard of the Easter Church—it's called the Osterkirche in German," I say.

Ray gives a confused look, like maybe we're idiots or something. I glance at Li and Gene, they too are looking at me.

"This is the Osterkirche," Ray explains, turning and waving his hand to the church in right in front of us.

WE HAD BEEN IN THE Osterkirche all along. Why hadn't mom just left the token with the supplies and ammunition? The answer comes quickly, as it is simple. Trusting others to hide supplies and pass a letter on to us is one thing, trusting them with the token is completely different. It must be hidden and kept secret from everyone save the Chosen. Ray knows nothing of the token, I'm willing to bet.

"Well I'll be …" Gene mutters as he stares up at the bell tower.

Li simply smiles.

"Corporal—er, I mean Ray—do you have any men by the name of Richard stationed here?" I inquire, pronouncing Richard like the French would: Ree-shaw.

Ray knits his brows together in thought for a moment.

"No," he says like only the French can; it sounds so much more impressive. "We are only a small unit here. There are many more soldiers at our headquarters. Maybe you will find this Richard there?"

I shake my head. It was a long shot and somehow, I don't think we are looking for a French soldier. That is why the name is curious to me, I still don't see how it fits with being in Berlin, Germany. What am I missing?

I realize everyone is staring at me, waiting.

"Ray, do you think you could give us a complete tour of the

church or ask someone who isn't on guard duty to do so?" I inquire.

Again, the knit brows and thoughtful look.

"The Captain may be suspicious if he sees you wandering the church again. Thankfully, he left for headquarters about an hour ago to attend a meeting," he informs us. "I cannot leave my post, and I don't know who I can trust. It may be best if you were to just give yourselves a tour, no?"

"How long will the Captain be gone?" I ask.

"He usually does not return until after dark. He likes to enjoy a long dinner with his fellow officers."

"Thank you for your help, Ray," Li says with a smile. "And sorry about what happened."

Ray reaches reflexively up to his wound, stops midway there, and drops his hand to his side.

"It is nothing. I am happy to help. If I see the Captain return or the other gentleman, I will come find you," he promises.

We each give our thanks to Ray and then head toward the main entrance of the church.

CHAPTER 17

MOLIÈRE

THE INTERIOR OF THE CHURCH is impressive. Having passed through the church while dark, I couldn't appreciate the beauty and magnitude of the building. As with many churches, the main focus is the altar and surrounding areas, and this church is no exception. Behind the altar, intricate murals decorate the walls, depicting Jesus in various settings.

The eye is drawn upward into the cavernous space, a deliberate architectural design to raise the eyes heavenward. It works here. The main worship hall is large with balconies for more seating on both sides of the room. Huge chandeliers hang down from the ceiling. This portion of the church appears to have survived most of the damage the rest of it has suffered from the war.

"What exactly are we looking for here?" Gene asks, breaking the silence in the room.

"Not sure," I say, without taking my eyes from the beautiful room. "Let's just look carefully at each of the areas of the church and see what we discover."

"So, the only clue we have is the name Richard, which could be an English name, like Richard the Lionheart, King of England, or it could be a last name of a Frenchman like … well, I don't know any famous French Richards. Or it could be somehow German," Li puzzles while walking through the huge space toward the altar.

After scrutinizing the altar and mosaics behind it up on the walls, we move through the balconies and back down to where we entered.

"Well, let's head through the rest of the church, it looks like there are quite a few rooms in the rear of the building," I remark without enthusiasm.

After searching the rest of the rooms, some of which are severely damaged from the war, we end up in the courtyard behind the church. We're all tired, hungry and depressed.

"We're missing something," I state the obvious.

"Yeah, we're missing the blasted token," Gene frets as he crumples into a heap on the ground.

"No, I mean that we are missing something about the clue," I persist, pulling out the envelope with the pages inside. "There must be more in the letter."

I find a place on the ground to sit and the others find spots on either side of me, with Gene sliding over from his already seated position.

I reread the letter. I cock my head to the side as I normally do when I am sorting through a problem. I close my eyes. "The first code is straightforward; it tells us the place where the token is hidden," I say, beginning to work through the problem. "It's the second code word that is incomplete."

The others sit silently waiting on me. I know if they have anything to add they'll speak up; otherwise they'll let me work through it.

"The second code's keyword comes from the famous line from Molière, 'Man's greatest weakness is his love of life.' We used Molière as the keyword to decipher the word Richard. We used Molière—" I feel like I'm getting close to something now.

"We used Molière for the second clue. We need to continue to use Molière for more help on this clue. 'Man's greatest weakness … love of life.' What is the opposite of loving life? Dying? Death. Not being afraid of death?" I shake my head in frustration.

"But what does death have to do with a church? The death of Jesus? Jesus also gave up his life for others. He didn't love life more than others … no …"

I open my eyes and stand, restless and angry that I can't see the answer. I move around the courtyard, still talking aloud. "What has a church got to do with death? Resurrection? Forgiveness of sin and a reborn life?"

IRUB MY HANDS OVER MY face in an attempt to scrub my thoughts clear. "No, this isn't about Jesus, it's about a guy with the first name or last name of Richard. What does an unknown guy named Richard have to do with death and a church?"

I snap my eyes open. I spin around the courtyard, then I run from one end to the other, searching for I know has to be here. It's where the answer lies.

"What is it, Jake?" Li calls out softly. Both Gene and Li are coming to their feet.

I stop my frenetic searching and turn to them. "Molière is the key again. Not only did he help solve the code, but his quote shows us where in the church we can find Richard." I rush through the words. "Molière says basically that strong men don't fear death. Death and churches. What do they have in common?"

I wait for the light to come on for them. When it doesn't, I continue. "Graveyards. Many churches include graveyards or crypts where they buried their dead. I bet the Richard we're looking for is buried here somewhere."

I resume my search in the back of the church. Rubble is strewn everywhere, and no clear graveyard is visible. I feel a hand on my shoulder.

"Uh, Jakers, this church is kinda in an urban area, ya know. I don't see any graveyard about," Gene points out.

"I know, but ..." I say, staring at the grounds.

Just then, a door opens from what I had assumed was a storage shed of some kind attached to the church. I thought it might house tools for upkeep, or maybe even electrical boxes and the like. An older man steps into the courtyard carrying a shovel and a wide broom.

He stops when he sees us staring at him. I step forward.

"Um ... excuse me sir, you must be the church's caretaker, yes?" I speak hesitantly, making deductions as I go.

The man gives a wary nod.

"The building you just left," I say, pointing to the door behind him. "Does it hold a crypt or lead to a graveyard?"

I'm leaning forward in anticipation, practically willing him to nod again.

"Who are you?" he asks gruffly, not willing to share the building's secrets. He inches closer to the door, acting as a guardian of whatever is within.

Gene, Li, and I have an unspoken conference sharing looks and questions among us. What do we say? What can we say? This lasts seconds.

Gene steps forward. "Sir, we have traveled a great distance in a search for something important left behind by our … loved ones. While this item has no value beyond our families, it is important to us," he explains with complete honesty. "We believe the family heirloom, so to speak, was left in this church's crypt or graveyard."

The caretaker does not move. Nor does his face register any expression at all. He may as well be made of stone, or brick like the building behind him. An eternity passes.

"Why would your loved ones hide something in the crypt of this church?" he questions. I take this as a good sign; at least he hasn't shut us down.

"The war, sir. What could be safer than something sacred like a church's crypt? It was the only place that our parents could think of to keep it safe. Please, sir," Gene begs, doing a good job of showing sincerity. "If you like, you can stay here by the door to make sure we don't do anything funny. We are just here to retrieve this item and then move on."

The man considers this for another eternity. I realize I'm holding my breath. I let it out slowly and concentrate on my breathing. If he doesn't allow entry, I don't know what plan B is, or even should be.

"I believe you. After a lifetime of caring for this church, I believe I am a pretty good judge of character," he finally answers, and I think you are acting honorably and telling me the truth." He steps aside and turns the knob on the door leading inside the building.

"This is the church's graveyard or crypt. It began as a graveyard and we later enclosed it as buildings were built around the church. The occupants of the other buildings complained about having a graveyard right outside their windows. As far as I know, I am the only person who spends any time in this building." This last part is said as a sort of warning to keep to our goal.

We rush forward, trying and failing to control our anticipation. Gene stops as we reach the man.

"My name is Gene. Gene Conklin, and it is a pleasure to make your acquaintance, sir." He reaches out a hand in an offer to shake.

"Thank you for your trust. We will not do anything to violate it."

The man shakes Gene's hand with what had to be a small smile, although it's hard to tell what with all of the crags and crevices in the man's worn face.

"Horst. Horst Schweinsteiger," he says and waves us forward into the building. At the last moment, he reaches inside the door, pulls a flashlight off a peg and hands it to Gene.

As we step into the building, I notice that it is larger than it looks from the outside. The entryway is lined with various tools; it seems the caretaker has turned the entry into a toolshed. I guess I was halfway right thinking it was just a shed or electrical building.

The structure is roughly twenty feet square with the same red brick lining the walls as with the rest of the church. Near the middle of the space, a stairway appears in the floor, leading down into the darkness.

Gene shivers.

"I hate graveyards. Have I mentioned that before? They give me the heebie jeebies," he shakes his body again and makes a sound that I think must be like a ghoul at a haunted house.

Gene flicks on the flashlight and points it down the stairwell. "Who wants to go down into the dark scary graveyard first?" he asks, letting us know it won't be him.

"Oh, please," Li says and snatches the flashlight from Gene. She marches down the stairs without looking back.

Gene and I look at each other. I shrug and move to follow Li into the dark scary graveyard. I notice the smell first. Musty, damp earth assaults the nostrils.

Li has already taken up the search of the headstones. The graveyard is small. I count maybe fifteen headstones. I move to Li's side and watch as she shines the beam on the nearest headstone. I don't think Gene has made it down yet.

"This *is* pretty creepy," Li admits. "Sealing up a graveyard inside a building is definitely weird."

"It looks like they turned the graveyard into a kind of crypt. I'm sure they knew that the grass would die and things could get … weird with the decomposition," I offer, but I don't think this helps.

Stone has replaced grass and I suppose the graves were moved while a cement foundation was poured. After that, crypts were probably constructed for the fifteen inhabitants of the space. The headstones still stand upright throughout the room, those who constructed this room staying true to the original layout, I guess.

"At least there are only fifteen headstones to check. Let's get it over with and back up to the living," I suggest.

A voice drifts into the crypt. "Please tell me that we are not going to be digging old Richard up. 'Cause I gotta tell ya, that's pretty much a deal breaker for Gene here," Gene says, suddenly referring to himself in the third person. "Gene doesn't do grave robbin'. Gene is gonna make a mental note to talk to his Pa when this is all over. What coulda been goin' through his noggin'?"

For the first time since I've known Gene, the little kid in him comes out here underneath a church in Germany.

Li turns to Gene. "Tell Gene to man up and get over here and help us," she orders, enjoying herself and referring to Gene in the third person as well.

Gene makes his way over to us slowly.

"This'll all be over in a few minutes, Gene," I promise, attempting to slap him on the shoulder like he does with me. Gene nods and squints his eyes to slits. I don't think he'll be any help.

"Jake, over here," Li calls. She's moved further away during my attempt to console Gene.

I walk over to her and see the name Richard in the flashlight beam. I lean forward reading the headstone. "Jean Francois Richard. A bishop of this church a long time ago, I see." I kneel down to the side of the headstone, careful to not step on the bishop. "How does a Frenchman become the bishop of a church in Berlin, Germany?"

"I'm not sure that's the question we need to be asking right now," Li observes. "We need to figure out what the token is and where it's located. As much as I hate to admit it, I, like Gene, do not want to be digging up graves."

"I heard that, Li," Gene says from a few feet away. He hasn't moved since I left him.

"I don't think we need to dig anybody or anything up. Our parents left this token behind recently, right? And if you look at the grave, there are no signs of disturbance. So if they didn't dig it up, then we won't have to either," I note.

I hear an audible sigh of relief from Gene.

"Okay, then where do you think the token is hidden?" Li asks.

I shake my head and begin to examine this particular crypt. I ask Li to shine the flashlight beam fully on the headstone. She does, and it lights up.

Most of the headstone is filled with a cross that is somewhat unfamiliar to me. This cross has two horizontal bars cutting across the vertical beam, the top one shorter than the bottom one. I lean back and reach into my memory bank. I have come across this particular cross and want some information on it now.

THE CROSS IS KNOWN AS the Cross of Lorraine and was used by the Knights Templar, Joan of Arc and more recently by the Free French Forces during World War II. The French had used it during the war as an answer to the Nazi symbol of the swastika. This cross has a rich symbolic history.

I lean closer to examine the cross, because something doesn't fit here. The Lutheran cross that this bishop would have used and worn would not have been the Cross of Lorraine. It didn't belong on this headstone. My eyes are about as close the cross now as I dare to get them. And that's when I notice it.

"This cross was added to this headstone recently!" I announce excitedly.

"What? What do you mean?" Li asks, leaning forward and staring at the cross.

"Gene, I need you to go back upstairs and see if you can find a chisel, a pick, pliers, or something like that among Horst's tools." I order, craning my neck toward him.

"Oh, c'mon, Jake, you said there wasn't going to be any grave diggin'," he complains, his voice half-whine, half-scared.

"Gene, don't tell me you're scared spitless right now," I say with a smile, remembering when he had told me the same thing a year ago. "Come on, I need you right now, buddy. Go get the tools for me, okay?"

A whimper escapes Gene's lips but he manages to turn around and head up the steps.

I reach out and run my finger along the cross. It is set into the marble of the headstone—someone had to chisel a snug groove into the headstone. It wouldn't have been impossible to carve a groove into the headstone and then set the cross into the groove.

"You think the cross is the token?" Li asks, reaching a hand out to touch the cross.

"I do," I say, consumed with examining the cross and its temporary home on the headstone. "Do you see where the bishop's name, birth and death dates have been carved into the headstone?"

Li nods.

"These are original carvings, but the grooves that the cross is set into are rough, more crudely done, can you see?"

Another nod.

"Plus, there is a slight color difference in and around these new grooves. So, I think our parents put this cross in place recently and we need to remove it. It is the first token," I proclaim.

"Pretty clever of our parents, don't you think?" Li marvels.

I nod, thinking about the fact that my mom was in this very same room as a teenager. It's weird to think about, because for her it was a long time ago, and yet in terms of our time travels, it was probably only a week or two ago. I smell the air again, irrationally thinking that maybe some of her scent still remains. I know that I don't even know what she smelled like when she was young; shampoo and soaps have most certainly changed, but I can't help myself.

Li must have sensed my change of mood, because I feel her hand slip into mine. She gives mine a little squeeze. I look at her and smile. She returns the smile.

"Your mom was here, in this creepy graveyard, with my dad and Gene's dad," she says gently. "I don't think we can smell them anymore, but we can sure feel their presence."

I think of Mom and will myself to visualize what she looked like when she was a teen, kneeling here in front of Bishop Richard's headstone. I can't do it. I can only picture her as my mom—as an adult. When I try again to visualize her, somehow she looks too much like Li. Yikes. I hope Li can't read that thought. I shake my head and turn back to see if Gene is back yet.

No sign of Gene.

Li slips her hand from mine and stands. I assume she is going to find Gene. She leaves the light with me and dissipates into the darkness beyond the halo of light provided by the flashlight.

I search the darkness in the direction of the stairs, leaving the light pointed toward the tombstone so Li and Gene can find their way back.

Finally, I hear Gene's heavy steps descending the stairs. I hope he found the tools we need.

"BOO!" Li's voice echoes loudly through the small chamber. Gene screams at the top of his lungs, a high-pitched shriek that sounds unworldly. Metal tools clang to the ground.

As those sounds fade, Li's laughter fills the air. Her laughter is deep and full.

"That was uncalled for, Li," Gene says between shallow breaths. I can tell that he is down on the floor. He must have fallen when Li scared him. "I'm serious, that was way out of bounds. Geez, Li, I'm as scared as a rabbit in a foxhole."

Li is still beside herself with laughter. I try to control my laughter—I want to make sure Gene can't hear me. I'm happy he can't see the tears running down my face and the shaking of my body due to the fits of laughter rolling through me.

"Well, you can pick up the dern tools yourself, Li, 'cause I think I'm gonna stay right here until we're done," Gene huffs.

"Suit yourself," Li chuckles through her laughter and begins picking up the tools. She makes her way over to me and sets the tools near the headstone. I pick up the flashlight and move it over the pile of tools. I select a chisel and needlenose pliers.

I have a thought as I move into position to remove the cross. "Hey Gene, does your dad do any carving, or anything like that?"

"Yeah, why? He loves to carve wood, he has a ton of truly ugly stuff that Ma won't let him keep in the house," he answers.

I'm hoping to distract him from his fear and anger. "Well, if I had to guess, I'd say it was your dad who carved this headstone so the cross would fit into it. It is a masterful job, really, the cross looks like it belongs." I get the reaction I'm hoping for when I hear him moving slowly toward our position.

"I'm a comin' over there to take a look, but I swear Li, if you try 'n' scare me again, I can't be responsible for my actions," Gene warns.

Li just laughs.

"Man, I think I peed myself a little," Gene declares.

"In that case, why don't you just stay over by the stairs," Li suggests with a grin.

"Har-har-har," Gene mocks in his fake laugh. "This means war,

Li. I'm not sure you understand what you've gotten yourself into now. My brothers and I have practical joke wars all the time, and feel like it's only fair to warn you that you are goin' down."

Li opens her mouth to respond, but I cut her off.

"Got it," I call to Gene.

I lift the cross out of the headstone with the pliers, carefully moving it to the ground. I suddenly feel like I'm playing the game Operation. I loved that game as a kid. As I get the cross to within a few inches of the floor it slips from the pliers and crashes to the floor.

It breaks into pieces. Li gasps. I just stare unbelieving. Gene leans down and looks at the cross.

"I don't think you broke it, Jake. It looks like it is supposed to separate into those three pieces," he points out.

I look down and see that the cross didn't break so much as separate into its three individual pieces. I start to breathe again. The two bars that make up the crosses on the long beam have separated and now lie on the ground.

"Huh," I mumble, a light beginning to glow in the back of my mind.

"What?" Li asks, picking up on my mumbling. "What did you figure out?"

"I don't know. It may be nothing, but these pieces separately remind me of puzzles. I just wonder if the token will need to be arranged in a certain way to give us the Key. It's not that important now; we'll find out as we go along, I guess."

Gene clears his throat. "Well, if we're done here then let's beat it. I can't wait to leave this place behind." He's already moving toward the stairs.

"I actually agree with Gene. Let's get this cross and move on. While I'm not at Gene's level, this place still creeps me out," Li admits while gathering the tools.

I pack the three pieces of the cross into a pocket and move with Li toward the stairs. We replace the tools as Gene found them and push the door open, ready to breathe in the fresh air.

Horst the caretaker is a few feet away shoveling rubble into a pile. He turns when he hears the sound of the door opening.

"Well, sir, I don't know how you survive down there, but thank you for allowing us to enter that sacred space," Gene says, slinging an arm around the man. "We found what we were looking for and did not disturb anything or anyone."

CHAPTER 18

DAY'S END

GENE LIKES HIS LITTLE JOKE. And to my surprise so does the caretaker. He gives a hearty slap to Gene and emits a hearty belly laugh.

"Young man, I try to never go down there if I don't have to," Horst replies.

Li and I shake Horst's hand and then move through the church to find Ray in the usual place. The sun is fading quickly now.

"Did you find what you came back for?" he asks as we approach him.

We nod in unison.

"What about dinner and a place to sleep?"

"We don't have any plans—or food or shelter for that matter," Gene answers, rubbing his belly absently. It's clear he isn't concerned about shelter so much as food.

Ray smiles. "I know a place that serves us when we get downtime. It's a miracle that the place didn't get hit during the war, but maybe it's just because it's the best food in the sector. And after that I know a place where you can spend the night safely."

"Perfect. Now about this food, what're we talking about, Ray? I'm a bit of a foodie back where I come from," Gene explains as he slings an arm around Ray and leads him off in front of Li and me.

I fall into step with Li, conscious of the fact that her arm brushes mine every other stride or so. I feel so awkward around her, I don't know what to do, how to act, how to start a conversation, or really anything. What is the jumping off point? I come up with something to start with and turn to Li. She beats me to it.

"Do you think I went too far with Gene back in the graveyard?" she blurts, and then blushes to red.

I look at her, momentarily thrown off by my own attempt to break the silence. I'm surprised by Li's blurt and blush. I wonder if she is going through the same thing that I am—does she not know how to begin either? But she is always so calm and cool, why would she need to feel awkward? She is the one in control. But then I think, maybe she doesn't think she's in control in these matters either. Maybe she doesn't know what to do or how to do it either. Well this is new! And it gives me hope.

"Jake?" Li begins again, uncertain of herself.

"What? Oh yeah, um, no, I don't think you went too far. I mean, seriously, what's too far when we're talking about Gene?" I say with a smile.

She smiles too. "But, I also need to give him credit for what he did back there with the caretaker. He showed a lot of integrity with him, and that's what this Key is all about, right? Showing integrity in all that we do?" Li says, comfortable now in our conversation.

"Yes, Gene is pretty incredible with people," I agree, watching him walk ten yards in front of us with Ray. He still has an arm around Ray and they are both laughing about something.

I wish it could be that easy for me. Some people just have that ability; they are born with it, I guess. I have to work on it, *unearth hidden talents*. I'll work on it, especially with Li. It feels scary and nerve-wracking with her, but also safe in some way. She won't judge or laugh at me and I need that, just like I felt safe with Master Shi over the past year.

"Where'd you go, Jake?" Li says, brushing my arm with her hand.

I'm pulled out of my thoughts. I look at Li. She looks fragile somehow. Well, here goes nothing.

"I ... um ... I was thinking about Master Shi from this past year. You know, just how comfortable he made me feel when I was trying to overcome my shyness and anxiety," I stumble over the words, wishing I was smooth like Gene. I sneak a glance at Li and realize I've said the wrong thing.

"And also, I was thinking that—" I might hyperventilate, and won't that be impressive.

"I was thinking that you also make me feel comfortable."

I take a heaving breath. Now I feel the heat rush up my neck and into my cheeks. I'm past the point of no return so … "It's just that I know that you won't judge or laugh when we talk and well, when I act like I'm acting right now," I finish with a shaky laugh to cover my flush.

Li turns her head straight ahead and walks in silence for a few seconds—a few seconds that feel like an eternity for me. Have I just made things weird between us? Did I blow it? My mind races through the possibilities. How do I salvage this situation? Do I take it back? How do I soften what I said, turn it into something different?

"Thank you, Jake," Li says so softly I barely hear her.

I don't know how to interpret this. It's an ambiguous statement. It could mean a thousand different things.

Li turns to me and we stop walking. She must have sensed that her statement was unclear.

"Jake, I feel comfortable with you too," she tells me. "I guess I don't know how to say it, but it's like we sort of just fit." She blushes fully and completely red now. She has just gone for it too.

"I don't know if that makes sense to you. I mean, I don't know what I'm saying. I don't know how to do this. But we're friends, right? We're close in some ways that others can't understand. Our moms. Our dads. Our lives in so many ways." Her eyes search mine, desperately looking for understanding, or agreement, or something shared.

I give a nod. It's all I can manage. I'm mesmerized by the intensity in her eyes, in her voice. This is important to her—*I'm* important to her. I wish I knew what to say at this very moment, the thing that the boy says in the movie to the girl as the music swells.

"I understand Li. We are friends. We do … fit together, because of everything you said. We … I … it's good," I end lamely. So much for the movie dialogue.

She smiles a huge, radiant smile. Then her arms are around me, squeezing me tightly—too tightly—but I don't care. As soon as the hug begins, it ends.

I follow her glance to Gene. I half expect him to be right next to us with some snarky comment about our hug. But, he's still moving away from us in deep conversation with Ray.

Li finds my hand with hers. She gives mine a squeeze. I think right then that we do fit. Together.

"We are good," Li agrees with an emotion that I still can't pin-point. She releases my hand and begins walking faster, toward Gene and Ray. "Let's catch up before Gene suspects anything," she says over her shoulder.

I just stand there. Suspects anything? What does that mean? What just happened? I'm sure that I just missed the point of our conversation. I stare at Li's back for a minute. Girls. I shrug and hustle to catch up.

CHAPTER 19

THE MÜLLERS

WE CATCH GENE JUST AS he and Ray are turning into a building. The building looks like a miracle. Everything around it is rubble, yet it stands like a little beacon of hope. It's small, a two-story structure with a restaurant on the ground floor and what I suppose is the owner's living quarters above.

Ray introduces us to a man who must be the owner. He introduces himself as Felix and quickly busies himself with preparing our food. The restaurant is almost empty, the only patrons are a couple of soldiers in a far corner. I guess Felix's business is mostly—if not all—soldiers. I can't imagine that many Berliners have the means to eat out right now. I see a small woman cooking in the back; she must be Felix's wife. Felix disappears into the kitchen and I see him reappear in the back. He leans down and kisses the woman who must be his wife. They look into each other eyes with love. I'm captivated by their interaction. Man, I need to get a grip.

"Whoa," Gene whispers under his breath. I turn to him and see he is looking in the direction of the kitchen too. But he isn't looking at Felix, he is looking at a girl who just came out from the back. She is carrying a tray full of water glasses and moving toward our table. I check Ray's expression and sure enough he is also staring at the girl.

She must be in her twenties and has long blond hair braided down her back. Her eyes are large and blue. She walks with a graceful ease. Now I know why all the soldiers seem to frequent this diner. Just to confirm my theory, I check the two soldiers in the corner. They are watching the girl too.

I switch my gaze over to Felix. He has stopped his cooking and is now watching out from behind the counter, scowling at the two soldiers in the corner. He knows what's going on, and he hovers carefully.

I smile. Felix looks like a bull ready to charge at the first sign of a move on his daughter. Li must have been following my gaze.

"Felix looks ready to destroy the first person who takes a shot at his daughter," she says with a lilt in her voice. "By the way, you passed the test. You haven't ogled her this whole time."

I turn to her, confused. Whose test? Felix's or hers? She just smiles.

"This should be fun," she murmurs to me.

I don't know what she means until I turn to see Ray and Gene stumbling over each other in an attempt to help the girl with the water glasses.

"Let me help you with those."

"You look like you could use a hand."

The girl brushes them both aside like she's shooing away flies. She sets the drinks down on the table, all business—until she sees Li. She smiles at her and reaches out a hand.

"Hello, it is so nice to meet another woman," the girl says and the two shake firmly. "My name is Elsa."

"I'm Li."

"Li, what a beautiful name. And you are gorgeous," Elsa gushes. The two girls fall into banter about girlish things; I suppose that Elsa has not had someone to talk to for a very long time. Eventually, she grabs Li's arm and they move off to the back to continue their talk.

Elsa's spell over Gene and Ray breaks when she disappears. Ray heaves a big sigh.

"So, is the actual food any good here?" I ask, bringing the two lovesick puppies back to reality.

"What? Oh yeah, it's excellent," Ray says. I still can't tell if he is referring to the food or not. I guess I'll have to wait and see.

After about fifteen minutes, Elsa and Li reappear with trays laden with food. The plates are spread over our table. The smell alone is worth it. At the sight of food, I realize how hungry I am.

The food turns out to be even better than it smells. I pack as much as I can fit into my slight frame, willing just a little bit more down before I figure I better stop. I find out that the Allied forces help provide Felix with the foodstuffs to feed the soldiers. I also learn that the Müllers (Felix's last name is Müller) also take all the leftovers around the neighborhood to feed those who cannot feed themselves.

That night after Ray leaves to return to his station at the church, we tag along with the Müllers on their trek through the neighborhood. We deliver food to many families scattered throughout the French sector. Elsa and Li fall in together, laughing and talking nonstop. Gene and Felix have become fast friends, sharing recipes and thoughts on food and life. Felix's wife, Marie, leads the way through the streets.

I stay behind, enjoying the solitude for now. I watch Gene talk effortlessly with his newfound friend. His manner is easygoing and affable. I want to learn from him, so I watch his interactions. I watch the way he talks and listens. I watch his body language and facial expressions. I catalogue all of this into my mind for later study. I watch Li and Elsa as well. Li is showing a side that I haven't seen before. She is pure teenage girl right now and is fully enjoying herself. I think Elsa feels the same way, soaking up companionship from someone like herself.

The Müllers are everyday heroes. You won't find their names in history books or in old newspapers. They won't be found accepting awards for humanitarianism. But everyone should know about them and what they do. I ask Marie why they do what they do every night. They must be exhausted at the end of every day. Marie shrugs and simply says, "We do this because it is the right thing to do." The Müllers won't leave anyone behind and alone. At one particular home, Marie and Felix sit with an elderly couple and feed them, because they are too weak to feed themselves. Elsa whirls around the apartment, cleaning and dusting, then she gathers the laundry and takes it with her.

"Elsa comes in the morning and at noon as well to feed, bathe, and clothe them," Felix tells me after he sees me looking at the laundry. "She also does their laundry and cleans up after them. They lost their son and his family to the war."

As we walk back to the diner, having delivered all of the food, Gene slips back to me. He throws his arm around me and we walk in silence for several yards. Li sees us and also slows to walk with us. She slides an arm around Gene and the three of us walk together the rest of the way.

We don't speak. We don't need to; the Müllers actions have said all that needs to be said this night.

The Müllers have done the things they have because they know it's the right thing to do.

We—the Chosen—will do the same.

I AWAKE TO SUNLIGHT STREAMING IN through gaps where shutters used to be. I look around and remember that Gene and I slept in the attic of the Müllers' place. It's cramped up here, but we don't need much space. Gene is stirring a few feet away. I sit up and feel my stomach growl. I hurry to dress, wanting to head down to the diner for a breakfast that I know will be delicious and filling. I feel like Gene for a moment, living a food-driven life. I smile.

I move down from the attic, through the Müllers' living room and down to the ground floor.

The Müllers and Li are already hard at work preparing for the day. Felix and Marie are busily unloading supplies from a French army truck, while Li and Elsa are putting together food packets, maybe for the old couple we visited last night. I move automatically to help with the unloading and stacking of food.

Gene joins us after a few minutes.

After unloading, we eat a huge breakfast and for the first time I feel like I am engaging with Gene in the food Olympics. I catch Li smirking at me as I shovel large quantities of food into my mouth.

"Looks like somebody is going through a growth spurt," she teases, the smirk never leaving her face.

"Boys," Elsa chides with a crinkled nose.

Gene and I are too busy to reply.

We say our goodbyes to the Müllers, lingering longer than we should, but unable to break away. Finally, after hugs all around and well wishes both ways, we set off toward the British sector.

It turns out we are very close to the British sector. After passing a few blocks in a southerly direction we encounter posted signs informing us that we are leaving the French sector and entering the British sector.

If the signs hadn't been there, I wouldn't have known that we'd passed from one sector to another. I don't know what I was expecting—maybe some huge change, or fence, or something. Which is ridiculous, I know. The city is still the city and these four sectors were just sort of drawn on somebody's map. If there is a difference, it's that there is even more destruction and rubble here.

The British sector is closer to the city center. Felix tells us that the British are headquartered down in the borough of Wilmersdorf, near the American sector. He's drawn a crude map for us that will send us south by southeast through the heart of west Berlin. He estimates that it is no more than 12 kilometers from Osterkirche to British headquarters. I do the conversion to about seven and a half miles.

The three of us cross over what looks like a river, but Felix has told us that it is a dam of some kind, and then we pass over train tracks and into the British sector. As we make our way down a wide road that—according to Felix—will carry us further south and into the borough of Tiergarten, I notice a soldier.

The soldier had been leaning against a wall with several other soldiers. If they were on patrol, they were being awfully casual about it. In fact, lots of people were moving about as if all the rubble around them just wasn't there. I saw men in business suits walking the streets, presumably heading to work. Women too, dressed and ready for a day of work behind a desk somewhere. Where, I wonder. Life is returning, finding some sense of new normal.

The soldier, I notice, is making a beeline directly toward us.

I turn to Li. She sees him too, and from her posture, she is ready for a confrontation. I become conscious of the weight of the pistol at the back of my pants.

Gene is oblivious. Or at least he is acting that way.

The soldier stops a few feet away, he's noticed our defensive posture. Or maybe he's just noticed Li's aggressive stance and demeanor.

"Hello. I've been waiting for you," he says with a clipped British accent. He's an officer, I see from his uniform. A lieutenant if I remember correctly.

All three of us just stare at him.

"Right, I believe you three are the people I am looking for," he begins again. "I was told to watch for two young gents and a lady.

And here you are."

Still nothing from the three of us.

"Look, I was given something by three young Americans, who look similar to you three—well, except for you," he corrects himself, pointing to Gene. Gene rolls his eyes. He travels back in time and still gets negatively compared to his dad.

"You look like the Asian guy in the last group," he observes, pointing to Li. "And you look just like the girl," he says in my direction.

He looks Gene up and down. "And you are gigantic just like the final guy." He stops as if this ends the matter. His proof is right in front of him.

Li shrugs. "What do you have for us?"

"It's not that easy," He cautions, putting up his hands in a stop gesture. "I was told that you would have something for me. Something I would recognize."

I knit my brows together wondering what it is he is demanding.

Gene doesn't share my confusion though. He has reached into his pocket, retrieved something, and is now offering it to the soldier. I catch a glimpse and see it is the item that his dad had given to him.

"Cheerio, mate! I think this is what ye are lookin' fer," Gene comments with an awful British accent mixed with his Texas drawl.

"Oh geez," Li mutters, shaking her head. Her shoulders slump in defeat.

Li and I both know that Gene will keep up his British act for as long as we are in this sector, which could be days, and we'll most likely offend every soldier in the sector. I watch the soldier for his reaction. I can't believe it. He laughs.

"Now I know that you are a match for the other gigantic fellow. He used the same, shall we say, peculiar accent." He reaches out and takes the coin-type item form Gene's hands. He examines it and appears satisfied.

"This is the same token I gave to your … friend. He assured me that you would return it to me as proof that you are those to whom I should give the letter," he explains, while bringing out a letter and offering it to Gene. The letter looks identical to the one in my pocket. The one from my mom.

The soldier moves off without another word.

CHAPTER 20

LETTER II

GENE OFFERS THE LETTER TO me, but I shake my head. "Gene, I think this letter is for you. It was your coin that got the letter and it sounds like it comes from your dad, just like the coin." "Let's find a spot out of the way," Gene says and we move over to the side of the wide street, looking for a small bit of solitude. It isn't too hard to come by.

Finding a spot in the shade, we sit down on some rubble and wait for Gene to get into the letter. He motions us closer, indicating he wants us to all read together. I flank Gene on one side and Li is on the other.

"Tally-ho, then!" Gene signals in his terrible accent. He holds the letter out so we can all see.

> *Chosen,*
> *This letter is unique, I think. We who write it and you who read it will surely know one another. The three of us, in our time, say to the three of you, we miss you!*
> *Now, the Quest to gather the Key is upon you. We have recovered the lost Key and placed in a protected place until you can retrieve it for the final time.*
> *The Key was difficult to get back from those evil ones who held it for so long.*
> *You will require four tokens to unlock the mystery of this Key. These tokens are spread throughout the city, one in each sector. You must not leave a sector of the city until that sector's token has been retrieved; you may not be allowed back in.*
> *To safeguard the Key, we have followed the usual proto-*

cols. Brain, Brawn, and Buddying will all be required for each token.

We have left communications behind with individuals you can trust in each sector who may assist you in your Quest. Use them wisely. Employ honor and honesty to find what you seek.

The second token is located in the British sector. We trust that you have found the soldier and given him your personal item in exchange for this letter.

Now, crack the code of the British token. Allow this time to be your finest hour and go forward to defeat the forces of Evil.

CMQSVVGPPMBKYKSP

ERXTTGPECURUS

May you be blessed in your Quest.
Thor Conklin
Brawn of the Quest

Remember the Motto. This is the war of the Unknown Warriors.

GENE FINISHES AND TURNS THE paper over. It's blank and it's the only paper in the envelope.

"Uh, there is more gobbledygook here in the letter," Gene says, turning to me.

"You're right, but those codes aren't meant for me, Gene," I say pointedly, fixing my gaze on Gene. "They are meant for you."

"What?" Gene says, taken aback.

"There is good news. It looks like we are to use the same Vigenère square from the first letter." I speak over Gene's confused protest. "This code is your code, Gene."

"I don't know any codes," Gene protests in a loud voice. "My Pa is a roughneck not a secret math genius."

Li is smiling. She continues to take pleasure from Gene's discomfort. I shoot her a look. She quickly wipes the smile from her face.

"Gene, the letter contains some hidden information that is just for you." Li encourages. "It's from your father."

Gene looks less than convinced. He stares at the letter for a long time. His shoulders slump and he turns to me. "Jake, I don't know what to tell ya. I don't have any memories of my dad telling to me to memorize famous quotes or hidden messages. We just rode the fences and wrangled livestock. We barely even spoke before this past year."

I hear the desperation in his voice, the defeat. I search for the right words to say, something to build him up and reassure him. I frantically try to channel my inner Gene.

"Gene, look at me," Li says, beating me to it. She grabs hold of Gene's shoulders, not in a rough way, but gently. "You have been Chosen, like your father before you. He did it, and he knows you can do it too. He prepared you for this moment. It probably wasn't a big deal, it was probably in his usual way. Something he said or did over and over again while you were growing up. Something he knew you would remember. Relax. Take your time. It will come."

I watch as Gene's posture changes; he relaxes fractionally. Li's words help.

"Gene, I'll help you talk it out, okay?" I say, doing for him what he has done for me. "Let's walk through your dad. Talk to us about him, his likes, his hobbies, his favorite things, his favorite people … whatever you can think of."

Gene smiles and straightens his shoulders.

"You're both right. Somethin' hasta pop up, right?" Gene remarks. "I mean the guy isn't a total mute and he was a Chosen, so he knows how this whole thing works. He wouldn'ta forgotten to tell me somethin' this important. Now I just need to remember."

He lays back and I can tell he's assuming his thinking position. He brings his hands up and puts them behind his head, nice and relaxed.

"Well, Pa loves all things western, so some possible keywords are John Wayne, maybe some famous quotes from his movies." Gene gets started. "Let's see, he also likes Johnny Cash—oh, and Garth Brooks."

"Good. Did he sing some song lyrics over and over again or quote John Wayne movie lines all over the place?" Li asks.

"Umm, not really," Gene admits. "Dern it all, I don't remember." He punches some rubble with a hand he has unlocked from behind his head. He shakes it like he hurt it and puts it back behind his head. He blows out a sigh.

"Wait. We're doing this wrong," I tell him, reaching over to the open letter on his chest. "We need you to look at the phrases in the letter, these will help bring the memories to the surface."

Gene sits up and begins to read the letter.

"Gene, most of the letter is identical to one Mom wrote to me. So, I would skip down to the part where the letter changes." I point to a spot on the page. "Here."

Gene reads aloud. "Now, crack the code of the British token. Allow this time to be your finest hour and go forward to defeat the forces of Evil." He pauses.

"Is there a movie line or song lyric that talks about a finest hour or going forward to defeat the forces of Evil …" I trail off, knowing the last part sounds lame. Who would sing or talk about defeating the forces of evil?

"No, you're right, Jakers, this part does sound familiar somehow." Gene says. "I can't place it exactly yet, but somethin' about the words 'Allow this time to be your finest hour' rings a bell."

"Now we're getting somewhere," I say. "Now let's go to the darker print at the end, after the signature."

"'Remember the Motto. This is the war of the Unknown Warriors,'" Gene reads aloud again. "I don't remember my Pa having a motto and it wasn't about unknown warriors. Pa didn't really talk like that, he was always giving my brothers and me practical advice about life and hard work. 'Life's hard, deal with it.' 'Worry is like a rockin' chair; it'll give ya somethin' to do, but it won't get ya anywhere.' Pa was always spoutin' stuff like that …" he falls back into silence. I can tell he is searching through his memories, hoping to unearth that little thought that would crack the code. Li and I wait patiently, allowing him the space and time he needs to move through his memory.

He reads the letter again. He stares at it for minutes. I can tell he is reading the parts that are different over, and over again.

"Oi, you lads cannot sleep here." We look up to see a British soldier standing over us. "Oh, accept my apologies, lass. I did not see you before," he quickly adds when he sees Li.

"Right you are, chap!" Gene says, moving to his feet. Li's eyes are already mid-roll by the time I glance at her. "My mate and this bonnie lass and I were just catchin' a little kip."

The soldier stares at Gene, unbelieving. Knowing we're American now, he says, "Have a good day."

"Cheers, mate!" Gene calls back as we move away. I glance back to see the soldier shaking his head as he moves in the opposite direction.

"Gene, you know your British accent makes you sound like a barmy git," Li comments with a smile.

"A what?" Gene says, confused. "What language is that?"

Li just laughs and shakes her head. I smile too, apparently Li knows more about British slang than Gene or I do.

"Hey, just so ya know, I'm pretty good with the Brits, my Pa and I used to—"

Gene breaks off what he's saying and stops dead in the road. He whips up the letter he'd been carrying by his side. Staring, he studies the paper for a moment and gives out a yelp.

"That's it! I got 'er," he cries out and does a little goofy dance in the middle of the street. He stops and looks at Li. "This is my process and you're just gonna have to deal with it."

CHAPTER 21

CHURCHILL

"SO, LET ME GET THIS straight," Li starts, enjoying herself now. "Your *process* is walking around the street offending every Brit you can see with your horrific accent and complete butchery of their language? That's your process."

Gene smiles. "Pretty much, yeah. And you know you love it, Li. I know Jakers does. Jake uses his genius. I channel my inner doofus. Come to think of it, I'm scared to see your process, Li. If I had to guess, Jake and I will be beaten to a pulp before you have your breakthrough."

"If you keep your *process* up, Gene, you won't have to wait for me to beat you to a pulp."

Gene throws back his head and laughs his trademark fake laugh.

"Seriously, though, I do got 'er figured out," he tells us again. "At least the first keyword. See, I had forgotten that Pa loves him some Winston Churchill and if you think my accent is bad, you should hear Pa do his Winston Churchill impression. It's hilariously bad."

Gene looks like he's going to launch into an impression of his Pa doing an impression of Churchill. Li moves quickly to prevent this from happening.

"So, what did you figure out?" she says, putting a hand out as an added measure to stop Gene. "What is the keyword?"

Gene looks disappointed that he won't get to do his Pa impression, but lets it go.

"Pa was always going on about how much he respected Churchill. He would find ways to shoehorn quotes from Churchill into our everyday lives. Half the time they didn't even really apply, but we all just went with it. Anyway, I shoulda seen it sooner, I mean the guy has a Churchill bust in the front room of our home—somethin' that irks my Ma something fierce."

I reach into my pocket and take out the scratch paper we used to solve the French sector codes. I also kept the Vigenère square out.

"Let's take a look at that first letter jumble. I'll write it out here on the paper and then we'll go from there, okay?" I say this to keep Gene focused on the task at hand.

"What? Oh, okay," he responds, pulling back from his memories of home. "Let's see here, the first bunch of hullabaloo is: CMQSV-VGPPMBKYKSP" he repeats each letter slowly as I write them. "And I think the keyword is WinstonChurchill."

I write the letter jumble down and just below that, matching up the letters, I write WinstonChurchill. The paper looks like this:

C M Q S V V G P P M B K Y K S P
W I N S T O N C H U R C H I L L

"It's a perfect match as far as length goes," I state. The others crowd around me now, and I hand the scratch paper out to Gene. "Why don't you copy down the letters as I use the square to decode them?"

Gene takes the paper and pencil.

I call out the letters one at a time as I decrypt them, using the identical method from last time. The W and C become a G. The I and M become an E. I continue through all 16 letters while Gene copies them down. As I finish, I look to Gene and see his brow furrowed in confusion.

"Maybe I didn't get the keyword right, 'cause this isn't a word; it's a long bunch of nonsense." Gene can't hide the frustration in his voice. He thrusts the paper toward me. I take it along with the pencil.

The paper now looks like this:

C M Q S V V G P P M B K Y K S P
W I N S T O N C H U R C H I L L
G E D A C H T N I S K I R C H E

I frown and hear a frustrated sigh escape Li's mouth.

"Wait, Gene, I think this might be another German word,"

I interrupt, noting that the translation again does nothing. "It's another proper noun, so no translation, but look at this last part of the word," I point to the end of the word. "Kirche was part of our last decrptyed word, remember? Osterkirche. So …" I begin writing on the paper, this time separating Gedachtnis and Kirche. I hold the paper up so all of us can see it. The translation appears under the separated words now.

GEDACHTNIS KIRCHE
MEMORY CHURCH

"Memory Church?" Gene says, expressing the confusion we all feel. "What in tarnation is a memory church?"

"Memory Church is a direct translation. I wonder if in English we might call it a Memorial Church or … well, I don't know what else we might call it. But let's show this to a German and see what they get from the word," I suggest. "Good idea, I was thinking the same thing," Gene says and casts his eyes about the street. He snags the paper from me and begins crossing the street toward a man dressed in a business suit and wearing a hat to match. Li and I hurry to follow.

"At least he won't be using his ridiculous accent," Li murmurs with a smile.

"Which one?" I say out of the corner of my mouth to Li.

"Good point," she retorts.

Gene reaches the man just ahead of us.

"Pardon me, sir, but I wonder if I might ask your assistance for just a brief moment," Gene says, no trace of any accent or drawl anywhere.

The man stops and nods in answer.

"Do you recognize this word? I'm afraid I don't recognize it," Gene explains, holding our scratch paper out toward the man and pointing to "Gedachtniskirche."

"Of course, this is the Memory Church built for Kaiser Wilhelm," he answers, looking up to Gene's eyes. "It was badly damaged during the bombing. I don't think much of it is standing anymore."

We share a look of fear.

"Do you know where we might find the church, or what's left

of it?" Gene asks somewhat fearfully.

"It is not far from here. A few kilometers maybe," the man says kindly. "You must pass over the Spree River and through the Tiergarten and it will be on the south of it." He finishes by pointing vaguely in a southerly direction.

Gene thanks the man and he moves on with a nod and smile.

I'm busy moving through the memory files of my brain. Something he said sparks a memory—something I studied in the Training Center.

"I know of the church that the man spoke of, it's now called the Kaiser Wilhelm Memorial Church. I don't know whether that has always been the English way of referring to the church. Anyway, the church was severely damaged, and a memorial tower was built next to its ruins. I think it still stands in our day. It's an important monument or memory according to what I read."

"Great! Now we know where exactly to head," Gene says with enthusiasm. "Let's move in that direction and in the meantime, I'll keep chewin' on this other keyword. Hey, do you think it's the same keyword?" He stares intently at the letter again.

"See here, Pa puts in a reference to Churchill when he says, 'Allow this time to be your finest hour.' Churchill gave a speech about the finest hour." Gene asserts, then moves his finger down to the final words of the letter. "And also, right here, Pa uses Churchill's words again. 'This is the war of the Unknown Warriors.' That's also from a speech that Churchill gave. Pa loved those words, he said them all the time to me."

Gene gets a faraway look for the briefest of moments but returns quickly to his thought. "So, he mentions two separate Churchill lines. Maybe he did that so we would know to use the same keyword twice." He shrugs. "I told ya, Pa is a simple guy, maybe he just decided to use the same keyword twice."

"Let's give it a shot," Li suggests.

And we do just that. We give it a shot, but soon discover that using the same keyword does not decrypt anything resembling words—not even German words. It's a bust.

"Hey, it was worth a shot." I say, trying to cheer Gene up. "Let's move ahead and get to the church. Maybe once we get there we'll have better luck with the second keyword." We move through the city slowly, the destruction seeming to grow more intense as we move toward the city center. As we walk in the summer heat, my mind wanders back to something from Gene's letter. Something that Churchill said. "This is the war of the Unknown Warriors." I wonder if Gene's dad had latched onto that because it so resembled our own situation, our parents and ours. The Chosen are unknown warriors, fighting to keep virtue safe for the world.

My thoughts turn to the Berliners that I pass on the streets. What war had they been fighting for the past several years? The horror of it all must be unforgettable, and yet the resilience of the human spirit is reflected in these men, women and children. They are moving quickly to rebuild their lives, to find purpose and meaning among the rubble of their city and their lives. Each person I pass is an unknown warrior of some kind. What has their experience been? What horrors have they witnessed? What secret pain do they carry in their hearts? How many have lost a husband, father, wife, mother, or child to the war of evil men—the very men who stole virtue and blackened it with their attempted eradication of good, the attempted eradication of the very soul of its people.

But evil men lost—they failed. Our parents, who were and are unknown warriors, recovered the key and safeguarded it until we could come and bring it to safety one final time. As I look into the eyes of these everyday heroes I pass on these streets, I know with certainty that the souls of these people have not been extinguished. Darkness could not overcome the light in their eyes. And now they are standing up again, searching for the good they know is out there to be found.

They will find it. And so will we find our Key.

I reach out and put an arm up and around Gene's shoulders. As I do, I realize that I am not the only one who has been deep in thought. Gene almost startles at my touch. He turns and I see that his eyes are shining. We share a look and I know that he has had much the same thoughts that I have had. We both then turn our eyes to Li. She moves close and slips an arm through Gene's— Gene, the tower between the two of us. Li's eyes shine as well.

As we continue, the streets close in on us, becoming more narrow and labyrinthine. Buildings in ruins loom over us on both sides. We turn off one narrow street into another, and I notice that these must be residential buildings, apartment blocks. Halfway down the street, a group of men step into the end of the street, blocking our way.

CHAPTER 22

FIGHT

WE SLOW TO A STOP, suddenly alert to danger. Hair stands up on my arms. I turn with Gene to head back the way we came. More men move into the street behind us, cutting off our retreat. We turn back to face the direction we had been walking.

A large man steps forward from the men in front of us. I count six total men at this end, with four to the rear.

"Oi," he shouts at us. That's it. Nothing more, just that short two-letter word.

The men in front of us look like soldiers, young hard men not much older than we, but old enough to have seen the ugliness of war. I swivel my head around to look closer at those approaching from behind. These men look different. They are just boys, and wear simple clothing that is in tatters from way too much use. They might be native Berliners, street toughs scavenging through the ruins of the city.

We must look like easy marks. But why are these two groups working together? Soldiers and street thugs. It doesn't make sense to me. I look at Gene to share with him my confusion. He has been studying them also, as has Li, and he simply shrugs at me as if to say, it doesn't matter why they are together, it only matters that we don't let them get us.

Li takes a half-step forward and speaks toward the guy who yelled, "Oi."

"What do you want?" she calls.

This brings laughter from the six guys blocking us from the front. The guy bows, an elaborate show of mock civility. "Why, we want you and your two little boys too." More laughter from his gang. "They call me Billy. Billy the Fib. I ain't a honest bloke." Again sneers and cackles follow the words. "Our boy Stevie sent us to ... collect you."

Stevie? I think. Who? And then I remember that Rat Face had called himself Steven.

"You work for Rat Face?" Li calls out. This brings the loudest laughter yet.

"Rat Face? That whatcha call 'im?" Billy the Fib chuckles. "Yeah, I guess that fits now, don't it?"

"Are you soldiers?" Li asks, eyes darting in every direction. I can tell that she is formulating a plan of attack.

"Not right now we ain't."

"What about the boys coming behind us?" Li jerks a thumb over her shoulder.

"Those are more a Stevie's friends, locals," he answers. "Enough rabbit and pork. Why dontcha come on wit' us? Stevie wants a minute."

"Rabbit and pork?" Gene murmurs.

"He means enough talk. He's a Cockney and they have their own little way of speaking," Li answers.

Gene and I both look her the same question. How does she know this?

"It's not important how I know right now, is it?" Li blows the question off. "Gene, I want you to take the four behind us. I'll take the others. Jake, stay put, we may need you if we get pushed back. Oh, and don't use your weapons if you don't need to. I don't want them to know we have them."

Stay put, I think. No way. As soon as I think this, my gorge boils up into my throat. Nerves spike and I feel sick. Perfect. Maybe I will just stay put.

Li turns back to Billy.

"We've already spoken to Rat Face and told him we have no more to say to him. I don't think we'll waste our time," Li says evenly.

Billy smiles wide. "I's hopin' you'd say tha'. Stevie said we could give ya a unscheduled meeting."

Huh? Apparently, our translator does not include a Cockney slang. Unscheduled meeting?

"A beating," Li murmurs. She is our translator. "Go now, Gene."

I turn and watch Gene move deliberately toward the four street thugs behind us. Li quickly reaches top speed as she sprints toward the six off-duty soldiers. Watching her closely, I can tell she will reach her group first.

I try to use Master Shi's training to track her movements. She is so quick. As she leaps into the air, I see Billy whip a hand signal to the soldiers. The soldiers spread out into a wide circle.

All of them, that is, except for one man. He runs straight for me.

I hear Li yell my name, but it seems so far away. I take one last glimpse at her as she is landing in the middle of the newly formed circle of soldiers. They have her surrounded. She leaps high again, but the soldiers scurry to expand their circle to keep her inside of it.

I've run out of time looking for help from Li. It's not coming. I'm on my own. Miraculously the bile pushes itself back down my throat, and I concentrate on my limited training with Master Shi.

I take a deep cleansing breath and assume a defensive stance, my left leg slightly in front of my right. My hands come up in front of me and I show the attacker the hard edges of my palms.

The man skids to a stop a few feet in front of me. He wears a sneer on a face that is crowded onto a too-small head. Every feature of his face crowds another. Eyes too close, nose too broad, forehead high and wide, and a mouth that looks like it's in danger of slipping right off his chin all combine to give the guy a frightening look.

He spits at me. Huh?

He waits for me to move. I don't. He shrugs and inches toward me. He takes a quick look back toward his buddies, and I wonder if he is waiting for help. Ironic. He wants help and I want help. I look beyond him when he glances back and see Li still in a circle of five soldiers. No real action there. Just like Too-Small Face and me. I don't dare chance a look behind me to Gene. I figure Gene has either beaten them all or befriended them all and they're swapping food stories. Probably the first one, I think.

My training had been centered around defending myself against attackers. This guy isn't attacking. We're just doing a slow dance from three feet away. Why? Why aren't they attacking Li? Why aren't they attacking me?

Gene. Gene is the answer. They want Gene.

I turn and break into a run toward Gene. He has his hands in the air. The four thugs have weapons in their hands and they are all pointed at Gene. I can tell he is talking to them, trying to buddy them.   .

I sense my attacker, or custodian, chasing me. He is closing in. I stop abruptly and move into a leg sweep, blindly moving my left leg around behind me, my hands on the ground helping with the torque. My leg makes contact with Too-Small Face. I don't pause to see what's happening, but I know he'll be going down.

I immediately reach behind me and grip the pistol that is tucked in the small of my back. I bring it around, sighting above the four thugs. I point and squeeze just like Li told me. As I do, I hear two more explosions to my left.

Li is also firing her weapons as she races past me. I empty my clip, careful now not to fire anywhere near Li's racing form. Li empties her clips also, then drops both guns to the ground and slides on her knees up under the nearest two thugs. Her hands move in blurry ferocity. Thugs and their weapons drop to the ground.

I see Gene hasn't been idle while we were shooting. He's moved in on the other two. I suppose they were distracted by our gunfire and moved their guns from Gene to return fire on Li and me.

I turn behind me, remembering Too-Small Face. He is almost on me, and I drop into a crouch, bringing my right palm forward in a punching motion. I land a solid blow to his chest. Air whooshes out. He doubles over. My left palm is already coming up to meet his downward-moving face. A sickening crunch sounds as my palm meets his nose. Blood spurts. Blood.

I've broken his nose. Too-Small Face crumples to the ground. I look beyond him and see the five remaining soldiers running in our direction, Billy leading the way, fists clenched and teeth bared.

Li's primal scream sounds in the narrow alley. Her streaking form zips by me in a blur. She doesn't leap or slide as she nears the five. She angles to the leftmost guy and drops him so quickly I can't see what happened. She moves with purpose through the others, finishing with Billy.

Billy catches her with a wild fist. Li's head snaps back and she wobbles, looking like she's going down. A heartbeat later, I recognize what she's doing. Rather than wobbling, she is actually rolling with the strike, deflecting some of the power and absorbing the rest. She spins with the blow and comes around quickly her palm coming around in an arc of kinetic force. Billy follows the normal motion after throwing a punch leaving his right kidney exposed. Li's palm strikes flesh.

I find myself running toward Li. I sense Gene beside me. Somehow, we both know. We know what Li plans to do. We need to stop her.

Billy the Fib's legs turn to jelly when Li's palm strikes; they buckle and he drops straight down, rolling onto his back. His anguished howl is matched only by Li's unholy fury. She drops easily onto him, one knee pinning his chest. Her left hand snatches a fistful of Billy's wavy hair. There isn't much to grab, but she manages. Her right hand raises high in the air, pauses, and then descends in a vicious decisive blow.

I dive for her arm and crash into her at full speed. We roll off Billy together in a tangle of limbs.

She looks at me with fire in her eyes. She pushes me away roughly. I feel the full force of her fury. I'm cast aside like a doll.

"LI," I IMPLORE. IT COMES out low and labored. I'm out of breath. "Don't." That's all I can manage. She casts a fiery gaze back at me and then turns back to the business at hand. I've failed. I can't stop her.

Gene stands between the prone Billy and Li now. His eyes are pleading, his arms out in front of his body in a pleading gesture.

"Li, think about what you're doing here," Gene beseeches desperately. "Just think for a minute."

Li shakes her head once but does not speak.

I pull myself up, working to control my breathing. Tears fill my eyes and I can't decide the reason for them. Am I hurt? Am I threatened? No, I'm afraid.

I'm afraid for Li. For what she is about to do. For what she is about to *become*.

She brushes by Gene. He reaches a hand out to stop her. She grabs his arm and twists it up behind his body. He spins in an effort to get away—to stop the pain.

I crash into Li for the second time. She releases Gene and rolls with my hit so that she lands on top of me. Her hand rears back, palm flat and rigid, ready to strike me.

"Li," I wheeze. I can't manage any other words.

She shakes her head and jumps up, leaving me behind on the ground. She moves back to Billy.

"Li, there is no honor in what you are thinking about doing. He is defenseless now," Gene speaks quietly, his voice strained and pleading.

"We cannot become like them," I find my voice at last. "If you do this, we lose. We become just like them."

I stand and my voice gains strength as I step to Li. "This is just what Rat Face wants. He wants you, Li, to become just like him. To give in to your anger … and fear. He wants to strip your integrity from you."

I say this while removing my key from beneath my shirt. I kneel down to face her. I clutch my key in my hand and show it to her. "We fight against evil with honor, keeping to a strict moral code. Integrity, Li. Integrity is what we fight with, this is our weapon."

I reach out slowly and point to her key, which has come out from under her clothing during the fight. It glints and shimmers against her shaking body.

She will not meet my gaze.

"Billy and Steven and whoever else won't stop coming after us," she says, anger punctuating each word. "They have to be stopped. I have to stop them. So they can never get to you and Gene again."

Gene joins me on his knees. We face her together. I slide closer to her, reaching out and taking her rigid hand into mine. "They grow weaker with every Key we protect. And we grow stronger." I squeeze her hand. Gene reaches over and adds his hand to ours. "We won't fail. You won't fail, Li. You will never fail us. So let Billy and his gang come for us again. Let Rat Face come. Let all of the forces of evil come against us. We will still prevail. We will beat them because we are right and good. Because we won't do what they do. Because we are not like them. And we will not become like them. Not today. Not tomorrow. Not ever."

I slump back onto my heels, my adrenaline spent and my courage waning. "I need you, Li," I say, tiredly but with conviction. "We need you. I need you."

This seems to break the spell. She turns slowly from Billy to

Gene and I. She searches Gene's eyes, like she's reaching deep into his soul. His gaze never wavers. She moves her eyes to mine. I know I have tears that threaten to spill over. She searches my eyes, seeing into my soul.

"I need you, too," she admits weakly and reaches out her arms to wrap them around Gene and me.

We hold onto each other as the tension and stress bleed away. Li's body shudders as she struggles for composure. I don't know how long we stay there in the narrow street, but I begin to think about moving on; someone has surely heard the shots.

"We should go." Gene is the one to speak first.

Li nods and pushes away from the embrace. We all stand and move zombie-like among the downed men. Li retrieves her pistols and hides them below her clothes again. We ensure that we have all that we left behind or cast aside during the fight. Li moves among the thugs and tosses away their weapons, emptying the guns of their bullets—real bullets—as she goes along.

CHAPTER 23

APOCALYPSE

WE MOVE AWAY QUICKLY, PUTTING as much distance as we can between the scene and ourselves. We cross over the Spree River and approach the Tiergarten. I had looked at images of our current day Tiergarten, and in some ways it resembles Central Park in New York City—at least from the air. It is a huge oasis of greenery right in the middle of a city.

So, when we reach Tiergarten, I am shocked. No post-apocalyptic vision can outdo what lays before me. The trees still standing are blackened and stripped of any foliage. They are stark reminders of the destruction that just ended. A beautiful garden has been reduced to a bleak, desolate stretch of destruction.

I see a graveyard for weapons of war. Planes that have been shot down lie in pieces, scattered around the grounds. Ironically, the Victory Column in the center of the gardens, surrounded by a roundabout of sorts, still stands, presiding over the visual reminders of defeat. Walking through this stretch is difficult. The visions and sights weigh down upon us like a depressing gravitational force.

"A testament to humans mistreating humans," Gene observes somberly as we move through the graveyard.

As we near the southern end, we ask for directions to the church. We are reminded each time we ask for directions that the church is in ruins. We are directed to pass by the zoo and then on to the church just beyond. The zoo is gone. Strangely, we see an elephant roaming the grounds of what used to be a zoo, but now looks more like a barren field. Only a few statues and statuettes still mark the grounds. A flak tower stands bulky and ominous as a reminder of the war. The tower, once used to shoot down aircraft, is now being converted into a hospital. The telltale sign of a red cross is adorning its walls. More irony. A building dedicated to harming the enemy is just weeks later dedicated to healing people.

"Everyone should be required to walk through what we just walked through," Gene states with conviction. "A testament to the destructive power of evil. Field trips should be guided through this place as it stands right now. Kids and adults alike should be made to run their hands along the broken planes, dead trees, and spend five minutes in that hospital."

Li and I nod silently, feeling somehow that we have been changed forever because of the walk through Tiergarten. Li seems particularly moved.

"I almost became part of the destruction. Part of the evil," her voice trembles, tears threatening again. She slips an arm through ours, now walking between the two of us. "Thanks to my heroes, I made it through the trial and am better because of it."

After several more minutes of walking beyond the zoo, we turn onto a wide street. A street sign nailed onto a pole designates it as Budapest Street. We get our first view of what must be our church. It is seriously damaged. We walk toward it, arriving at the church and staring upward. We continue to walk beyond it and walk in a slow circle around the blocks surrounding the church.

A sign just beyond the church designates the border between the British sector and the American sector. The church is just barely in the British sector.

"As soon as we find this token, we'll know exactly where to go to find the American sector, I guess," Gene points out the obvious. He's probably nervous about decrypting the second line of code.

After our slow circle to get our new bearings, we approach the church again. It was once a magnificent structure, with a central spire reaching toward heaven. There are four other smaller spires at each corner. One corner tower at the front remains largely intact, as does one at the rear. The other two look as though some giant hand came through and cut them in half. The huge central spire is missing half of its cone. I'm reminded of what the Coliseum in Rome looks like today. It's half a building, and so is this church.

"WELL, HERE WE ARE AT the Kaiser Wilhelm Memorial Church. Now what?" Gene says. "Just kidding; I know what's next. I need to figure out the second keyword. But before I do, do you think we could have some grub? I'm starvin'."

"Good idea, Gene," Li agrees, smiling at last. "I'm sure you think better on a full stomach."

We begin to look for a comfortable spot to have an impromptu meal. I wonder if people will think it strange that we will be eating out in the open, and then decide this might the least strange thing they have experienced in the past few years. We decide on a spot on the church grounds, a wall that still stands but had to have been an interior wall before the bombs. The wall offers some privacy for us; it tucks us in away from the main streets and most eyes.

"Ya know, the one thing we don't have that would be mighty fine, is a cold drink. Water. Coke. Anything cold, really," Gene muses, almost to himself.

Li seizes upon this thought.

"Gene, why don't you get settled in here and go over that second keyword. Jake and I will go find some cold drinks." Li says, then adds, "I'm with you, I could use a cold drink."

I tense up. "Do you think it's a good idea to separate?"

"Well, Jake, how about you come with me. We'll leave Gene alone to concentrate on breaking his father's keyword. I think he'll be fine here. It's a pretty secluded spot and I haven't seen anyone come near the church itself since we arrived."

"Plus, I can take of myself, Jakers," Gene adds in support of Li's suggestion. I can't tell if he just really wants a cold drink or he wants some alone time to think through the message. I decide on a 60 percent need for a drink and a 40 percent need for solitude.

"I don't know …" I mumble, memories of Rat Face and his buddies accosting me in China are still vivid.

"Think of my incredible thirst, Jakers. How am I supposed to solve this riddle if I can't quench my thirst?" Gene says with a wide smile.

I readjust my earlier percentages to 85 percent need for a drink and 15 percent need for solitude to solve the puzzle. I shrug and give in to them both. I still don't like it, but I go along anyway. Gene can take care of himself and I'll be with Li, so we should be fine.

I'll be with Li. Wait, what was I thinking? This is a great idea!

We leave Gene snacking on some bread from the Müllers and staring at his letter. Li and I head away from the church, instinctively following the groups of people. They must have a good idea of where to go. Not wanting to leave the British sector of the city, we head north and west of the church.

Soon we are well away from the church and fall into a rhythm. We scan the streets looking for a place that still sells goods to the public. I realize this may be harder than we thought.

I'm jolted out of my thoughts by a new sensation.

Li has taken hold of my hand. We're holding hands! I turn to her with a questioning look. She smiles that brilliant smile at me. Butterflies activate in my belly, anxiety fills my body. I don't know what to do or say. So I don't.

"Thank you, Jake, for … um, well, for tackling me back in that narrow street." She says, coming a bit closer to me. The butterflies intensify, but they're mixed with a feeling of giddiness. "You saved me back there—you and Gene, both."

I look at her, my tongue still tied in knots. I hope she can see that I am trying. My eyes practically plead for her understanding. She smiles, and I know she understands my silence.

"I kind of lost myself back there for a minute. Dark feelings filled me up and I knew what I had to do. I shut you out of my thoughts, because I knew that you would stop me from what I was going to do. I fought within myself then, and after you tackled me, I knew you would win. I wanted you to win. To save me from myself. To bring me back from the darkness.

"I almost compromised my integrity in that street, Jake." There is desperation in her voice now. "I would've have been lost. I would've failed. I would've had to give my Key over, right?"

I look into her eyes and see the wetness there. And the fear. I have not seen fear in those eyes before. Li seems suddenly fragile. I squeeze her hand reassuringly.

"I won't let that happen, Li. Just like you won't let me give in or give up," I reassure her with a smile, eyes never leaving hers. "We fit, remember?"

Li throws her arms around me in a fierce hug. She is squeezing me so tightly, I cannot breathe in any air. And I don't care. The hug is perfect. I hug her back, less fiercely, but just barely so. After a few seconds—or a lifetime, I can't decide which—Li pulls back and finds my hand again. We begin walking again.

"I have a theory about Rat Face and our attacks," I tell her, beginning the conversation again after several strides of blissfully enjoying her touch and proximity.

"Oh? Well let's hear it."

"My theory is simply that Rat Face is just scaring us with these little episodes. He doesn't know where the tokens are located, and he doesn't have the letters that point the way. He needs us to do the work for him in order to retrieve the Key for himself and his master."

"Then why have us attacked at all?"

"I think he does it to learn."

"Learn?"

"Yes, to learn how we fight, to learn what we have learned over the last year, to understand how we work together. He will use all of this information to beat us when we have the Key in our sights. Right now, he is sitting back, watching us carefully, and learning how to defeat us."

Li nods her head, allowing me to continue.

"Take our last little skirmish. The men knew to stay away from your leaps and they also knew to keep you encircled. By the way, how did you escape their little trap anyway?" I ask, turning to face her.

She smiles, a slightly wicked. "I used the walls of the buildings. The monks have taught me much about their mysterious ways. I ran along the wall for a few steps until I could leap outside of their circle."

"And now, Rat Face has that little piece of intelligence to add to his file, so to speak," I muse with a serious look. "Rat Face is compiling notes on all three of us. He's looking for weakness in our defenses, both physically and mentally. You can bet he knows that you almost … well, finished that guy back there. He'll work on that weakness and try to get you to have another go at some-body, maybe even him."

"You think Rat Face would sacrifice himself in order to get me to … to go over to evil?" she gasps with alarm. The fragility is back in her voice.

"I do. Rat Face is like a zealot for his cause, a crazed guy completely given over to his evil master. There is no telling what he might do, up to and including dying himself."

"So what do we do? How do we defend ourselves against this?" Li pulls herself together, all business now.

"Well, I think subconsciously you already knew this in some ways. I mean, I saw that you fired all of your wax bullets above the four thugs in the alley," I remark with a coy smile, like I'm revealing a secret. "And I know that you hit what you aim at, so I can only conclude that you shot high on purpose. I think you didn't want anyone knowing that we are using wax bullets."

She smiles like she's impressed. "That's right. Well, look at you, Jake. You've come a long way in a year. Instead of puking, you are coolly observing the battlefield. I didn't want these guys knowing we aren't playing for keeps."

"I didn't think of that until after the fight. Trust me, during the whole thing I was this close to hurling," I inform her, holding my index finger a fraction of an inch away from my thumb. "But, anyway, I think it's smart to keep some our cards hidden from Rat Face."

I squeeze her hand again. I like that I can do this with Li.

"The most important factor for us is our ability to keep together mentally," I say carefully, not wanting to dredge up bad memories again. "We cannot allow each other to give in to our darkest thoughts and motives. We cannot compromise our moral high ground. Once we do, we become just like those we fight against."

Li's shoulders slump slightly and she refuses to meet my eyes. I stop walking and reach my hand toward her face. I'd like to say I do this smoothly like you see in the movies, but truthfully, my hand shakes and jerks on its way to her chin. I miss her chin slightly and rub up against her neck. I quickly move it to her chin and gently move it to face me. I lower my eyes so I can see her downcast eyes.

She tentatively meets my gaze.

"Li, you won. You fought your battle back in that street and you won. You have made your decision. You will not have to fight that battle again—at least not as you did then. Once you make a decision like that it gets easier the next time.

"I'm also not as worried about Gene. He faced his battle over integrity back at the Easter Church with the caretaker. He could've made up a story to try and convince the caretaker or stretched the truth about what we sought. He didn't. He stuck to the truth. He kept his integrity intact, just as you did.

"Li, I haven't been faced with my choice yet. I'm scared I'm not up to the task," I admit, dropping my hand from her chin. I reveal all of my insecurities to her now. "I don't know how I'll react. I can say that I'll do the right thing, but I've seen how hard it was for the both of you and—" I can't say it out loud.

Now it's Li turn to find my eyes.

"And you think you are not as strong as Gene and I," she finishes my sentence. "That's what you want to say isn't it? You think you're not as tough, or strong, or whatever."

Li turns her head away in frustration. When she turns back to me, the fire is back in her eyes.

"Jake, you're mistaking physical toughness for mental strength. And in that category, you are our leader. You will be strong enough." She takes my hand in hers once more and we start walking again.

"And besides, Gene and I will be with you. We're a team, remember," she reminds me gently. We walk in silence for a few steps when she adds one more thing. "*I* will always be with you." She leans her body into mine as she says this, her shoulder contacting mine. Comfortable warmth spreads through me at her touch. I suck in a deep breath. She feels it and turns into me with a smile. Quick as can be, she reaches up and pecks me on my cheek.

CHAPTER 24

BASEMENT

L I SEES A SIZEABLE GROUP of soldiers off to the right of our current position and leads me over to them. "Excuse me, gentlemen," Li begins, addressing them formally and speaking directly to the leader of the group who wears the uniform of an officer. "We are looking for some cold drinks, water or Coca-Cola. Do you know where we might purchase some?"

I notice every soldier in the group stands a little taller at the sight of Li. They glance curiously at our clasped hands, trying to decide the nature of our relationship. Our hands are clasped in the way you would shake a hand rather than having our fingers intertwined. I see some of the soldiers take this to mean we must somehow be friends rather than anything more than that. Most of them can't be much more than 18 or 19 years old. Li carries herself as much older than 14, so these men probably misjudge her age. I stare at them impassively.

Li seems not to notice the attention she receives.

"Right. Miss, we have these items back at our HQ," the officer says crisply. "I'll have two of my men fetch them for you straightaway."

He turns his head to two of the boys in the back. They get the message and immediately take off.

"Thank you for your kindness, sir." Li responds gratefully.

"We are happy to be of service," the officer returns. He turns to the remainder of his men. "Carry on." The men snap out of their trance-like state and resume their cleanup of the rubble.

The officer looks as if he wants to ask us more questions. He surely wonders what a couple of young kids are doing wandering the streets of Berlin. Propriety keeps him from asking the questions however, so we just wait in silence.

The two boys return carrying two containers that must hold water and also two Coke bottles.

We offer our sincere thanks and then begin to retrace our steps back toward Gene and the church. I would be completely lost if Li weren't with me. I realize I had spent the whole walk in some sort of Li-induced stupor. I hadn't paid attention to the streets or turns we had taken. I had no idea how to get back to the church.

Li suffered from no such stupor. She walked confidently through the streets, comfortable with her surroundings.

I began to carefully scrutinize the buildings in varying states of ruin as we pass them. These had been homes to people and business. We pass a burned-out building, the bottom floor of which looks like it used to be a café or restaurant of some kind. I imagine that kids just like Li and me might've once sat in the booths, tentatively holding hands and blushing at one another. Life had been cruelly interrupted, and in some cases extinguished, because evil men were allowed to go about enacting their murderous plans.

Li must sense a shift in my mood, because she moves in closer to me.

My thoughts turn to the buildings themselves. They are symbolic in many ways of the lives of the people who once inhabited them. They are in shambles—rubble and dust are their only occupants now. But they will rise up, be rebuilt and shine once again. I picture in my mind the maps and photos of Berlin that I studied in the Training Center. Photos before the war, and also photos of current day Berlin.

I think of another of the speeches that Winston Churchill gave along the way, one I read back at the Training Center.

"A penny for your thoughts?" Li says, breaking into my reverie. I smile at her.

"You know, with Gene's dad using Winston Churchill as a keyword, I've just been thinking about something else Churchill said during this war," I begin, waving my free hand in front me. "It's stuck with me and as we walk among these buildings, I think it's appropriate to us now. He said, 'we shape our buildings and afterwards our buildings shape us.' We have the benefit of knowing that these buildings we walk by will be rebuilt and reshape a new generation of people.

"I can't help but think of my house back home. My great-grand-father built it, shaped it, and I think of how it has shaped my life. Our parents have left these tokens in buildings that now shape our lives as we seek the Key. I don't know, it seems like these buildings are somehow just like us. They need to be shaped and cared for, not destroyed and cast aside."

I run out of things to say. I wonder if I've made any sense, again struggling to take my thoughts and put them into words.

Li walks silently beside me, gazing up at the buildings as we pass by. She is quiet for a long minute. "The shape of our lives," she murmurs and leans in close to me.

When we turn the corner toward the church, having released one another's hands, we see Gene, who is positively giddy. It's hard to tell if he's excited by our return, or the Coca-Cola bottles he sees us pulling out of our sacks. Turns out it's neither of these two things.

"I've solved it! I figured out the second keyword," he shouts.

"I knew you could do it!" Li enthuses, and she hurries to give Gene a hug.

I move in and give him a slap to the shoulder by way of con-gratulations.

"Well, let's sit down and eat and drink while I tell ya'll about it," Gene says, eyeing the drinks greedily.

We sit down and bring out the Müllers' food. We add the Cokes and water to the feast and start right in on it. I smile as Gene tells us his story as food spittle flies in every direction. Li and I exchange a smile, knowing this is our Gene, food spittle and all.

"So, I'm sittin' here starin' at the letter and cursin' my pa for making it so difficult. I mean why couldn't he justa made it obvi-ous throughout my life with repeated references to the keywords. But no, Pa makes everything harder than it needs to be. Gene sits up and clears his throat. An impression is coming.

"'Eugene, ma boy, life is hard, ya see, an' knowin' as such, ya might as well get used to it. Just remember to keep calm and carry on,'" Gene intones, apparently mimicking his dad's words and mannerisms. He turns to us and spreads his arms in a "ta-da!"

manner.

"That is sorta Pa's motto, I guess. He's always sayin' it to me,"
Gene continues. "So, as I'm readin' the letter, I realize it talks about
a motto at the end." He picks up the letter and points to the last
line. "'Remember the motto', Pa wrote and then put a period after
it. See, so he wasn't saying remember the motto to make ya think
the next sentence is the motto. It's not 'Remember the motto' and
then a colon, but 'Remember the motto' Period." Gene emphasizes this with a finger tapping the period on the paper, lest we
miss the point.

"So, the second sentence was like a second clue to Winston
Churchill in case I missed the first clue about the finest hour.
But this 'remember the motto, period' points me to the second keyword. Which I believe is, "Keep calm and carry on."
Gene hands me the scratch paper and pencil. He picks up the
square and begins decrypting the letter jumble using this new
code.

He has already written the jumble and keyword on the paper
for me:

ERXTTGPECURUS
KEEPCALMANDCA

He begins reading off the newly decrypted letters. The first is
a U, then comes N. He continues until our paper looks like this:

ERXTTGPECURUS
KEEPCALMANDCA
UNTERGESCHOSS

I quickly copy the new word's letters again in a manner closer to
a word: UNTERGESCHOSS.

Gene and Li lean in to take a look at the word. It translates
before our eyes into English for "basement."

"I guess untergeschoss is the German word for basement," I the-
orize, looking carefully at the German word. I recognize the first
part *unter*. It looks very close to our English word *under*. I quickly
separate the *unter* and the *geschoss* on the paper with my pencil.
The separate words now translate as *under* and *floor*.

"Huh, so the token will be found under the floor or in the basement of this church?" Gene wonders.

"Looks like it," Li agrees while hoisting herself up. She begins packing away all of our supplies.

"It'd better not be another underground graveyard," Gene mumbles to himself.

I catch the corner of a smile forming on Li's lips and I can't help but smile too.

"I'm sure it'll be fine, Gene," I assure him, not believing my own words.

"We have two immediate concerns," Li says, voice sharp and ready for action. "And, no, Gene one of them is not about graveyards."

This earns Li a smirk from Gene.

"The first concern is we are losing daylight quickly and the second is we don't have any flashlights. If we are heading underground again, we'll need light."

"Yes, we do," Gene says matter-of-factly.

"Yes, we do what?" Li asks.

"We have a flashlight. I have one in my army supplies here," Gene says digging through his gear.

"Why didn't you use it back at the last church?" Li exclaims with exasperation.

"Cause I was tryin' not to pee ma pants, remember," Gene says with mock exasperation. "I didn't think about nothin' 'cept getting outta there alive."

Li rolls her eyes. "Well, then I guess we only have one concern, we need to find the entrance to the basement while we still have sunlight. It'll be harder in the dark with just one flashlight beam between the three of us."

CHAPTER 25

DESCENT

WITHOUT FURTHER DISCUSSION, WE MOVE into the church proper and begin to search for an underground entrance. We start at the front end of the church, or what used to be the front end and moved deliberately through the building. It seems weird to be in here without the roof, the church has lost its reverential quality. The sacredness has been replaced by rubble and debris.

It takes me a good fifteen minutes to realize that being in this structure is probably dangerous. We climb over stones and portions of the roof large enough to have crushed the pews underneath. I look up to see portions of the roof clinging tenuously to the walls. I search with more urgency now.

Gene finds the stairway to an underground level near the rear of the building. It seems appropriate that Gene finds the stairs that lead downward for two reasons. First, this is his search in a way, the letter having come from his dad. Second, he's found the dark scary pathway to his fears.

I catch up to Gene as he is using trembling hands to search through his pack for the flashlight. I put a hand on his shaking arm and give a look that tells him that I'll find it. I pull the light out of the pack and flick the switch. The light is dull at best. I decide on a whim to shine the light into his pack and I see a second flashlight. It lights up, but it's also a weak beam.

"Of course." Gene says, shaking his head.

"If it makes you feel any better, Gene, I don't think a flashlight was standard issue in the army. I think our parents found these and provided them for you." Li says, grabbing one of the lights as she moves toward the stairs. "Let's go."

I wait for Gene to follow Li down, taking up the rear, and making sure that Gene follows us down into the basement. The air changes almost immediately into a stale musty combination. I wonder if we are the first people down here since our parents.

Li is waiting for us. We stand in a hallway that runs back under the length of the church. The walls are narrow and the ceilings too small for Gene to stand fully upright.

I hand the light to Li and she leads us down the hall. We traverse the entire distance without seeing any doors or hallways on either side of us. The hall ends in a doorway, where Li is holding the light close to the door, as if she is inspecting something.

"Take a look," she says without turning her head.

Gene and I crowd in around her, focusing on the beam of light on the door. There is the faintest of scratches on the door. They form the shape of the coin that Gene handed over to the soldier in exchange for the letter. The coin Gene's dad had given him.

"I guess this means we go through this door," Li remarks.

A sound comes out of Gene that sounds like a whimper. Li turns and gives Gene an incredulous look. Gene just shrugs pitifully.

Li pushes the door open. Gene reaches out quickly and pulls it shut again.

"Wait," he breathes. "I don't want any shenanigans down here, okay? No fake screams or wailing. No grabbing me out of the darkness. No nonsense."

"Whatever could you mean, Eugene?" Li says in an overly sweet voice.

"I'm just sayin' I can't be responsible for my actions if somebody were to scare me," Gene clarifies, looking pointedly at Li. She just smiles innocently in return.

Li pushes the door open again and steps inside. I wait for Gene to follow and then bring up the rear.

We've stepped into some deep underground cavern. We stand on a raised platform with stairs that appear to descend into the cavern. The weak beam of the flashlight barely reaches to the ground below us. It does not provide enough light to see the entire space. I hear the drip-drip of water somewhere in the darkness.

We follow Li down the stairs. They turn back on themselves

twice before we reach the ground.

When Li steps off the last stair, her shoes splashes into water. She shines the beam toward her foot. Shallow puddles of water are gathered sporadically around the floor. The ground consists of cracked cement from what I can see.

Li slowly shines the flashlight in a wide circle attempting to get a picture of the space. She ends with the flashlight on the wall to the left of the stairs. She takes a few steps forward, light fixed on the wall.

"Another door," Li says. As she shines her beam on the wall, a door materializes out of the gloom. I immediately see the now familiar faint scratches on the door. Gene's coin again.

Gene's breathing is coming in shallow gasps.

"Hold on a second, Li," I say, then put an arm out to Gene, finding his shoulder. "Gene, you need to take some deep breaths for a minute. Follow my breathing, okay?"

I take deep, slow breaths, exaggerating the sound so Gene can mimic me. He starts haltingly and then eventually normalizes his breathing.

"It's funny," he says.

"What's funny?" I continue to keep him talking.

"You helping me to beat back my anxiety." Gene says, attempting a laugh. "The tables have turned, haven't they?"

"I guess they have, Gene. And I'm happy to be the one to help you. You saved my life many times in China with your help in calming my nerves and fears."

I feel more than see Gene nod.

"Let's get this token and then get outta here. The sooner the better," Gene shivers.

Li takes that as her cue and opens the door. She steps inside, and I think I hear her stifle a laugh. Gene steps inside and I follow in after him. I can't see beyond Gene, but when I hear him moan and turn into me I know what lies beyond the door.

"No. No. No. Not again," he mutters as he tries to push past me. I grab him and do my best to keep him from running by me.

"Gene, we got you, okay?" I say, looking beyond him to get Li's attention. She is already moving over to help. I shoot her a look about not teasing Gene. *No games*, I tell her with my eyes. She looks momentarily disappointed but nods.

"Gene, I promise no shenanigans." Li says, repeating Gene's own words, which are unfamiliar to her. "No jokes, no tricks, no teasing, okay?"

"Keep calm and carry on." Gene recites his father's motto. This seems to do the trick. He heaves a deep breath. "I can do this."

I pat him on the shoulder and let him go. The flashlight catches Li's face for a second and I catch her battling with herself over some joke or tease. I call her name in warning. She pretends not to hear. But she doesn't tease Gene, she only moves over and closes the door behind us.

"Can't we leave the door open? I mean, it won't hurt, will it?" Gene pleads.

Li shrugs and leaves the door open a crack. After she moves away from the door and begins showing the light through the room, Gene opens the door wide.

The room is a crypt. A large one with many headstones and larger stone monuments spread throughout the space.

"Okay, so last time, we had a name to search for," Li notes, getting down to the business at hand. "This time, we don't have a name or anything else to look for."

"Actually, I think we do have something to look for," I counter. "I believe we should look for that same marking of Gene's coin somewhere on a headstone or monument."

"Oh right, smart thinking yet again, Jake," Li replies. "Should we spread out? There's a lot of ground to cover in here."

Gene still stands next to me and makes a terrified sound at the thought of splitting up.

"How about Gene and I start back here near the door and make our way toward the middle while you start at the back," I suggest, wanting to help Gene stay calm.

"Good." Li is in agreement and moves toward the back of the room.

As it turns out, we met in the middle and saw the symbol at roughly the same time.

"I've got something here," Li reports.

"Really? So do I, over here," I call back to her.

We shine our lights on one another and realized we are examining different ends of the same sarcophagus-like stone box. I move around the decorative stone and shine my light on the point that

Li is showing me. It's the same symbol from Gene's coin.

"I found the same symbol on the other end of this sarcophagus," I tell her. "This must be the one, let's take a look around it and find the token. It's probably etched into the stone like the last one."

"Wait, did you say sarcophagus? I thought those were just for pharaohs and ancient Egyptian people," Gene comments. It's nice that he's diverted from thinking about the dark scary graveyard.

"These types of stone monuments originated in ancient Egypt, but you can find sarcophagi in Greek and Roman times. They can even be found in America in certain places. It's really just an aboveground monument to the person usually buried beneath." I explain while moving my light over the surface of the stone.

"Here it is. I found it." Li's voice carries over to Gene and me. She is on the opposite side of the sarcophagus, bent down low.

Gene casts a quick glance to the open door, some subconscious check on his safety outlet. Upon seeing the door still open and available for his escape, he moves in Li's direction. I follow.

"It looks like your father spent some time down here etching another set of grooves in the stone." Li says pointing to the token embedded in the stone.

"That looks like the British flag." Gene says leaning forward and tracing a finger along the lines of metal embedded in the stone.

"At the risk of boring you both to death." I begin, forgetting where we are. Gene shoots me a "not-funny" look. "Oops, I mean I don't want to bore you to tears. Anyway, the British flag came to look as it does now when the English flag was merged with the Scottish and Irish versions. The horizontal and vertical lines represent the English cross—the red cross of Saint George. The crosses or x-like lines are representations of the crosses of St. Patrick and St. Andrew. Thus, we have the Union Jack."

Gene makes a snoring sound and receives a slug from Li for his trouble.

"Just kidding, maybe that'll come in handy at some point later in my life," Gene says, clearly doubting that this knowledge will have any impact.

"My point is, the Union Jack actually represents crosses of different kinds. Just like the French cross token we retrieved from the Osterkirche," I explain, a touch exasperated.

"Oh, I see. So you're saying that both tokens so far are crosses of different kinds. That is the common theme," Li says, making the connection. I suspect she is trying to make me feel better about launching into my nerdist history.

CHAPTER 26

TRAPPED

"LET'S JUST GET THESE SPECIAL crosses out of the dead guy's tomb and get back up to some fresh air." Gene says, working to free the metal Union Jack from the stone.

Li shimmies up next to Gene and begins helping him with the extraction process. I figure the two of them can handle it, so I decide to satisfy my curiosity about the sarcophagus.

As soon as I lean in to see who lies within our stone box, I hear the metal door leading into the room clang shut. I whip my head in the direction of the door but see nothing but black. I hear the panic in Gene's voice clearly.

"What just happened?" he cries out. "Jake, not funny. Seriously, I asked you two to not tease me. This is crossing the line, dude. No shenanigans, I said!"

A light flashes across my face causing me to blink and turn my head.

"Gene, Jake is standing right there." Li says firmly. "He didn't shut the door. And neither did I, I was right next to you freeing the metal Union Jack. It probably just swung shut somehow."

Li's light swings to the door, the weak beam barely strong enough to reveal its outlines.

"Let's get this token packed up and then I'll go reopen the door for you Gene." Li says, command in her tone.

I've come around to their side again, abandoning my curiosity about the occupant of the stone box. I see that Gene has the token free and just as with the previous token, it separates into pieces.

This time there are four straight metal pieces. Gene shoves them into a pack quickly.

"Let's get out of here." He says, trying to keep the panic out of his voice.

Sounds come from behind the door. I can't place them. I strain my ear hoping to discern what exactly is happening on the other side of the door.

Li apparently knows. She scrambles toward the door, her light bobbing crazily as she moves. I move my light over to her. She is working at the door, but it doesn't open.

"It's sealed," Li announces, an edge of anxiety now in her voice.

"Whatdaya mean, it's sealed?" Gene asks, his voice an octave higher than usual.

"I mean that somebody came behind us just now and locked us in. The door is sealed shut. Completely. If..." Li trails off and leans closer to the door, as if listening. After a long second, she pulls backs and kicks at something on the floor.

"They must've welded the door shut," she says as she quickly makes her way back to us. "It's completely sealed, except for at the bottom..."

Gene makes a sound like an injured animal. Li grabs him by the shoulders and gives him a firm shake. She keeps a hold on him.

"It gets worse. They are pumping some sort of gas in under the door. My guess is we'll be unconscious or dead in a few minutes. We need to find another way out of here." Li reaches into Gene's pack, flashing her light around as she does. She comes out with a gas mask—standard issue to soldiers—and pulls it over Gene's head.

"Keep this on, Gene. You're breathing is already shallow and we need you to stay awake," Li instructs him, in total command now.

Gene starts to remove the mask, protesting, his voice distorted and weird. "No, Jake or you should be wearin' it."

Li stops Gene from removing the mask, a bit roughly I notice. She doesn't have time for niceties. "Gene, you have to wear it. I don't think Jake and I will be able to carry you out of here when we find an escape route. We need you conscious. If Jake or I go out, you'll be able to carry us."

She says this last part as she is turning and grabbing me roughly. "Jake, I gave you the smoke grenades, right?" She doesn't wait for an answer. She finds them in one of my pockets and pulls both of them free. She fixes me with an intense gaze. "Jake, I need you to detonate this grenade over by the back wall. When you do, smoke will begin filling the area…"

I feel hands on my shoulders. "Jake, are you with me? Are you listening?" Li's voice is sharp, but there is an edge of worry. "I need you to listen to me. Okay?"

I nod shakily.

"The smoke will rise out of the grenade rapidly and fill the space. I need you to watch the smoke carefully. We need to find a place where the smoke escapes into the walls. Do you understand? The smoke will tell us where moving air is and then we can get out. Okay?" Her words come out rapid-fire.

I nod, more resolutely this time.

"I'm going to do the same thing with the other smoke grenade on the right wall over there," she continues, pointing to a wall. "We have no time. Do you understand? We need a way out right now!"

She gives me a little shove toward the back wall. I stumble around the headstone and grave markers and reach the back wall. My fingers feel thick and useless and I struggle to grab the pin. I finally get it, pull it, and release the smoke bomb. It clatters to the floor and immediately thick smoke begins filling the air.

I have no idea what Gene and Li are doing. It doesn't matter. I need to watch the smoke, I tell myself. I feel light-headed and my head feels fuzzy. I shake it. That makes it worse.

The smoke is thick and burns my eyes. I actually think this helps me focus my mind. I begin to cough and can't decide if it's from the invisible gas working to put me to sleep, or the thick smoke.

I squeeze my eyes shut for a second and then reopen them. I focus on the smoke. It clings to the walls, but I don't see any signs of it being sucked into the walls and out to some unseen fresh air.

I move sluggishly along the wall, hoping against hope that I'll see an escape.

Nothing.

I feel funny. I look around to find Li and Gene. I don't see them. Only smoke.

This is end then, I think, then sink to my knees. I let my eyes close, a peaceful warmth overcomes me. I've failed but it doesn't seem to matter so much right now.

I'm jolted. Ouch! I scream, but I realize no sound has come out of my mouth. I'm just screaming in my head. I see an alien life form standing over me, bending down and hauling me up over its shoulder like I'm a sack of flour.

I'm carried for a few steps and then set down against a wall. Good. I can sleep now. I close my eyes. Something is roughly shoved over my head. I'm being kidnapped like in the movies, I think. A bag-over-the-head job.

I take a few ragged breaths. My mind clears with the breaths. I realize I am now wearing the gas mask. I move my heavy head up to see Gene and Li banging and kicking against the wall. I see tendrils of smoke zipping into the opening. They are being carried away by some unseen wind. Fresh air.

Li slumps against the wall. She is pale and sleepy.

I heave several breaths in and out. I force as much of this clean recycled air into my lungs and I then I rip the mask off and force it onto Li's head. She doesn't fight me.

I'm holding my breath and turn to Gene. He hasn't stopped ramming the stone wall. I pick up the flashlight Li was using as a ramming instrument and join Gene in pummeling the stone wall.

I'm forced to take a breath and I feel dizzy immediately. I hold my breath again.

Gene breaks through the wall. It's a tomb, a horizontal tomb, barely large enough for a corpse to lie flat. Thankfully, this corpse must have been large in death, because the space is large enough for us to crawl through. I shine the weak light into the space.

Bones.

Gene's not going to be happy. I turn to look at him. Li is forcing the mask over his face. He accepts it with wide eyes and a look of pure terror. His eyes are locked on the bones.

Li reaches into the chamber and pulls the bones out onto the floor unceremoniously. I calculate we have seconds left before unconsciousness takes over. No time for niceties.

Li does make time for a pained look at me and then a quick peck to my cheek. And then she is shoving me into the space. I feel her right behind me.

I scramble down the space, maybe ten feet until I reach the end. I flash my light at the stone. It's cracked and smoke seeps out into the beyond.

I thrust the flashlight forward like I would in a poke move with a staff. The metal of the flashlight crashed through the stone wall. My knuckles scrape against the stone as my hand passes through it. I don't even feel it.

I frantically poke thrust again and again, clearing more space, until the hole is wide enough for me to squeeze through. I shove through, taking more stone with my shoulders and fall clumsily head over feet to the ground. I look up just in time to Li falling toward me. I try to shield myself from her falling body and manage to protect the important parts.

Li rolls off of me and we both look up to see Gene's alien-gas-masked head pop out. He has to take another few seconds to punch out more stone so he can make it through. I scramble out from under his imminent drop and concentrate on sucking in giant breaths of air into my lungs. Li is next to me doing the same thing.

Gene finally wriggles out of the horizontal chamber and falls awkwardly to the ground. There is no graceful way to climb out of a crypt, I decide.

Gene rips off the gas mask looking ready to vomit.

"I can't believe …" he croaks out between heaving, shuddering breaths. "I can't believe … that just happened …"

As often happens after an adrenaline-infused life-and-death situation, the three of collapse in fits of hysterical laughter.

"Shhh …" Li sputters, trying to control her own laughter. "We don't want to give away our escape. We need to put some distance between ourselves and the jerks who just locked us into that death chamber."

She hauls herself to her feet and begins checking herself and her supplies. I stand wearily, the effects of the gas still lingering in my head and limbs. I concentrate on my breathing for a moment. I reach down to grab the flashlight I used to break through the wall. It's no longer working. The other light is in Gene's hands. It still works.

"Which way?" he asks, shining the weak beam to his left and right.

"This must be a subway tunnel or whatever they call it here," Li notes. "Let's go this way." She sets off immediately. One thing

I've learned about Li is that she has an uncanny sense of direction. She always knew where to go in the caves of the Training Center when Gene and I were lost and turned around. Gene knows this too, because he sets off behind her without a word.

As we trudge through the tunnel, my hand begins to throb and I realized that blood drips from my fingertips. I don't say anything to the others, knowing there is nothing to be done about it at the moment. Gene senses me falling off the pace and falls back to help me walk. I lean into him, grateful for the help.

I don't know how long we walk. Time has no meaning underground, I decide. After some time, the ground begins to rise in a gentle slope up toward the surface. The air freshens noticeably, we must be arriving near the surface. Sure enough, after another hundred yards, I see stars blinking in the heavens.

After climbing out of the tunnel and back onto the surface, we make our way into the shadows of a burnt-out building to catch our collective breath. We fall against the wall almost in unison, working to shake off the effects of all that has happened.

The street and buildings are eerily silent. Night has fully fallen and the city is sleeping. The moon and stars are bright enough to allow us to take in our surroundings. If we had the energy to, that is.

Li's hand reaches out to take mine. She's taken hold of my injured hand, I jerk it away in a jolt of pain. She lets out a gasp and then seems to understand.

"Gene, can I use the light?" she asks.

A second later, a light shines on my hand. "Oh," Li says in a small whisper.

My hand is covered in blood. It throbs to the beat of my heart.

"It's not as bad as it looks. I scraped my knuckles on the stone when I was punching it clear." I let out a small laugh. "I guess I was pretty anxious to get out of that death chamber, because I didn't feel a thing at the time."

Gene takes in the blood on my hand and also the blood that is now smeared on Li's hand. Recognition flickers in his eyes. He knows we were holding hands. He doesn't comment.

"I got some water left in ma canteen, let's wash that out and bandage it up for now. Come daylight, we'll hafta get it looked at." Gene says.

"Hey, look," I say, pointing down the street wanting to take the focus off my hand. "There's the church we just escaped."

I think we're all surprised that we haven't put as much distance as we thought between ourselves and the scene of our imprisonment.

"I see the signs right over there that we saw yesterday. I think those are the signs telling us that the American sector is close. Let's move into that sector and put some more distance between our attackers and us. Then we can find a place to get some rest." Li says while hauling herself up.

Gene and I follow suit, not wasting energy on words. We cross into the American sector; it's close, just as we had seen yesterday on our walk around the church grounds. We pass beyond the signs and I somehow feel safer simply because we passed a sign that said we are entering the United States sector of Berlin. Nonsensical, I know, but still comforting.

I'm certain that the gas we inhaled is contributing to our fatigue, because I notice that all three of us are moving slower than normal. My limbs feel heavy, and slow to respond to my brain's commands. Gene and Li look to be struggling in the same manner.

An American soldier slips from the shadows and begins making his way over to us. I see Li move her hands fractionally closer to the pistols I know are hidden beneath her clothing. The soldier looks friendly and open, a wide smile on his face.

CHAPTER 27

POSTCARD

"**W**ELL, I WAS HOPIN' Y'ALL'D show up soon." he says, then looks appraisingly at the three of us. "It sure looks like y'all could use some shuteye. Am I right?"

We stand close together, careful not to expose ourselves unnecessarily. I can see Li's eyes roaming in all directions assessing the possible danger.

"Oh, I beg yer pardon, lemme introduce myself here first off." He says. "My name is Eriksson. Richard Eriksson. I been asked to wait fer y'all over here with that there church in my sights." He waves a hand at the church we have just left behind. "I saw ya earlier in the day but was told not to talk to ya until you crossed over into the good ole U S of A sector." He offers another smile. "I was beginnin' to fret about y'all though. You disappeared and didn't show yerselves for a right good long time."

He claps his hands together. "Anyhoo ... y'all don't wannabe spendin' yer time listenin' to a duffer like me. So I guess I need to be askin' bout the item you should have in yer possession to exchange for the item I have in my possession. Yer ... er ... friends were positively adamant about the exchange."

I feel like I'm listening to Gene's long-lost uncle, although I know this soldier's accent is more deep south than Texan.

Both Gene and I turn to Li. It's Li's call here, she carries the final item to exchange for a letter – a letter from her dad. She hesitates only a moment longer before reaching under her bulky clothes and removing the item.

The postcard.

Richard grins as he reaches out for the postcard.

"Perfect. Just the one I gave over to yer friends." He says and reaches into his pocket to remove a letter. He hands the letter to Li with an air of formality.

"Now, if I may, it looks like y'all need a place to sleep. I know just the place."

Li shrugs and nods to the soldier. We follow him through winding streets covering maybe a quarter mile, moving deeper into the U.S. sector and away from our unknown attackers.

Gene moves up and falls into conversation with Richard. He's back to his usual self, instantly making a friend and falling into friendly discussion.

My hands still throbs, but the bleeding seems to have stopped.

Li falls into step next to me but doesn't reach for my hand. "Do you trust this soldier?" she asks.

"Yeah, I guess," I say. "He seems like a nice enough guy. I don't get any weird vibes from him, but I'm also impossibly tired, so …"

"I know. I'm so tired too. But I get a good feeling from this soldier. He just feels safe," Li tells me, not used to using her emotions to make these kinds of decisions.

I nod and we continue in comfortable silence until we reach a set of buildings that are lighted and mostly intact. It's always a wonder to me how some buildings escape damage while those right next to them are completely obliterated. Just like our lives in many ways. I'm an ordinary kid thrust into extraordinary circumstances. By contrast, my neighbor continues on normally.

Li must sense my thoughts while following my gaze. She leans into me and whispers in my ear.

"The shape of our lives," she says, knowing just what I'm thinking and also knowing just what to say. What can I say? We fit.

I turn to her, hoping she can see my face in the reflected light of the buildings. I smile and nod to her, leaning into her, enjoying the closeness.

"Uh … I hate to break up whatever it is that's goin' on between you two, but we are here," Gene announces with a wide smile. "Ricky here is gonna leave us now and head back to his post. He says there are proper beds here we can use to sleep off the effects of … our night."

We shake the hand of our newest benefactor and watch him melt back into the darkness. We move into the building, which is glowing with light, and are greeted by an older German couple.

I'm taken by surprise. I assumed that this was some kind of military headquarters.

"Hello, welcome to our home," the man says in greeting, his welcome sounding to my ears like velcome. He must be speaking English accented with German, otherwise our translators wouldn't offer any accent. "We are happy to host you for as long as you need, we have beds ready for you and warm food as well."

The woman, who I assume is the man's wife, moves past him and reaches carefully out to my hand.

"You are injured, young man. Come with me and I'll tend to your wounds," she says in a motherly way and gently pulls me along behind her toward a back room. I twist my head around to see Gene and Li smiling at me.

"My name is Hanna and my husband is Gunter. We have opened our home to the American soldiers and any other who may be homeless or in need." She says kindly, her accent even heavier than her husband's. She begins washing my hand, cleaning the blood off and revealing the cuts and scrapes along the knuckles.

"Is not so bad," she murmurs and sets to cleaning the wounds and then wraps my hand in a cloth. "You should be fine. Are any of the fingers broken do you think?"

I make a fist and then flex my fingers outward and back. "I think I'm fine, thank you for your help, ma'am." I say. I'd like to get back to Gene and Li. I'm uneasy without them, even though I feel safe in this home.

"I see you are anxious to rejoin your friend," she says with a knowing look and a wink. What? How does she know about Li and me? "A woman always knows, young man," she says with a twinkle in her eye, reading my thoughts.

Ten minutes have passed since I left Li and Gene behind. Hanna leads me upstairs after a brief conversation in German with her husband that she believes I won't understand. Gunter tells her that Gene and Li have already been escorted to bedrooms and that there is room in Gene's room for me.

I enter the room that houses Gene. The lights are out and I can hear Gene's low purring snores coming from one side of the room. I leave the door open long enough to plot a course to the bed opposite Gene's, then close the door returning the room to darkness. I step carefully over to the bed and collapse on it. Sleep comes almost immediately.

CHAPTER 28

LETTER III

I WAKE WITH MEMORIES OR MAYBE dreams trailing in the wake of the journey from sleep to consciousness. Lost in these dreams I open my eyes, expecting to see Mr. Wang's bedroom with Gene rolling around to find shelter from the sunlight. I shake my head to clear the memories and remember when and where I am.

I turn my gaze to Gene's bed, but it's empty. I fight a brief moment of panic, I'm sure he's fine, but I don't want to be alone, so I jump up and begin moving to the door.

Halfway to the door, I hear a soft knock.

"Are you decent in there?" Li's voice carries through the door.

I finish moving to the door and open it with a smile. Relief floods my body at the sight of her. Her hair glistens from a recent shower or bath and her skin is radiant and pink, scrubbed clean of the dirt and grime of the previous days. Her gaze flits up to my hair and she tries to suppress a smile.

I reach my hand up to my hair automatically and can tell it's going in all directions. Bed head in 1945 Berlin.

"You look rested, Jake," she says, a faint blush rising. Her hands move in a way that tells me she doesn't know what to do with them. I'm familiar with the motions. "You look good."

She finally makes a decision about her hands when she moves into me and gives a quick hug. I barely have enough time to hug her back.

"I think Gene's in the bath and then it can be your turn if you want." Li says, back to business. "Then on to breakfast. We need to read the letter and solve it quickly, the forces against us are gathering and getting bolder."

Last night's close call come back to mind. I nod, not trusting my voice. "Well … I'll see you downstairs." She rocks from her toes to her heels, again unsure.

My move! I realize with suddenness. She's waiting for you, you idiot. I quickly reach a hand out to her, catching her forearm clumsily. I let my hand slide down to hers and give it a squeeze. I smile at her, showing my pleasure.

"I'll see you in a few minutes then." I say, but it sounds like someone else's voice. It sounds confident and bold. Cool.

She returns the squeeze and then turns away, moving down the hall toward the stairs.

"Heya, loverboy!" Gene calls, he is moving toward me from the opposite direction of Li's departure. He must have watched the whole thing. "You and Li, huh? I guess I already knew."

Gene moves into the room and closes the door.

I just stand there, not knowing what to say.

He laughs. "Jake, snap out of it, go get a bath and meet us downstairs for breakfast. Li wants to hurry up with the letter."

I move to the door woodenly.

"Oh and Jakers? Good for you, buddy," Gene says with his back turned to me. I stare at his back for a second and then move out the door.

"Okay, Li, let's get that letter open and grab the next token. We still have two more to find, and time's a wastin'" Gene says, leaning back onto a couch, rubbing his hands over his belly.

Breakfast was a feast and we ate a ton of food. I'm surprised by my appetite; I'm always hungry. Gene tells me I must be going through a growth spurt. Secretly I hope so.

We've made our way to Gunter's den at his invitation. Gunter and Hanna must be incredibly wealthy because their home is huge—as big as a hotel. And his study is filled with books, old paintings, and plush leather furniture. I can't help myself as I move through the space, gazing lustily at all of the books. I could spend hours in here. Or days.

Li brings me back to reality. "Why don't the two of you join me over here so we call all read the letter together."

I move to the couch and sit on Li's left. Gene moves from his loveseat to join us on the larger couch. He sits on Li's right. We crowd together as she opens the letter and removes the single sheet of paper. She holds it out so we can all read it together.

Chosen,

This letter is unique, I think. We who write it and you who read it will surely know one another. The three of us, in our time, say to the three of you, we miss you!

Now, the Quest to gather the Key is upon you. We have recovered the lost Key and placed in a protected place until you can retrieve it for the final time.

The Key was difficult to get back from those evil ones who held it for so long.

You will require four tokens to unlock the mystery of this Key. These tokens are spread throughout the city, one in each sector. You must not leave a sector of the city until that sector's token has been retrieved, you may not be allowed back.

To safeguard the Key, we have followed the usual protocols. Brain, Brawn, and Buddying will all be required for each token.

We have left communications behind with individuals you can trust in each sector who may assist you in your Quest. Use them wisely. Employ honor and honesty to find what you seek.

The third token is located in the American sector. We trust that you have found the soldier and given him your personal item in exchange for this letter.

Now, crack the code of the American token. With two tokens in hand, we have so little time in which to do so much to find the final tokens and that which was once lost.

CIHZIMOTKTVS

KFWSFHRYZUDSXOPG

May you be blessed in your Quest.
Zhang Ming Wun
Brain of the Quest

we trained together. It was sort of our mantra for martial arts—don't do more harm than you need; do what you feel in your heart is right."

I smile at her, partly because she has solved the puzzle so quickly, but also partly because I can see that this is bringing her closer to her dad. I know how important that is to her, and I'm happy for her.

"Okay, I'll use the square to decrypt the letter jumble. Why don't you write the letters as I call them out," she says briskly, taking the square from my lap.

Once again, I nod and ready the pencil. Gene leans in to follow along.

Li runs her finger down the column at the left-hand side of the square to the letter R and then over to the letter C—the first letter in the jumble. When she hits C she moves her finger along that column up to the top row. Her finger settles on the letter L. She calls out L and I dutifully write it on the paper. She follows this pattern, using Roosevelt as the keyword and needing to use Roo over again at the end.

I've written out the keyword and jumble on the paper and write the decrypted letters below them, so my paper ends up looking like this:

R O O S E V E L T R O O
C I H Z I M O T K T V S
L U T H E R K I R C H E

CHAPTER 29

UNDERGROUND BELLS

THE WORD DECRYPTED IS: LUTHERKIRCHE.
I immediately notice the word kirche from our previous decryptions. I know it means church. I look to Li and see that she notices the same thing.

"The word translates as Luther Church," Gene says as he sees the word translate before his eyes. "Another church. Perfect. If we hafta go into another crypt I'm gonna scream."

"Well, that won't be any different from the other crypts we've been in so far," Li teases, unable to resist a playful jab at Gene.

"Har-har-har," Gene returns laconically. "And wipe that smile off ya face there, Jakers. What're you two, gangin' up on me now? Geez, I wish I had Chloe here to defend me."

Li snorts and somehow it's cute when she does it.

"You think Chloe would defend you if she saw you down in the crypt screaming and carrying on like you do? I don't think so. You should count yourself lucky that she isn't here to see you like that."

Gene stares at Li, and for a brief moment I think he's going to explode on her. I tense up, thinking I might have to get between the two of them, then Gene breaks into laughter.

"Yer right, I'm glad she isn't around for all this," he admits, waving a hand around in the air. "Actually, I'm glad nobody's around to see me like this, except fer you two—my friends."

"Awww, look at Gene sharing with us what gives him the scaredy pox," Li says with a smile. "Now that we know what gives Jake and Gene the scaredy pox, we can help each other out in those situations."

"What gives you the scaredy pox, Li?" I ask, beating Gene to it. Li just hikes her shoulders up and lets them fall.

"Nothing," she gives us both a wicked smile, and we know she's hiding something. "But let's get back to the issue at hand. I'm sure we can get directions to this Lutherkirche, so let's move to the second encrypted word. I think we should use Eleanor Roosevelt on this word. It's long for one thing, and my father always referred to her as Eleanor."

I write Eleanor Roosevelt on the paper and then underneath it our long-lettered jumble. I motion that I'm ready for Li to begin the decryption. She reads off the decrypted letters one at a time until I have this on the paper:

E L E A N O R R O O S E V E L T
K F W S F H R Y Z U D S X O P G
G U S S S T A H L G L O C K E N

I hold the paper up so we can all see the new word, which again I'm assuming is in German. As I look at the word it translates before my eyes to: cast steel bell.

"Cast steel bell?" Gene says. "Does that mean what I think it means?" He sounds hopeful to the point of giddiness.

"Yeah, Gene, I think that means that we'll find the third token in the bell tower of this church rather than in a crypt," I reply.

I try to remember the last time I've seen Gene this excited.

"Let's get going. I don't think my father's warning about having so little time was simply a convenient way to point me to Roosevelt; I think we're really running out of time," Li emphasizes as she stands and moves toward the door.

Gene and I jump up and hustle to catch up to her.

HANNA WAS HAPPY TO GIVE us directions to the Lutherkirche, which is less than two miles from our current position, but she was quick to add something that has us all sort of confused.

"The Lutherkirche was destroyed by bombs two years or so ago," she says with a furrowed brow. "I don't believe much if any of it still stands today."

We thank her for her kindness, Li offering up an embrace, and are now nearing the church. We are walking eastward along a wide street and I wonder if we are nearing the border of east and west Berlin. For some reason, I feel a shiver travel down my spine as I think of going into Soviet-occupied east Berlin. Up to this point we have traveled exclusively in the Allied sections of the city, people friendly to three American teens, but soon we'll need to enter enemy territory.

I shake off this line of thinking and concentrate on the task at hand. We'll need to cross that next bridge, so to speak, soon enough. I'm brought back to the present by a soft *whoa* from Gene. I look in the direction of his gaze and see the ruins of what must be the Lutherkirche in front of us.

"I don't think the bells are still in the bell tower," Gene says, his imagination running wild I'm sure with the possibility that the bells have somehow found their way to a crypt below ground.

Li reaches out a reassuring hand to steady Gene.

As we arrive at the church, I see that the walls and portions of the roof are blackened from hot fire. I had read about the phosphorus "fire" bomb that had been dropped on Berlin during World War II. I find myself hoping that nobody was inside during the bombing.

"Let's find the token and move on," Li says, giving voice to my thoughts. I'm sure all three of us are dreading picking through the rubble to find the bells.

I remind myself that our parents had to have done the same thing to hide the token in the first place, so they wouldn't lead us into a true graveyard—one where the bodies have yet to be buried. Of course, they led us into two crypts, so maybe I'm off in my presumption.

Li leads us into the church, although it's hard to imagine that what we are climbing through what was at one point a church.

"The remnants of the bell tower are over here," Li points forward. "Watch your step."

"It feels strange walking through a church and feel the sun shine down on your back as you climb over ruins and rubble. This is weird," Gene says.

We pick our way over to Li, who is standing looking down at something in the floor. This is odd, because she should be looking up into the tower for the bells. Except they aren't in the tower. The tower, or what's left of it, is empty. No bells. No nothing.

I move my head from craning up to the exact opposite, mirroring Li's bowed head.

"Of course," Gene groans. "Of course—the bells have fallen through the floor and now lie underground in the dark scary hole."

"Look on the bright side, Gene, it doesn't look like a graveyard down there; just an empty, broken cavern," Li encourages with a slap to Gene's shoulder.

"What don't you understand about dark scary holes? There cannot be a 'bright side' to them," Gene huffs, putting air quotes on the words *bright side*.

"Well, then, just stay up here and wait while Jake and I climb down and grab the token," Li offers.

"Good idea, I'll just keep watch up here while the two of you descend into the depths of darkness, never to return," Gene mutters.

Li turns her head to Gene, her face a mixture of frustration and mirth. "Gene, what are you talking about? I can see the bells from here. They can't be more than a few feet down," Li chides. "It's not like they have fallen all the way to the center of the earth. And speaking of the center of the earth, how come you weren't afraid when we went into the Old Dragon's Head in China? That was underground."

"Yeah, but there were no crypts or graveyards—*and* it was built by Chosen, so I knew everything would be fine. We always had a way out."

I think to myself that Gene's not making sense; we didn't always have a way out. We were trapped by the Wang brothers and their goons. But, there is no way I'm going to bring this up to Gene, especially right now. I know firsthand that phobias are not rational.

I can tell Li doesn't understand Gene's logic either, but thankfully she shrugs it off.

"Well, it's only a few feet down and I don't see any graves or sarcophagi or crypts or anything, so I think it's safe. Plus, we'll always be able to see up through this opening in the floor, right?" Li says confidently while she is looking for the easiest way down into the hole in the floor. "It looks like a basement of some kind was under this portion of the floor."

Thick wooden beams crisscross the opening; they look like they were the support beams for the bells. I can see one of the bells lying on its side, the underside of it partially showing.

She reaches into her new pack provided by Gunter or the American soldiers, we don't know which; they were just left outside our rooms this morning. Food, flashlights, rope, smoke grenades, and water canteens fill our new supply packs. Li removes her rope and gets to work.

After several minutes of working and shifting around the hole, she stands and appears to be satisfied with her work. Gene and I have just been standing idly by, looking dumb not knowing how to help.

Li drops the rope into the darkness and turns to face Gene and me. "I'll go down first to make sure the rope will hold," she says seriously. "Gene, why don't you come next, and then Jake can come last."

"I thought I was going to wait up here, ya know, keep watch and whatever. Do ya really think all three of us need to go down?" Gene protests weakly, a rising panic edging into his voice.

"Gene, we may need your help down there—your brute strength, or height, or some combination of both," Li counters. "I was joking when I said you could wait. We're a team, remember?"

"Yeah, okay," Gene says morosely, his voice betraying his words. It's definitely not okay for him.

Li dips into the open hole and finds footholds on the fallen wooden beams. As I watch her, I carefully note exactly how she is moving and where she places her feet. I'll need all the help I can get to get down. There is no safety harness or net keeping me from a fall.

Li's voice come up from the darkness and it's Gene's turn. He looks at me for a second, letting me know that he is not happy with this situation. I attempt a smile, but think it comes out more like a pained lip curl. I'm nervous too, buddy.

Gene grabs the rope and descends into the hole. After a few minutes of grunting and maneuvering he too disappears into the darkness below.

CHAPTER 30

LIBERATING THE TOKEN

I LOOK AROUND AT THE RUINS of the church, cataloguing burned pews and fallen columns. I stare at what looks like a balcony fallen to the floor. Again, I absently wonder if there were any people in the building at the time it fell.

I spin around quickly at the sudden feeling that I'm being watched. I scan the ruins and then look beyond them, the hairs on my arms and neck standing up like cold goosebumps. I don't see anybody, or anything at all. The area is as quiet as a ... well, as a graveyard. I smile a little, thinking of Gene.

Soon I hear my name called from below and grab the rope and begin my descent. I call to mind the footholds and movements of Li's descent, mimicking the process the best I can. She and I are roughly the same height, so I knew that I would have no trouble matching her movements.

I reach the ground with no trouble, although my hands burn from the death grip I had around the rope. I flex them as soon as I let go, and let the blood work its way back into all of the fingers and spaces in between.

I reach into my pack and pull out my flashlight. I turn it on and see the now familiar weak beam penetrate the darkness. Li has been busy with the bells, which are lined up on their sides. The bottommost bell has gouged a deep groove into the floor. The second bell hangs as if defying gravity, skewed toward the ground and the bottom bell, but not touching it. The third bell hangs in much the same position of the second bell, it is the bell we could see from up above. I'm amazed that the three bells have remained in their thick steel and wooden harness. The fall of the bells could've damaged all of the bells beyond repair had they come loose from their harness. Instead, the second two bells hang suspended in air, looking ready to ring out their notes.

Li is searching the grounded bell thoroughly with the light. Gene has moved off as if he is searching the chamber we have descended into, no doubt checking to make sure we are not in an underground crypt of any kind.

"I found the door back here. It's still in working order, I wonder if we coulda just used some stairs at the back and then made our way back through the hallway," Gene says, his voice is not upset with our rope descent, he simply sounds curious. For a moment, I think he's going to disappear down the hallway, but he just closes the door and heads back to us.

"I've got it!" Li says with excitement. She's up inside the bottommost bell, I can only see her feet and a faint glow from her flashlight. "I think I need some help dislodging the token from the …"

Li's grunts of exertion carry over to me and I sidestep my way over beams and rubble to get to her. Gene meets me at the bell's opening.

"What's the deal?" Gene asks, wanting to know how to help.

"Well, it's like the token is welded to the bell in some way." Li says between her exertions. "I can't pry it loose."

"Is it another cross?" I ask, I can't contain my curiosity.

"No. It's a star," she calls back. "It's like the last tokens, though, in that it's made up of separate metal pieces."

Gene starts digging through his packs, he still carries the original pack of an American soldier. He comes out with a couple of items.

"I have an old set of pliers—at least I think that's what they are— and a small hammer with a wooden handle," Gene calls. "What'd these soldiers need with these things anyway?"

"Gene, really, you want to discuss a soldier's supply kit right now?" Li snaps. She's frustrated from her efforts and lack of success. "Why don't you hand me a stake, if it's metal, and the hammer." I watch as Li shimmies out of the bell and stretches her body for a moment. Gene goes back into his supply pack and removes a metal stake, like you would see used to hold a tent pole securely in the ground, and hands it and the hammer to Li.

"Would you like some help?" Gene offers, trying to soothe Li's frayed nerves.

"No, it's too crowded up inside the bell for two of us" she says as she takes the two items from Gene. "Thanks," she adds sweetly as an afterthought.

CHAPTER 31

BUSHWHACKED

SOON WE HEAR A HAMMER strike the metal of the stake. A few more strikes and then a loud yelp. A soft mumble follows but I can't decipher it.

"Can someone shine light up in here; I can't see what I'm doing."

Gene and I both jump into action and we both shine our lights up into the bell.

Li waits for the light and then places the stake against something and swings the hammer a few times. I hear something come loose.

"Finally." Li mutters. More clanging follows and a minute later, Li begins to slide backward out of the bell.

She stands up holding five long metal objects. They look to be the same length and they look just like long metal sticks the way Li holds them. She hands the token to me and turns back to the bell. She retrieves the hammer and stake, and hands them over to Gene.

I quickly examine the token and see that that small grooves are cut into all but one of the metal pieces. I figure that this is how they lay atop one another to form the shape of a star.

"Let's get out of here." Gene says, already making his way over to the rope. Li takes the token from me and packs it away safely into her pack.

"We'll be right behind—"

Li is cut off by the opening of the door behind us. The three of us whip our heads around like we're synchronized together. A familiar voice booms across the space.

"I trust I've given you plenty of time to retrieve the third token," Rat Face says as he steps into the ruined room. He is just a shadow to my eyes, but I can see more shadows standing behind him. "I wouldn't trust that rope to hold out this time, why don't the three of you come with me."

I hear the sound of a weapon being cocked.

"Please," Rat Face adds with mock pleasantness.

I turn to Li. Her eyes are darting around the cavernous space, searching for an escape, wanting to formulate a plan. I can tell from her body language that nothing reveals itself. I flash my light in Gene's direction. I see the rope falling down to him; somebody above us cut the rope.

"I said please," Rat Face says with amusement in his voice. He knows we're out of options. Gene makes his way over to us.

"Stay close," Li whispers into my ear and then does the same with Gene.

We make our way out of the mess of beams and steel and head across the room. For the first time I notice the chairs and table stacked up near the walls. This room must have been used for storage before the bells came crashing through the floor. I look to get my bearings, noting that we are moving away from the front of the church. The passageway beyond probably runs the length of the church, with other rooms opening to the left and right.

Rat Face moves aside and indicates that we should precede him through the door. As we do, Gene and I closely flanking Li, I notice that I am right about the hallway. It's long and straight with a few doors in my line of sight.

I notice Billy the Fib is in Rat Face's group of men. He gives me a sneer, but saves most of his attention for Li. His sneer shifts to a leer as his eyes move from me to Li. Bile and anger rise within me. The bile I force down. The anger I allow to rise and bloom within me.

We take a few steps beyond the soldiers moving slowly down the hallway when I'm struck violently at the base of my neck.

Everything turns to black.

I COME AWAKE SLOWLY, THE DARKNESS receding at a snail's pace. I keep my eyes closed, but can tell that light fills the space

I occupy. I want to check the back of my head for blood, but realize my hands are bound to the chair that I slump in. My chest is
bound to the chair as well. A check of my legs and feet tells me
they're free of bindings.

I risk a peek with one squinted eye. I'm in a room that is well lit
by portable lamps of some kind, I also hear the hum of a generator.
A see a body slumped into a chair opposite me, fifteen feet separate us. At first I think it must be Gene, but when open my eye a
bit more, I realize it's not Gene or Li.

CHAPTER 32

WARFARE

I SLOWLY TURN MY HEAD TO my right and emptiness fills my view. A wall stands about eight feet away from me. I am positioned near the back of the room, whereas the human form across from me is near the front. I swivel my head slowly to the left, attempting to minimize the pain of movement, and I see Li sitting alert in her chair.

Seeing her awake, I open my eyes fully. Gene sits beyond Li, he is also awake.

Li notices my movement and turns to me. "Jake, so glad you're awake. How do you feel?" she asks, her only concern at the moment is me.

"I'm fine, probably feel a lot like you and Gene," I answer, hurrying on to other more important things. "Where are we? What happened? Who is the other person over there?"

"I think we're still underground in the church. We were knocked unconscious and brought to this room. The other guy looks like Richard Eriksson, our American soldier and helper," Li answers my questions in order. She asks me a question of her own. "Can you get free?"

I wrench and wriggle against my bindings, but they don't budge. I shake my head.

"Well, it was worth a shot. Gene and I can't get free either," she tells me. "We need to get out of here."

"Let's just ask Rat Face nicely, maybe he'll let us go," Gene tries and fails to inject some humor into his voice.

The door swings open on rusty hinges and Rat Face steps into the room.

"Well speak of the devil," Gene says with bravado. "And I mean that literally. We were just wonderin' if you'd be kind enough to let us go."

"I intend to do just that, Gene. But before I do, I wanted to take a minute and discuss something with you." Rat Face talks while playing at his manicured fingernails like we're in a fine restaurant sitting down for tea.

"Haven't we had this discussion before with your flunkies, Rat Face? I mean we're not gonna give up our Keys and go over to Evil, so why don't you just let us go?" Gene says mimicking Rat Face's tone.

"Now, why can't we be civilized about all of this? My name is Steven," Rat Face protests with exasperation. "I don't call you three hurtful names. Why can't you show me the same courtesy?"

"By showing courtesy, do you mean attacking us, beating us, and knocking us unconscious? Or do you mean holding us against our will and trying to cajole us into doing something against our will? It's hard to know how you define courtesy," Li analyzes his words, not bothering to hide her contempt.

Before Rat Face can respond, Gene jumps in, assuming an aristocratic voice. "This guy acts like he's some kind of gentleman villain. Gentlemen and lady, why can't we all just get along? Let's agree to destroy the world over tea and crumpets," he makes a snort of disgust at the end.

Rat Face shows just a hint of anger that is quickly replaced with a neutral look. "I didn't bring you here to ask you to join us," he begins. "I've already tried that personally and through others. No, I brought you here to demonstrate that this world isn't as simple as you make it out to be. Sometimes hard decisions must be made, and sacrifices are often required. I feel strongly that you need to understand this personally." Rat Face finishes with a wicked grin, one that sends chills up and down my spine. I let out an involuntary shiver. Rat Face sees it and his smile grows wider.

"Yes, Jake, hard decisions that will make your spine tingle and have you reliving them over and over and over again in your dreams and waking nightmares."

I feel an overwhelming sense of dread come over me. It fills the room quickly and completely, seeming to suffocate all other emotion and feeling. I have a hard time breathing. Whatever is coming will shape our lives from this moment forward. I know it. And I know Rat Face knows it.

"I have prepared an … exercise for the *Chosen*." Rat Face looks like he's eaten a lemon when he says Chosen. "A demonstration of what it means to make real world decisions. I, for one, am intrigued to see how you decide the fate of the world." Rat Face walks over to the man slumped unconscious in the chair. He nods to one of his thugs, who walks over with a bucket and splashes water into the man's face. He comes back to consciousness with a jerk. Only one eye opens; the other is swollen shut. Dried blood and bright purple bruises cover his face and exposed arms. I imagine by the way he holds himself that his torso and legs are no better. He has been beaten mercilessly. His open eye seeks out ours. He makes eye contact briefly and then lowers his head to his chest again, the effort of holding it up is too much.

"You may or may not recognize this man, so allow me reintroduce you to Corporal Richard Eriksson of the United States Army. He is your in-sector contact, the man who helped you with the letter and guided you to shelter." Rat Face turns away from Richard and walks back to us.

"My men have … worked hard at extracting all of the information from him that they could. To be honest, he wasn't much help in the end. He doesn't know much. Your parents were careful in compartmentalizing their secrets. But, I decided Richard could serve a good purpose for us after all." He pauses and spreads his arms dramatically. "The good Corporal will serve as the focal point of the demonstration. He will represent the problem you will have in making your decision."

Rat Face returns to Richard's side. "You see, Richard has been strapped to a bomb." He lifts the man's shirt and I see the wires and explosives running on and around his body.

I HEAR LI SUCK IN A breath of air. Gene is ominously silent. I feel my gorge rising and hives pushing to the surface of my skin. My breathing becomes rapid and shallow.

"I have set the timer for ten minutes." Rat Face points to the face of a watch that is attached to Richard's wrist. "As soon as I activate the timer, you will have ten minutes to decide who you will save. This one man, or the entire world by saving yourselves. You must know that if you sacrifice yourselves, the Keys will be lost and your Quest will end. End in death and misery."

Another dramatic pause from this vile merchant of pain and death. Anger begins to burble up in my stomach replacing the bile, I feel the heat of fury burn through my body.

"So, who will you choose?" Rat Face speaks as if he is casually lecturing a class with an air of self-importance. "This is what I mean by real-life decisions. You three walk through your so-called Quest all high-and-mighty, thinking you are above the down-and-dirty decisions of power. Well, now you have all the power in your hands. What will you do? I can't wait to find out!"

Rat Face gives another nod and men step up to us and begin cutting our bindings. Strong hands hold me from behind as our bindings are loosed. Rat Face takes no chances of a sudden attack. I see Li and Gene struggling against those holding them. They want to fight right now.

Rat Face is shaking his head. "No, no, no. It won't be as simple as fighting my men and me. We will leave you now to your decision. Good luck." He walks out of the room without another glance. I hear the soldiers shuffling out as well. Only a few remain, those holding us and several with weapons pointing at us.

Rat Face pokes his head back in the room; he is smiling wickedly. "Oh, I almost forgot, shoot all three of them with their own weapons. Real-life decisions are usually made under stress and pain."

He disappears again. Three soldiers holding weapons immediately begin firing at us. Out of the corner of my eye I see Li moving to duck and dodge. There are too many shooters and they are too close. I see her hit. And then I go down under the weight of several bullets. I'm hit in the shoulder, gut, and both legs. Pain blooms. And then the shooting stops and the door slams shut.

We're alone with Richard.

I let out a groan and sit up carefully rubbing the tender spots on my body. I look over at my friends. Gene is moaning and rolling over in an attempt to push himself up. Li is holding her neck and gasping for air while coming to her knees.

Rat Face has had us shot with our own wax bullets.

I manage to struggle to my feet. I think I escaped the worst of it. From the looks of Li and Gene, they took way more wax than I. I walk drunkenly over to Richard. He is barely conscious. Seeing him this close, tears spring to my eyes. He is terribly beaten; it appears so much worse up close.

I tear my eyes from his wounds and focus on the ticking clock on his wrist. Forty-five seconds have passed, we have just over nine minutes. "Jake, we have to go. We have to be well clear of this area when that bomb goes off," Gene urges. I stare disbelieving at him. How can he be so callous? But as I look closely I see his cheeks are stained with streaks of tears. He shakes his head. "Richard would tell us to go. Look at him, look at his eye."

I do. I bend down and carefully raise his head. His open eye is wide and I can tell he is trying to speak. His eyes are fierce. He wants us to leave—to save ourselves.

I feel a hand on my arm. A soft hand. Li's hand. "We have to think about the world, all the people in the future who are relying us to find and protect the Key. As much as I hate this, we need to go." Her eyes are pleading, filled with sadness.

I shake my head. I can't believe we have to make this decision. I just stare between my friends and Richard, a new friend. I'm frozen. I can't move. I can't make a decision like this. Who am I to decide who lives and who dies? My teeth grind together as my vision fills with the memory of Rat Face and his smarmy smile.

I feel Li and Gene gently pulling me away from Richard and toward the door. I can't help looking back toward Richard, his head has slumped back down on his chest.

Something I studied in the Training Center comes into my mind. Something a creator of the atomic bomb said when he saw a bomb test detonated in the deserts of New Mexico. "'I am become death, the destroyer of worlds'." I mumble as I'm being pulled toward the door.

"What?" Li asks mildly, concern in her eyes as she meets mine.

I shake free of their hands and stand facing Richard.

"That is what Oppenheimer said when he saw the atomic bomb detonated. I am become death, destroyer of worlds." I say with anger in my voice. "I will not ... I cannot leave this man to die. I'm staying."

"What?" This time Li's voice is high-pitched and panicky.

I turn to my friends. "This is the insidious nature of power. And nuclear power pales in comparison to the threat of destroying human life—human virtue," I start, my voice strong. "That is what they come seeking. This is why they want the Key. We seek the Key to protect life. To embolden virtue within us. To build something bigger than ourselves."

I begin to cross the room to Richard. "They seek the Key to destroy life. To subvert virtue and therefore subject humankind. To build themselves bigger than life." I point to Richard and stare into the faces of my friends. "This man is our Quest, don't you see? He is symbolic of us all. Without the Keys, we are bound and ticking down to our own destruction. No virtue. No character. No humanity. No future.

"I know we must live. But so must Richard, and all the Richards to come. I need him to live for me to live. I need him. We need him. In my mind, if I leave him to die, then I am no better than Rat Face. I don't decide who lives and who dies and neither does he. My decision is simple. I need Richard because Richard represents everything that I am fighting for on this crazy Quest.

My shoulders slump a little and I take a heaving breath. My eyes never leave theirs. "I need to save him."

I search their faces for some clue as to what they are thinking. "Gene and Li. Our needs become our dreams. Our dreams become our visions. Our visions become our salvation. Let's turn our need to vision, and figure out how to get him out of here with us," I beseech them, my voice desperate and pleading now.

Li and Gene share a look. "Okay, Jakers, tell us what to do," Gene says simply.

Relief floods my body.

I turn to Richard and mark the time. We have just over six minutes left. "Six minutes," I say and then inspect the bomb. "Two sets of wires run from the explosives to this box behind him. "Li, keep the time. Gene come over here with me."

CHAPTER 33

BOMB

I KNEEL DOWN AT THE BOX behind Richard.

"Do you know how to disarm a bomb?" Gene asks hopefully. "Did you study it in the Training Center?"

I flick a quick look at Gene, then Li. They both look hopeful. "No. I've never even seen a bomb in person before. This wasn't part of my studies. But necessity is the mother of invention, right?" I add this last part in a pathetic attempt to keep hope alive.

The breaths I hear from both of them tell me all I need to know. They think we're going to die. And I guess I think so, too.

"Okay, think …" I mutter, mostly to myself. I squeeze my eyes shut for a minute. "A bomb has a timer, some source of power to send the charge, detonators and explosives. This box must hold the power." I reach out and carefully remove the lid on the box.

A battery.

That's what it looks like inside. I'm reminded of watching my dad help jump start a car. Wires are attached to two nodes – red and black. I trace these wires back along the ground and then up into the explosives strapped to Richard.

Richard sees me out of his good eye. His body goes rigid and he struggles to speak. "Get out …" Richard manages to croak. "Leave …" His eyes are fierce and angry.

I meet his gaze with a fierceness of my own. "No."

I watch tears well up in his eye. His head slumps back down to his chest, the effort of speaking sapping his energy.

"Five minutes," Li whispers.

"Okay, these two wires run to the battery back here. So, is it reasonable to think that if we detach the correct wire the bomb will be rendered useless?"

"Uh, Jake, we have no earthly idea," Gene says, panic in full bloom.

"I'm just talking out loud now, Gene." I try to smile at him. "Remember, it's our process. I bounce ideas off of you and we find our answer."

I take a half-second to wonder how I am so calm at this time. I guess my decision has been made, my destiny thrown in with Richard's, and I'm comfortable with that. Plus, I've never failed to solve a puzzle, so is this any different? Okay, I admit that it's a lot different.

"One of these wires must be the grounding wire and the other is the one that sends the charge to detonate and make the stuff go boom. But which one?"

I try and think of that old battery. Red and black. Positive and negative. Charged and grounded. "Is red positive or negative?" I say aloud.

"Are ya talkin' 'bout a battery, like in a car?" Gene says with his full drawl. Again I see this is his natural state of being.

I nod.

"Red is positive. Black is negative and can be used to ground," he says with confidence. "I help Pa out with maintenance of the trucks."

I look at the battery and the red and black wires attached to the metal nodes protruding from the battery. "So, do we detach the positive or the negative?" I hesitantly reach out toward the wires.

"Four minutes," Li calls.

I reach forward toward the black wire. "Here goes nothing."

"Please, please, please be nothin,'" Gene prays.

As I touch the black wire at the node, I receive a shock, like when you rub your feet around on the carpet and then touch something. I pull my hand back quickly and let out a gasp. Gene lets out a yelp and Li screams.

My heart beats so fast I think it's going to burst right out of my chest. I sit back and take several moments to calm my beating heart. I need to think clearly.

"Geez, Jakers, what was that?"

"It gave me a little shock. Sorry about that," I say. "Actually though, I think I'm going to unwind the red wire—that's the one carrying the charge into the explosives, so I think that is the one to remove.

I close my eyes and take a deep breath. As I reach toward the red wire I realize that I'm now holding my breath, and that seems appropriate.

"Three minutes," Li tells me, her voice cracking a little.

I turn to her. Really? Already? That was fast. Her eyes are pleading with mine, pleading to save not only Richard's life, but hers.

I begin to unwind the red wire from the battery node.

"Wait!" I yell to myself and move my shaking hand away from the red wire.

Gene is holding his chest like he's trying to massage his heart. "I can't believe I dinnit die right then. Jake, you are scarin' me ta death."

"Me, too, Gene ... me, too," I mutter as I stand and move back to Richard. "I just remembered something very important. There are two set of wires running from Richard's body."

I point to the twin sets of wires. The set that runs to the battery we have been working with, and a second set running off to the other side of him. I follow these wires to a bench. Behind the bench is hidden a second box—a second battery.

"Oh, crap," I say as I stumble to the floor next to the box. "There is a second battery. A back up power source. A fail-safe."

I look up at Li, then Gene. "If I had detached that red wire it would have triggered this one," I swallow dryly, realizing I have no spit in my mouth. Reflexively, I lick my lips.

"Two minutes," Li calls.

"Seriously? I swear that thing is speeding up," Gene says, not bothering to try and hide his panic.

"Gene, we're going to need to do this together, okay? Now's the time to test your theory of knowing exactly what's going on in my head, because we need to remove the wires from the battery at the exact same time. So when I send the nerve impulse in my brain, you need to send yours," I say with a smile, trying to get a smile from Gene.

He just stares at me disbelieving, mouth agape. "Jake, I don't really—"

"I know, Gene, just do your best," I say reassuringly, although I don't feel anything near sure. "Let's unwind the wrapped wire that is exposed and touching the metal node, but do not remove it from the node yet. Just get it ready."

Gene nods shakily and sets to work. I do the same on mine.

"Mine's really twisted tight on this here node." Gene says without looking up. Mine is tougher than I thought, as well. The bare wire is stiff and difficult to unwind. Rat Face must've used tools to tighten the wires.

The flesh on my fingers is torn as I work the wire and blood mixes with the wire. I grit my teeth and struggle with the wire.

"One minute!" Li calls desperately.

I double my effort on the wires. I glance at Gene and see he has as well.

"Forty-five seconds."

I'm almost there. Just a few more twists of the wire.

"Thirty seconds."

"I got mine ready!" Gene calls, never moving his eyes from the wire.

"Okay, I'm ready too."

"Fifteen seconds."

On the count of three, remove the wires." I call to Gene.

"One, two, thr—"

"Wait!" Gene yells.

"Ten seconds!" Li's voice cracks in panic.

"Do we remove at three or one, two, three, go?" Gene asks wildly.

"Go!" I say. "One, two, three—go!"

I pull the wires away from the metal. I look up to see Gene has done the same. We both look to Li.

"Zero," she says so softly I barely hear her. Her eyes are tightly shut. I realize my eyes are shut also. I open them.

The room is quiet. No sound. No explosion. I carefully tuck the red wire away from the battery.

A slow smile spreads across my face. I look to Gene then Li. Li fills my vision as she bowls me over in an adrenaline spike hug. Next thing I know, Gene has joined us and we are on the ground in a euphoric group hug.

After a few long moments, we untangle and sit up.

Li slugs Gene in the arm. "Seriously, Gene, with the whole, 'Do we do it on three or go?' I thought we were dead right then. I'm watching that stupid watch tick down and then you yell, 'Wait!'"

Gene shrugs. "I had ta get 'er right. I woulda hated ta kill us 'cause I pulled mine away on three, with Jake waitin' for go."

Li smiles a wild smile and turns to me. "I'm proud of you, Jake. You made the right decision The need became the vision."

I reach out to touch her neck carefully, there is a nasty looking red welt swelling.

"Are you okay?" I ask.

She reaches up and folds her hand around mine. "I'm fine. One of those jerks hit me with a wax bullet right in the throat. I thought it was over for me. I couldn't breathe for a minute, but it worked out. I owe that guy one, though."

I turn to Gene, meaning to ask how he feels from the wax, but my question stops in my throat. He is watching Li and me with a twisted smile.

"So how long have you two been holdin' hands?" Gene asks, our near-death experience firmly in the background now, as he has a new joke to focus on. "'Cause from where I'm sittin', I can tell this isn't the first time you two have found each other's hands. Am I right?"

Li lets go of my hand and pushes herself up, all business now.

CHAPTER 34

TWO GENERALS

"WE NEED TO GET OUT of here and to somewhere safe. Rat Face will know now that the bomb didn't detonate. He might be on his way back here already," she says, moving to untie Richard.

"Li, I see whatcha doin', but seein' as how yer right, I'm gonna leave this hand-holdin' discussion for another time, but don't think that I'm forgettin' 'bout it." Gene says, moving over to help Li.

Li doesn't acknowledge Gene. She just continues to work on Richard. Richard is hefted up with his weight spread between Gene and Li. I move over to the chairs we were held in and find that our packs sit behind them. Why didn't Rat Face take the tokens? The answer comes immediately. He expected us to leave Richard behind and save ourselves. And he needs us to find the Key, so he can take it from us.

Or maybe he doesn't need that much from us, but he does need us to find the fourth token, so he left the others with us, thinking he'll take all four from us at the same time.

"Let's move," Li urges, as she and Gene pass me with Richard between them.

I gather up all of our packs and awkwardly swing them over my shoulders. We move as quickly as we can with Richard in tow. I hustle ahead of them to scout out the hallway. The room we were being kept in is near the end of the long hallway. I can see a stairway leading up and out of the basement.

"Careful, Jake. We don't know where Rat Face and his men

went, they could be waiting for us upstairs," Li calls, her breathing labored as she struggles under Richard's weight.

"They wouldn't wait this close; they were expecting the bomb to go off," I call back to her and head up the stairs.

"Jake!" Li yells at me, but I continue upward.

The sun shines down on my face and I have to squint to see anything. I'd almost forgotten that we're underneath a church that has been destroyed. No roof to protect my eyes from the sun.

I squint around as my eyes adjust to the light. I don't see any-body nearby. This area seems deserted, like when we arrived. After a moment to get my bearings, I see now that the sun is actually on its way down for the day. We must have been unconscious longer than I thought.

I hear the others struggling up the stairs. I turn and offer assis-tance to them in getting out of the stairwell. Gene and Li help Richard down onto the floor, leaning him against a portion of rear wall that still stands.

"Stay with Richard while I do a quick scout of the area," Li doesn't wait for a reply. She disappears out the back of the dam-aged structure.

I kneel and rummage through the packs until I find a canteen. I shake it to ensure water is inside. I put it up to Richard's lips and help him get some water down his throat. He licks at it thirstily, although most of the water runs down his chin.

I move to return the canteen to the pack when a firm hand grips my arm. I turn, expecting Gene, and am surprised when I see it's Richard who has hold of my arm. His grip is surprisingly strong. His mouth forms the words *thank you*. Tears stream down his face. I blink away my own as soon as I see his.

"You're welcome," I return, unable to say more. Enough has passed between us in unspoken ways, however. I pat his arm and find a place for the canteen.

Li is gone longer than I anticipate, and I begin to feel nervous about her absence. I'm just about to tell Gene that I'm going to look for her when she reappears around the wall.

"I found some soldiers to bring Corporal Eriksson to a nearby hospital here in the American sector," she says when wonder of wonders, several men come around the wall behind her. She directs them in lifting Richard, and soon they are lumbering off into the growing dusk. Li watches them for a bit and then turns back to Gene and me.

"We need to move. On the way back with the soldiers, I asked them about passing over into the Russian sector. They gave me directions along with some warnings. I think we should head for the sector right now. There is no time to lose."

Gene and I form up next to her.

"What did we lose besides our weapons?" Li asks me.

"I don't think we lost anything," I say, motioning to the packs. "The tokens are still all there and our other supplies, so …" I'm still thinking about why Rat Face would leave us with the tokens and our packs.

"Rat Face still needs us," Li concludes. "Otherwise, why would he leave the tokens behind? He doesn't know where to find the fourth token, or where to find the Key, that much is clear."

"Neither do we," Gene comments, reminding us that we are no closer to the Key and have no idea where to begin looking for the fourth token.

"We've always sort of run into a soldier that our parents left a letter with, right? So I guess that will have to do in the Soviet sector as well," Li concludes.

I nod in agreement.

We set out, leaving the ruined church behind and moving quickly in a northerly direction. Toward East Berlin. This could be tricky, I think, as we move forward.

"Isn't East Berlin to the east?" I ask Li.

Without turning she answers. "The quickest route to the Russian sector is north and east of our current position."

I shrug, knowing I can trust Li. We walk in silence for about a mile, covering the distance quickly, our little group running almost completely on adrenaline. We come to a wide road that must be a main thoroughfare through the heart of Berlin and turn right. Now we are walking almost due east.

After covering another several hundred yards, we come to signs that tell us that we are entering the Soviet sector of Berlin. This barrier is more noticeable than all of the other sectors we have crossed over. Passing from the French to British to American sectors meant little more than seeing a small sign and crossing a street. However, here the military presence of both Americans and Russians is more evident.

We pass ruined buildings, burnt-out cars with tires and doors strewn everywhere. As we step up to the barrier between the Soviet and American sectors, an American soldier stops us.

"Do you have business in east Berlin?" he asks, careful to keep his tone friendly.

"Yes. Something of ours was left behind there and we were sent to retrieve it." Li says firmly.

"You were sent?" the soldier asks dubiously.

Li nods.

"Be careful. I can't keep you from passing over, but we can't offer you any protection either," he tells us. We must look to him like beggars, homeless and wandering the streets. Our clothes don't fit and have obviously been scrounged from others, our faces are dirty and bodies worn. Add the giant welt on Li's neck and we must be quite a show.

Li nods again and moves forward, boldly leaving the west behind. Full dark has now fallen and I realize I desperately need rest. I turn to tell Gene about my weariness when I see a Russian soldier approaching us.

"I couldn't help but overhear you conversation with the G.I. Joe there," the soldier says, waving to the American soldier who is still watching us.

None of the three of us speak.

"I've been waiting for you to come," he says with a smile. "Please follow me, you look like you need food and sleep."

Although we have been half-expecting this, we are still wary. Maybe it's the Russian military that has us hesitant. Li finally moves forward after a few wordless exchanges between the three of us.

I realize as we walk with our new guide that we have nothing to give the soldier in exchange for a letter that he surely must be carrying. I wonder how we are to verify one another's credentials.

The soldier leads us around a corner and I realize we are disappearing from the view of the American. Just as I think this, strong hands grab me and a rag or cloth is held up over my mouth and nose. The fumes are noxious and I cough a bit. I strain to turn my head, wondering about Li and Gene. The hands holding me don't allow my head to turn. My eyes go wide as I realize I am slipping into unconsciousness.

FOR THE SECOND TIME IN twenty-four hours I come awake slowly, although this time with no crack on the back of head. Whatever took me to unconsciousness did however leave me with a splitting headache that runs from my eyeballs all the way to the rear of my head.

I try to move my hand up to my head to cradle it and give it some relief, but again, my hands are bound to a chair.

Rat Face was waiting for us after all, I think.

"Wake up!" A voice shouts next to my ear. I might go deaf from the proximity of the shout. I lean my head away from the noise and slowly open my eyes. Li and Gene are bound next to me, this time we form a sort of ragged circle in the middle of a bare room. A single light bulb hangs from the ceiling in the center of the room, directly over where we are seated.

A man stands over the three of us, staring maliciously at us.

Not Rat Face.

I don't recognize the man. He is dressed in a Russian military uniform with quite a few ribbons and medals hanging from his chest. He must be someone fairly important. The man has dark eyes that look black as coal separated by a wide nose, and full lips droop below the nose. His most prominent features are thick dark eyebrows and a high forehead with wavy hair sitting atop it.

"My name is General Nikolai Berzarin, and I am the man in charge here in Soviet Berlin," he says, spittle flying from his mouth. I catch a couple of droplets on my cheek. "You are looking for something that was … lost, I understand."

"Well, hello there, General Nikolai, I—"

Gene's head snaps back from the vicious slap delivered by the General.

"I did not ask you to speak." More spittle flies from the General's mouth. "You will not speak to me unless I give you permission to do so. And then you will do so in as few words as possible. Save your pathetic buddy routine for someone else."

Gene does not speak again but does give the General a murderous stare.

The General waits as if he is goading Gene into speaking again. Finally, a wicked smile spreads across his vile face.

"No? You don't want to be hit again? Good. Now, shut up and listen." The General says. "You three are going to—"

"Wait," Gene interrupts, head cast down for the moment. "Did you just refer to what you did to me as a 'hit'? Gene raises his head up proudly now, still wearing a ferocious look. "'Cause where I come from that's a slap. And only cowards slap."

General Berzarin's face moves through all of the shades of red and purple. His anger is boiling over.

"So, listen, General Nikolai whatever-you-said-your-last-name was, if yer gonna hit a fella, go ahead and make a fist like a real man."

The General lets out a low growl and steps toward Gene, fist clenching and cocking back behind him.

The door swings open behind the General, and I see a man dressed similarly to our current General.

"General! Stop. Right. Now." This new military man says, his voice deep and commanding. This is a man who is used to having all of his orders obeyed immediately.

General Berzarin stops bringing his fist forward as soon as he hears the voice. But he leaves it cocked and ready. He seems to be deciding how to proceed.

The new man walks briskly to the General's side. He towers over the General and his authority alone practically pushes the General back a step.

"Drop that fist, soldier," the new man says. "These are my prisoners. I have had my soldiers on alert for them for days now. I would watch my step, Nikolai." When the man finishes, he is inches away from the General's face, leaning down and forcing the General to arch his back away in a clear sign of submission.

"This isn't the end," General Berzarin spits, then turns and moves out of the room. Before he reaches the door, Gene can't help himself and speaks. "Oh and General? Stop slapping people like some little coward, okay?"

The General slows briefly and I think he's going to turn around, but his hesitation is brief and he continues out without a backward glance. The new man orders all soldiers out of the room and has the door closed behind the departing soldiers. He moves a chair from the corner over to where the three of us are bound.

"Hello, my name is G.K. Zhukov, and for the time being I have more authority than that man," he says warmly, then his voice turns cautionary. "I would advise that you not cross him, however, he is a dangerous man. Most of the soldiers in the city are his, if you know my meaning."

Li gives Gene a withering look, as if to say thanks for pushing the buttons of the most dangerous man in east Berlin. Gene gives her his best *I'm innocent* look.

"Now, we must hurry if you are to accomplish your goals here in Berlin," he says, removing something from a pocket of his coat. "I, like General Berzarin, am well aware of your … situation here. I have something for you to read." He hands over the letter, he reaches out and places it into my bound hand. "Please read it quickly."

All three of us are about to protest at about the same time, how can we read something when we are bound to these chairs? G.K. stands and flicks a knife open and gets to work on freeing each one of us. In seconds, we are free. I flex my fingers and wrists for a few seconds to get the blood pumping through them again, and then move somewhat clumsily to open the envelope.

It looks just as the others, and I know what we will find inside. I hold the letter out so Li and Gene can read it with me. They scoot their chairs in close for a better look.

> *Chosen,*
>
> *This letter is unique, I think. We who write it and you who read it will surely know one another. The three of us, in our time, say to the three of you, we miss you!*
>
> *Now, the Quest to gather the Key is upon you. We have recovered the lost Key and placed in a protected place until you can retrieve it for the final time.*
>
> *The Key was difficult to get back from those evil ones who held it for so long.*
>
> *You will require four tokens to unlock the mystery of this Key. These tokens are spread throughout the city, one in each sector. You must not leave a sector of the city until that sector's token has been retrieved, you may not be allowed back.*
>
> *To safeguard the Key, we have followed the usual proto-cols. Brain, Brawn, and Buddying will all be required for each*

token.

We have left communications behind with individuals you can trust in each sector who may assist you in your Quest, use them wisely. Employ honor and honesty to find what you seek.

The final token is located in the Soviet sector. This final token will be held in the possession of a trusted friend. There is no code to decrypt in this sector. Time is of the essence at this point.

You may not know it, but there are many forces seeking the Key for their own purposes. Each government that has descended upon Berlin divided up the city in an effort to locate the Key for its own purpose. Some seek it for evil purposes, some believe they are doing it to protect the Key from the others, but the Key cannot fall into any government's hands. On top of this, the remnants of the Nazi regime also seek to recover the Key. And of course, you know about the forces of evil seeking the Key; we assume you have already had encounters with them.

So the final step in recovering the Key is a sort of race. But this is a race where only you have the tokens that will give you access to the Key.

Do not leave the tokens behind.

The man who gave you this letter is part of our cause. He does not want his government or any of the forces of evil to have the Key. He is trustworthy. He is General G.K. Zhukov.

And he is the final token! As a sign between you, please provide him with the three previous letters and papers.

May you be blessed in your Quest.

Sarah Sigurdsson
Thor Conklin
Zhang Ming Wun
Chosen of the Quest

We wish you smooth sailing!

CHAPTER 35

UNDERGROUND

I FINISH AND LOOK TO MY friends. Their confusion and wonder matches my own. I then look to General Zhukov. While we were engrossed with the letter, he has removed something else from his pocket. He holds pieces of metal in his hands, similar to those that make up our tokens.

"Do you have the previous letters and papers?" He asks.

I reach into my pack and remove the Vigenère square and the letter from my mom. Gene retrieves his letter. Li does the same. We are reluctant to hand over these letters. They are memories – keepsakes – from our parents. Finally, I hand my letter, Vigenère square and scrap of paper over to the General. Gene and Li follow suit after a moment.

The General accepts them as if they are valuable historical documents, which I guess they are. He is staring at the three of us oddly, like he is trying to solve some internal puzzle. As I study him, something clicks into place in his eyes. This seems to jolt him a bit in his chair. He begins speaking slowly, testing his newfound knowledge.

"You … are their children," he says slowly, moving his eyes from Li to Gene and finally to me. His voice holds awe. "I suspected they had somehow come to me from a different time and now here you are, the close images of them, with many of their same mannerisms."

We say nothing, but I think he confirms his theory from the look on my face. I've never been one to conceal my thoughts and emotions. Now is no different. His eyes lock into mine. "Sarah …

is your mother," G.K. says this as a question. His eyes penetrate mine. I drop my eyes and give a small nod. "And Thor is your father, and Michael is your father." Gene and Li both nod almost imperceptibly. *Michael?* I think. But now isn't the time.

The General strikes a match and set fire to the papers we have handed to him. He waits for the fire to consume them, dropping them to the floor as the flames burn close to his fingers. He stomps a boot over the ashes and scatters them across the floor. Another connection to my mom gone. A pang of heartache slams into me. I take a huge breath to cover my anguish. Gene's arm comes around my shoulders reassuringly. The General notices my bare emotion.

"I'm sorry," he composes himself and stands. "We must hurry. I have new packs with fresh supplies waiting for you, as well as transportation."

He begins moving toward the door. We follow. He stops and turns back to us. "I almost forgot to give you these," he holds the metal pieces out to us. "Your ... parents gave these to me to pass on to you."

I take them and slide them into my pack alongside the French cross.

"I hope you understand that I must keep us some appearances; therefore, I cannot take you to your destination personally, but I have drawn up a map that will deliver you to the destination." The General pushes some papers into Li's hands. "Also, I have provided a personal letter that will allow you to pass into your destination without trouble. Just show the letter to the soldiers posted at the entrance and you will be allowed to enter ... I guess in that way I am your token." He finishes with a small smile.

"Where are we goin'?" Gene asks.

The General stops with his hand on the door and ensures that all three of us are listening. "Underground."

Gene seems to deflate in front of us all.

"The underground tunnels of Berlin are shrouded in mystery. It is believed the Nazis greatly expanded the tunnels in secret, housing great wealth and treasure there. But of course, these are just rumors." The General waves a dismissive hand and then seems to reconsider. "Obviously, your parents found something under-ground, so there must be some truth to the rumors."

The General holds out a hand and we each grasp it in turn sharing a warm handshake. "Go to the Brandenburg Gate and present my letter to the Captain charge, a Captain Ivanovich. He will show you to the underground staircase. Good Luck … and say hello to your parents."

He moves to turn the doorknob, hesitates and then turns back to us, roughly embracing each of us in a large bear hug. As soon as the hug begins, it ends, and the General is opening the door. In the hallway, his rough manner is back in place as he barks orders and we all head out.

General Zhukov shows us to our transportation. Motorcycles. Two of them, not three. One has a sidecar attached. He apologizes for the lack of a third, then points us to the new supply packs tucked into the sidecar. He moves away to his car and disappears.

"I can't fit into that tiny sidecar, so I'll let the two of you figure that out." Gene says with a smile. He swings a leg over the other motorcycle and fires it up.

"I am not sitting in that sidecar," Li says with finality and she swings a leg up and over the motorcycle seat. I wonder for a second if I should be offended or argue with her. Then I remember that I have no idea how to operate a motorcycle, so I just shrug my way into the sidecar, shoving the packs aside and wedging myself into the space. I hear Gene laughing over the roar of the engines and show him a wide smile.

"You don't know how to ride one of these babies, do ya?" Gene yells to me. I shake my head and reach over and pat Li's leg, showing him that I have a chauffeur. He laughs louder now and turns to Li. "You have the map, right? I'll follow you. Apparently, we have to hustle."

With that, Li hands me the map and leans down to my ear. She looks funny in her goggles and helmet. And so do I, I'm sure. "Hold the map and help me out. I've memorized it, but might need your help with navigation."

We run into no trouble while covering the miles between our current destination and the Brandenburg Gate. It turns out that after we were rendered unconscious by General Berzarin's soldiers, we were brought to Karlshorst and the Soviet military headquarters of Berlin. Karlshorst is the furthest we have been from the center of Berlin, and it takes us a half an hour to wind our way through rubble and the scattered hulks of burnt-out cars.

The sun is setting on the city as we near the gate. We must've have been unconscious for the better part of the day. My body clock is completely messed up. I think I should be hungry and tired, but my mind isn't sure what to think. Sometimes, adrenaline is a wonderful thing.

We slow as we near the city center. More traffic, mostly pedestrian or military, congests the streets. I motion for Li to pull over and yell into her ear that we should find a place to eat before we head underground. She tells me this is a good idea, and pulls over into an alley.

"Did you study anything about the underground at the Training Center?" Gene asks me as he plows through some meat, cheese, and bread that he has made into a crude sandwich. He's trying to hide his anxiety over going back underground.

"There wasn't much information. Just as General Zhukov said, there isn't much known about the tunnels, other than it was a massive project undertaken by the Nazis, but never completed and maybe even destroyed by them near the end of the war. Perhaps the most famous underground area is the Furherbunker, where Hitler killed himself at the end—I guess not too far distant in history from when we are now."

Gene looks less than pleased.

"Gene, these are tunnels and bunkers created strategically for military and government purposes – they are not a bunch of crypts and bones. You have nothing to worry about. This will be more like the Old Dragon's Head or the Training Center, and you did fine in those places." I end with a smile to reassure him.

He smiles also and chuckles. "I'm sure you're right, little sidecar buddy." He can't resist a jab at me to take the attention away from his personal phobia. I let it go.

"Let's go." Li says, sounding too much like General Zhukov with her commanding tone. "We are in a race, remember."

Gene and I share a smile. Li is mentally gearing up for whatever may come, and her skills will most likely be needed. With her back to Gene, she slips out of her tough persona and gives me a smile and wink. I'm pretty sure Gene sees the color rise in my cheeks, but he doesn't say anything as he starts his bike again.

"We have a letter for Captain Ivanovich," Li says with authority, her hands clasped behind her rigid back. Gene and I stand just behind her, trying to match her intensity. The soldier looks over us for a second longer than he should, and Li takes advantage of his hesitation. "Is there a problem, soldier?"

This snaps him out of his thoughts and he moves smartly out of view, presumably going to inform the Captain of our presence. A few minutes pass and I can tell Li is beginning to feel nervous. She is shifting her weight from one foot to the other and back in an effort to stay loose and ready for a fight.

After another minute the soldier returns trailing a tall, thin man who moves with the grace of an athlete—or a predator.

"I am Captain Ivanovich; my aide tells me that you have a letter from General Zhukov," he curtly informs us.

Li nods and produces the letter without a word. The Captain also takes it wordlessly and opens the letter, careful not to let the prying eyes of his aide see the words. After he finishes, he tucks the letter carefully into an inside pocket of his uniform and asks us to follow him.

"Stay here," he says to the aide, who looks disappointed, but does not question his superior.

We follow the Captain, who is moving briskly through the area of the gate. The Brandenburg Gate, much like most of Berlin, has seen better days. Although, we have come to the gate from the east I can see the faint outlines of trees that mark the end of the Tiergarten on the west of the gate. This marks the symbolic center of Berlin, with the British occupied sector to the west of the gate, and the Soviet sector to the east. The American sector is not too far to the south, with what would become the famous Checkpoint Charlie a stone's throw south of the gate, and the southern tip of the French sector just to the north. The Brandenburg Gate acts as sort of a hub of a wheel with the four sectors branching off from it.

Rubble and what looks like metal rebar are piled everywhere along the wide street that leads east from the gate. Bullet pockmarks are everywhere along the buildings, and even in the burnt-out husks of cars along the side of the road. Cleanup of this area has begun in earnest, as the wide street is relatively clear of debris, until we get quite near the Gate itself.

The Gate is decorative in nature, with twelve large columns holding up the archway and a decorative chariot and horses atop.

The twelve gates create five passageways through which a person can walk.

We end up on the northern side in the final of the five passageways. Captain Ivanovich stops halfway through the gate and feels his way along the wall. I hear a popping sound and then air releasing as a hidden door opens inward. I never would've guessed that a door was along this walkway. It is completely hidden and blends in with the rest of the wall so well that unless you know it's there, you would walk right by.

The Captain stands aside and motions us inside with quick waves of his hands. His eyes scan every direction in an effort to ensure that our entrance goes unnoticed. He doesn't follow us inside, and before we know it the door is swinging shut. Gene and I stand there staring as the door shuts us into total darkness. I'm sure our mouths hang open in dumb wonder. Li rustles quickly through her new pack and produced a flashlight. It's beam shines like a beacon in the narrow space.

The air is musty and stale. I wonder how much oxygen hangs in this narrow space. Enough, I guess, although I don't want to stay here for long. The walls run all the way up to the top of the gate, and I realize the entire portion of this wall is hollow. I run my hand along the wall, as if to ensure that what I am seeing is real. The rough stone registers in my senses and I know it's real. The narrow passageway runs for thirty feet, east to west.

"Don't just stand there looking dumb; get your flashlight out and let's figure out where this leads," Li says, the command clear in her voice.

Gene and I take a minute to fumble through our packs and produce our lights. Their beams join Li's in searching the narrow passageway.

"Only one way to go, I guess," Gene offers, stating the obvious. We make our way along the narrow passageway toward what must be the end of the column wall. Dead-end. Li's light moves to the floor, and a stairway downward is revealed.

"I'll lead us down with Gene bringing up the rear," she says in the commanding voice.

The staircase is metal and spirals down in a tight circle. It looks like a decorative staircase in a museum or mansion, out of place here in the darkness. The metal creaks and moans as our weight presses down on it, and I hope it holds.

"Do we know where we're headed down here?" Gene calls from above us. "I mean, we don't know where to go from here. Our parents didn't leave us a map did they?" Gene knows full well that our parents didn't leave us a map, he's just talking, and I sense it's to keep his own mind occupied and off the claustrophobic nature of this underground space.

"I'm certain that there will be markers down here to point us to our destination," I call back over my shoulder, not nearly as confident as I sound. We reach the bottom of the stairs and I calculate that we have descended twenty feet below the road above.

We flash our lights around, in an effort to get our bearings. We are standing in a small cavern that has been carved roughly out of the rock. Heavy wooden support beams line the walls, with two placed along the center line of the room for added protection. The room appears to be sealed. I don't see a door or passageway on any of the walls. Thinking of what we have just done, I point my beam to the floor and walk the room scanning for a hatch or opening in the floor. Nothing.

"Over here," Gene calls while he examines something along the wall farthest from the staircase. Li and I form up next to him and look at the point of light on the wall where we discern marks etched on the surface of the wall. "They're faint, barely even scratches, but I think they are our map."

Li leans even closer to the wall, coming up on her tiptoes to see what Gene is seeing. "The signs of the Chosen," she murmurs. "And then a key, but the key is pointing downward, like it's falling."

I can barely make out the faint scratches, and I lean in so close my nose is almost touching the wall. As I do, the key beneath my shirt clanks against the wall like a magnet. It lines up exactly with the hanging key scratched into the wall.

Rumbling sounds follow and then a portion of the wall next to the markings slides open revealing a passageway that leads off into the darkness. I peel myself away from the wall; the magnetic connection is stronger than I imagine.

"Well done, Jakers," Gene says with a smile and a slap to my back.

"I didn't mean to do that, I was just trying to see what you were looking at," I say sheepishly.

"Maybe your mom knew you'd need glasses and need to get close," Gene says.

"Mom had perfect vision and how would she know that my eyes would be bad?" I say, scoffing at Gene's ridiculous theory.

"My father has terrible vision. Well at least he did until he had Lasik surgery, but my point is my father was the Brain and maybe they assumed that the next Brain would also need to get close," Li muses, then adds, "plus, the scratches were pretty faint—the odds of one of us stepping close enough to trigger the magnet were pretty high."

"Can't argue with that," Gene says with a grin, shining his flashlight on his face and holding it just below his chin to give his face an eerie glow.

I can't tell if he means *can't* argue with Li, or *won't* argue with her. This brings a smile to my face as I think of either Gene or me disputing Li's wisdom down here in the dark underground. It doesn't seem smart to cross Li, especially down here.

"I missed whatever the two of you are sharing a secret laugh about," Li tells us, and then moves off down the hallway. Over her shoulder she calls, "Gene, watch our rear."

The carefree walk through Berlin with Li, holding hands and talking easily, seems so far away and long ago. Now, she is a different person, focused and precise. How can she send a warm shiver through me with a soft touch at one minute and then send a cold shiver through me the next? *Girls*. Especially this girl.

"Check the walls carefully. Based upon the last scratches, our next sign will be hard to see. Only for our eyes, I guess," she turns around to look at us while she talks.

We spend an eternity traversing this hallway, carefully examining the walls for the next scratches. The hallway must be unending. We haven't passed any cross hallways, or doors, or anything to break up the monotony of the walls. If I have my bearings correct from above, we are moving in a northerly direction; other than this, I don't know what is above us.

I calculate that we have covered roughly 3,300 feet or two-thirds of a mile. At a brisk pace, we could cover this distance in a matter of minutes, but with our careful search of the walls, it has taken us over thirty minutes.

At this point, we see our first change from the endless walls and walkway. A door is set into the wall on the right-hand side. There is no knob or handle. We stop to investigate our first change of scenery since we entered the hallway. The door is flat with no markings. Gene pushes on the door without success. He even holds his key out to the door. Nothing happens.

CHAPTER 36

BRUSH WITH THE ENEMY

"WELL, I'M FRESH OUT OF ideas," he admits, turning to Li and me. "Maybe this isn't even a door that we need to worry about."

Li and I shake our heads at the same time.

"No markings and no handle mean this is exactly the door we are looking for," Li murmurs, closely examining the door.

"Do you hear that?" I say, cocking my head toward the hallway that we have yet to walk through. "It sounds like running."

Li immediately forgets the door and shines her light further down the hallway. She moves another twenty feet down the walkway and then disappears around a corner. A corner? Another break in the long, straight hallway? She returns quickly.

"A group is coming toward us. I guess is between eight and ten of them. I can't be sure, they're too far away." She while moves quickly to her pack and removrd two pistols, several of the flash grenades, and a short baton-like rubber stick.

"Uh, Li?" Gene prompts her for more information.

"There must be other ways into this underground maze, and people are coming for us, maybe looking for the Key, or maybe looking for us. Either way, we have the element of surprise on our side. And we're going to use it."

Gene and I take that as our cue to remove our own weapons and grenades. I see I have a pistol and several smoke grenades in my pack, just like before. I make sure the pistol is loaded with the now familiar wax bullets and check the grenades. I pack everything into pouches along my body. Gene breaches his shotgun, checking for wax shells and then moves to the pistol that he found alongside. He shoves it into the back of his pants and gives the shotgun a theatric cocking. He dumps extra shells into his pockets. We both shove earplugs into our ears and wait on Li.

"You look like a gunslinger from the wild west, Li," Gene observes with pride. "What's the plan?"

"That corner," Li hooks a thumb over her shoulder toward the corner she had disappeared behind before, "offers us perfect cover. Gene, I want you stationed on the far side, ready to provide cover fire. We don't need to worry about giving away the fact that we use wax bullets; they probably already know. Give 'em everything you got. I'll be attacking down the near side of the hallway, so keep your fire down the center and right."

She turns to me. "Jake, you take cover on this far corner, as well. Kneel and fire below Gene. Fire at anything that moves—except me, of course." A wicked smile spreads over her face.

"I'm going to launch the attack with the flash grenades. They will be enough to stun and blind the group. I will then run at them as fast as I can, emptying my weapons along the way. I'll take them out as fast as I can."

"Don't come around the corner until I say it's safe. And don't start firing until I throw the flashbang. Oh, and cover your own ears and eyes when I throw the grenade."

I lean my body against the wall and close my eyes. I work on controlling my breathing. In. Out. Just bring air in, don't let any bile out. I visualize kneeling and firing wax bullets at the oncoming intruders. I convince myself that no one will get hurt, especially none of the Chosen. I can feel my hands shaking in a combination of fear and adrenaline. This won't help my aim. I focus my mind on my hands, the motions of firing and targeting, breathing and relaxing.

The telltale sound of a pin being pulled from a grenade moves through my consciousness. I open my eyes and move into a crouch. Gene sidles in next to me, readying his shotgun above my position. Li stands ready opposite us. The rushing feet sound uncomfortably close now. I watch Li's hand swing back and then forward in an underhand motion. The flashbang grenade flies into the air. In a graceful, fluid motion, Li's hand moves to her side and come away with her weapon. I notice her left arm is matching her right's motion. Two guns are coming up.

I realize my hand is also moving, a pistol acting as an extension of my arm. I apply pressure to the trigger as I sight in on the nearest soldier. At my level, I make a split-second decision to fire at knees and legs.

Even with the earplugs, I hear the deafening roar of Gene's shotgun, signaling the beginning of chaos. This snaps me out of my mental fog and I just remember to squeeze my eyes shut before the grenade goes off.

The light and sounds almost knock me backward onto my backside. I fall against Gene's legs instead and quickly right myself. I cautiously open my eyes and see mayhem in all of its glory not more than twenty feet in front of me. Soldiers are struggling to bring weapons to bear on their unseen and unknown targets. Our advantage is clear.

Gene's shotgun sounds again. Almost automatically, my preprogrammed reflexive response activates, and I am aiming my pistol at legs and knees. Soldiers go down, the wax bullets enough to send them to their knees. The soldiers have nowhere to hide, no room to duck into, no wall to crouch behind. While this works to our advantage, it also stirs a determined panic among their ranks.

In my peripheral vision, I see Li scything through the space between them and us. She covers the ground in a flash and is upon the soldiers, wreaking her special brand of havoc. Her palms and feet fly with precise power, landing blows that render men unconscious.

I decide to stop firing as Li is now fully in the mix. I don't want to be the cause of a blow that knocks her off balance and allows a soldier to gain the upper hand. Their bullets are real and deadly. Gene moves around the corner, his shotgun ready, he quickly moves over to the downed soldiers kicking aside weapons and ensuring the men are subdued completely.

And just like that, it's over. I remain in my kneeling crouch, frozen against the cold wall. I search the scene carefully to ensure that all the soldiers lie unmoving on the ground. I concentrate on breathing again. The act of breathing seems more difficult now as the adrenaline fades. I want to get up and move to my friends. I want to help them secure the soldiers and empty their weapons, but I can't. I can't move.

Long minutes pass and then Gene is by my side, lifting me up with strong arms. His voice penetrates my foggy brain and I realize he is speaking to me.

"… the big fella in the back took some doin', but he finally went to sleep with a blow to the neck from Li," he says as he's helping me move back toward the knob-less door. "You did real good there, Jakers. A steady hand fired that pistol and quite a few soldiers will have sore knees and legs 'cause a you."

Gene slips into his talk-to-Jake-so-he-won't-hyperventilate mode with ease, and I am grateful. I start to regain myself and feel like I can focus on the problem we put on hold to defend ourselves.

"Li says the soldiers were French. Neither one of us recognized any of 'em. It wasn't Rat Face or Billy the Fib; at least they weren't with those guys." Gene carries on his conversation while he carries most of my weight back to the door. "Li thinks they might've been sent by the French government, like G.K. talked about. That's all we need, more people trying to take us out."

By this time, we've reached the door. I lean against the wall next to the door and try to put the pieces together. Where did the soldiers come from? It's obvious there are more passageways leading down to these tunnels than the one we entered. Is the unmarked, knob-less door even the right door to go through?

"Those soldiers had come along way, I think," Li remarks as she joins us at the door. "They had been sweating for a while; it had begun to seep through their clothes. I overheard one of them call the passageway the French corridor, whatever that means." She takes a big swig of water from her canteen.

French soldiers. French corridor. The spark of an idea pushes through the fatigue in my brain. I stand upright and move in front of the door. I reach into my pack and remove the three metal pieces that make up the French cross—the three pieces we found in the French sector of the city. By feel I separate the longest metal piece from the other two, moving the shorter pieces to my left hand while bring the long piece up to the door with my right.

I move the piece against the door, sliding it around like I'm rubbing the door with the metal. As I move it higher on the door, I feel the piece grab the door in a magnetic seal. I carefully remove my hand. The piece stays attached to the door in a vertical line. I quickly bring the other two pieces up and set them against the other, forming once again the French cross—two horizontal lines on the long vertical line.

As soon as the third piece magnetically seals itself into place against the door, a thunk and whoosh sound echoes through the hallway and the door swings slowly open.

"Well I'll be," Gene says with a slap to my back. I almost go down from the slap. "Oops, sorry. Just excited. You did it again, Jake."

"Li got me to thinking that if this was somehow the French corridor then maybe our first token would somehow get us through. I remembered the magnetic key from before and decided to give this cross a try on the door," I shrug. "Just lucky, I guess."

"That's not luck, Jake," Gene says admiringly. "That's genius."

The three of us move into the new hallway, except the new space isn't a corridor at all. It's a small room. I mean small, like five feet by five feet. In the exact center of the room a thin wire hangs down from the ceiling.

A key hangs suspended from the wire.

"Is that ... the Key?" Gene says in confusion.

"No, it's *a* key, not *the* Key," I say with a smile. I think of my mom. This has her fingerprints all over it. What would she use to recover a key? A key, of course. To demonstrate to the others that this is a normal key, I reach up and remove the key from the wire. I bring it to the Key around my neck and touch them together. Nothing happens. "This key will help us get into whatever or wherever the Key of Integrity is at." I put the key into my pack and move to the opposite side of the tiny room. A door is set into the wall. Again, no handle, no knob.

Li sees the door too and immediately moves to the door we've already passed through, removes the French cross pieces from the door, handing them back to me.

"Thanks," I say, showing her a big smile. "You read my mind."

"Hey now, that's my job, ya hear?" Gene says indignantly. "You can be Jake's girlfriend and go around holding hands in secret, but knock it off with the mind reading. That's my job," he says this while poking his chest with a finger to emphasize his point.

I roll my eyes, trying to hide my embarrassment at the truth of his words. Li recognizes the hurt in Gene's voice and moves to put a hand on his arm. "Gene, nobody can take your place with Jake. What you did back there in talking him out of his frozen fear, helping him to move past the shock of battle—only you have that bond with him." Li smiles at him and moves into him with a side hug. "I didn't read Jake's mind—I can't read his mind, trust me, I've tried." Now Li is blushing. "I just saw the door without a handle and knew we needed the cross again. I read the situation, not Jake's mind."

Gene smiles and returns Li's hug. He clears his throat. "Well, then, just as long as we're all clear about the importance of being Gene …"

Li laughs and shoves away from Gene playfully.

I turn my attention to the door, affixing the cross to the door. A thunk and whoosh later, we are moving through this door. Our flashlights reveal a corridor similar to one we left behind. We begin to move into this new space when I turn back quickly to the open door.

I swiftly enter the small room and close the first door on the hallway. I don't want anyone coming behind us and without the French token, the door won't open. I move back through the small room, remove the cross from the door and shove it back into my pack. After I have the cross pieces stowed away, I shut the door, sealing us into the new hallway.

Li and Gene both stare at me with pride. "Good thinking, Jakers." I shrug at them both. "I don't want anyone following us – and we might need the cross pieces again.

We form up and begin moving through the hallway. After only ten yards, the hallway takes a right turn and I calculate in my head that we are now heading south, back toward the Brandenburg Gate in a parallel corridor from the one we had come through to get to the key room.

I also notice the floor sloping downward; we are going deeper into the earth. After another twenty yards the hallway takes another right turn, and floor drops away steeply.

"We must be passing under the original corridor we came through on the way to the key room. We're moving west now, right?" I say my thoughts aloud.

"Yes," Li responds, her sense of direction and navigation as keen as ever. "This corridor is taking us into the British sector. "Oh, and now we are turning left and heading back south," she states as we reach another turn in the corridor. The ground has leveled out now, I suppose we are now twice as far underground as we had been.

Once we make the left turn heading south, the corridor stretches out into a long straight line as far as our flashlight beams reach. We settle into a quick walk rhythm and fall into silence. Our breathing keeps time. I keep count of my steps to occupy my mind as I go.

The corridor stretches on and I realize that my steps are coming up on the fifty-three hundred mark, which means we are closing in on having walked this stretch for a full mile.

"Lights," Li speaks in a whisper and switches off her flashlight. Gene and I snap out of our stupor and fumble to turn ours off. Li brings us in close. "We are coming up on a left turn. We don't know what's ahead of us and I think we should be cautious."

She looks at us both with intensity. Our breathing is heavy from our quick march and sounds deafening in the silence. Tension fills the void.

"Let's take a little break, drink some water, and stretch our muscles," she says looking pointedly at Gene. He immediately slumps against the wall and slides down into a sitting position. He pulls out his canteen and drinks thirstily, swallowing large gulps at a time. I join him against the wall and drink my own water. Li hands us both some dried meat and hard bread. As soon as we have eaten it, Li beckons us up with her hand and motions to follow her. Last, she presses a finger to her lips in the universal sign for quiet.

She leads us around the corner. I hear movement up ahead, but can't see anything or anyone. Li stops us and whispers in my ear to move back around the corner. She moves to Gene and I assume gives the same direction. Now back around the corner, Li brings us close again.

"Obviously we have more visitors up ahead." Li whispers. "I'm guessing now, but I bet they've beat us to our second door and are waiting for us to arrive. I also think they have come from a different direction, so they won't be expecting us to come up on them. My final guess is that they are British, based upon the order in which we got our tokens. Stay here while I go find out."

Li moves to sneak away, but Gene stops her. "Wait. What are you going to do? Maybe I should come along to help."

She comes close again. "I'm not going to show myself. I'm just going to get close enough to test my guesses. I won't engage them, promise. Be right back."

I feel Gene shrug. Li waits a heartbeat for any further protest. None comes, so she disappears around the corner.

I wait next to Gene and count the seconds. Four-hundred-thirty seconds pass before Li comes back around the corner. Over seven minutes that seem like an hour. I didn't even hear a scuffle the entire time she was gone.

"The men are soldiers – British judging by their accents." Li says with a little triumph in her voice. "They are milling about in front of a door that I assume we need to go through. Most of them are facing toward a hallway that juts off to the west from us, it must be the direction they came from. This one," she points to the hallway she had come from, "dead-ends just beyond the door, so the only way they could've come is from the hallway from the west."

I nod and wonder how we are going to get to the door, let alone through it.

"We have no cover from our approach and I don't want to risk another fight where the opposition has the cover of the hallway while we are in the open. Too many bad things can happen." She is thinking. I can tell her tactical mind is churning through possibilities. Gene and I both wait on her.

She finally gives a frustrated shake of her head. She's come up with a plan that she clearly doesn't like. Taking a breath, she turns to Gene. "How do you feel about playing the American idiot boy?" There is a crooked smile on her face as she watches Gene.

His smile grows wide and mischievousness sparks in his eyes. "I fancy another go at the blighters," he responds in his ridiculous British accent. I don't know what he means, and I'm pretty sure even he doesn't know what he's saying.

"Good," Li pronounces, even though she grimaces when she hears his accent. "Here's the plan: Gene is going to lead us out, making as much noise as possible. We're playing the clumsy Americans lost and in need of help. Gene will lead us. We need to act chummy so we can get our rings in contact with three soldiers. Gene will render the leader."

"You mean we get to use bacon fat to render those guys? I've been wanting to try out my new ring!" Gene blurts in excitement. "This is awesome! First I get to use my British accent to play the bumbling American, and then I get to use my bacon fat. This can't get any better!"

I can't help but smile at Gene, and I see Li is trying to stifle her smile.

"This is dangerous, boys, they have real guns with real bullets; let's not forget that okay? Jake, you and I will pick out the biggest and meanest of the soldiers. That will leave three. Gene, you take one and I'll take the other two out as quickly as possible. Questions?" she asks and looks at the two of us. Neither one of us says anything.

"Good, let's get ready and then we'll head out." She moves to ensure her ring is in place and she also checks her weapons, reloading as needed. I follow her lead, reload my pistol and move my ring into position. Gene does the same and then seems to be getting into character as he tests out his accent and certain words that I'm not sure he knows the correct meaning and usage of.

We move around the corner, Li tucks me behind her and Gene in the lead with a protective gesture that should make me angry, but doesn't. Gene moves us forward and immediately launches into character.

"These here hallways just go on and on, don't they?" he says, more loudly than necessary and huffing like he's out of breath. "I can't believe we's lost. I'm tired and hungry … and scared," his voice creeps up an octave when he says scared, and he pronounces it like "skeered." His drawl is in full effect.

We keep moving forward, matching Gene's wobbly, tired gait. "Hey, d'ya hear that? I think someone's up there. Oh please, let us find us some help."

CHAPTER 37

BRITS AND YANKS

THE SOLDIERS HAVE ALL TURNED in our direction. They seem content to wait for us to come to them. They aren't stupid; they know they have the safety of the corner for cover. They fan out in a defensive position and their leader steps slightly ahead of the rest.

"Keep your hands visible and empty," Li whispers.

"Howdy!" Gene calls out to the waiting soldiers. "We's lost our way in these dern tunnels." He raises his hands in a surrender gesture and leans forward like he's about to share a secret. "An' ya know what? We have something we needa find, pronto." I catch Gene winking, or blinking, I guess.

We reach the soldiers and lower our flashlights.

"How do you do?" the leader says in a cultured British accent. He looks over our little group, trying to assess the situation. He looks wary but not overly concerned. Perfect.

"We do mighty fine, gent," Gene responds, continuing to move forward with his arm outstretched in an offer to shake hands. "I'm right proper glad that we've run into you Brits."

Gene's accent is atrocious. I watch as the leader and the others wince at his butchery of their language. Perfect.

Gene shakes the leader's hand firmly in two exaggerated pumps. "Cheers!" he says with gusto.

"I am Major Joshua Ferguson," the British leader says. "How may we be of assistance to you?"

Gene slings an arm around the Major and brings him in tight, ignoring the man's discomfort. I take this as a cue to move toward one of the men. I focus on a small man whose eyes are dark and dead looking. He scares me, so I decide to take him down with my ring. I see Li move to a huge soldier and reach out her hand in an offer to shake.

I offer my hand to Dead Eyes and he hesitates, looking at my hand in disgust. He'd rather not shake, but propriety moves his hand forward to mine. I sneak a quick glance to Gene. He is watching me, and Li move into position.

"Well, Josh—do ya mind if I call you Josh?" Gene begins, not waiting for a response. "I dunno what we would've done without ya. I's about ready to give up when we turn the corner back there; ready to just sit down and die on the spot. But whatdya know, we flash our lights up ahead and we see you lot, and Bob's your uncle!" Gene is blatantly going between Texas drawl and horrible British accent, throwing in words and phrases that don't even fit together.

Major Ferguson looks completely flummoxed. Gene gives him a squeeze of the shoulder and I know the Major has just been injected. I bring my left hand up to Dead Eye's hand that is still clasped in my right. I act like I'm grateful with my two hands squeezing his. I feel the bacon fat inject into the back of his hand. Dead Eyes pulls his hand away, not because he felt the prick of the needle, but because he doesn't like me.

I smile, and then turn my face into a look of concern. "Are you okay?" I ask Dead Eye.

"Major Josh, yer lookin' green, ma friend," Gene adds simultaneously.

Li doesn't speak; she just moves into her huge soldier and tries to ease him down to the ground.

I'm unable to help Dead Eyes to the ground. He goes down too quickly.

"A little help here, boys," Gene calls to a couple of the soldiers. They move to help their Major, but when they try to get their arms around him, Gene grabs their heads and brings them together with a crack. The Major goes down in a heap and the other two fall on top of him.

Li is left with just one. I turn to her and see that she has already delivered a blow to the poor guy's neck. He is already slumping to the ground. She then moves quickly to bind the soldiers and empty their weapons of bullets.

Gene reaches into his pack and removes the metal pieces that form the Union Jack symbol—the two crosses. He steps to the door and moves the vertical piece around the door until it seals in place magnetically. He looks at the pieces to ensure he is placing them in the correct order, with the grooves sliding into place. Soon he has the pieces in place correctly, and the door opens with the usual sounds.

Gene moves inside, and I follow. Li joins us after finishing her work with the soldiers. The room is identical to the last room we opened. Five feet by five feet with an old key hanging from the ceiling. Gene takes the key and drops it into his pack. Li has already removed the union jack pieces and hands them back to Gene.

He moves to the far door while Li swings the other door shut. Gene quickly has the door open and the metal pieces go back into his pack. After Li and I follow him through, she turns and seals this door shut as well.

"I guess we have a date with Americans coming up," she says as she catches up to us, flashlight in hand.

The corridor we are in ends after ten yards and turns left. But this corridor only runs for five yards before it turns right. We're headed north again, back toward the Brandenburg Gate. What a maze of tunnels!

After a few yards heading north, a group of soldiers step into the corridor with weapons raised menacingly at us. They are no more than fifteen yards ahead of us.

That was fast. No mile-long walk this time, I think to myself as I slowly raise my hands.

"Howdy guys! Boy, are we glad to see fellow Americans," Gene starts.

"Shut it," a soldier barks. "No talking. Remove your weapons and packs and place them on the ground. Slowly."

I turn to Li. She nods slowly and begins removing her pistols. I follow her lead and place my pistol on the ground. I hear the clatter of Gene's shotgun meeting the ground.

"Grenades too" the man snaps sharply.

I lower my pack with the smoke grenades to the ground. Li lowers her flashbangs as well. Gene has no grenades, so he makes no move. We all stand upright, keeping our arms high in the air in surrender. I cast another glance at Li, but she is staring straight ahead. Her eyes move quickly though, assessing the situation.

The soldier giving orders turns his head back to the corner and gives a nod. More soldiers come around the corner and move quickly toward us. They collect our weapons and packs, then move back behind the others.

From what we can see, there are nine soldiers total. The leader, four pointing their weapons at us, and the four who collected our weapons. There may be more around the corner though.

"Nine," I mutter in Li's direction.

A gun fires and I duck instinctively, but way too late. A bullet has struck the wall near my head.

"No talking," the lead soldier holds his pistol in his hand now. He must be the one who shot at me.

Several snarky comebacks run through my head, but I don't give voice to any of them. For one, I don't want to get shot. For two, I am scared spitless, so I can't speak anyway. So I settle for what I hope is an angry, defiant glare at the man.

The four who collected our weapons reappear with bindings in their hands.

"Move slowly to the corner here," the lead soldier orders.

"Why are you doing this? You're Americans, right?" Li grinds out with steel in her voice.

"Orders from the government. They need to secure what you are looking for, so nobody else can use it against us, ma'am," the soldier says, his voice softening by his embarrassment of treating fellow Americans like he is. "I'm sorry."

Li takes this opening and apology and goes with it. "No government should have what we seek. We are here to take it and protect it for good. No one will be able to take it, not even our government. Help us."

"Sorry, ma'am. No more talking," He says, reverting back to his coarse persona—his way of hiding from his real feelings.

"What's your name, soldier?" Li asks in her most commanding voice.

He flinches for a brief second and looks like he's going to tell us out of habit before he catches himself and shakes his head. "Please, ma'am, no more talking."

"You'll just have to shoot me, soldier!" Li rears up to her fullest height. The man still towers over her, but you wouldn't know it from their body language. "Are you going to shoot an unarmed American female soldier? Is that who you've become now?" she demands.

I see the hesitancy in his eyes. The other soldiers' shoulders slump slightly and I can tell none of them want any part of shooting us. Uncertainty hangs in the air like a thick, encompassing smoke.

Li steps forward and puts her chest against the barrel of the lead soldier's pistol. "You're going to have to shoot me then, soldier, and after that you're going to have to live with yourself. And I don't think you can—neither the shooting nor the living with yourself afterward."

She takes a breath, her chest rising and falling against the barrel of the pistol. "What is it going to be?" she spits out harshly.

The man pulls his pistol away and holsters it at his hip. "I'm not going to shoot you. I don't need to," the soldier says, then turns his head to those waiting behind him. "Bind them tightly. No mistakes."

Before I can register these words, Li flies into action, her arms sweeping in an arc through the still-raised rifles of the four soldiers directly in front of Gene and me. The rifles are swept aside, with two of them dropping to the ground. Gene doesn't hesitate, and moves in close to the two who still hold their rifles. He brings their heads together in a loud crack.

I turn in time to see Li's open palm crashing into the lead soldier's chest, knocking him back into the wall. Not wasting a second, Li turns her attention to the four guards who have dropped the bindings and are reaching for their holstered weapons.

I do the first thing that comes into my mind and drop to a knee, thrusting a closed fist forward into the groin of the soldier closest to me. He had already been bending down to grab up the rifle Li had knocked from his hands. The blow to his private area brings him down faster. My hand is already moving upward, this time in an open rigid palm. The heel of my palm meets his chin in a sickening crack. Reverberations run through my arm and also through his head. His eyes roll up and he crashes to the ground, out of the fight.

The second soldier who dropped his rifle is on me now. His

arms come around my shoulders in an attempt to grab me. I slip through his arms down to the ground, landing on my back. The man is above me now, continuing downward in his effort to grab me. I rear back on my shoulders, bringing my legs up like I'm looking to roll over, but instead I kick the soldier in the head with my right leg, and I continue with my left leg into his shoulder. He's falling down on top of me, but I let my leg fall quickly to the ground and use the momentum to propel my open palm up into his face. I miss his face, miscalculating his fall and my upward momentum. I catch him awkwardly in the throat. It has the desired effect as he falls on me, clutching his trachea in an attempt to allow air into his lungs.

I roll out from under him and cast my eyes around at the scene.

Gene has the four soldiers down, arms and legs akimbo. Sweat drips from his face and I guess he has just put his final combatant out of the fight. That makes six soldiers Gene has taken down.

I turn the other direction and see that Li is locked in combat with the lead soldier. I quickly recalculate. Li must've stunned him with her palm to his chest and then moved over to the four with Gene. I do notice that the lead soldier's holster is empty. Okay, so Li took the time to relieve him of his weapon before moving on.

The two move in slow circles around each other, each looking for an opening. As Li moves around the man in some macabre slow dance, I notice that she is bruised and bleeding. Her nose gushes blood. The soldier does too, from the nose and a cut on his cheekbone.

I'm ashamed to admit that my first thought when I saw Li's bloody nose was that I hope this guy hasn't ruined Li's perfect face.

"Li!" Gene calls roughly; anger permeates his voice. He's seen the blood too. "The soldiers are all down, except for the Neanderthal that gave you that bloody nose."

He moves forward to engage the lone soldier. The leader. I take a closer look and see the man is tall and muscular, but not a bodybuilder type. He is strong and quick on his feet. He must be if he's keeping up with Li. I wonder if he's just too strong for her. Sometimes I forget that Li is a fourteen-year-old girl and can't possibly defeat everyone she faces. The man's straw-colored hair is cut high and tight, and his eyes register every movement from each of the three of us, but especially Li.

"Your men are all down, out of the fight, soldier," Li says as she continues to circle. "Let us carry on with our mission and you can tend to your men."

He smiles and shakes his head. "I'm sorry, ma'am, I can't do that. I've never failed a mission and I'm not about to start now with three teenagers—no matter how tough they might be."

Li shrugs as if she expected this answer. "Well then, I apologize in advance. You seem like an honorable man, and you certainly have taught me much about hand-to-hand combat, but time is not on our side, so …"

She leaps into action, and with two quick strides her feet are on the wall. Here she is, defying gravity again. Her feet leave the wall, her right cocked and whipping toward the soldier's head. He seems transfixed by her movements, paralyzed by her grace. I know I am. At the last second, he makes an effort to move his head by pivoting his body around his back leg. A forearm also comes up in an effort to deflect the oncoming leg kick.

Li is too fast. Her leg compensates for his movement and her shin connects with the man at the base of the neck, where it meets the shoulder. My knees go weak just from the sound of the contact. His knees buckle and he crumples to a kneel, but no further. I can't help but think that any other human would have been out of the fight after that blow.

Not this man. He raises a forearm to block Li's continuation punch and lands his own blow to Li's thigh. This knocks her off balance and she falls flat, catching herself in a pushup-like pose and quickly pushing back to her feet. This gives the soldier the time he needs to regain some sense of composure, the blow to his neck and shoulder has shaken him, but incredibly, he is still fighting.

I see Gene moving toward him and I feel my own legs propelling me forward also. Our need to protect Li runs deep within both of us, even though she does most of the protecting.

"No," Li warns us quietly. "Leave him to me." The quiet menace is laced with a certainty in her voice. She is confident and determined.

"Li, maybe just this once we can help you take care of this guy," Gene pleads.

"He's dangerous, Gene, and you and Jake will get hurt—maybe seriously—and we can't have that; we still have much to do." She gently shoves Gene away and gives me a look that warns me off. I hesitate, then nod to her. Gene also capitulates and stands aside.

Li wipes an arm across her nose, smearing the blood across her cheek and along her arm. The blood has slowed a bit, but she does look more pale than usual.

The soldier's eyes seem to have lost some of their focus and he pants, trying to regain his senses. Li doesn't give him any additional time. All of this has taken place in a matter of seconds. The man is still down on a knee, and his attempts to stand have failed to this point.

Li takes two strides, which bring her to full speed and she races up the wall again, looking as though she is going to repeat her kicking move. The man thinks this as well and moves quickly to block her. I realize he must have been faking his struggle to stand. However, her movements prove to be a feint as well. She sails over and behind the man, landing behind his back. As he wheels to face his opponent, she already has her leading leg cocked as though she is going to violently stomp on a spider.

Her leg lashes out and connects with his ankle. The subsequent snap of bone echoes in my ears. I think it's loud enough to bring the other soldiers back to consciousness.

Li continues her movement, using her momentum to drop into a crouch where she uses her forward and downward motion to her advantage. Her right arm is cocked back, palm open and rigid, and then it shoots forward and makes contact with the soldier's opposite knee. Another loud crack.

The soldier is falling, a damaged ankle on one leg and a ruined knee on the other. Even he can't shrug off these blows. As he falls, helpless to stop himself, Li catches him along the jaw with another strike of her left palm. He crumples to the ground. Li remains coiled in on herself, ready to strike again. She warily leans toward the man, concerned that he is playing possum. He's not. He's out.

"Thanks for the playtime," she whispers into his ear. "You should've let us go, I'm truly sorry about your ankle and knee, they should be repairable, though."

"Yowsers, Li!" Gene says, a little breathless. I realize I have been holding my breath and guess Gene had been doing the same. "Why didn't you start with the cracking-bones thing?"

"I didn't want to do that to him if I didn't have to, but this soldier is one tough guy," Li says, breathing heavily while she carefully binds his hands. She doesn't bother with his feet. "I respect

this soldier, he's just following orders. There was no anger or malice in his actions."

Li rolls the man over and looks carefully at his dog tags, squinting her eyes in the dim light. "Sergeant Russell Dix. D – I – X. You are one tough soldier. I salute you."

With this, she moves to her packs and begins to rummage through them. Over her shoulder, she calls to Gene and me. "Gather up our things. Make sure we have everything; we'll probably need everything we've got to get through this and get that Key."

I move with Gene to recover our weapons and packs. When we have everything back together, I see that Li has already placed the metal pieces on the door behind the Sergeant Dix's unconscious form. The door is open now and Li is gathering her things together. When she sees us approaching, she waves us toward the door. I see she has stuffed a piece of torn cloth into each of her nostrils. She gives me an embarrassed smile when she catches me staring at her nose. "Is it broken?" I ask, concentrating on looking her in the eye rather than staring at the bloody cloth sticking out of her nose.

Li shakes her head and moves a hand up to cover her nose, then thinks better of it and lets her hand drop to her side. "No, it's fine. It just bled a lot; he caught me with a glancing blow. I'm still mad about not ducking it properly."

"That's a real good look, for ya, Li. Wear stuff hanging outta your nose this summer while you're in Hong Kong and it'll become fashionable in about two weeks, I reckon." Gene says with a smile. "They'll call 'em Nose Plugs and it'll be the new fad to sweep the country."

"Funny, Gene," Li comments, her voice sounding nasal because of the cloths. "Maybe I'll start the new fad with you, what do you say? I'll give you a quick punch to the nose, and bam, the fad moves to Texas."

"Us Texans are way too smart to be taken in by some silly fad," Gene brags with an upturned nose and nasally voice to match Li's.

I laugh a little, but try to stifle it, worried that Li will give me a reason to start my own Nose Plug fad. Instead, she laughs and gives Gene a quick hug.

"You're an idiot," she says through the hug.

"I know," Gene says as he returns the hug.

The three of us enjoy a quick break from the tension and stress of our Quest, but it passes too soon, and we turn our attention back to the door we must pass through.

CHAPTER 38

EPIPHANY

T HE INTERIOR IS IDENTICAL TO the other rooms we have opened: five by five with a Key dangling in the center. Li removes the Key and tucks it into her pack. She then moves to the metal star and removes it from the door we have come through and moves toward the back door. She hesitates for a minute.

"Let's take a minute to think this whole thing through, okay?" she says while she swings the one door closed, leaving the American soldiers behind and sealing us in the little room. "What do we know at this point?"

"We've moved through the first three tokens or areas, I guess. Is that what you mean?" I say.

"Yes, here's what I'm thinking," Li picks us from my statement. "We've passed through three doors now and collected three keys. But, we still have to pass through the Russians, and according to General Zhukov, possibly the remnants of the Nazi leadership. Plus, I'm sure we'll see Rat Face and his little gang before this is all over, right?"

"So ... we still have the Russians, Nazis, and Rat Face to go through before we reach the Key? Man, I'm already tuckered out, ya know? I'm as tired as a bear in hibernation," Gene's drawl is creeping out again.

"I'm worried that as we're getting closer to our final destination, we weren't ready for these last guys. We didn't plan on running into a new group so soon. We need to be more careful from here on out," Li declares.

"And we're still heading right back toward the Brandenburg Gate and where we started, right?" I ask Li.

"Yes. This door will lead us out pointing due north, back the way we came," she says tapping on the closed door. "Unless we take more turns, of course."

"Okay, so now what?" Gene says.

"Let's take a quick inventory of our gear, just so I know what we have available to us against the upcoming forces."

We turn out our packs and set our weapons on the floor. We have our usual compliment of weapons—Li's two pistols, Gene's shotgun, and my pistol. We take a moment to ensure they are all fully loaded and then tuck them away. We have two smoke grenades and plenty of wax of ammunition, but no more flash grenades.

We move to our other packs and lay out our French cross, Union Jack, and US star, flashlights, food, canteens and ammo.

"Hey, would ya look at this," Gene sounds confused. He pulls out more metal pieces, pieces we haven't seen before, but they match the workmanship of our other tokens. Gene spreads them out on the floor in front of us.

There are three total pieces of metal. The first looks like the hook that a pirate would wear in place of a missing hand. The other two are straight pieces, one much longer than the other.

I recognize them immediately. "General Zhukov put these in the pack. He is the token," I say, working out my thoughts aloud. "He got us into these tunnels, but also left the fourth token for us to find." I reach out and arrange the hook with the other two pieces. I place the hook first and then lay the long straight piece over top, fitting it into the notch along the hook. Finally, I place the short metal piece at the top end of the long straight piece.

"The hammer and sickle. The symbol of Soviet Russia. This hook is actually a sickle, which in communism represents peasants, while this other image, the hammer, symbolizes the worker."

"This completes our four tokens, representative of the four nations now occupying Berlin," Li says, then shifts gears as she shifts her body against the wall. "Let's grab some food and water while we're breaking a minute."

We eat more of the bread and dried meat, and drink more water from our canteens. This seems to freshen our little group, and we repack all of our gear away and prepare to carry on.

Li places the star pieces magnetically on the exit door and as the door thunks open, we warily pass into the new passage. Nothing is in sight, no waiting attack or soldiers. Nothing. Li removes the metal star and shoves it quickly into her pack. Our lights shine on an empty stretch of corridor. Our light fades long before the corridor ends.

Li leads us forward, quickly resuming her brisk pace. We travel for a quarter mile before we reach the end of this stretch and a left turn. Li slows, and with our flashlights extinguished, peeks around the corner. She disappears around the corner for a minute and then returns with her flashlight on. She waves us onward.

With the left turn, we now are headed west again, away from the Brandenburg Gate and toward the large open parks of the Tiergarten. The tunnels slope downward again on this westward stretch, gradually taking us further under the earth.

We don't have to travel long before we hear sounds of life. We slow our progress and creep forward without the aid of our flashlights. The sounds grow louder as we move down the corridor. Li brings us in close and whispers for Gene and me to stay put while she scouts ahead.

She disappears and I keep time by counting my breathing, working to relax as much as possible. I hear Li's voice, and panic rises as I realize she is not speaking to us. Her voice is too far away. Has she been caught? Her voice doesn't sound panicked. What's happening?

Li returns and her flashlight cuts suddenly through the darkness. "Guess who is waiting for us?" Her face is bright with a wide smile. She doesn't wait for an answer, which is good, because I don't think Gene nor I could've mustered an intelligent sound at that point. "It's General G.K. Zhukov, our token," she surprises us.

With that, she picks up her packs and moves away toward the voices. Gene and I share a look and a shrug, then scramble to follow Li's receding form.

General Zhukov stands with seven other Russian soldiers, all of whom look relaxed and nonthreatening. Li is talking easily with the General. He is bending toward her face with an expression of concern. He passes her on to another of his soldiers who is reaching into a medic pack.

"Boys!" the General calls out as he sees Gene and me. "Miss Li has told me of your progress to this point. I have her being tended to by my young medic. Now, if the British knew we were under their sector, they wouldn't be happy, but no one will know, will they?" he chuckles softly.

"Sir, thank you for all of your assistance," I say quietly and sincerely.

"I am honored to protect you who protect things most important to a better way of life," he says as he claps me on the shoulder. He slings his other arm around Gene and leads us over to a metal staircase spiraling upward. And downward, I see. I hadn't noticed the staircase until now. My eyes crane upward to see the stairs end a floor above us. Moving my eyes downward, I see the stairs disappear into darkness in the ground below.

"We took these stairs down to this level according to another note and map from your parents," General Zhukov explains. "This leads from our sector in the east over to here. The note directed me to wait here for you, and to point you toward the downward stairs."

Li joins us at the staircase. The nose plugs are gone, and the perfectly symmetrical face has been restored to its original state. Li must've caught me calculating, because she offers me a quick smile.

"Would you like my soldiers to accompany you? I have chosen each of them because of their fidelity to me. And for their integrity in choosing to do right in the face of ugly wartime conditions," the General offers.

"I believe we'll accept your kind offer, General," Li says. This shocks me a bit; Li is usually careful to go it alone. "If you say they are trustworthy, that is good enough for me."

"Excellent. I believe you already know Captain Ivanovich. He will lead these men at your direction," the General notes, pointing to the Captain. He gives a nod to us and offers his first smile. "Good luck."

With this, the General turns on his heels and ascends the staircase. We watch until he disappears above us.

Li turns to Captain Ivanovich. "Would you be so good as to lead us down?"

The Captain gives his men instructions, then leads the way down the stairs. Four soldiers, including the captain go ahead of us while the three remaining follow us, guarding our rear.

CHΛPTΞR 39

ATTACK

THE TIGHT SPIRAL STAIRCASE IS just like the one we descended at the Brandenburg Gate. At the bottom, we find ourselves facing a door without a handle.

"Shall we attempt to blow the door?" the Captain asks Li.

"Not necessary, Captain," she assures him and motions to Gene.

Gene is already moving toward the door, rummaging through his pack. He brings the hammer and sickle pieces out and slides the sickle over the door until it locks magnetically. He fits the other pieces over the hammer, and the door thunks open. This brings murmurs from our new companions.

"Stay here for a moment; the next room is a tight fit," Li tells the Captain.

The three of us move into the room and Gene takes the Key from the dangling wire and puts it into the pack. He moves to the door, takes the hammer and sickle down and moves to the far door.

Li pokes her head back out the near door and waves the soldiers forward. As we pass through the far door, we stop just inside, seeing something we didn't expect to see.

There is no corridor this time.

A huge, cavernous room spreads out before us. It looks like a large domed cave, but it is certainly man-made. Unlike the rest of our underground journey, this space is lit by hundreds of electric bulbs. There are 1940s era desks and partitions spread throughout the space, which looks like an abandoned command center of some kind. The Nazi flag still hangs by one corner along the far wall. The room looks like the equivalent of a modern day cubicle farm on the floor of a high-rise office building, complete with maze-like pathways through the desks and partitions.

We move into the room, heads swiveling left and right attempting to take in our new situation. My eyes stop on five doors that are set into the walls of the cavern, evenly spaced around the circular walls. I can only see the tops of the three furthest away. These three have handles attached to the doors.

I turn back to the doorway we've just come through to see Gene removing the hammer and sickle metal and placing it back into his pack. He then moves to close the door and I see what I expected to see. A handle on this side of the door.

"Including the door we've just come through, there are six points of ingress in this cavern," Li remarks. I turn and realize she's talking to Captain Ivanovich. "That makes me nervous." The Captain nods his agreement.

"I think we should head for the door opposite this one," I suggest.

"Why do you say that?" Li turns her attention to me.

I shrug. "I can't say for sure, but we need to find a doorway without a handle and I can see the nearest doors have handles. I'm guessing that our door will either have a magnetic lock or four keyholes."

"Let's move through the center of the cubicles, then directly over to the far side," she says, and I'm happy that she refers to them as cubicles too. Not important, but still.

Li sets out with Captain Ivanovich and two soldiers at the head of our group. Gene and I follow with four soldiers trailing us. As we near the center, the tall Captain goes up on tiptoes and confirms that five doors beginning with the one we have passed through do have handles.

We can't see the door opposite us, because the path through the desks and partitions is not a straight line. As I said, it is maze-like.

Suddenly an explosion sounds to our left. Instinctively our group ducks and looks for the source of the explosion. The door has been damaged, but still holds firm. A second explosion rocks the cavern and this time the door gives way.

"You've gotta be kidding me," Gene groans after a second or

two.

Rat Face and Billy the Fib lead the way through the smoke and dust.

"That is the enemy, Captain!" Li shouts, pointing toward the men pouring through the blast.

The Captain turns and barks out orders to his men.

Rat Face sees us. His beady rat eyes meet mine. For a second, time stands still and all I hear is my own breathing as something passes through our gaze. There is finality in his gaze, as if this is the last stop for us. Only one of us is leaving this room, and he is confident that it will be him.

A third explosion rocks the cavern, this time from the opposite side. Instead of looking in that direction, I turn my head upward. The top of the cavern sends dust and small particles of rock down toward us. This place can't take many more explosions.

"Uh … Li," Gene says, spinning her by the shoulders to take in the new threat. "Nazis," He points out needlessly while pointing a finger at the newcomers.

A sound of disgust escapes Li's lips. "Captain, Nazis at your six o'clock," she uses the terminology of a soldier. Six o'clock refers to an analog clock face and the six would be behind you. Three is directly to your right and nine is directly to your left. Twelve o'clock is straight ahead.

The Captain spins around to see the Nazi soldiers coming through the new blast site. He begins shouting again, redirecting some of his men.

Gunfire sounds in the cavern, and Li drags me down behind a desk and partition.

I use Li's clock analogy to get a picture in my mind. If the door we need to get is at twelve o'clock—straight ahead—then the door we came through is at our six. Rat Face is at our eight and the Nazi soldiers are at our four. Counting our door, the three rear doors have been used. The three doors near to what I consider the front of the cavern are still closed.

As I think this, another explosion rips through the cavern. I peek up with Li to see the door at our ten o'clock has been breached.

"This isn't getting any better," I mutter to Li. She doesn't respond. She is looking off to the right. I see her head shake.

"Two doors blew simultaneously. The door to our ten and our

two," she indicates, pointing her arm first in one direction and then in the other.

I stand up to get a look at the men coming through the two o'clock door. I squint my eyes in an attempt to see clearly through the dust and smoke. I stand up straight in shock.

"I think—"

Li yanks me down roughly. "Stay down, Jake."

"I think the men coming through the two o'clock door are Americans," I say to her with wide eyes. "And I think Captain Eriksson is leading them!"

Li forgets her own advice and stands up straight, craning her head to see over the desks and partitions.

"Gene? Jake? Li?" A familiar voice shouts from our front left— our ten o'clock.

There is a French accent attached to the voice.

"Corporal LeGendre?" Li murmurs, then cups her hand and shouts the name again.

"Yes!" comes the reply.

We hear shouting from the Americans too now. Captain Eriksson is also shouting our names.

Gene joins Li and me in our crouched position.

"The cavalry has arrived, people," he pronounces with a wide smile.

Li turns and beckons Captain Ivanovich over with a wave.

"Captain, more of our friends have arrived. The French soldiers to our ten and the American soldiers to our two are both here to help us. Tell your soldiers to concentrate only on the others," Li instructs him.

Captain Ivanovich nods and moves away in a crouch, already barking orders to his men.

Gene stands up a little and yells out in his loud voice, "Corporal LeGendre and Captain Eriksson, good to see you! We have trouble to the back left and right of us. Nazis and Evils," Gene turns to us and shrugs at his designation of Rat Face and his gang as Evils. We shrug back; now is not the time to quibble over a proper name for our enemies.

"Roger that!" Captain Eriksson's voice carries over to us.

"Understood!" Corporal LeGendre calls out.

The cavern quickly becomes a cacophony of noise—of the

sounds of war. The acoustics are terrible and my ears ring even with my ear plugs

Li scuttles over to Captain Ivanovich and begins giving instructions. I can tell because her arms are waving and pointing in various directions. She quickly returns to us.

"Here's the plan," she starts, her words rushing out and mixing together in my ears. "We are going to make our way to the door Jake wants to see while Captain Ivanovich keeps an eye on our backs. From the sound of things, the Americans are engaging the Nazis on their side and the French are keeping Rat Face's forces pinned down. Each group of bad guys has to contend with forces on two fronts. This should keep us free to get to the door."

As soon as the words are out of her mouth, she moves out. Gene and I follow mutely. I try as hard as I can to block out the screams of men who've been hit. I can't think about it right now—it will paralyze me. I focus on Li and Gene.

We slowly make our way toward the door. As we near it, we see the French being pushed back toward us. The Americans too are inching back toward our target door.

"Duck!" Li shouts and knocks Gene and me over, landing on top of us in a tangle of bodies. Hot searing flames shoot over us a second later. Li sucks in a breath and I can tell she's hurt. The minute the flames recede, she jumps up and fires her pistols in the direction they came from. I hear grunts of wax bullets hitting their targets.

"Move." Li says.

I see that her pack is still burning. She must realize it too, because she spins the pack around, shucks it off her body and onto the ground. She stomps it with a foot and then gingerly picks through it, removing the metal pieces of the star token and an old key. She shoves these to Gene without a word. He crams them into his own pack.

I carefully reach out to touch her back, her jacket is blackened in several spots but the damage looks superficial. She feels my tentative touch and calls over her shoulder, "I'm fine. No burns on my skin."

Gene looks at me with a wry smile. He looks like he wants to say something, but finally decides to let it pass. I shake my head at him.

We reach the end of the cubicles and Li holds up a fist to signal a stop. Between the end of the desks and partitions that act as short walls, there is a ten-foot gap to the door. No cover, and no means of protection against the enemy forces. Li crouches at the final partition and peers first one way, then the other, and finally straight ahead.

I see the door and the four old-time keyholes, and I know they match the four keys we have in our packs.

"The keyholes," I whisper into Li's ear. She throws me a quick nod and then turns to face Gene and me.

"The good news is we've found our door. The bad news is we'll be exposed out there," she jerks a thumb over her shoulder to the door. "Here's what we're going to do: Jake you're going to use the keys to open the door while Gene and I protect you the best we can. Gene take the American side and I'll take the French side of the room. I'll ask Captain Ivanovich to form up here to protect this middle area."

As soon as she says this, she heads back down the winding center aisle. Less than a minute later she returns with Captain Ivanovich in tow. Only three soldiers follow the Captain. His face looks grim, his eyes sad yet somehow determined, as if he's pushing the sadness to the edges.

The Captain gives quick orders to the three soldiers who then form up around the opening to the door facing inward. They will protect this inner passageway.

I turn to look for Li, expecting her to be near, but she has gone again, over to where the French soldiers are battling with Rat Face's gang. After she has words with Corporal LeGendre, she retreats to our partition. She rests only a moment before she heads over to the American side of the rounded wall. I see a battered Captain Eriksson with several soldiers entrenched behind some desks and partition walls that they have dragged from the center of the space and leaned against the cavern walls. Li speaks briefly with Eriksson and then returns.

The French force is our largest, and several men break off behind the Corporal and begin shoving desks across the ten-foot gap of open space. Partition walls follow and soon a crude shelter is thrown up for the three of us to crouch behind while I go to work on the door.

Li gives the signal and we perform a crouching run over to the door.

"Go!" Li gives me the one-word command, and then immediately turns and unloads her dual pistols toward the oncoming enemy. Gene yells at the American soldiers and waves them over. They get to work on building a desk and partition banker on their side of our door. After another minute I am completely surrounded by metal desks and partitions.

I take a quick breath in a pathetic effort to steady my hands and reach into my pack for my key. I notice for the first time that Li and Gene have thrown their packs onto the ground by the door. Gene has two keys and Li has one. I fall to my knees and dig through the packs, quickly finding the keys. I lay all four on the ground in front of me. I hear grunts and sounds of men struck with bullets. I feel nausea rise within me.

I feel strong hands on my shoulders. "Jake, look at me," Li's voice comes through my panic-induced haze. I manage to move my eyes to hers. They shine brightly with affection. This shocks me; I expected to see the warrior within her at this crazy juncture in our journey. I decide that for a moment, she has hidden this for me. I'm grateful.

"Push everything else aside and focus on getting us through that door—fast." She leans in and brushes her lips against my cheek, then whispers into my ear. "I know you can do it." And then I catch a glimpse of her eyes as she moves away to face the onslaught. I see the warrior return, and I'm somehow comforted by that as much as her words and the heat on my cheek.

I turn to the door. Each keyhole is rimmed with brass that gleams brightly, which seems out of place in this underground cavern. I bring my eyes close to the keyholes trying to figure out which key goes where. I do my best to push away the sounds of fighting that loom over me, and for the most part I succeed. I get lost in the problem at hand that needs solving.

Faint scratches on the brass reveal the four tokens—a cross on the topmost keyhole. I reach for my key and shove it into the hole, I turn the key and feel something tumble into place. One down. The next one down shows the Union Jack etched faintly into the brass. I find Gene's first key with a similar etching and push it into the keyhole. A twist locks it into place. I quickly follow suit with the final two keys. As I twist the final key, one with the hammer and sickle, I twist it to the right as I had the other three, expecting to hear the now familiar thunk of the door opening. But nothing happens.

CHAPTER 40

STEVE AND BILLY

PANIC RISES, AND I FORGET the danger to stand upright and frantically twist each key, thinking one must be stuck. I feel each one fall into place, but the door doesn't open. Maybe the door is stuck.

"Gene, I need you!" I call without turning from the door.

I hear Gene's heavy breathing before anything else. "Whatdya need?" He says without looking at me. His shotgun explodes twice before I can get a word out of my mouth.

"Put your shoulder into this door. It must be stuck," I tell him, hearing my voice as if it's coming from someone else. I hear the panic. I hear the worry that I've failed and we're trapped.

Gene shoves the shotgun into my arms and rocks back onto the heels of his feet and then lunges forward putting his shoulder into the door, with all of his weight following against the door.

It doesn't budge.

"Still locked, buddy," he says shortly and then grabs his gun and turns away from me. I watch him kneel down and begin reloading his shotgun, pushing shells into the breached weapon. I stare around the room and see the dust and smoke. I smell the burning smell that hovers around the discharged weapons. I'm lost now, adrift in my doubt and despair. I can't open the door. I've missed something, and I can't think what it could be.

I'm jerked back to my senses as I'm pulled down roughly by Li. She looks at me like I'm the biggest idiot in the room for standing up, showing myself a target for all to see. "Stay down!"

"I can't open it," I mumble.

Li had already begun moving back to her defensive position. Her hands drop to her sides, the guns idling at her fingertips. "What?" The warrior is gone again, and my friend returns.

I look into her eyes, showing her my full-bodied panic. "I can't open it. I turned the keys, they fell into place, but it won't open."

Li whips her head around in all directions, assessing our situation. From her face, I can tell we won't hold out here much longer. She turns back to me.

And smiles. Her thousand-watt smile. The one that turns my knees to jelly and drops my jaw slack. "Unlock that brilliant mind of yours, Jake, the answer is in there." She holds her smile on me for a moment longer, then gently turns me back to the door.

I barely hear her words. The words don't spread through me and bathe me with confidence. It's her smile that does that. That smile. She believes in me. And this is what I need.

I look at the door. What am I missing? What is the door missing? Suddenly it seems so obvious.

I turn to the packs and rummage through them until I pull out a long piece of metal. I lay the piece flat against the door and run it around until I feel it catch. I need the tokens for this door, of course. The keys aren't enough. I quickly place the tokens on the door. They run vertically down, in order: the French cross, the Union Jack, the US Star, and finally near the bottom, the Hammer and Sickle. As soon as they are placed, I reach for the keys and turn them, one by one. They turn further now, a full three-hundred-sixty degrees. As the final key makes its revolution I hear the thunk I've been craving.

"Stop!" a voice calls from behind. The voice sends chills down my spine. I freeze. The gunfire slowly comes to a halt and now my ears ring for the lack of thunderous din. "Well done, Jake. Once again you prove your worth. Now turn around slowly." Rat Face's voice is hoarse, giving it an even more sinister quality. I shiver again as I pivot around to face the scene.

I draw in a shaky breath as I see the destruction all around me. Two Nazi soldiers stand over two American soldiers on their knees. Rat Face's thugs have three French soldiers on their knees—Corporal LeGendre among them. Rat Face stands next to Billy the Fib who has Captain Ivanovich on his knees.

Rat Face himself stands over Captain Eriksson.

"I see that you saved the good Captain, after all," he sneers, while prodding the shoulder of the kneeling Eriksson. "Well done, you three. I would ask how you did it, but it's of no consequence to me. You continually surprise me."

"Let these men go, Rat Face, you have us now," Li snaps, unable to keep the contempt out of her voice.

Rat Face turns to her and makes a pouty face, as if he's hurt by her words.

"It's Steven. The name is Steven," Rat Face says with a shake of his head. "Is it too much to show me the courtesy of calling me Steven? Or Steve. Or Stever. Even Stevie'll work for me."

"Don't blame us, Rat Face. Blame yer parents for givin' ya that ugly mug," Gene says in a tone that suggests we're all out for a nice after-dinner stroll together.

Rat Face turns his beady eyes to Gene and anger flares in his eyes. His voice remains pleasant, however. "I wish I could, Eugene, but my parents abandoned me on the front steps of some orphanage when I was born."

Gene hangs his head. "Oh. I'm sorry." He waits a beat, then adds, "They couldn't stand your ugly mug either, I guess."

Anger threatens to spread from Rat Face's eyes out through his body. He struggles for composure for a moment and then pushes the anger away and smiles at Gene. "I'm going to enjoy this, Eugene." Rat Face moves his pistol to the shoulder of the kneeling Captain Eriksson.

I want to squeeze my eyes shut, but can't keep from staring wide-eyed at Rat Face. I see his finger adding pressure to the trigger of his pistol. I know there aren't rubber bullets in his gun. My eyes go to Captain Erikson's eyes. His head is held high, and even though his bruises have yet to heal from his earlier beating, I see pride there. Tears spring to my eyes.

"Say goodbye to Captain Eriksson, Gene. This time you can't save him. In fact, your smart mouth has done this to him."

A gun fires.

I finally manage to squeeze my eyes shut. But before they do, I see the damage done. Not to Captain Eriksson, though.

It's Rat Face instead. His hand is blown back and his pistol clatters to the floor.

Instantly everyone is in motion. I realize for the first time that not one shot was fired, but two. Both shots from Li's two pistols. Billy the Fib's gun has also been blasted from his hand, which he now cradles in his other.

I work hard to follow all of the movement. The Americans are moving and overwhelming their captors. The French are doing the same. Captain Ivanovich has the upper hand on Billy the Fib now, and Gene is rushing at Rat Face. Captain Eriksson is too weak to do much at this point.

And then Li is shoving me through the door. "Get the keys and tokens from the door and then find cover behind it. Wait for us to come through and then slam it shut," and then she is gone. I see her taking quick steps and am amazed all over again at how quickly she gets up to top speed.

I work at freeing the keys from the keyholes, my shaking hands not helping the cause. I drop to the ground, momentarily giving up on the keys and grab a pack. I turn it upside down and empty out all of its contents. Food, ammo, and assorted items spill out onto the floor. I move the bag to the door and set to work on the keys again.

A bullet sparks against the metal door and wings away. My eyes go wide and I turn around stupidly to see who is shooting at me. Rat Face and Gene are locked in a mortal struggle, they both have hands on a pistol. Same goes for the others. Our friends are fighting against the thugs of Rat Face and the Nazis.

I whip around to concentrate on my job. Keys are yanked free and dropped into the pack. Next come the tokens. I have to drop the pack to the ground and use two hands on the magnetized metal pieces. I shove them into the pack and pick it up, rising again to my feet. I need to get through the door.

It's then that I'm hit.

A body barrels into me and the two of us knock into the door and then through the opening as the door swings open against our combined weight. I take the brunt of the blow as my attacker lands on top of me. The ground is hard and unforgiving. I feel bone give way with a snapping sound. My head strikes the ground and bright light flashes just before darkness creeps in at the edges of my vision.

I'm rolled onto my back roughly and I see a fuzzy vision of Rat

Face kneeling over me. He has me pinned and cocks a fist back, readying a devastating blow to my head. I almost welcome the imminent darkness. I won't make it beyond this punch. I know my body, and I'm more than halfway to unconsciousness now.

My eyes jump to the fist, my brain demanding to see the blow coming, and I see that Rat Face's fist isn't empty. His fingers are wrapped around a knife. In that instant I realize Rat Face isn't going to knock me out—he's going to put me out of the game for good. The Key must be in this room and he must feel confident he doesn't need my help anymore.

These thoughts run through my mind in a nanosecond. The knife adds an element that triggers something in my mind. I don't want to see the knife coming toward me. I want to close my eyes. Maybe this way I won't feel anything.

Distantly, as if from miles away, I hear an explosion.

And then I see bright red liquid bloom on Rat Face's shoulder. The knife clatters to the floor.

CHAPTER 41

EVERYDAY HEROES

GENE IS ON RAT FACE now. A blow to the back of his skull from the butt of Gene's shotgun, and Rat Face's body goes limp on top of mine. I squirm out from under him and turn to the door.

Li is silhouetted in the door frame. She is holding a pistol in both of her hands. Her hands are shaking. She seems frozen on that spot unable to move. I squint my eyes and she that tears are running freely down her cheeks.

The warrior is gone. The girl remains.

Li shot Rat Face. Not with wax bullets. A real bullet.

I watch as Gene moves carefully to Li's side and gently pulls the pistol from her grip. I see him throw the gun through the doorway back into the cavern. I see Li fold herself into Gene's huge frame, disappearing into his arms.

I move to push myself up and pain spears through my shoulder and down my left arm. I remember the snap from my crash with Rat Face. I cradle my left arm across my chest and hold it there. This position offers that least pain. I use my right arm to push myself to my feet awkwardly and slowly move over to Gene and Li. My vision swims drunkenly from the effects of my fall and head banging. After an eternity, I finally reach Gene and Li.

I must have said something or made a sound of some kind, because Li pulls away from Gene and looks at me. Her eyes are grief stricken, the light seems to have left them entirely.

"I thought he was going to ..." Li stammers. "He was going

to …"

"I know," I say, my voice shaky, but stronger than I would've guessed. "But he didn't, because you saved me. You saved me again."

Captain Ivanovich and Corporal LeGendre are with us now. A few of their soldiers along with an American soldier move to Rat Face. The American works on him for a minute and I realize he is a medic. He turns to us. "He'll make it."

The soldier almost seems disappointed. I feel Li exhale loudly in relief. I'm certain Gene mumbles something about it being a bummer. I don't feel anything right now. Li and I move to the wall just inside the new room and slide down to the ground with our backs against the wall. I wince in pain as my shoulder and arm flare up with the movement.

"You're hurt!" Li exclaims, and I sense she is happy to have something to focus on other than what just happened. "Medic!" she shouts, and then begins probing my shoulder and arm. I suck in air through my teeth when she hits the right spots.

I see Rat Face being hauled out by some of the soldiers, and the medic arrives at my side.

"I think he's broken his collarbone," Li says while scooting out of the way.

The medic quickly confirms the diagnosis and creates a make-shift sling from some clothing remnants he rummages around to find.

The soldiers all gather around Li and me. Gene sidles up to me and stands protectively over the two of us. Captain Eriksson is leaning on Corporal LeGendre, looking like he could use a month-long vacation.

Captain Ivanovich speaks for the group. "This door will be difficult to breach. We've inspected it and it's unlike the other door leading into the room. It's similar to a bank vault door," he motions to the door we've come through, his voice full of admiration at the craftsmanship.

"Thank you for your help and sacrifice," Gene says, speaking to all of the soldiers. His voice is full of admiration. "We'll be safe in here. Please tend to your wounded and guard the prisoners carefully. We'll go alone from here."

The soldiers nod. "There is a switch here on the wall that I presume will light this space," Captain Ivanovich says, pointing to a knob on the wall.

I nudge Gene and motion for him to help me. He smiles and pulls me up, holding my good arm. Gene turns to the soldiers who are holding out their hands in an offer to shake. Gene ignores them and pulls each one into a firm hug. Much back-slapping and hugging follows. I take my turn moving through the men offering hugs. They appear to hesitate with Li. She doesn't appear to see their hesitation, because she steps right in and hugs each one fiercely.

We stand together silently, knowing that something special has occurred here underneath the city of Berlin. I look at each of these men and wonder about their lives. These are everyday heroes, once again lifting us and saving us in our Quest. I make a promise to myself that I will look up their families and try somehow to let their grandchildren and great-grandchildren know that they were uncommon heroes.

"You are heroes. Our heroes, and unknown heroes to the world," Gene says, giving voice to my thoughts. "We would not have succeeded without your help. Your integrity and moral principles are an example to each one of us. We'll never forget you."

I take a hesitant step toward them and add something that has popped into my mind. "Later, many years from now, you will be called the Greatest Generation, because you fought not for money or fame, but because it was the right thing to do," I say remembering a famous journalist's words from my studies.

The men smile and seem to stand a bit taller. The look like giants in my eyes.

As they move out of the room, Gene moves and twists the knob that will light the space. The giant door swings shut, sealing us in, and at the same moment the lights flicker to life. I turn and see something incredible.

The cavern now revealed is enormous. It is exponentially larger than the cavern we have just passed through, something that seemed impossible a few moments ago.

At the far end a large battleship fills the space.

I blink my eyes, thinking I must be seeing incorrectly. Maybe that blow to my head did some real damage.

"Stop blinking, Jake, you're seeing what we're all seeing," Li chides gently as she slips an arm through mine.

The ship must be over four hundred feet in length and stretches from one side of the cavern to the other. I begin walking toward it, knowing I'll cover more than that length just walking over to the massive ship.

"What is a ship doing buried underneath Berlin?" Li asks, speaking to no one in particular.

"Yeah, an' how'd it git here?" Gene adds.

I don't respond to either question. I'm busy taking in the ship. Two masts spear up into the air from the ship with two funnels rising up from the deck in between the two masts. The funnels were where the steam would be released from the engines below. Gun turrets jut from both ends of the ship and along the sides as well.

"HMS Ocean," I mutter as I see the name of the ship.

I turn to the others in excitement.

"I know this ship! The Master had me study this and other ships from the British Empire. He told me that the Key had been lost during the period near the turn of the century. I wondered why I was reading about old battleships that had sunk long before World War II."

CHAPTER 42

QUESTIONS AND ANSWERS

I'M ALMOST TALKING TO MYSELF now as I increase my pace toward the ship. "This ship was reported sunk by a mine in 1915, during World War I, but I wonder if this battleship was captured with precious cargo on board and brought here or somewhere near here while a rough duplicate was produced and then sunk in its place.

"What if those who held the Key were aboard this ship and defected to the side of Evil. We know that only Elizabeth was true to her Key, it's possible that the others gave themselves over to Evil and allowed themselves to be captured on this ship. They betrayed their fellow soldiers." My voice trails off as my mind whirls with the implications.

"Either Hitler built this place and brought the ship here by dismantling it piece by piece and rebuilding it here, or someone before him did it and he just sort of took over."

"But why keep the ship? Why not just take the Key itself and leave the ship behind?" Li wonders.

"I don't know, but I bet we're going to find out in a minute," I say with a hike of my shoulders.

A ramp or gangway runs from the ground up to the ship. I lead the way up the ramp and onto the deck. It creaks and moans like the old ship that it is. I hope we don't crash through the floorboards at any point. My eyes wander over the deck and I see an open door with stairs leading down into the bowels of the ship.

I take the stairs down, with Li and Gene following me. We wander through the ship, seeing rooms that have been opened up wide to accommodate many more people than the original ship intended. I see machines that look like encoding machines like the famous Enigma, and also mounds of radio equipment.

We pass through these rooms until we come to a door closed off down a hallway. These were originally the officers' quarters. At the end stands what must be the door to the Captain's quarters.

I reach my hand out and turn the handle. It's locked. I search the door looking for signs of how to open it, wondering if we are to use our keys and tokens.

A huge foot flies by me and crashes into the door. "I've got the key to this one, little buddy," Gene says with a laugh. He's just banged open the door with one of his giant feet. "Okay …" I say, taken by surprise. My breath catches as I step into the room.

In the dim light, I see two skeletons propped on the bed. Slim chains run around their neck vertebrae, and a key rests on what would be their chests.

"I think we just found Elizabeth's defector friends," Gene blurts.

"Show some respect, Gene. These two were Chosen at one point," Li murmurs quietly.

"Yeah, and they went over to the dark side and caused quite a load of mayhem and death because of it," Gene returns.

"What if they had a change of heart?" I say, almost to myself as I move further into the room. "Look, they still have their keys around their necks. Maybe they didn't give them away but changed their minds when it was too late—after they had given over the Key of Integrity."

"That's why the ship is here, and their bodies are here too," Li says, picking up for me. "Whoever gained possession of the Key didn't understand how it worked, but they did know that they couldn't take the two keys from these men's necks. So they took the whole ship and kept the men here with their keys."

"That is how they wielded the power of the Key. They kept these men imprisoned here and used the Key power from here, because they couldn't remove it from the men's necks," I continue, finishing the thought.

"So how'd our parents get it?" Gene asks, confusion written all over his face.

"They put their keys up to these keys." Li says pointing to the keys on the skeletons. "Only Chosen can take them into their own keys. Our parents freed the Key from these men and then hid it here …" she begins looking around the room.

"It's more likely that they took the Key into their own keys and returned to the Training Center as we have done. And then had to return with the Key to place it here in a safe place for us," I say, connecting the dots of lost Keys in my mind.

"You're right," Li says. "Theirs was a two-part mission. First retrieving the Key and then returning to keep it hidden from the world until we could come and retrieve it for the final time."

"How does that work?" Gene asks, scratching his head.

"We don't know," I say. "We aren't tasked with hiding Keys; we need to find them and bring them safely home."

"Huh?" Gene sounds unsure and leans over the two skeletons, placing his key onto theirs. Nothing happens. "So they don't have it anymore. Well then, where is it?"

"Here," I say, pointing to a huge chest in a far corner. "Help me pull this out into the middle of the room.

The three of us push and pull on the heavy chest until we can see all four side of it. Unfortunately, I'm not much help with just one good arm, but my comrades don't seem to hold it against me.

"Seriously, this thing looks like a pirate's chest," Gene says in awe. "And look, it even has an X on it marking the spot," he smiles at Li and me, happy with his joke.

"You're right," I say seriously.

Gene's smile disappears. "Whatdya mean, I'm right? Right about what?" he wonders.

The chest is just over three feet tall and does look like a traditional pirate chest, like something you'd see in a move. It's four feet in length and two feet wide with a domed lid secured by several locks. Four locks, to be precise.

I motion to Gene with my good arm; he has been carrying the pack with the keys and tokens, and hands it over to me. "The X marking the spot on the lid of the chest is actually part of the Union Jack token. Gene will you put that in place?" I ask, handing him the pieces.

Li reaches over, takes the star pieces and moves to the backside of the chest. "I see the star goes over here." She busies herself with placing the pieces.

I find the French cross on one end of the chest and slide the hammer and sickle pieces to Gene. "Gene, the hammer and sickle is probably on the opposite end."

I place the cross into the chest and feel the familiar tug of the magnet pull the cross into position. I move back to the front of the chest and lay the keys out in front of me. Gene and Li join me at the front.

Four keyholes run horizontally along the chest, just below where the lid meets the bottom portion of the chest. Bright symbols of the four tokens are etched below each keyhole. No more faint markings apparently.

I push the four keys into the proper holes. I stop and take a breath to steady my nerves.

"Gene why don't you take the two keys to the left," I suggest. "Li, take the key to my right. I'll take this one here," I suggest and rest my hand on the middle-right key. "On the count of three, turn the keys."

"Wait!" Gene shouts. Li and I both turn to him expectantly. My eyes go wide.

"Do we go on three or are you gonna say—"

"Shut it, Gene," Li cuts him off, trying and failing to hide her smile. Gene laughs loudly. "Hey, I'm just makin' sure that we time this thing just right. I mean who knows? This thing could be boo-by-trapped."

Li and I just stare at him.

"Oh wow, now both of you are giving me identical looks," Gene says, his grin still in place. "Jake, I'm disappointed in you. Li is changing you, man."

I still just stare at him. I begin a dramatic start to the countdown. "One. Two. Three!"

We turn our keys and the chest's lid separates, revealing a sliver of space. As if our minds are connected, the three of us reach for the lid at the same time. Red velvet lines the interior. The chest holds just one item.

The Key.

Our mind connection holds as we move our keys out from under our clothing and dip down toward the Key.

Our keys touch simultaneously. No need to have a countdown.

There is a certain sadness in my mind as I lean toward the Key. Something has changed here underneath the earth. We're different. Older somehow.

My thoughts are interrupted as I am sucked into the chest—into the Key.

CHAPTER 43

FINISHED

WE FALL ONTO THE FLOOR of the office, keys held tightly. I remember the heat from last time and quickly release the key.

The key has added to its weight again. One more key added.

I know the flowing script will appear now, and I wait to see it appear. I don't need to wait long.

Integrity.

Integrity joins Faithfulness on our key. I begin to pull myself up off the floor, which is not easy with my injured left arm in a sling.

I feel a hand wrap around my good arm and ease me up. I turn my head up to see Elizabeth, our Guide for this Quest.

"Well done," she says, her eyes moist with tears. A smile touches her lips, but it can't completely erase the sadness that I see in her eyes. I realize she is watching Li.

I turn to Li and notice her own eyes are drawn, clouded over with something I can't place. I sit in the middle chair out of habit and Gene plops down into the chair on my left. Li sits on my right. Concerned, I reach out and fold her hand into mine. Right now, I'm not concerned about Gene or the Guide seeing, or knowing, or whatever. I'm just worried about Li.

The Guide clears her throat softly. "Thank you for bringing my Key back to safety. My friends, the other two Chosen, took the Key and went over to Evil. They were seduced by promises that even they can't remember now. However, just as you surmised, Jake, they had a change of heart. Too late, of course. They had taken the Key from me and separated themselves from me, the third Chosen, but they would not give over their Keys. Therefore, the Key of Integrity had no placeholder and therefore had to be kept with the men. Even after their deaths, the keys could not be removed from their bodies. The Key had to travel with them or they with it. That is why you saw the battleship and their bodies aligned as you did." Elizabeth takes in a huge breath and we all sit in silence for a moment until she continues.

"The Lost Key has caused so much death and destruction. But never again, thanks to your parents and to you." She then stands to her full height. She offers us an elegant bow. "You are my heroes."

This catches me off guard, and emotion wells up. I quickly glance at Gene and then Li. Tears shine in their eyes as well.

"I suppose that you will want some time to yourselves to talk things out before you return to your lives and homes," the Guide says with a smile. "When the time comes, and you will know, you will be taken back."

The Guide moves out from behind the desk. She's almost past us when she stops and turns to us again. "The men who aided you in your quest. They all were rotated to their homes shortly after you left. They went on to live exceptional lives. You should know that they knew your parents and aided them as well. These men reunited late in their lives and shared their stories with one another one final time. Corporal LeGendre immigrated to America and started a partnership with Captain Eriksson in the construction business. After the fall of the Soviet Union, Captain Ivanovich joined them some forty years later. I thought you might want to know."

The Guide then quietly moves to the door, opens it and passes through without a backward glance. The door closes softly.

We are left alone together.

Gene twists himself around in the chair as if he's looking around the room for something. "Is there a comment card or a suggestion box in here somewhere, 'cause I'd like to request Elizabeth for our future Quests. I mean, the old Guide just whooshed us off to our houses without so much as a warning."

He settles into his chair with a great big smile. "This is much better now that we have some time to chat," he adds. "I'd like to get your numbers and emails, so we can text and email over the next year. Also, how 'bout y'all coming out to my place this summer for a week or two? Whatdya think?"

Both Li and I smile and nod at Gene. I find a scrap of paper and a pencil on the Guide's desk (it's like she left them for us knowingly), and scribble out my phone number and email address, then hand the paper to Li. She does the same. I hand it to Gene.

"You have our info, so when you get back, send us a text or email with your info," I say.

"Oh no. Yer not puttin' that on me," Gene says and then rises for more paper. He tears a sheet in half then writes out his info twice, once on each paper. He hands them both over to Li and me. "You two can exchange numbers and stuff too," he winks at the two of us.

"Gene, you were amazing during this Quest," Li says, standing and moving over to him. She hugs him tightly. "Thank you."

"Aw shucks, Li. You're gonna embarrass a fella now," Gene falls right into his full drawl, just like he always does when he's embarrassed. "We're a team, right? We help each other out."

Li moves back to her chair and sits. I guess it's my turn, so I stand and turn to Gene. Before I know it, he's got me in a huge bear hug. He puts me down and gives me a poke in the chest. "I'm serious about ya comin' to ma ranch this summer."

"Let's do it," I say with a smile.

I shift a little awkwardly on my feet, not knowing what to say now.

Gene gives me a look and then moves his eyes to Li. "I guess you two want to talk a bit … I get it. See ya soon," he says with his trademark grin.

And then he's gone. I've never watched anyone do that before. Usually I'm the one doing the vanishing. It's a little strange. From this perspective, there is no falling, or tunnel, or whatever. Gene's just gone.

I turn to Li. She reaches for my hand. I sit back down, her hand in mine.

Jake … I shot him …" she says, her breath suddenly ragged and the tears are back.

I crease my brow, not understanding. "But you saved my life, Li. You know he was going to …"

Li leans forward as though she is desperate to have me understand, and to get this off her chest, too. "But, Jake, I *wanted* to shoot him. I took a real gun from that American tough guy, knowing I wanted to shoot Rat Face …"

I don't know what to say. I sense that I am not supposed to say anything. Just listen, I say to myself. I squeeze her hand in what I hope is a reassuring gesture.

"Don't you see, Jake? Rat Face wasn't going to kill you. He just wanted me to think he was going to, so I would shoot him … so I would become like him. And I did!"

Li is frantic now. She thinks she has become like Rat Face, or is becoming like him, bit by bit. I shake my head.

"Li, you shot him in the shoulder. Doesn't that mean something?" I urge, searching for an anchor.

"I don't know. Maybe I just missed because I was scared of what he might do to you … or … I don't know."

I shake my head again. I rise from my chair and move in front of her. Her head is down on her chest. She won't look me in the eye. I kneel down, so I can look into her eyes.

"Li, please look me," I ask softly. She hesitates and then meets my gaze. "You are not Rat Face. You are not like him and you will *never* be like him. You did what was necessary. And I am alive because you did. You can't know what he was about to do. From my perspective, he certainly looked ready to … to end me. You shot him in the shoulder, knowing that it would cause him to drop his knife, and also knowing it wouldn't kill him. You don't miss. I've seen your aim. Don't tell yourself anything but this: You did right."

I reach and cup her face gently with my good hand. "You did right. And you always will. You are Chosen." I let my hand fall back to my side. She seeks it out again and holds my hand in hers.

"We fit, remember? I'm not going over to Evil and neither are you. I can't. You can't. It's just not going to happen. You aren't like him … like them. Feel the weight of your Key, search inside yourself and you will know the truth just as I do." I fall silent.

We stay like this for minutes, or hours, or maybe days. I don't know. Her eyes search mine for the truth as if I hold her truth within me. And maybe I do. Maybe we all hold parts of one another within after a bond has been forged. Some unseen force binding the best of ourselves within a friend or loved one. Part of

Gene is within me now. And Li. And Mom. Mom lives within me, part of her truth—of her being—lives on inside those whom she has touched.

I felt it with those men in Berlin. They knew my mom and therefore I saw something in them, some part left behind by mom for me to find, for me to know.

Li leans into me, breaking off my thoughts, and hugs me tightly, fiercely. "Thank you, Jake. Thank you."

She pulls away and color flushes her neck and cheeks. I love that I do that to her. She grins and holds out the torn sheet of paper that Gene had given her. "Can I have your number and email?"

We both laugh a little. I take the papers and write out my info while she does the same. I hold her paper in my hand, reluctant to give it to her. I know what this means. It means leaving. She hesitates too, and I know she is doing so for the same reason.

We both laugh again.

"I don't want to hand this back to you," she admits, giving voice to our thoughts.

"I know. Neither do I," my smile reinforces my words.

Li leans forward and hands me the paper, while taking her paper out of my hand. She continues forward. I stay absolutely still. Her lips brush my cheek. A shiver ripples down my body. A good shiver.

"See you in the stars."

And then she's gone. And I'm rushing through wherever.

I'm on my bed at home now. But I still feel her breath on my ear and her lips on my cheek. I reach my hand up to my cheek illogically, thinking I'll be able to touch her.

I start to breathe again and stand. I walk over to the window of my bedroom. It's still light outside and suddenly I can't wait for nightfall.

I need to see the stars.

———◆———

D EAR READER,

Thank you for continuing the journey of THE QUEST FOR THE LOST KEYS – I hope you enjoyed The Lost!

If you did, I would appreciate it if you could write a short review on Amazon. It doesn't need to be long, a sentence or two is all. Every review makes a difference to me and helps other readers find the book and series.

I am also thrilled to announce that Book III, The Broken, will be available this summer!

Please head to *www.elwoodjohnson.com* and sign up for my newsletter to be notified on all new releases. (Your email will be kept 100% private and you can unsubscribe at any time)

As always, I'd love to hear from you on social media if you prefer. Twitter, Instagram, or Facebook. I always try to respond!

Live your Quest!

Elwood Johnson

ALSO BY ELWOOD JOHNSON

QUEST FOR THE LOST KEYS

The Chosen (Book 1)

The Lost (Book 2)

AND Coming Summer 2018

The Broken (Book 3)

The Unbowed (Book 4)

The Noble (Book 5)

The Ancient (Book 6)

The Oracle (Book 7)

The Free (Book 8)